EMMA HART

and the

DEMI-GODS

A.L. Stephens

Rock Creek Press

Published by Rock Creek Press

Rock Creek Press

First Edition. Printed in the United States of America.

Books may be purchased in quantity by contacting:

Rock Creek Press at 541-580-4717.

PB ISBN: 978-1-946353-35-1 (pbk.)

PB ISBN: 978-1-946353-32-0 (EPUB)

For Rick Stephens and Nicole Bowman, because of you, this was possible.

CONTENTS

CHAPTER 1 - PAIN

P ain. Nothing but pain is all I've known for... I don't even know how long. Oh, and darkness. I blackout and go somewhere where it's pitch black. At least when I'm there, I can't feel the pain. I know I'm awake when I can feel. And feeling isn't something I want to do, ever again. Not just because of physical pain but emotional too.

My mom is dead. I know she is. She must be.

We were riding in a taxi to our hotel in Athens, Greece, when two black SUV's slammed into us. I remember my head hitting the window of my door and my mom falling on top of me. There was ringing in my ears that made me think my head was about to explode.

Then two men pulled me from the car and I could hear my mom screaming my name. She was calling for help and telling the men to let me go. I looked over my shoulder to see two other men pulling my mom out of the crushed taxi and saw them throw her to the ground on the other side of the car where I couldn't see her anymore. By the way they were acting, they were kicking her. Then one pulled out a gun and fired two shots. She stopped yelling.

I remember screaming and kicking at that point. That's when the man on my left hit me across the face with his fist and knocked me out.

When I woke, I woke up in this... well for a lack of a better word, room. I don't know how long I've been here. I don't know how long my blackouts last. Minutes? Hours? Days? I don't know. I get a bread roll and a tin can of water, I think three times a day. But again, I really don't know.

I've tried pretending to be asleep or knocked out, but that doesn't stop the men from beating me. They used to demand me to show them Mark or my "mark". I used to cry and tell them I didn't know a Mark and didn't know what they were talking about. I didn't have a mark on me, not a scar, not a freckle, not a birth-mark, nothing. After a while they stopped asking but the beatings kept coming. I heard one of them say, just before I passed out and as they were leaving, he didn't know how I was still alive. They were basically told to beat me to death and they were surprised at how long it was taking. I wasn't who they were looking for appar-ently, they mentioned that too.

I don't know why they just don't let me go. I don't know what they look like. I only know their different smells.

One smells like tobacco. One smells like pine needles. One smells like alcohol. And the last, and the worst, smells like mint. There's also a lady. I only know that she's a lady because she wears a perfume. It's a musty perfume that kind of smells familiar but I can't think of where I know it. It's one that probably costs hundreds of dollars, but it doesn't smell good. Or maybe the smell of it makes me sick because of the situation I'm in currently. She never speaks or at least she never speaks when she's around me.

She hasn't came in for a while. Pretty much since they decided I wasn't "The One". And apparently that meant to continue to beat me until I was dead. Why couldn't they just shoot me? Wouldn't that be faster?

Tobacco-man is the one I hate least. He only slaps me around and he's the one that brings me food and water. He's also the one I hate the least because he came in once when Mint-man was the one who had come to torture me for the day. Mint-man had tried to full on kill me within, what I can only assume was, the first couple of days of me being here but Tobacco-man stopped him. I hate Tobacco-man for what he's done but I was thankful he stopped Mint-man from trying to kill me. But now, I wonder if it would have been better to have died then, than to endure all of these beatings. Mint-man hasn't been here alone with me since then either and hasn't been in for a quite a while period, I'm just now realizing that.

All I can do while I wait in between beatings and

blackouts, is remember who I am. If I can keep hold of who I am, maybe I can bare this Hell until someone saves me. But if I'm honest with myself, who's going to save me? My mom was my only family. I didn't have any friends. No one knows what happened to us. We didn't have anyone to tell we were leaving for our Greece trip, so no one is expecting us home at a specific time.

So, here I suffer on my dirt floor with a sheet to keep me warm. I mentally recite what I know, it's kind of a speech I have memorized.

My name is Emma Hart. My birthday is June 13th. I'm 17 years old. I graduated from high school and as a surprise graduation gift, my mom had bought us an all-inclusive trip to Greece, a place I'd always wanted to go. I know my mom is dead, two gunshots will do that. I know I'm probably going to die soon. I know that it's probably not going to be soon enough. I know...

My thoughts are cut off as I hear boots coming to my door. The door unlocks and someone walks in.

Alcohol-man is here now. I can hear him unzipping his coat and throwing it down on the ground. He walks over to me and grabs me by the hair and throws me into the middle of the room, where I land in a heap. He starts to kick me and with every kick my breath gets shorter and shorter. He reaches down, grabs me by the hair again, and pulls my head back. I feel his fist come down onto my nose again and again until finally, my black place takes over.

CHAPTER 2 - TY (SAVED)

"Ty, Charlie, Clay, Max, you guys take the left side. We'll take the right. We'll meet at the end of the corridor where there's a large room. Use your Magikida's if they have them, most likely they'll just try to out-Talent you. Do what you must. We need to get in and out as quickly as possible but sweep every room carefully. Ty says there's a Demi here. They might be the one we've been looking for all these years. Ty, if you find him or her, you guys get out and meet us back at the hotel," Bill says.

I nod in understanding.

Bill's the Guard Commander and our Unit Chief. Charlie, Clay, Max, and I have been in his Unit ever since we joined the Guard, two years ago. We might only be 20 years old but Bill says we are better than his most seasoned Guardians. He takes us with him when he's got an important mission to complete.

Today's mission is a dangerous one. There are known Rifts here, lots of them, but if my information and Bill's intel are correct and the Demi is here, we have to get them out. He or she could be the key to our people's freedom.

Bill nods to his group and they go right.

As we get into formation, I tap Clay on the shoulder, and we move to the left. The building isn't big but the way it was built was like a box with a yard in the middle, with a corridor wrapping around it.

We check the first few rooms and find nothing. The doors aren't even shut.

We come to the second to last room in our corridor, I try the door handle but it's locked. This has to be it. I tap Clay twice on the shoulder and he stills.

I pull out my key and unlock the door. We all have keys like this. They can unlock any locked door.

When I open the door, the smell of blood, sweat, dirt, and mold sweep over us. We step in and let our eyes adjust to the darkness.

At first, I don't see anything of importance until I see a small foot sticking out from underneath a sheet that's so dirty it looked like the dirt floor at first glance.

We sweep the room to make sure there aren't any other hidden bodies in the room and then make our way to the one laying under the sheet.

I reach down and pull the sheet from off the face and I'm stunned by what I see and check for a pulse.

"It's a girl," Max says.

"A severely beaten girl," Clay adds.

"She's got a weak pulse, but she's got one. I'll check

her for a Mark, watch the door Charlie," I say.

"Duh, bro. I'm already on it," Charlie says. I know I don't need to tell the guys their jobs, we work like a well-oiled machine.

I pull the sheet down a little more and find that she doesn't have a shirt on, just her bra. I cover her back up after I pull her right arm out from under her. I notice her arm is broken in multiple places and take it easy, lying it down as carefully as I possibly can. I search on her wrist, just below her palm for her Mark. There isn't one.

"No Mark," I say.

"Well, she doesn't look like she's old enough to have gotten it yet," Max says, looking down at the girl's face.

"Clay, let Bill know what we've found," I say. He nods back and then closes his eyes. His Telepathy really comes in handy on missions.

"Bill says it's up to you. If you want to take her, she's your responsibility," Clay says back keeping his eyes closed.

I don't even have to think about it.

"Tell him, we're getting her out of here. We'll check the last room and meet them at the room at the end of the corridor," I say.

Max pats me on the back and smiles as he walks over to Charlie, who just shakes his head.

"Bill says they are clearing their last room and for

us to just clear our last room and then leave. He thinks the Demi you tracked is the girl you have. We've been here for too long. If you sense a Demi is here after we get back to The Pit, we'll come back as soon as possible," Clay says, opening his eyes.

"Alright, Max take my packs. I'm going to wrap her up in my jacket," Max walks back over to me and takes my packs from me and slings them over his shoulders. I toss the sheet off of the girl and see she's just in her underwear also but is covered in bruises from head to toe.

Charlie walks over and looks at her, "She may be small, but man, look at her ti--" but I interrupt him before he can finish.

"Come on man, not cool," I take my jacket off and wrap it around her twice. I pick her up as gently as I can and walk to the door. Charlie walks back over to the door, looks out, and nods. Clay walks out first, then me, and then Max, with Charlie covering our rear.

We get to the next room and find the door open. It's empty just like the others.

As we're getting ready to leave, I hear voices.

"Clay, are those our guys?" I ask.

Clay closes his eyes and listens.

"Negative, they're Rifts. We need to get out of here. They're coming to check on the girl. We've got maybe five minutes before they're here. If we run they'll hear us and we can't Run with her either," Clay says, opening his eyes.

"I'll Jump us. I'll take the girl and Ty first, then come back for you two," Charlie says, looking at Clay and Max.

"Have you done more than one person before?" Clay asks, looking concerned for his twin.

"I've been practicing. I'm only going to do outside the building by the dumpster we saw before we came in. We'll have to go on foot the rest of the way," Charlie says.

"Alright, let's go. Max, Clay, do what you have to, to stay safe but stay in this room. Charlie will be back in a few seconds," I whisper.

Max and Clay nod and go stand closer to the door, drawing their Magikida's.

Charlie comes and stands in front of me and puts a hand on my shoulder and one on the girl.

"I hope she's worth it," he says.

The next second we're outside and then Charlie is gone.

Five seconds pass and then Charlie, Clay, and Max appear out of thin air, pointing their Magikida's at me and the girl.

"What happened?" I ask.

"Rifts passed the room we were in, but one must have Sensed we were in there, because they came running back just as Charlie showed up. We had just raised our Magikida's when he Jumped us out," Max says, shaking his head.

"They'll know she's gone soon. Tell Bill to get out of there," I say to Clay.

"Got it," Clay says, closing his eyes again.

"Good job, Charlie. How do you feel?" I ask.

"Winded... but... fine," he says, taking deep breaths.

I give him a nod, then say, "Let's get out of here. We'll meet Bill back at the hotel."

We start running towards the road we'd came in on and find our trucks still hidden in the brush.

Charlie jumps in the driver's seat, I normally drive but since I'm holding the girl, I can't and he knows it. Like I said, a well-oiled machine.

We speed down the dirt road and hit the pavement going 110 mph. We get to the hotel room in half the time it took us to get to the Rift hideout.

We jump out and run inside.

"I've got to check her injuries and see if I can Heal her before Bill gets here. Maybe she'll be awake by then and can answer some questions. Charlie, Clay, keep an eye out. Max, will you give me a hand?" I ask as I lay the girl down on one of the beds.

"Sure," Max says coming to stand beside me.

I touch the girl on the forehead to get a Sense of her injuries.

"Uhh...," I say. I lift my hand and shake it and then place it back on her head.

"What's wrong?" Max asks.

"I can't get a Reading."

"Try her heart. Maybe she's so badly hurt, her mind has shut down."

I nod and then I place my hand under my jacket, on top of her heart.

"I can feel a faint heartbeat, but I can't Sense anything," I say.

"Is that normal?" Max asks.

"No. Even if she was on the brink of death, I should still be able to tell where her broken bones are, but I'm getting nothing."

"Bill and the guys are here, maybe he'll have better luck," Clay says, going to open the door.

Bill walks in as Charlie goes out. The other guys must be taking positions outside.

"What do we have here? What happened back there?" Bill asks.

I fill him in on what happened and tell him I can't get a Reading on the girl.

He puts one hand on her forehead, the other on her heart, and closes his eyes.

"Huh, I can't get a Reading either. We'll just have to do it old school and check her manually. Max, Clay, run down to that convenience store on the corner and get all of the first aid supplies they have and tell Charlie to run down and get some ice. Ty, help me feel for breaks."

The guys leave just as I'm checking her right arm for broken bones.

"Bill, her arm is broken at her elbow and wrist. Her pinkie, ring, and middle fingers are broken also," I say, feeling slightly sick.

"That's better than this arm," he says back, looking up at me with a disgusted expression all over his face.

"How is she alive?" I ask.

"I have no idea. We better get her back to The Pit where Doc can help her."

"I hope he can before she wakes up. Nobody should have to feel what she no doubt is feeling," I shake my head and keep checking for injuries, disbelief crossing both our faces.

CHAPTER 3 - WAKING UP

I'm starting to feel again so I must be coming out of my dark place. As hard as I try, I can never make myself stay. I really hoped that last beating had done it, had ended this torture but as I feel myself waking up, that hope is crushed, and I feel a heaviness settle in my heart.

As I feel myself becoming more aware, I can tell something is different this time. I can't smell the nastiness of the room or feel the hardness of the floor that I've come to expect when I wake up. Now it smells like soap and laundry detergent, it smells clean. And the most significant thing that's different, the pain is gone. My body just feels really heavy.

I try to open my eyes, something I haven't tried doing in so long, but I can't. It's not that they are too heavy from sleep, it's because I can't physically open them. They won't budge. I guess I'll just have to use my other senses.

I can hear beeping coming from nearby on my left and I can feel that I'm lying on an actual bed with a pillow and blanket.

That's it. That's all I can hear. No dripping of water or whatever it was I had to listen to while I was in that last room.

Can it be possible that I'm in a hospital? That would explain the lack of pain, they must have given me some pain medicine.

So, have I been saved? Or just let go?

I hear a door open on my left and someone with soft footsteps walks towards me.

Someone who smells like fresh cut grass comes to stand beside me. They reach down and touch my neck, checking my pulse.

I hear the door open again. Heavy footsteps and another set of soft footsteps come in.

"How's she doing, Sara?" it's a man's gravelly voice.

"About the same. She confuses me like no one I've ever met," the woman, Sara, says, brushing my hair away from my face.

"Why's that?" the man asks.

"Well, because she doesn't have a Mark yet, but she must have Talents because she's Shielding us from Healing her and that is something I've never seen. Not to mention she's hurt far worse than anyone I've ever had to Heal and yet she can still Shield herself. I don't understand," Sara says.

"She might be a Shield but just hasn't received her Mark yet," a different man's voice says from my right side. I jump inside because I didn't know he was here, I hadn't heard him come in.

"Maybe, but she's so small, she doesn't look like she's much older than 15," the other person says who came in with the gravelly voiced man, it's another female voice. Her comment on my size hits me hard. I was made fun of growing up for my size, for being five feet and only weighing 105 pounds. Even my Senior year, I had been told I was in the wrong building, that the middle school was across the street. I couldn't believe that those people, the people I went to high school with for four years, still didn't know I was in their class. Now I'm going to have to hear it from these strangers. I should be used to it, but it still stings a little when someone makes a comment about my size.

"Maybe. I'm going to go do some research," Sara says. I hear her leave the room.

The guy on my right stands up and removes his hand from my foot. I hadn't noticed him touching me until now. Just as soon as his hand leaves my foot, the pain returns. Only it feels a thousand times worse, maybe because my mind had gotten used to it being gone.

I feel my back arch and my heart race. I can also hear the monitor going crazy, it must be a heart monitor. When my back hits the bed again, I start spasming.

I just want this pain to stop! I'm in too much pain to scream, to tell these people to help me.

"Ty, don't let go!" the man shouts, pushing my shoulders down into the bed, he smells like hand soap.

The other girl runs to my right side to help hold my shoulders down. She smells like lilacs.

"Crap..." Ty, the guy who had been touching my foot, says under his breath and then grabs hold of my foot again. And just as fast as the pain came on, it's gone. Completely gone.

As I lay listening to my heart pounding in my ears and try to calm my breathing, Ty says, "I seriously have to sit here until she wakes up and we tell her to lower her Shield?"

"We *ask* her to lower her Shield, you mean? We can't make her do anything," the girl says. "And yes, you're the only thing that takes her pain away. Pain meds didn't ease it at all. For whatever reason, your touch relieves her pain. You might not be able to Heal her, but you can make her comfortable until we figure out how to help her."

"But I have to take a leak and I'm starving," Ty says.

"Well, I'll bring you something to eat and you can use the bedpan at the foot of the bed if you *have* to go that bad," the girl says, snorting at her last statement.

"HA, real funny, Libby," Ty says.

"She'll wake up soon and when she does, we'll talk to her," the other man says. They haven't said his name yet, I wish they would. It's nice having names for people again.

"I'll go get you something to eat and then maybe I can take over for you so you can run to the bathroom. Maybe since we're related, I can help her too," Libby says sounding hopeful.

"Maybe," Ty comments back.

"I'll go get Meredith. I think our little gal will be waking up soon," the older man says.

I hear him and Libby leave. Ty sighs and I hear the legs of the chair scrape a little on the floor as he sits back down beside me. I'm going to have to make my consciousness known when they get back. I don't want Ty to be stuck sitting here with me because of something they're calling my Shield. I have no idea what they're talking about, I'm not doing anything.

Quite frankly, they sound insane to me. They talk like they have special powers or something. Like stuff you'd see in movies or comic books. But if they don't have powers, how is it that just the touch from Ty can make my pain go away? That's not normal.

Yeah, as soon as Libby and the other guy gets back, with Meredith, whoever she is, I'm going to have to make a noise or something. Could I still talk? It's been so long since I've spoken a word. Screamed, yes, but talked, no. How long? I don't know. I don't even know what today's date is or if it's day or night.

Ty starts to hum a song. It doesn't sound familiar, but the melody is soothing. He starts to rub my foot with his thumb, whether he means to or it's a subconscious thing, I don't know but it sends a shock up my leg and into my heart.

Who is this guy? Maybe I should just make a noise now and try and talk to him.

Just as I'm about to try to say something, I hear the door open.

"What are you doing here?" Ty asks, sounding slightly annoyed.

"I brought you something to eat. I saw Libby in the Great Room and I insisted on bringing you your food. And plus, Doc needed her help bringing back some supplies for this... child," a girl says.

I can hear Ty's teeth grinding and he lets out a long breath. It doesn't seem like he's fond of this girl.

"Well thank you, Alysa, I'm starving," Ty finally says. I hear a paper bag being ripped open.

"So, nothing has changed with her then?" Alysa asks.

"Mmnope," Ty says, around a mouth full of food.

"I wonder who she is, she doesn't look like anything special," Alysa says. Now my teeth are grinding. She doesn't even know me, how can she say that?

"Well, she is something. She's got a pretty strong Shield. We can't Heal her, but as long as I'm touching her, her pain goes away," Ty says, then I hear the crunch of some kind of food as he puts it in his mouth.

"I see that," Alysa says with a slight bit of... jealousy? No that can't be it, he's just touching my foot.

Ty clears his throat and says, "Well, thanks for the food."

"Anytime. Anything you ever need, you know you only have to ask," Alysa says, giggling a little.

I internally roll my eyes, what kind of line is that?

Apparently not a very good one because Ty awkwardly says, "Umm, thanks..."

"You'll come around," Alysa says flirtatiously as she walks back to the door.

"Doubt it," Ty says under his breath.

Not a minute later I hear the door opening again and I can hear three separate footsteps.

"Did Alysa bring you your food?" Libby asks.

"Yeah, thanks for that," Ty says sarcastically.

"Ha. Ha. Ha. Anytime!" Libby says laughing.

"It's not funny," Ty says, but I can hear a little bit of humor in his voice.

"How's our girl doing?" a lady's voice asks from the foot of my bed.

"Same ol', same ol'," Ty says.

"I think she'll be waking up soon," the man from earlier says. So, the lady must be Meredith.

I guess it's now or never, I need to let them know I'm awake.

I try to talk but nothing comes out, so I try to clear my throat.

Ty's chair scratches on the floor as I hear him stand up quickly. The other three gasp and all goes silent in the room except for the sound of my heart monitor. They're holding their breath, waiting for me to do something else.

I try to talk again but again I can't. If my throat wasn't so dry maybe I could say something. I try to lift my left hand but it's so heavy I can't. I raise my right hand just a little bit and try to bend it but it wont bed.

"Holy crap, she's waking up," Libby says. "Doc did you know she was going to wake up? Can you Read her?"

"No, I didn't really know but I could hear a difference in her heartbeat," Doc says. I'm so glad they finally said his name.

I hear Meredith walk around Ty and come stand on my right side.

She touches my shoulder and says, "Honey, can you hear me?"

Well, yeah, I can, but how do I tell her I can? I can't say anything. How else do I let them know I can hear them?

I raise my right hand again and extend my fingers, which is really just my pointer finger and thumb, I can't move the other ones.

"Oh, thank the gods," Libby says.

"Can you talk?" Doc asks.

I don't know what to do to say no, so I just lie here.

"Are you still with us, Hun?" Meredith asks.

I raise my hand.

"Okay, so you can't talk?" Libby asks.

I raise my hand.

"Maybe she's thirsty," Ty says. "When my throat is really dry, I can't talk."

I raise my hand.

"Oh, Oh!" Libby says and runs to the other side of the room. I hear the faucet turn on and I hear running water. She runs back over and holds a cup to my mouth.

"Just sip it, don't drink too much too fast," she says.

I open my mouth, which isn't very far. Libby tries to give me a sip, but it just spills down my chin.

"Can you open your mouth a little more?" she asks.

I don't move my hand because no, I can't. My mouth is locked or something.

"I'll find a syringe," Doc says. He runs off and opens the door they've been coming in and out of and seconds later he's back. "Here, put a little in here and squirt it in. It's the best we can do."

I feel the tip of the syringe touch my lips and then cool water slowly leaks into my mouth. I want to groan from the taste. I haven't had cool, fresh water in I don't know how long. I try to clear my throat, but nothing happens. Libby gives me another sip and I try again. This time a little cough comes out.

"Have one more sip and then try to talk," Libby says as she puts the syringe back to my mouth.

I cough again and through clenched teeth I say, "Thank you." It's the first thing I've said in a long, long time. I don't know if these people are as good as they seem or if they are evil like the last people I was with, but everything they've done and said make me believe they're good. Either way, I am thankful for the water.

They all sigh and let out a little laugh.

Ty lets go of my foot for just a second, to do what? I don't know but I start screaming from the pain. Head to toe, excruciating pain.

"Damn it!! Sorry, sorry!!" Ty says and plants his hand back on my foot.

I take deep breaths to slow my breath again.

"It's.... okay...," I cough out.

"Hun, can you tell us who you are?" Meredith asks.

"Can we let her get a little more water, before we start asking questions?" Libby asks, sounding slightly irritated.

"No, we can't," Meredith says.

"It's okay. I'm okay for now," I say, hoarsely.

"Can you tell us who you are?" Meredith asks again but more gently.

"My name is Emma Hart," I answer.

"Emma, my name is Meredith. Jim, Libby, and Ty are here as well. It's so nice to finally meet you," Meredith says.

"Umm thanks," I respond shyly.

"How old are you, Emma?" Doc asks, whose actual name must be Jim.

"17," I answer.

Ty's hold squeezes just a little and he says in a surprised tone, "You're 17?"

"Yeah. I know my size is deceiving," I reply.

"When's your birthday?" Libby asks.

"June 13th," I say.

They all clear their throats and shift their feet.

"Umm, Emma, do you know what today's date is?" Doc asks.

"I don't know the exact date but I'm guessing sometime in May," I answer back.

Meredith puts her hand on my right hand and squeezes.

"Emma, it's June. June 11th," Libby says.

My heart stops for just a second.

"Wait, what?" I say, trying to sit up. This can't be right!

"Don't sit up," Doc says, trying to push my shoulders down.

"Emma, calm down, it's going to be okay," Libby says.

"But you just said it's June 11th!! How is that possible!?" I cough out, starting to hyperventilate.

Ty's hand tightens on my foot just a little.

"Do you remember where you were at before waking up here?" Ty asks.

I shudder before I answer, "I remember the room. I didn't see the actual place."

"When did you get there?" he asks.

I laugh a hysterical laugh and say, "Three weeks ago, today."

"Can you tell us what happened?" Meredith asks calmly.

I sigh, I knew this was going to happen. I haven't told this story out loud before, only in my head.

"My...." I have to clear my throat before I can go on while fighting back tears, "My mom and I had just gotten to Greece. We were in a taxi going to our hotel when we were hit by two black SUV's. Two men grabbed me and dragged me away, towards another SUV. Two other men stopped my mom from coming after me, they.... they shot her. I started to freak out so one of the guys holding me, hit me in the face and I blacked out. When I woke up, I was in a room with a dirt floor. I don't think I ever left there."

I take a deep, calming breath, and continue, "Four men and a woman would come in and the men would ask me about Mark or a Mark or something. I couldn't show them any Mark, so they'd beat me. After a while when they decided I wasn't who they were looking for, I'm guessing the lady told the men to 'take care' of me. So, I got beat, I'm guessing, every day. I'd black out and wake up pretty much in time to get knocked out again. I thought this last beating was going to be the last, that it was going to kill me, but obviously it didn't."

Ty's hold on my foot slowly got tighter as I told my story.

"They beat you that often?" he asks.

"Yeah, I'm pretty sure it was daily. They didn't care if I was conscious or not," I answer. "I woke up a couple times to one of the men hitting me."

"That's sick," Libby says.

"I'm so sorry you had to go through that," Doc says.

I just shrug. There's nothing I can do about it.

"So, ummm... who are *you*?" I ask.

"Don't worry, Emma. We're the good guys," Meredith says.

"Before we go into detail about what's going on, we'd like to get you feeling better," Doc says. "Could you do something for me?"

"Sure," I say.

"Can you try and relax and think about letting us heal you?" Doc asks.

"Ummm... what?" I say with an embarrassed giggle.

"Heal you," Ty says.

"I'm not stopping you from healing me, don't you have me hooked up to monitors and what not?" I ask.

"Yes, we do, and this might come as a shock, but we have... powers, we call them Talents. Some of us can Heal people by touching them," Meredith says.

"You seem to be blocking us from Healing you, we think you have a dormant Shield Talent. We need you to relax and allow us to Heal you," Doc says.

"You're kidding, right?" I ask. If I could only open my eyes, maybe I could see their faces, to see for sure that they are kidding.

"As hard as it is to believe, we are not. So please, just try to relax. Think of something soothing," Meredith suggests.

"OOOOkay, I guess I can try," I say, not really sure what they want me to do.

I take a deep breath and think about not having any pain. I think about how Ty's hands take the pain away. I think about being whole again.

"That's it," Doc says. "Keep doing that. Ty, you keep your hand on her. Libby and I will Heal."

I'm not sure what I'm doing so I just keep repeating the same thing over and over in my head.

"I'll do her face and arms if you want to do her legs and midsection," Libby says.

"Perfect idea," Doc replies.

I feel Libby put her hands on my face and a warmness spreads out from my nose to my ears and then down my jaw. I hear and feel a pop on my jawline and then it cools and then warms up again. I feel the same warmth on my feet where Doc is touching. The same pop, coolness, and warmth happens about every five seconds. It's quiet in the room for about 20 minutes before anyone says anything.

"Okay, I think that's it," Doc says.

"Ty, take your hands away," Libby says.

I brace myself for pain but the only thing that I feel is a dull throb.

"How do you feel?" Ty asks.

"Nowhere near the pain I had before. It feels like how you'd feel a day or two after working out and have sore muscles," I respond. I try moving my arms. "My arms are a bit stiff."

"You didn't let us Heal you completely, so you'll be sore and stiff for a few days and you'll still have your bruises, but your broken bones are Healed. I'll unhook you from the monitors." Doc says as he takes something off my finger and sticky things off my upper chest.

"Open your eyes," Libby encourages.

I slowly try to open my eyes and find that I can actually open them. They're still a little puffy so I can't open them all the way, but I can finally see. The lighting isn't as bright as I was expecting, which helps. I can't remember the last time I was able to see something. By the sound of it, it's been pretty much a month. That's crazy.

I look over to my left at where Libby and Doc are standing.

Libby looks about my age. She's tall though. Really tall, maybe five-ten, maybe even six feet tall. She's got the body I've always wanted, model like. Curves where there's supposed to be curves and athletic looking. She's got long brown hair with honey color highlights and really pretty light green eyes. She's gorgeous.

She smiles at me and says, "Hi there, I'm Libby Conner."

I laugh a little and wave at her.

I look over at Doc and see a man who looks to be in his late 20's to early 30's standing there. He's got dark brown hair and kind, brown eyes. Like Libby, he's tall. He's quite a bit taller than her so I'd say he's about six-six and has a football linemen's build, he is very strong looking. He's not what I expected him to look like at all.

Doc also smiles and says "Hi! I'm Jim Riserson but everyone calls me Doc, except for my wife."

I smile and nod at him.

Meredith walks around to stand next to Doc and smiles at me when my eyes meet hers.

"Hi Emma, I'm Meredith Riserson, Jim's wife," Meredith is just as gorgeous as Libby with the model like figure. She's about Doc's age. She has chin length blonde hair and light blue eyes, that are kind as well.

The chair to my right moves and as I look over, I see Ty standing up.

And OH... MY... GOSH!!!

CHAPTER 4 - DEMI-GODS

If I was still hooked up to the heart monitor it would be going crazy.

Ty is the hottest guy I have ever seen in my life. He's tall, just like Doc. Not as big in size but I can see his shirt is tight around his biceps and chest. My eyes slowly rise to his face where I see a strong jawline and an angular nose that looks similar to Libby's. He also has the same color of hair as she does only it's short but kind of spiky messy on top. His eyes! Holy crap! It's like two emeralds staring back at me. And they twinkle! How can a guy's eyes twinkle so much?

He clears his throat, which probably means I've been staring at him for too long. I quickly look down at my hands and feel my face turn bright red. I'm hoping my face is bruised enough to not let it show.

"And that's Ty," Libby says. "He's my brother, well twin if you want to get technical."

I glance at her and then at Ty and see that they are just about as identical as a brother and sister can get.

"Hi," I say to him, shyly.

"Hi," he says back.

It gets quiet, kind of awkwardly quiet, so I start to fiddle with my fingers. Trying to get them to loosen up.

To break the tension I ask, "Can I ask you guys some questions?" I only have a million of them.

"Sure," Doc says as he grabs two chairs and gives them to Meredith and Libby. He goes back for one more for himself and they all take a seat. Even Ty, who sits back down in his chair. I guess he's forgotten about his bathroom needs for the time being.

"Okay, I guess my first question is, how did I get here?" I ask.

"Ty, why don't you take this one," Meredith says.

"Umm, okay," he says.

I look over at him and he adjusts the way he's sitting.

"I'm a Tracker and in the Guard. I had Sensed that someone was at that place you were being held. Bill, he's the Guardian Commander, checked with some recon, and found out that the Rifts were holding someone there. We decided to do an extraction. My team and I found you. So, we brought you back here," Ty says, leaning back in his chair when he was done talking.

"You saved me?" I ask slowly.

"Well, me and my team did but yeah," he says hesitantly, like he didn't want to take credit.

"The way I heard it was that Bill gave him the choice to leave you or take you and he didn't think twice. He took you away from that hell hole," Libby says, smiling over at her brother.

Ty just rolls his eyes and looks away.

Hmm, so he could have left me but chose not to, so he is a good guy.

"Why did Bill give you a choice? I thought you guys came for someone, for me? Just curious," I ask.

"Well, we've all been waiting... looking for someone. And when I told him you didn't have a Mark, he gave me the choice," Ty says.

"So basically, since I'm not the one you're looking for, he was okay with leaving me there?" I ask. This Bill guy doesn't sound nice.

"It wasn't like that," Ty says, trying to stick up for Bill. "You have to understand, we were in a very dangerous situation by just being there."

"Oh, believe me, I know just how dangerous it was there," I say back, I'm getting a little irritated.

"I didn't mean... You obviously know... it's just that we were on a specific mission," Ty says, standing up.

"Well, I'm thankful you thought my life was worth saving even though I'm not 'The One'," I say back.

"Bill... he... I didn't mean for it to sound like he didn't want to save you. You don't understand. He gave me the choice," Ty says, sounding like he's getting angry with me.

"Okay," I say, maybe I was taking it too personally but if it weren't for Ty, Bill would have been fine with leaving me there? That's not okay.

Ty starts walking away and I hear him mumbling something under his breath as he goes to the door and walks out. My heart sinks just a little as he leaves. I don't even know him, how can I have feelings for him? Because he's hot? How shallow can I get? Or maybe I feel like this because I actually feel safe when he's around, from either knowing he made my pain go away or because he saved me or both. I don't know.

I shake my head a little to clear it.

I look over at Libby and she's grinning ear to ear at me.

"What?" I ask.

"My brother never has a hard time talking and for the first time in our life, he was stammering like an idiot. I just find it funny and interesting," she laughs.

"Hmm," I say, awkwardly.

"What other questions do you have for us?" Doc asks.

"Well, I have about a 100 more to add to them after hearing Ty's story," I answer back.

They all laugh.

"What is a 'Tracker' and what's a 'Guardian'?" I ask. They sound self-explanatory but I want to know everything for sure before I assume anything.

"A 'Tracker' is a Talent that a few of us have," Meredith says.

I interrupt and ask, "A talent, like a power? Like a

superpower?"

Meredith smiles and says, "Yes, like a superpower. We call them Talents though. Tracker's can locate people. The Tracker's we have here look for unknown Talents and then our Guardians go out and find them to bring them back here. The Guardians are like our military. The Guardians protects us from the Rifts. Certain Talents qualify you to be a Guardian. Take Ty for example. His Talents are Healer, Protector, and Tracker."

"I'm pretty sure I know what a Healer can do, but what's a Protector?" I ask.

"A Protector has Super Strength, Super Hearing, and Super Eyesight. And yes, a Healer is pretty self-explanatory. They can Heal anyone that has a cold to a broken bone to a gaping cut, anything. They can't, however, bring someone back from death," Meredith explains.

"We all have Super Strength, but Protectors are even stronger. We all have Super Speed and can heal faster than Inepties. It takes a lot for us to die but it can happen in extreme circumstances and it involves Talents," Libby adds.

"Wait, what do you mean, Inepties?" I ask, confused.

"Inepties are what we call normal humans," Meredith states.

"Are you guys not normal humans?" I ask slightly frightened now.

"We are but we aren't," Doc says. "We come from a long line of people called Demi-gods, Demi's for short."

"Like Poseidon and Zeus, those kind of gods?" I ask.

"Yes, exactly. We get part of our Talents from our parents and the rest from a god themselves," Meredith answers.

"How do you get Talents from the gods?" I ask. Man, the more we talk the more questions I think of to ask.

"Well, we are all born with a certain Talent, inherited in our DNA from our parents. Sometimes it's one Talent from one parent or it's multiple from both. After we turn 18, the gods will gift us with a Mark, which will give us stronger power for our original Talents, the ones we inherit, or they give us a different one that becomes our more dominant Talent," Meredith replies.

"Oh okay. So, the Mark those people were looking for makes sense now," I say.

"We are all curious about that too. You have a Talent called Shield. It allows you to protect your mind and body from other Talents. So, like, how we couldn't Heal you until we asked you to allow us to, that was you Shielding. And the fact that you were hurt so badly and yet your Shield was so powerful, we're confused on why you don't have a Mark yet, especially since your birthday is in a couple of days," Doc says, scratching his head

"Wait, I'm a Demi-god too?" I ask, totally surprised.

"Yes," Meredith answers matter-of-factly.

"No," I say.

"Yes," they say in unison.

"No. I can't be. I'm just me, nothing special," I say, and I remember that Alysa girl saying it to Ty.

"You are and I'm guessing a very Talented one," Meredith says.

"And my Talent is Shield?" I ask.

"Yes, and you might have others we don't know about," Libby says.

My head is spinning. Am I crazy for wanting to believe them? Probably.

"So, I should have a Mark? Where should it be?" I ask them.

"On your right wrist, just below your palm. See look, here's mine," Libby says, pulling up the sleeve of her jacket and shows me her arm.

And just like she said, on her wrist was a symbol I'd seen when we were boarding our jet leaving for Greece. A man had a big tattoo of it on his shoulder. He was telling another passenger he was in the Army Medical Department and the tattoo was the symbol for it.

"What is that symbol called?" I asked.

"Caduceus," Libby says.

"It looks like a tattoo," I say.

Libby laughs and says, "Yeah, I love it."

"If you don't mind me asking, what does it mean?" I'm not really sure if asking about these kinds of things is okay or not.

"Oh, no, I don't mind. We're allowed to talk about our Talents with other Demi's but not with Inepties," Libby says. "My talents are Healer and Shifter."

"Shifter?" I ask, sitting up more.

"I can change my appearance. Anything from my hair color to my size. I can also change into any animal or bird or water creature. Anything," Libby says grinning at me from ear to ear.

My mouth fell open at 'hair color'.

"That's awesome!" I exclaim.

"Yeah, it's pretty fun. Scared me half to death the first time it happened, though," she laughs, thinking back to that first time, no doubt.

Doc leans forward and shows me his Mark. He has a Caduceus also.

"I know you're a Healer because you helped me, so is the Caduceus the Mark for Healers?" I ask him.

"Yes, and I'm also a Mentalist which Caduceus is the Mark for that Talent also," Doc answers.

"And a Mentalist, I'm guessing, has something to do with the mind?"

"That's correct, I can do anything with the mind. For example, I can read minds, move things with it, talk to someone in their head, make people forget things or add/change their memories. Things like that," Doc says, shrugging like it's no big deal.

"Wow...." is all I can think of to say.

"He's pretty impressive," says Meredith, looking at her husband lovingly.

"Not that impressive, I can't Read your mind, Emma. You're the first I've ever met who I haven't been able to Read," Doc says, tilting his head, looking at me with interest.

"Is something wrong with me? Because I'm not doing anything," I say.

"Nothing is wrong with you, it's just your Talent protecting you. It's a very strong Talent if you can protect yourself without thinking about doing it. Usually, Shields have to think about it before they do it. For instance, if I was trying to Read someone's mind that is a Shield, they could block me, but they'd have to concentrate," says Doc.

"I see," but I really don't. I don't get how I could be doing something without actually doing it.

"Would you like to see my Mark?" Meredith asks.

"Sure," I say, looking up excitedly.

She walks to my right side and places her arm in my hands. Her Mark is a Lightning Bolt.

"This is cool," I say and then look at Libby and Doc and say, "Not that yours aren't cool." I feel my face turn red a little, I hope I didn't offend them.

But they just laugh, and Libby says, "The Lightning Bolt is pretty awesome."

We all laugh at that.

"My Talents are Silver Tongue, Truth Speaker, and

just like Jim, I'm a Mentalist," Meredith says and then explains. "Silver Tongues can talk, or in most cases, manipulate, people into saying or doing anything they want them to do. They also can get them to tell the truth. So, if I were talking to someone and needed information, I could make them tell me the truth if I thought they were lying. Truth Speaker means that I speak the truth, I can't lie. And you know about Mentalist."

"Wow, this is all so unbelievable!" I say, in awe.

"It's a lot to take in, especially if your parents didn't talk to you about any of this." Libby says. "And I'm guessing they didn't say anything to you?"

"Not a thing," I say. "Although, we were going to Greece. Maybe my mom was going to tell me once we got there. You know, set the mood and everything. After all, we were in Athens."

"What about your dad?" Doc asks.

"He died when I was a baby, I never met him," I reply.

"Do you know his name?" Libby asks.

"No, my mom didn't like talking about him, so I stopped asking after I turned 10. I didn't like seeing her upset," I answer.

"What was your mom's name?" Meredith asks.

I wince at the word 'was'. I still can't believe my mom is gone.

"Nessa Hart," I answer with tears starting to fill my

already swollen eyes.

"Oh, I'm sorry Emma, I didn't mean to make you sad," Meredith says, rubbing my back.

"It's okay. It still feels like it happened yesterday. It still blows me away," I say as I wipe away a tear that rolls down my cheek. I'm going to need to spend some time mourning my mom and then I need to move on. She always told me to be strong and never dwell on anything that I couldn't change. I'd be strong for her.

"That's understandable," Doc says.

"Can I ask another question?" I ask.

"Go for it, that's why we're here," Meredith says.

"Where is here, exactly?" I ask.

"Oh yes, we haven't told you about The Pit," Meredith says, smiling. "About 10 years ago we had to find a new safe haven for Demi's. It's built underground, under a dry cleaners of all places, in Boise, ID. We run electricity from the building. We bought the building and put the dry cleaners' business in because it takes a lot of electricity to run the machinery. We can run electrical wires down into The Pit and it won't raise any questions. The 'owners' of the dry cleaners are Inepties who have been loyal to the Demi's since the beginning, loyalty passed down through generations. They are the Fitzgeralds. We have some Seekers out looking for a new place for us but for now we have to hide because of the Rifts. My sister, Beth, put an Untraceable Shield around the dry cleaners which includes The Pit and everyone inside of it. The Rifts can't Track us"

"What are Seekers? Rifts?" I look at each of them.

"Seekers are a group of Trackers sent out to look for Demi's still in hiding. If they find any, they alert The Guardians. Rifts are Demi's who have stolen other Demi's Talents," Libby says with a sour look on her face.

"How do they do that?"

"Well, there's a Talent that's called Borrower. It allows the person with the Talent to borrow another Talent from someone else. They can only borrow it for a little while, an hour tops, before they have to borrow it again. While they are borrowing the Talent, the person it belongs to can't use it. So, if someone borrowed my Healing Talent, I wouldn't be able to Heal anyone. But I could Shift. Also, the person has to allow the Talent to be borrowed. If not, it doesn't work, with one exception. Within the first month of getting our Mark, our Talents can be borrowed without our permission. Normal Demi's would never take a Talent without permission though," Libby explains.

"Rifts have figured out how to take the Talent away from a Demi, permanently. Sadly, we think they end up killing the person after because we never see them again. We think they kill them so they can't escape and tell us how their Talent was taken," Meredith finishes.

"So, their greedy Demi-gods?" I ask.

"Essentially, yes," Doc says. "They aren't satisfied with what they have been given or they are jealous of what others were given and they've figured out how to steal what they want."

"Chris and Vanessa Walters are the ones who began doing it 20 years ago," Meredith says. "They started getting followers, groupies that wanted different Talents. They started calling themselves Rifts. They asked Jim and I if we wanted to help them figure out how to switch Talents. They weren't happy with us when we turned them down."

"The people that had me, were Rifts?" I ask.

"Yes, and Bill's getting more information about that right now. He and a team went back to get some photos of the people that are there. We're hoping we'll know more by tomorrow," Libby says.

"You said school, is there a school for Demi's to go to?" I ask.

"There used to be, it's where we used to live. Meredith was the Headmistress and we were both Professors. Chris and Vanessa showed up one day and a battle broke out between their people, and everyone at the school. Meredith didn't think we could win so we got all the students out before we were all killed. Over half of the Professors gave their lives that day so that we could save the students," Doc answers me, reaching across my bed to take Meredith's hand. They look very sad.

"Then you moved here," I say.

"Yeah, they haven't been able to find us yet. We're

hoping to keep it that way," Libby says.

I yawn and lean back. Even though I've been out of it for so long, I feel really tired.

Doc looks at his watch and says, "It's late, we'll let you get some sleep. It'll help the healing process. We can talk more tomorrow."

"Okay, thank you! I don't know why I'm so tired. I feel like I've done nothing but sleep," I say.

"It wasn't really the best way to sleep, so your body needs actual rest," Libby says.

They get up and put their chairs back where Doc had gotten them.

"You're safe now, sleep well," Libby says as she follows Doc and Meredith through the door.

I close my eyes and feel myself falling into a deep sleep.

CHAPTER 5 - NIGHTMARE

I wake up and I am surprised to be waking up in the hospital room.

"It wasn't a dream," I say out loud.

"Nope," someone says to my right.

I nearly jump out of bed. I didn't know anyone was in here. I sit up and see that it's Ty.

"You scared the crap out of me! What are you doing?" I ask, breathing hard.

"Sorry about that, I thought you were talking to me," Ty says. "I'm here because I wanted to check on you. I must have fallen asleep, I'll go."

And just like that he walks out of the room.

He must feel responsible for me because he brought me here. I'll never be able to thank him enough for saving my life, but I'll figure out a way.

I wonder how long I'm going to have to stay in here. Surely since I can see and my bones are all healed up, Doc will let me leave. I really want to go explore The Pit. They never went into detail what it looked like, I'm really interested in finding out for myself.

I stretch my arms out and find that I'm still pretty sore around my right elbow. My left shoulder feels like it was punched 100 times but at least I can move them. I swing my legs to the side of the bed and carefully try to stand. I instantly crumple to the floor in a heap.

I try to pull myself up but end up pulling the tray that was next to my bed, down on top of me. Water from a pitcher dumps over my head and a plate of food goes flying. I hadn't even noticed the food.

I must have made quite the racket because Ty comes running in. He looks at the bed and his eyes get really big when he doesn't see me there, but he quickly finds me on the floor and rushes over.

"What happened?" he asks, sounding slightly irritated.

"I was trying to stand," I say back.

"Well don't!" he snaps back.

"I can if I want! Unless I'm a prisoner here too!!" I shout back at him.

"You are not a prisoner, but you haven't stood in... how long?" Ty growls.

"Why are you angry at me?"

"Because you're yelling at me. I don't do well with being yelled at by a little girl," Ty says nastily as he puts an arm under my knees and around my back.

"Little girl!!?? I WILL BE 18 TOMORROW!! Just because I'm a little small in size does NOT mean I'm A LITTLE GIRL!" Now I'm really yelling, and I push away from him which causes me to fall awkwardly from his arms, and I whack my face on the side table.

Blood starts to run down my chin from a split lip.

"What is going on here?" Libby says as she rushes through the door. Her eyes get huge when she sees me on the floor, bleeding.

"Emma thinks she can just take off and get out of bed without anyone helping her. I came in and found her on the floor and when I tried to help her back into bed, she started yelling at me and then practically jumped out of my arms. She hit her face on the table when she fell," Ty explains to his sister, who is glaring at him as she bends down to check me out.

"You called me a little girl, that's why I was yelling. You started yelling at me first," I say around my hand. I was trying to keep my blood from going all over. My upper lip was starting to throb.

"No, I didn't," Ty says back.

"What!? Yes, you did. You snapped at me about not getting out of bed and standing," I say, my voice getting a little louder.

"See, Libby, this is what she was doing! It's not my fault," Ty says, glaring at me.

"You both need to stop hollering. Emma, we need to get you back into bed. Ty was right about one thing, you shouldn't be trying to stand or walk without someone in here to help you. It's been almost a month since you were last on your feet, right?" Libby says, sternly.

I sigh. She's right, it has been a really long time. But this is ridiculous, I feel fine.

Ty bends down again and effortlessly picks me up and puts me back on my bed and not very gently. I glare up at him and try to ignore the pounding my heart had started to make again when his arms wrapped around me.

"OUT!" Libby shouts at him.

He shakes his head and mutters something under his breath as he leaves.

When Libby turns towards me again, she's smiling.

"I've never seen him act like this. He doesn't usually raise his voice to anyone but me and it's usually in a playful way. You rile him up, Emma. I like it!" Libby says.

I shake my head and say, "You're crazy!" but then I laugh.

"You must be feeling better? Or you were before you hit your face? Here let me Heal it and then you can talk," she grabs my face and places her hand over my mouth.

I feel heat, then a tingle, then coolness, then heat again, and then Libby moves her hand. She hands me a mirror and I look at myself for the first time in a long time.

Holy crap, I look awful! I have bruises around my eyes and over the bridge of my nose but they look a little yellow, so they'll be gone soon. I look at my mouth and see that I have a faint pink line where I was cut. It's still a little swollen but it doesn't feel as big as it did a minute ago. I turn my head to the right and see a nasty bruise covering my jaw down to my neck. I turn to the left and see a faint pink scar that starts behind my ear and runs down to my chin.

I have bruises around my neck like someone tried to choke me, how nice. I shake my head and put the mirror down. Tears fill my eyes.

"Emma, it's okay. You're safe now. They can't hurt you anymore," Libby says, sitting on the bed, taking my hand.

"I know, I just haven't seen my reflection in a long time and it just reminds me of how my life has been. Kind of sucks," I say back. "Libby, can you tell me how bad I was hurt? What were all my injuries?"

"Do you really want to know?" she asks.

"Yes," I reply, honestly. "If I'm going to get over what happened, I need to know everything."

"Okay. Head to toe or toe to head?" she asks, scrunching up her nose.

"Head to toe," I say, not that either one seems like the better option.

"As you saw, your nose was broken, multiple times. Luckily, the last time it started healing properly, so all we had to do was speed it along. Both eye sockets were broken just below the outside corner. Your jaw was broken on both sides. You had a deep gash from your left ear to your chin, which you saw also. You had some cuts on your eyebrows and forehead, but we were able to heal those up completely because they weren't very deep," Libby takes a breath and squeezes my hand. Then she continues. "Your right collarbone was broken, along with your elbow and wrist on your right side. Your left shoulder was dislocated and put back into place, we don't know how many times, but it was to the point it was just hanging there. On both hands your pinkies, ring fingers, and middle fingers were broken. Your left thumb was dislocated."

Libby takes another breath before saying, "You had eight broken ribs on your right side and six broken on your left. You had a punctured lung that had collapsed. And your sternum was broken in three places. Your left femur was broken along with your left ankle. Your right kneecap was busted and all the bones in your right foot were shattered," Libby finishes, looking at me with sad eyes.

I lean back into my pillow and let all this settle. How in the hell did I survive all of that?

"Doc's sister, Sara, who is second in charge of the Hospital Wing, did a full exam to make sure every injury was accounted for, there were a lot," Libby states.

I just nod and then I yawn again and realize I could take a nap.

Libby looks at her watch and says, "Breakfast is in 3 hours, why don't you sleep? I'll come get you and take you to get some food when it's time to eat. Sound good?"

"Yeah, thanks, Libby," I say, squeezing her hand, trying to convey some of my gratitude towards her.

She smiles at me and says, "If you need me, I'll be in the office just outside the door. I can hear you if you holler at me. So, anything at all, just give me a shout."

I nod at her and she leaves the room.

I close my eyes and I'm instantly asleep.

I wake up and there's a familiar smell in the room, mint. I sit up and see that Mint-man has found me in the hospital. As I try to get up, he runs over and throws me out of my bed and starts kicking me. I try to crawl away, and I get halfway under the bed next to mine but he grabs me, pulls me out, and throws me onto the bed. He crawls on top of me and starts kissing me. I start screaming for him to stop but he keeps kissing me all over. I try to punch him, but he grabs both my wrists and slams them above my head. I try to kick him, but my legs are pinned beneath his legs. He lays on me and I can feel my breath being pushed out of my lungs and all I smell is mint. I feel bile rising in my throat. I swallow it back down so that I can scream again and again as loud as I can.

He starts calling my name in my ear, "Emma....

Emma... Emma... Emma...."

I start crying, trying to pull my arms free but he won't let go. I get a slap across the face and when I open my eyes, I see Ty staring down at me.

I look around frantically trying to find Mint-man but he's nowhere to be found. I see Libby at the foot of the bed holding my feet.

It was a nightmare? But I can smell mint.

"Was he here? Where is he?" I scream while crying.

"Who?" Libby asks, coming over to my left side.

"Mint-man! I can smell him!" I scream again.

"It's just us. I brought you some mint tea, it helps with stomach issues caused by malnutrition," Libby says, grabbing a cup.

"Get it away, get it away! It smells like him!" I start to sob.

She runs over to the sink and dumps it out and then rinses it out a couple of times.

Ty pulls me into his arms and says, "Shhh Emma, it's okay, it's okay. Shh, I've got you," as he rubs my back.

I don't know how long we sit like this, but I've been sobbing for a long time. Libby comes over and tries to get me to drink some water but all it does is make me choke. Ty tells her to go get Doc.

Doc, Libby, and Meredith come running back in about five minutes later. I have slowed to just crying but I'm hiccupping horribly.

"Emma, can you tell us what happened?" Doc asks.

"Libby said something about how you thought some-one was in the room with you, someone that smelled like mint?"

"It was... a nightmare... but it felt... so real," I say be-tween breaths.

"Do you want to tell us what it was about?" Mere-dith asks.

I tremble in Ty's arms, he squeezes me and says, "It's okay, he can't hurt you. Talking about it might help."

Taking a deep breath to calm myself, I say, "I dreamt that I woke up and he was here, I could smell the mint. I only know him as Mint-man because he smells like it so bad. I tried to get up, but he threw me to the ground and started kicking me. I tried to get away, but he grabbed me and threw me on a bed and then climbed on top of me. I tried punching him to get him to stop but he pinned my hands above my head and my legs were pinned under him. I was slapped and when I opened my eyes, that's when I was really awake because I saw Ty and Libby," I say, breathing easier. Ty was right, it helped to talk about it. It also helped not having the tea here.

"We heard her screaming so we came running in. Ty tried to wake her, but she started punching him. That's when he grabbed her hands, we didn't want her hurt-ing herself. She started to swing her legs around wildly, so I grabbed her feet to keep them from flying around. We were calling her name, but she wasn't waking up,"

Libby says, looking at Ty.

"So, I slapped her, not real hard, but enough to wake her up," he says, looking down at me with sad eyes, "Sorry about that. Seems like I can take your pain away, but I cause you pain as well."

I pull back and look at his shirt. It's soaked with my tears and probably my snot. I wipe my face off with my hands and say, "I've ruined your shirt."

Ty looks down and shrugs, "I've got more." Then smiles at me for the first time and my heart stops.

My goodness, he's gorgeous!!!!

"Libby, when did you bring the tea in for Emma?" Doc asks. "After you heard her screaming or before?"

"Before, I thought she could drink it before breakfast," Libby states and then realization seems to hit. "Oooh shoot, the smell must have triggered the memory of that man which caused her to have that nightmare. Oh Emma, I'm so sorry."

"You didn't know. I didn't know. Well, I knew I would have issues with the smells from the men that tortured me, but I didn't know it would cause me to have nightmares if I smelled them after I'd fallen asleep," I was going to have to make sure mint was nowhere near me until I could handle the smell again.

"What other smells?" Ty asks.

"Tobacco, pine needles, and alcohol. And the lady wore a very musky perfume," I answer back.

"I see. Well, you won't have to worry about the

tobacco and pine tree smells. We do allow alcohol but only on the weekends. As for the perfume, that'll be trickier," Meredith says.

I nod and lay back down.

"Do you want to sleep some more, or would you like to go eat?" Libby asks.

"No, no sleep. I'm not really tired. I just feel... weak," I say.

"You need to eat something, it's been far too long since you've had a decent meal," Doc states.

"I could probably eat," I say, smiling.

Ty stands up and picks me up.

"Wait, ummm could I change into some clothes instead of this hospital gown?" I ask. I really didn't want my rear hanging out if Ty was going to insist on carrying me around. He sets me back down on the hospital bed.

"Of course," Meredith says, "I'll Run to your room and get some clothes for you. I had my sister, Beth, get some things for you. What would you like to wear?"

"I have a room?" I ask.

"Yes," Meredith answers but she makes it sound like a question. "You can stay in it from now on. What would you like to wear?"

"Oh, jeans and hoodie if possible, please," I'm getting a little chilly. Jeans and a hoodie are my go-to clothes of choice no matter the temperature. Well, I guess except when it gets extremely hot in the summer.

"Okay, I'll be back in a second," and in a flash she's gone.

Blinking rapidly at how fast she left, I shake my head. It's starting to hurt so I lie it back and close my eyes.

"Are you feeling alright, Emma?" Ty asks.

"My head just hurts," I answer him. I'm starting to feel bad that he feels like he has to keep an eye on me.

"I can fix that," Libby says. She walks over and places her hands on my head so that her thumbs were touching each other on my forehead. I feel, what's starting to be the familiar feeling of Healing, the warm, tingle, cool, and then warm again, a soothing sensation. And just like that, the pain is gone.

"Thank you! I don't know if I'll ever get used to that," I say, smiling up at her.

Meredith reappears at the foot of my bed with blue jeans and a light blue hoodie. She also grabbed a pair of tennis shoes, underwear, a bra, and socks for me.

"Thank you, Meredith!" I say.

"Uuuhh.... Ty and I will step out until you're done," Doc says. He and Ty rush out.

Meredith and Libby help me get dressed. Since I can't stand on my own, Meredith has to hold me while Libby pulls my pants up.

"Well this isn't embarrassing or anything," I say.

They both laugh. Libby says, "It's okay, what are

friends for?"

I look up at her and grin. No one had ever referred to me as a friend.

Meredith sits me back on the bed while Libby walks behind me and runs a brush through my hair. Meredith goes and gets Doc and Ty.

"Umm question, did someone give me a bath?" I ask.

"Yes," Libby says, sounding puzzled.

"Who gave it to me?" I ask.

"My sister did," Doc says.

"Sara?" I ask, trying to remember if that was the name Libby told me.

"Yeah, that's her. How did you know?" Doc asks.

"Oh, Libby told me how she double checked my injuries," I say.

"Oh, yes," Doc says nodding.

"Do you want me to braid it?" Libby asks, playing with my hair.

"That'd be great," I say. I haven't had anyone braid my hair before, besides my mom.

"Your hair is really pretty. I love how black it is. I wish mine had this natural wavy curl. It looks like you spent all morning taking a large curling iron to it. If I want it to look like this and I don't want to spend any time on it, I have to use my Talent," Libby says as she whips my hair into a braid. She started up by the left side of my forehead and then braided down over to my right shoulder.

"Thanks, that feels much better than having it in my face," I say, smiling up at her.

She smiles back at me and says, "Anytime, now let's go get some breakfast."

Ty sighs, steps forward, and picks me up.

"You don't have to carry me. Isn't there a wheelchair around here somewhere that I could use for a day or two? Just until the strength in my legs come back," I ask, once again feeling annoyed that Ty is acting like this is a big inconvenience to him, I didn't and haven't asked him to be my personal carrier.

"We don't have wheelchairs here," he says. I see him roll his eyes as he shakes his head.

We leave the hospital wing and I get to see The Pit for the first time. The hall outside the Hospital Wing has dirt walls and floors, with a light hanging from the dirt ceiling, every six or so feet. It is the complete opposite of the room we just left. That room had actual linoleum floors and a lot of fluorescent light bars, and actual walls. They probably tried to make the hospital as sterile as possible and all the light is necessary to see what they're working on.

There's a wood door on both sides, in the hall just outside the hospital door. The hospital door looks like a double door from an actual hospital.

"What's in there?" I ask, pointing to the wood doors.

"Those are the Healer offices," Doc says.

Oh right, they had said their office was right out-side the door.

We keep walking and it gradually starts to slope down and it gets a bit chillier. I'm glad I asked for a hoodie and jeans.

I see light ahead and when we step out, we are in a huge, square, cavernous room. I look up and see lights about 20 feet up. There's also lights on the walls and just like in the tunnel we just came from, they're set about six or so feet apart. There's mostly tables and chairs but in the far right corner there's a bunch of couches and comfy chairs. There's a lot of people in here, also.

"How big is this room?" I ask, in awe.

"It's 50 yards by 50 yards and 25 feet tall," Libby says.

"So, about half of a football field," it's the only thing I can think of to compare it too.

Ty laughs and says, "Yeah, pretty much."

I look up at him and see that he's got a weird look on his face.

"What?" I ask.

"Oh nothing, it's just that I wouldn't have figured you would know what a football field looks like," he an-swers, snickering.

I shake my head and look back out into the room. We had stopped, I'm guessing so that I could take it all in. There were two tunnel openings on each side of the room, so six in total, except for the side we just came out of, there is only one.

"Where do those tunnels lead to?" I ask.

"The two on the left, lead to the Quarters, which are our bedrooms, and the bathrooms. Straight ahead, those two lead to the Gym and The Pub. And the tunnels on the right wall lead to the elevator that will take you to the kitchen and dry cleaners above us and the other one takes you to the Guard Room," Meredith says.

"About halfway down each tunnel is another tunnel that cuts off so that it connects to the tunnel next to it. So, if you're in your room and you have to go to the bathroom, you don't have to walk all the way back down to the Great Room and then walk back down to the bathroom. The Gym tunnel connects to The Pub tunnel. The entrance and Guard Room tunnels connect. But they don't all connect together," Libby says, trying to explain how the tunnels work.

"I gotcha. So, there's an actual Gym down here?" I ask. I wasn't allowed to participate in sports. I asked to play every year, but my mom wouldn't let me. Although, I was allowed to go to the pool every weekend.

"Yeah, they did a pretty good job building it. There's a natural hot springs that runs through here. We built the bathrooms to run off of it, as well," Libby says, smiling over at me. "When we're done eating, we'll take you on a tour, won't we Ty?"

I look up at Ty who's looking at his sister with the most annoyed look on his face.

"No, it's okay. We don't have to," I say. I was not going to be some annoyance Ty was going to have to put up with all day.

"Ty doesn't mind, do you?" Libby says, glaring up at her brother.

"Well actually, Bill's supposed to be back in a little bit, and he called a meeting so I actually can't," Ty snaps at her.

"Well, then I'll just take her," Libby says.

"No, really. We can wait until later. Maybe my legs will be better this afternoon," I say hopefully.

We start walking again and as we get closer to the tables, people start turning in their chairs to stare at me. I can hear the whispers of "Is that her?", "Is she The One?"

How disappointing it's going to be for them when they find out that I am, in fact, *not* the person they've been waiting for, for so long.

I see that in the left corner there's tables set up with food on them.

"The food comes from the kitchen above us?" I ask.

"Cooky refurbished the second floor of the building into a kitchen. She cooks up there and then brings it down here for us to eat. She does that three times a day. If we want a snack, we have to go to her," Libby answers.

"So, we can leave The Pit? I was under the impression we weren't allowed to leave."

"It's not advised, but yes you can. This isn't a prison, Emma. But you need to understand the dangers of leaving. Rifts are everywhere, so most of us stay here or go up into the building if we want some fresh air and sunlight," Meredith says.

Ty sets me down at an empty table and takes off towards the food tables.

"I'll bring you some food," Libby says as she walks off.

"I need to go find out if Bill's back. Walk with me?" Meredith asks Doc.

"Of course, my dear," he replies. They both smile and wave at me as they walk away.

I look around the room and find that everyone is looking in my direction.

I swing my legs under the table so that I can focus on my hands, rather than looking at everyone staring at me. Out of the corner of my left eye, I see something red coming towards me, so I look over. It's a gorgeous girl with the reddest hair I have ever seen in my life. What was it with this place? Did all the girls have to be so pretty?

CHAPTER 6 - VANESSA WALTER

T he redhead stops in front of me and extends her hand and says, "Hi, I'm Alysa Shae. You're the one the Guardians brought back a couple nights ago?"

"Ummm, hi Alysa. I'm Emma, Emma Hart. And yeah, that's me," I say back, shaking her hand. I recognize her voice. She's the one that had brought Ty food. I grit my teeth, I'm sure this isn't going to be a pleasant conversation.

She pulls the chair out and sits down across from me. I see her look over to where she was just standing and nods her head and waves at someone. I look over and see two more beautiful girls coming over.

"Emma, this is my sister Malysa and my best-friend, Malory Foster. Girls, this is Emma Hart. And she is the one the Guardians brought back," Alysa says smugly.

Malory has beautiful chocolate brown skin, brown eyes, and gorgeous brown hair.

"My gods, you're tiny!" Malory says, laughing. "How

old are you? 12?"

"Actually, I'll be 18 tomorrow," I say back shyly.

"Ignore her, we all do," Malysa says. She extends her hand and when I reach out to shake it, she says, "And you can call me Shae."

I grin at her, she seems nice.

"No, you're the only one that ignores me," Malory says.

"Only the brightest of us do, Malory," Shae says.

"Whatever Maaaalllyyyyssaaa," Malory says, drawing out her name. "Alysa, I'm bored. Let's go."

"Hang on," Alysa says. She leans in and says, "Just so you know, Ty is mine."

"Umm, oookay," I say, not sure why she's telling me this or where this is going.

"Don't be thinking that he likes you just because he *has* to watch over you right now and carry you everywhere because your legs aren't working yet. In fact, he told me he thinks you're an annoying little girl. He wishes you'd hurry up and walk so he didn't have to haul you around all the time," Alysa says nastily.

"Well, first, I just met him. And second, it didn't sound like he was that into you when you brought him food. In fact, he sounded more annoyed with you than he does with me," I shoot back.

She glares at me and says, "You were eavesdropping?"

Kind of hard not to hear when you're standing next

to the bed I'm lying in," I say.

Alysa raises her hand, points her finger at me, and says, "I'll teach you a thing or two right now. As far as you're concerned, I'm the queen bee around here. Watch what you say! And remember, Ty is mine!!" At the tip of her finger I see fire, actual fire start to flame out towards me. I try to lean back before it can get to me, Shae shoots water from her hand and it hits her sister's hand, putting the flame out.

"Knock it off, Alysa. You've had your fun, now go away," Shae says, handing her a towel.

"You've been warned," Alysa says as she walks away. Malory follows, glaring over her shoulder at me.

"Thanks, but isn't she going to be mad at you?" I ask Shae.

"Probably, but I don't care," she answers.

I look at Shae and realize something.

"You guys aren't just sisters, you're twins?" I ask.

Shae sighs and says grudgingly, "Yeah, unfortunately."

Alysa has red hair, but Shae has brown but everything else was identical. Same nose, mouth, and brown eyes. They seemed to be the same height also and had that perfect model form I was seeing a lot of here.

"You have brown hair though?" I didn't mean to ask it like a question, but it came out as one.

"I make Libby change it for me. I have natural red hair like my sister, but I got tired of getting in trouble for all the nasty things she used to do and still does, so I decided to change my hair color. I used to dye it, but it never looked natural. I go to Libby once a week now and have her change it for me. I have to go once a week or my hair goes back to red. Libby is the only Shifter I know that can transfer her Talent to someone even if the person doesn't have the Borrow talent. I'm really grateful to have her as my best friend," Shae says.

Now I know why I thought I could like her. If she and Libby were best friends, then I, for sure, was going to like her. Unlike Alysa, Shae had kind eyes. She also had a way of making me feel comfortable.

"Can I ask what your Talents are?" I'm still unsure on how to ask about a person's Talent.

"Sure!" She says enthusiastically. "Well, you saw my Water Talent. I can conjure it up out of thin air and I can also manipulate it. So, like if we came to a river and it was too fast for us to cross, I could calm it down and make it shallow so we could cross. I can also swim really fast and I feel at home in the water. I can't stay under indefinitely but longer than most Demi's. I also have the Psychic Talent."

"Wait? You're a Psychic? As in, you can see the future?" I'm stunned.

"I'm still learning how to control it. It's mainly in my dreams. I'm learning how to figure out if it's a dream or a premonition. I'm also learning how to concentrate while I'm sleeping, when I know I'm having a premonition, so that I can extend it, otherwise I don't get the full length of it. Take you for example, I 'dreamt' the Guardians were going to be bringing someone back but I couldn't concentrate long enough to find out who," Shae explains. She shows me her Mark, it's a Trident crossed with a Caduceus.

"Have you seen anything else?" I ask.

"No, I haven't been sleeping very well. Professor Densmore thinks it's because something big is about to happen so my mind and body are overexerting themselves to the point I can't sleep. I'm half tempted to have Madam Olivia make me a sleeping potion so that I can finally sleep and see what's going on."

"Who is Professor Densmore and Madam Olivia?" I ask. There are so many people to meet.

"Professor Densmore is one of the instructors for Mentalist Talents and Madam Olivia is our Potions Master. She makes things for the Guardians to use. Like sleep bombs, which is just the sleeping potion but in gas form so that the Guardians can throw it into a room and knock out anyone that's in there, Rifts or Inepties. She can also make quick healing spray for Demi's that aren't Healers, who are going out without a Healer. I don't think there's anything she can't make," Shae says, yawning.

"Why would the Guardians need stuff like that? Don't get me wrong, that's really cool but isn't there a Demi that has those Talents?" I question her.

"There are but not enough to send out every time the Guardians go out and if multiple Units go out, there's definitely not enough. Over half of them left with the Seekers. That's why she makes them, so that they can protect themselves."

Thinking about that, I look around again, and see that most of the people that were staring earlier have gone back to their breakfast. Most of the people in here are around my age if not a little older. I look all around the room and see that there aren't any kids or elderly people. I'm about to ask Shae why that is but Ty walks up and puts a tray in front of me.

"I wasn't sure what you liked so I got you some fruit and toast. It should be easy to digest. I'm guessing your kidnappers didn't feed you often or well enough, so you need to eat slowly so you don't get sick," he says, then he walks away.

I look over at Shae and she shrugs.

"Who beat me to it?" Libby asks. I look up and see her standing in front of me.

"Ty," Shae answers her, shooting her a look I don't recognize.

Libby smiles and places the two trays she's carrying down on the table, then sits down where Alysa had been sitting.

"What?" I ask.

"Nothing," Libby says as she bites into an apple, still smiling.

I shake my head and stare down at my food. I haven't had anything but bread and water for a month. My mouth waters at the sight of the grapes, pineapples, and strawberries.

I take Ty's advice and start eating slowly, cutting each piece of fruit in half and chew it up and swallowing it before I put another piece in my mouth. It's hard going slow, this fruit is amazing. I don't want to eat the toast, it will taste too much like the rolls I'd come to expect for my meals. I glance at the tray Libby had brought me and see she had brought me the same thing as Ty, only there were eggs on it.

"Umm... would it be okay if I had that fruit and the eggs?" I ask her.

"Sure, I brought it for you but stop eating if you feel full. We don't need you getting sick," she says, sliding the tray over to me. She also hands me two glasses, one has orange juice and the other has milk.

I drink the juice and then start in on the fruit. Once the fruit and juice are gone, I start eating the eggs and down the milk. For the first time in a long time I actually feel good, good and full.

"Thank you, Libby," I say as I stack my trays on top of each other. "That was delicious."

"Just wait until dinner, Cooky is the most amazing cook," she says, smiling.

I look around and once again I'm surprised at the lack of age difference here.

"Can I ask you guys a question?" I ask, looking at Libby and Shae.

"Sure," they say in unison.

"Where are all the kids? Is it a school day or something?"

Even if it was a school day, surely it's still early enough they'd be here eating.

Libby and Shae exchange sad glances and then look down at their hands.

I look back and forth between them, waiting for an answer but they don't say anything.

"What? Why aren't there any kids?" I ask quietly.

Libby sighs and looks up at me with tears in her eyes and says, "They've all been captured by Rifts or murdered in the process. We don't think those that were kidnapped are still alive. The Rift will kidnap the kids and we think they keep them until their 18th birthday and then they take their Talents. We never see or hear from the kids again. You are the youngest of us here. You are the only one that we know of that's survived for so long without the Rifts finding you."

"No kids, at all?" I ask.

"None that we know of because most Demi's are scared to have their kids taken. Everyone has stopped having kids, it's kind of become an unspoken promise to not have any until the Rifts are taken care of or we figure out a way to keep the children safe. There might be the random loner Demi couple that have found a hiding place and they have a kid or two but the Rifts will un-doubtedly find them, unless we of course can find them first," Shae says, looking really upset.

"What about the elderly?" I'm not really sure if I want to know the answer.

Again, they look at each other but this time it's not so sad.

"Well... After we get our Marks, we don't really age," Shae says.

"Wait, what!?!" I ask. No way this was true.

"Yeah, for example, Doc looks like he's maybe 30 but he's really 62 years old. Meredith is 60," Libby says, smiling at me.

"Holy crap!" I say. This totally blows my mind.

They both laugh.

"Uhh, how old are you guys?" I ask.

"We're both 20," Shae says, laughing. "You should see your face."

I laugh and say, "Well, I don't know. You guys could be 200 years old, I wouldn't know."

We all laugh for a good couple of minutes. I've never had friends before, but I could tell that Libby and Shae are fast becoming my very first ones.

"Most of the professors that died in the fight at the old school, were some of our oldest Demi's. They were 200-300 years old. The rest of the older Demi's live in different countries, in their private homes, that only they and their personal Guardians know about.

The oldest, some of the first Demi's made, make up our Elder Council. We just call them The Elders. There are only seven Elders left. All the others were killed in battles. The Leaders only contact them when something really serious happens. The Elders live in their own village, somewhere near the base of Mt Olympus in Greece. The Leaders are the only ones that have been there," Libby says.

I'm about to ask some questions about The Elder's and The Leader's but Ty says from behind me, causing me to jump, "Emma? Bill and Meredith would like you to come talk to them."

"Jeez-oh-pete! Don't you make sounds when you walk?" I say to him as I look up at him.

He just shrugs and grins a crooked smile at me. My heart starts to beat fast, I really wish it would stop doing that.

"You should make a sound to let someone know you're coming up behind them," I snap at him.

"Where would the fun be in that?" he chuckles as he scoops me up in his arms.

I just glare at him.

"We'll see you later Emma. Ty, will you bring her to my room when you guys are done?" Libby asks as she stands up.

"Maybe," he says as he walks away.

I look up at Ty and think about what the girls had just told me. Since he and Libby are twins, he's 20 also.

I thought he was somewhere around 25 or 26. His size is what confuses me, I guess. I can feel his arm muscles tighten around me as we start to climb up the tunnel leading to the Guard Room, but his breathing is steady, as if he was taking a stroll by himself on a flat surface.

"How are you feeling?" he asks, startling me out of my thoughts.

"Oh, fine, thanks. Eating and drinking something has really helped," I answer him. Unsure why he's asking, maybe to be polite and start a conversation while we walk.

That's good. Your strength should be coming back to you the more you eat and rest," he says as he stops at a door. He adjusts me in his arms and raises his hand and knocks on it three times, it's opens.

We walk into a room about the size of the Hospital Wing, but it's got huge computer monitors on the walls and a large table in the middle of the room where about 20 people were sitting. Meredith and Doc are sitting amongst them and she's sitting next to two empty chairs. Ty walks towards the chairs and sits me in the one closest to Meredith and then he sits next to me. I look back at the door and see two men standing on either side of it.

"Thanks for joining us, Miss Hart. How are you feeling?" a man on the other side of Doc asks.

"I'm doing better, thanks."

"This is Bill Johnson," Meredith says.

"Oh, hi," I say. I wasn't sure if I liked Bill or not. I guess I'll just have to get to know him before I decide. I can't take what happened too personally, he was just trying to do what was best for his people.

Doc leans behind Meredith, smiles, and says, "We'll start your physical therapy once we're done here, if you want to. I think you should be strong enough by then."

I smile back. I can't wait to start walking again. Maybe then Ty wouldn't feel like I was a nuisance anymore.

Bill stands up and clears his throat, all the conversation quiets and all attention goes to him. He grabs papers from in front of him and starts to hand them out.

"First off, let me introduce you to Miss Emma Hart. This is the girl that Ty and his team saved Wednesday. Let's go around the table and introduce yourselves to her," Bill says looking to his right where a man is sitting.

He stands up and says, "I'm Luke Harris and this is my wife, Mikayla," Luke looks to his right and Mikayla stands and waves. I wave back and they sit down.

Sitting next to her is a lady who has to be her twin, they are identical. She stands and says, "I'm Ginny Schultz and this is my husband Fred." The man next to her stands and waves. His twin stands next to him and says, "I'm Fred's brother, Mark. This is my wife Lauri," Lauri waves and then they all sit back down.

We went around the room, each person standing

and telling me who they were married to or related to. What was with all the twins? It was kind of freaky. We get to the last three guys, who are sitting on the other side of Ty.

Two tall, blonde guys, stand up. One has a shaggy haircut and the other with a short, military haircut. And yup, they are twins. The one with the longer hair says, "I'm Charlie O'Neal," he winks at me, "and this is my brother Clay." Clay smiles and says hi. They sit down as the guy next to them and Ty, stands.

He looks just like Malory, he must be her twin. He says, "I'm Max Foster." I say hi and he sits down. I look around the room and try to smile at everyone but find it hard to, they were all staring at me.

Bill clears his throat again and says, "Okay, now on to business. We were able to get some pictures of the people that had Miss Hart. I've made copies so everyone should have some now."

We all look down at the papers in front of us.

I see, for the first time, the face of one of the men that had kidnapped me. Whether he's one that tortured me or not, I don't know.

"There were 26 men in total and one woman. We all know who she is, Vanessa Walters. Chris Walters wasn't there and we aren't sure where he's at right now. We haven't been in contact with our spies, for their safety and for the sake of their mission, so we don't know the men. We have no information on them. Miss Hart, can you tell us anything about them?" Bill asks, drawing all attention back to me.

I clear my throat and look through some of the pictures of the men. "I'm sorry, I don't know. I never got to see their faces. The room I was kept in had no windows and no lights. And even if there was light enough to see them, I probably wouldn't have been able to anyways, my eyes were pretty much swollen shut the entire time."

I heard murmurs around the room. They're probably disappointed in the lack of information I have for them. They continue to talk about how to get information about the men and if they should try to make contact with their spies. It sounds like there are two of them there.

As they're talking, I glance down and look at the rest of the pictures. When I get to one of the last pictures, I freeze. My mom-- they have pictures of my mom.

"When... when did you take these?" I try to stand but find my legs are still not quite strong enough, but I push through the weakness and make myself stand.

Bill glances at the picture I'm holding and says, "Yesterday, the same day as the others, why?"

"This is my mom, Nessa Hart. You have to go back and bring her here. You have to save her!" I'm shouting now, clutching at the pictures, panting from trying to keep myself standing.

They all search through the pictures to find what picture I'm talking about. Meredith stands behind me and tries to get me to sit. I shake her off.

"You have to go! Now! She's in danger! I thought they'd killed her!" I shout and then finally fall back down into my chair, mostly because Ty makes me.

He looks at Meredith, who glances at Doc and Bill. They all have looks of concern on their faces.

"That's your mom?" Doc asks.

"Yes!" I shout again. Why aren't they moving? Why aren't they making plans to go get her?

"Emma, calm down, and look at the picture. Does she look like she's in distress?" Ty asks, pointing at a picture of my mom standing next to a car.

I look closer and see that she doesn't look like she's been hurt or anything. In fact, she looks completely comfortable. She looks different though, her hair is chopped short to her chin, it's not long anymore, and she's wearing all black. Black pants and a black turtle-neck.

"I don't understand," I say, shaking my head to try to figure out what this means. "I saw them shoot her."

"That's not your mom," Bill says. "That's Vanessa Walters."

I look over at him and back down at the picture.

"No, that's my mom. Her hair is shorter but that's her."

They all look at the picture and then at each other

again.

"Your mom is Vanessa Walters?" Charlie asks.

"No, her name is Nessa Hart," I snap at him.

"Emma, that is Vanessa Walters. She's married to Chris Walters. They are the leaders of the Rifts," Doc says, coming to stand beside me.

I look at the picture. Maybe I saw wrong. "No, that's my mom. She has the scar on her upper lip. She told me she got it from a dog, which was why I could never have one. She didn't like dogs after her attack."

"Oh gods!" exclaims a woman who I think said her name is Kathryn, she stands up.

"What is it Kathryn?" Bill says, confirming her name for me.

She looks at me with wide eyes and says, "I... I remember something about Vanessa and a baby. Someone had seen her with a newborn, but she had never been seen pregnant. I just assumed it was another kidnapping."

A rumble of murmuring and whispering goes around the table. Everyone shifting in their chairs slightly.

"That could be why Vanessa hasn't been seen until now. She's been MIA from all the Rift attacks and recon missions we've gone on in the last 17 years. She wanted to raise the infant herself," Luke says.

They all look at me.

"What?" I ask, I'm not sure what they're trying to

say.

"You must be the baby," Meredith says, putting her hand to her mouth.

"No... No...," shaking my head violently in protest, "No, I'm not. This Vanessa woman is not my mom. My mom loved me. She never hurt me, not once. Plus, we have the same smile."

"That doesn't matter. She needed you to grow up and feel dependent on her so that you would never leave her. Did you feel like you could ever be independent of her?" Bill asks.

I think about that for a minute. Come to think of it, Mom was the reason I didn't have any friends. Anytime someone would act like they wanted to befriend me, Mom would make an excuse as to why they couldn't come over or why I couldn't go to their house. I couldn't do sports. I couldn't be in any clubs. She made it so that she was my only friend, so that I needed her more than anyone else in the world, more than just a daughter needing her mother.

"I wasn't allowed to do anything. I didn't have any friends. I left the house to go to school and swim on the weekends. She isolated me but called it being studious. That I'd have time after I graduated high school to make friends but for now I just needed to focus on getting good grades," I answer Bill. I look at Meredith and say, "If who I thought was my mom, is really Vanessa, then she was there the entire time I was being beaten?

She was there when I was tortured so close to death? She's the one who told those... those men to get rid of me because she realized I wasn't who they were looking for?" I can feel tears running down my face.

Meredith looks at me with despair in her eyes. She reaches for me, but I pull away.

"No, I don't--- I can't believe this. If she's not my mom, who is? Who are my parents?" I ask, looking at Bill.

He looks at Kathryn.

"I'll see if I can figure something out," she says. She stands up and disappears from the room, I can't focus on the fact she just literally disappeared into thin air. My world is spinning out of control.

I start crying harder. How could this be happening? My world had been turned upside down when I thought my mom had been shot and I was kidnapped and tortured. But now, I'm being flung into another dizzying mess. The woman who I thought was my mom, the one who took care of me, raised me, isn't actually my mom at all? In fact, she was the reason I was being tortured. She could have just let me go after she realized I was the wrong person, but she wanted them to kill me. Does she not have a heart? She spent 17 years with me. Watching and hearing me get the crap kicked out of me every day, how could she not feel anything?

My crying turns into quiet sobs and it gets harder to breath. Doc comes over and tries to talk to me, but

I can't hear him. I just hear my heart thundering in my ears. Ty's face flashes in front of me, he's saying something, but I can't hear him.

My world has exploded again, my life is a complete lie. Who am I? Who are my parents? Are they still alive? Did that woman murder them like she tried to murder me?

I feel that familiar darkness pulling at my vision, so I close my eyes and let it swallow me up.

CHAPTER 7 - FRIENDS

When I wake up, I'm in a room with dirt walls. I sit up fast, thinking I'm back with my kidnappers but there's a light on the walls on both sides of me. I lay back down and breathe back the hysteria that was about to escape from my lips and also, sitting up so fast has made me dizzy.

I turn to my side and look at the room. It's big enough for the bed I'm lying on, a small dresser, and a small bookshelf. Instead of a door there's a sheet hanging from a rod that has been pushed into the top part of the dirt doorway.

I can't believe how different this place is from my old home. My mom ....

The thought of my mom, no of Vanessa, brings tears to my eyes again. How much more change can one person endure before they have a total mental breakdown? Not to mention being tortured for three weeks. I can't imagine I'll be able to handle much more.

"Emma, are you awake?" Libby asks from the other side of the sheet.

"Yeah, come on in," I answer, sitting up, slowly this time.

"How are you?" she asks as she sits next to me. I know she's not just asking how I'm feeling.

"Confused, I guess," I reply. "I don't know what to believe. Did they tell you what happened?"

"Yeah, Ty filled me in. He went with Kathryn to make some notes so that they can figure out who your real parents were," she says.

"Were? So, they really think they're dead?" I already know the answer.

Libby looks at the floor and sighs, " Yeah, Bill and Meredith figure if they were still alive, they would have gone to someone for help. And also, Chris and Vanessa aren't known for leaving people alive after they've gotten what they want from the person or people."

"Right," I say. How could Vanessa and Nessa be the same person? Now that I think of the two names in my head, it makes sense that she wouldn't fully change her name, just tweak it enough it wouldn't be hard to adjust to people calling her by it. But really, the Nessa I knew, was fairly kind and caring towards me. She at least never raised her voice at me, let alone raised a hand. She seemed to love me like I was her daughter, granted she did make sure I was isolated from anyone and everyone that ever wanted to become friends.

"You gonna be okay?" Libby asks, taking me out of my thoughts.

"I don't know, maybe. It might take a while before all this really sinks in."

Libby looks at her watch and says, "It's dinner time, you haven't eaten anything since breakfast. Let's go get some food."

I look towards the door, expecting Ty to walk in on cue like he usually does but he doesn't. I look back at Libby and she says, "Why don't you try out your legs?"

"You think I can walk?"

"Maybe, let's try."

Libby stands up in front of me and offers me her hands. I grab them and slowly try to stand. And I do without them shaking too horribly bad.

I look up with a huge grin and see she's smiling just as big.

"Okay, let's try a step," she says, taking a couple steps back while still holding onto my hands.

I nod and try to take a step and then another and another. Libby lets go of my hands and I stumble a little.

"Maybe you should hold on to my arm, just for now, " she says, grabbing me before I can fall.

"Good idea," I say.

We leave the room and start walking down the tunnel. I notice that all of the entry ways have different things being used as doors. There is a fridge door, a car door, and a sports team's flag.

"Hey, whose room was I just in?" I ask.

"That's your room. We'll stop by The Closet on our way back from dinner and get you some more clothes and things," she says.

"The Closet?" I ask looking up at her.

"It's kind of like a store. Meredith sends her sister, Beth, out shopping once a month for clothes, shoes, books, CD's, things like that. We'll pass it just before we get to the Great Room," she answers, smiling at me.

"How do we pay for things if we want to get something?" I don't have any money, how am I supposed to get more clothes?

"When our Demi leaders realized we were going to have to go into hiding, they pooled all of their money and put it into one account under the name of the Inepties who run the dry cleaner. Not only is Beth a Shield, she's also a Shifter like me and she changes herself to look like Mrs. Fitzgerald so that she can use her driver's license and bank card. We earn credit by going to our Talent classes and trainings, and helping around The Pit," Libby says, stopping in front of a purple door. "This is The Closet. I'd show you but you'll want to go in and we need to get some food in you before we do any shopping."

"I haven't been here long enough to earn credit, how am I supposed to pay for anything?" I ask. Speaking my concern out loud makes me feel a little better.

"Oh, all newcomers are given a certain amount of free credit. It's enough to get the essentials," she says as we step out into The Pit. It took us about 15 minutes to get here, I'm guessing it doesn't normally take this long

Libby takes us over to a table where Shae is sitting with Max, Alysa, Malory, Clay, and Charlie.

I tighten my grip on her and she pats my hand.

"It'll be okay. Shae will make sure Alysa behaves herself. Gods know she's the only one that can," Libby says as we reach the table.

"Oh Emma, how are you?" Shae asks, pulling the chair out next to her so I can sit by her.

"I'm okay," I say.

I hear Alysa snort and when I look at her she rolls her eyes and then whispers something into Malory's ear, they both bust up laughing.

"Something you'd like to share with the group?" Shae asks, staring at her sister.

"I was just telling Malory that I remembered when I was two and still needed to take naps," Alysa says, smirking at me.

"And you guys were laughing because?" Shae asks. "No seriously, it's not even funny. Or clever. Yeah, Emma is small, but she doesn't look like a two-year-old."

I giggle a little out loud. Alysa's teasing is nothing new, in fact a lot of the kids back at my high school used to call me, The Toddler.

"Whatever," Alysa says and starts talking to Malory again.

"Sorry about her," Shae says to me.

"It's okay. It's nothing new, I had to deal with about the same at my school," I say back, smiling.

Charlie comes to sit on the table between me and Shae and says, "I'm sure you hear this a lot, but you have gorgeous eyes. What color of blue are they? Oh, and I'm sure you remember but supposing you don't, let me reintroduce myself, I'm Charlie O'Neal," he reaches down, takes my hand, and kisses me on the knuckles. Normally, if a cute guy were to ever do something like this to me, I would feel embarrassed or giddy, but I feel more uncertain than anything.

"Yeah, I remember you," I say to him, as I pull my hand back. I try to ignore Charlie as much as I can, he's sitting awfully close to me. I look at the two guys sitting across from me, and ask, "You're Clay and you're Max, right?"

Clay smiles and says, "Yeah, hi."

Max just nods and smiles.

"No but seriously, what color blue are your eyes? I've never seen such pretty eyes," Charlie says, trying to draw my attention back to him.

"I don't know. I guess you could call it dark cobalt," I say to him so that he'll stop leaning in towards me.

A tray of food gets set in front of me and Charlie jumps up out of the way. I glance behind me and see Ty walking off.

"What's his problem?" Charlie asks.

"He's probably tired of playing waiter," Alysa says.

"I didn't ask him to bring me anything, I can get my own food," I say, but I'm secretly thankful that he'd brought me something. I didn't want to make a fool out of myself if I ended up falling or something, while carrying my tray back. I'd have to thank him the next time I saw him. I didn't even know he was in here but now he's gone again.

"Whatever, let's go Malory," Alysa says getting up and leaving the table before Malory can answer. She glances down at her half-eaten plate of food and sighs before she gets up, gives Clay a kiss, and then follows Alysa out of the Great Room, walking towards what I think is the Gym.

"Can you show me around?" I ask Libby.

"Sure, as soon as we're done eating. We've got to make sure to hit The Closet before seven o'clock though, that's when Beth locks up for the night," Libby says.

"Locks up? There was only a purple sheet for a door," I say.

"With her Shield Talent, she can project it out into a small space for an extended amount of time. She can make it so no one can enter The Closet after she's left, and no one can take it down but her. Beth has tried to do The Pit so that the Guardians don't have to always be on duty, but her Talent isn't strong enough. She can do the Great Room, but it doesn't last very long or she gets worn out from doing it for too long. We did a drill to see if she could do it, she lasted five hours but she slept for the next three days straight. Five hours would be enough to keep us safe and figure out a plan if we were under attack but she's not sure how she would do with Rifts attacking her barrier," Libby answers, looking around the room.

"That's pretty cool. I wonder if I'll be able to do something like that," I say.

"Maybe. Doc says your Talent will be a strong one, once you get your Mark," Libby says, grinning at me.

As Shae stands up, she says, "I have to use the bathroom, don't leave without me. I wanna go on your tour with you."

I smile at her. It was nice having people want to spend time with me. I'm not used to people actually wanting to hang around. Although, who knows how many friends I would have had if my mom... if Vanessa would have let me have any. Shaking my head, I try to think about something else.

"Clay, do you mind me asking what Talents you have? I'm just curious about what different ones are out there."

"I'm a Protector, Shifter, and Mentalist," he says and then pulls his sleeve up so I can see his Mark.

"Is that a sword?" I ask.

"Yeah," he says, pulling his arm back. "Most of us that are Guardians, have a sword."

"Which god does it signify?" I ask, curious as to which Mark belongs to which god.

"Ares, god of War and raw violence," he answers, looking proud.

"So, if you have that Mark, you're a good fighter?" I ask again. So many questions. I hope I don't start annoying people with all of them.

"Yeah, pretty much," Clay answers, laughing. At least he doesn't seem bothered by my questions, thank goodness.

I look over at Max and ask, "Do you mind me asking about yours?"

"Not at all. I'm a Protector, Animal Shifter, and Wind Mover," he pulls up his sleeve and shows me his Mark which is a Crescent Moon with a sword across it.

I look up at him, confused, "Two Marks?"

Max laughs and says, "It's one Mark, but it's from two different gods. Ares and Artemis. Artemis, goddess of natural environment. I can summon wind or change the air around us."

"So, some people can have multiple dominant Talents from different gods?" I ask.

"It's rare but yes," Max says matter-of-factly.

"I guess you'd like to know my Talents now?" Charlie says, sliding into the chair Shae had been sitting in.

I grudgingly look at him. I'm weighing my hunger to know more about Talents and my need to get as far away from Charlie as possible. I still can't decide if I'm attracted to him or if the feelings in my stomach are from my instincts telling me to stay away. I have to admit, he is really good looking but so far everyone I've met here, has been. I decide to just go with feeding my need for more information.

"Sure, Charlie, what is your Talent?" I ask.

"Other than being an excellent kisser," he winks at me which makes my stomach flip. Good or bad? I'm not sure. But he continues, "I'm a Protector, Earth Mover, and Jumper."

"Earth Mover and Jumper?" I'm glad I decided to find out what his Talents are, I hadn't heard of these ones yet.

"I can move the ground, you know, make a hole or canyon if I need one. Or build a mountain or hill. As a Jumper, I can move, anywhere I want to, without walking. I just have to think about where I want to go, and I'll appear there. I just have to have been to where I want to go, or I have to see or have seen a picture of the place. As of now, I can take up to two people with me. That's how we got out of the place you were being held," Charlie says, winking at me as he shows me his Crescent Moon and Sword Mark.

"Wait, you were there?" I ask, stunned by this news.

"Yeah, me, Clay, and Max are Ty's comrades," he says, smiling at me ear to ear.

"Really?" I say, looking at Clay and Max for confirmation.

"Yeah," Clay says. "I Telepathically told Bill we'd found you. Charlie Jumped you and Ty out of the building first because some of the Rifts were coming towards us sooner than we thought they would. Charlie got back to us and Jumped us out to where you and Ty were waiting."

"I didn't know that," I say, dumbfounded by this information. "Thank you! Thanks for getting me out of there."

"It's what we do," Max says. "And it sounds like we got you out of there in the nick of time. With the amount of injuries you had, I bet you wouldn't have lasted much longer. You still look like hell, no offense."

I laugh, "None taken. But I do feel much better. Still a little sore but nowhere near the pain I was in and I look far worse than I actually feel. My face is more color than anything."

"We heard your birthday is tomorrow," Clay says. "How old will you be?"

"18."

Charlie chokes on his drink he had just swallowed and spits out what's left in his mouth. Coughing, he asks, "You're going to be 18?"

"Yup," I answer shrugging.

"No way," he says. "Maybe 15, 16 at the oldest."

"Nope, I'll be 18," I say. Feeling slightly grossed out that he thought I was that young and yet he was still flirting really bad with me.

"You're so----- "

"Small?" I interrupt Clay.

"Some parts aren't so small," I hear Charlie whisper. I glance over at him and see him trying to be sly but failing, he's totally staring at my chest.

"Dude... show some class," Max says. Charlie quickly looks away. I nonchalantly cross my arms over my chest.

"Well yeah, why *are* you so small?" Clay asks but then turns red. "Sorry, that was rude."

"It's okay, I'm used to it. And I don't know. Why are you guys so tall? I mean *all* of you. Boys and girls. You all could be pro football or basketball players and you girls could all be models for crying out loud," I say, looking at Libby.

She laughs and says, "You are just as pretty, if not prettier. We look like this because it's in our DNA. Our parents look the same way."

"What does that say about my parents?" I ask, saddened once again that I actually don't know anything about them.

"Maybe when Ty gets back, he can answer that. Hopefully Kathryn was able to find her information on your parents," Shae says from behind me, causing me to jump.

I shake off the surprise of Shae's return and ask, "So how old are you guys?"

"We're all 20. Ty and Libby turned 20 in January.

Charlie and Clay were in February. Alysa and I turned 20 in April. And Max and Malory were in March," Shae says, taking a seat next to Libby.

"That's a relief," I say, making the others laugh. "Can I ask one more question before we go look around?"

"Sure," Libby says.

"Why do you all have twins? I mean, does every single person here have a twin? Is that in the DNA also?" I'd been wondering this ever since the meeting with the Guardians, they all had a twin.

"Yeah, pretty much. Our parents have twins and their parents and theirs before them. We've been wondering about your twin, if you had one but it was murdered or if you weren't born with one," Libby says but then looks like she probably shouldn't have said anything about my lack of a twin. "Sorry, I don't mean to bring up more about your family."

"It's okay, I have been wondering the same thing," I sigh.

"Let's get out of here and take your mind off of things until Ty gets back, wanna go for that walk?" Shae asks.

"Yeah, but I have just one more question first," I say.

"Of course you do," Libby says winking at me.

They all laugh, as do I.

"No really, after this we can go," I say smiling but then stop and ask, "Where are your parents?"

They all look at each other and Max is the one that

answers me, "They are all Seekers, out looking for another place for us to have as an Institute. We haven't heard from any of them for over a year. We knew it would happen. We don't have any communication with the outside world. No cell phones, no internet. Those things are just another way for the Rifts to find us. So we figure they are too far away to Telecommunicate with us which would mean they are on the other side of the country or in a different country altogether. Meredith has ways of tracking them down if she needs to talk to one of them."

More questions pop up but there'll be more time to ask them later. I really want to go check out the rest of The Pit.

"Do you mind if I join you?" Max asks.

"Ummm..." I don't know what to say, I'm not used to people, let alone boys asking to tag along when I'm involved. "Sure."

"Awesome," he says, walking over and grabbing Libby's hand as she stands up. I look at them and their hands.

Libby turns a little red and says, "Yeah, he's kind of my boyfriend."

"Kind of? I'd say 'kind of' went out the window two years ago when we first started dating," Max says, kissing her on the cheek.

She giggles and gives him a quick peck on the lips, "I know but every day feels like the first with you."

Aww, how sweet.

"You're going to make me sick," Shae says but she just laughs and stands up. "So lovey-dovey and sweet, I can't stand it."

"You're just jealous cause you don't have a boyfriend as awesome as me," Max says.

Charlie puts his arm around Shae's shoulder and says, "We could always give it another go?"

She throws his arm off and says, "Really? You want to go there?"

Charlie looks taken aback and slightly ashamed. After half a second though, he shrugs. He looks at me and is about to say something, but Shae says, "Don't even think about it," and loops her arm through mine and starts walking, forgetting that I'm still a little weak in the leg department.

I stumble and almost fall except someone catches me. I look up and see Ty.

"Ooops, sorry Em, I forgot," Shae says.

"It's okay," I say as Ty sets me back on my feet, a tingling sensation spreads out from where his hands are touching me. Libby comes over and takes one of my hands. I look at Ty and ask, "Where'd you come from?"

"I just walked in," he replies, stepping back.

"Oh, well, thanks," I awkwardly say.

He just shrugs and looks around.

Max asks him, "Wanna tag along, Ty? We're gonna go show Emma around."

"Sure, I guess. I'm just waiting for Kathryn to get back to me," he answers like he's anxious.

"Where do you want to go first?" Libby asks me.

"Can we check out the Gym? I've been dying to see it."

"Okay, let's go," she says.

I look back and see that Clay and Charlie are following us. Shae is on my left side, with Ty on her other side. Libby has my right arm and Max is holding her right hand.

This was so different than anywhere I'd ever been. I seem to have friends now. I think I'm going to really like it here.

CHAPTER 8 - THE PIT

I'm able to walk a little bit faster than before, so making it down to the Gym doesn't take as long as it had to walk from my room. Even though the Gym is further down the tunnel than what we had walked from my room to the Great Room.

As we step into the room my mouth hits the floor. If I thought the Great room was big, it's nothing compared to the Gym. The ceiling is at least twice as high as the ceiling in the Great Room. There is a basketball court, a tennis court, and in between both courts was a boxing ring and then work out areas around it.

There are people practicing hand to hand combat right now on the mat behind the boxing ring. There is a basketball game going on, some girls are sitting on the floor watching.

"What do you think?" Shae asks, smiling down at me.

"This is incredible!" I say in awe. "How far down are we, exactly."

"Far enough," Clay says from behind me, laughing.

"If you think this is cool, wait until you see the bathrooms," Libby says.

"The bathrooms?" I snort out a laugh.

Libby laughs, "Yeah, the bathrooms. They're awesome!"

I just shake my head and look around. The size of this place is absolutely amazing!

"What sports do you like?" Max asks me.

"I like all sports but my mom... err... Vanessa, only let me swim on the weekends," I answer sadly.

"Well, here, you can play whatever sport your little heart desires," Libby says, wrapping her arm around my shoulder and squeezing.

"Let's go show her the bathroom," Shae says, taking my shoulder and turning me back down the tunnel.

"You good to walk?" Libby asks before she lets her pull me too far away.

"Yeah, I won't be running a marathon anytime soon, but I can walk," I say.

We all turn and start walking out of the tunnel. Charlie comes up beside me and puts his arm around my back and onto my shoulders.

He leans in and whispers in my ear, "I've got a secret to tell you."

"Oh yeah, what's that?" I say wondering if the chills I just got were good ones or bad ones.

"I've got an early birthday present for you," he says quietly.

"Oh really?" I ask, not believing him.

"Yup," he says slyly, smiling down at me.

"What is it?" I ask.

"You can open it after you're done with the bathroom tour," Charlie says, running his hand down my back and then back up to my shoulder.

Again, a chill runs down my spine.

"Oookay," I say.

"Move along Charlie," Shae says, coming up from behind us.

"Don't be jealous, Shae. There's plenty of me to go around," he says, flexing his arms as he walks backwards in front of us.

"Oh please," she says, rolling her eyes at him.

Charlie stares at her before he turns around and sprints off towards Max and Libby.

"Let me know if he bothers you," Shae says.

"Nothing I can't handle," I say back smiling, "but thanks."

"He's kind of a man whore, sleaze bag. We dated for a bit but then I came to my senses," she admits shaking her head.

I laugh and keep walking. We take the connecting tunnel to the left and I can hear a roaring from somewhere ahead. We turn left again to walk down to the end of the tunnel and the roaring gets louder.

We walk into what looks like a main bathing area and I stop dead in my tracks which causes the person behind me to run into me, knocking me to the floor.

Before I roll over to my butt, I already know who knocked me down, the shock that went through my body told me enough. I look up and see Ty looking down at me.

"Could warn a person if you're going to stop walking," he says, reaching down to help me up. I ignore his hand and get up on my own.

"And you could let a person know you're walking behind them, so they know you're there," I snap back.

Ty rolls his eyes and shrugs. He walks past me towards the bathing pool.

I shake my head and then focus again on the bathroom. I have never been to a water park, but I always imagined it would look like this.

The ceiling was just as high as the Gym ceiling which allowed for a tall waterfall. They had put lights around it so that the water looked like it was glowing in the dark. It looks so amazing!

Libby comes skipping back to me and says, "What do you think?"

I just stare and she laughs. I finally find my voice and say, "You were right, it's amazing! I mean, it's better than amazing but I can't think of the right word right now. This is fantastic! It's all-natural hot springs?"

"Yup. The waterfall is where the springs come together, that's why it's so large and loud," she says, pointing to the waterfall.

"I think this is going to be my favorite place," I say, truly smiling for the first time since I got here. As crazy as that sounds, I never thought I could love a bathroom as much as I love this one.

"So how does this all work? We don't all bathe together, do we?" I ask.

Libby laughs and says, "No, just past this bathing pool there are two separate areas. One for guys and one for girls. There are showers in there and kind of toilets. There's a separate stream that washes the waste away. This bathing pool is more just for fun. Kind of like a regular pool but the Leaders don't want us spending too much time in it as it is the bathrooms and to many people would cause congestion. Most people will just jump in and then get back out, a quick rinse off if they don't have time to go take a real shower."

"That's understandable," I say.

Libby looks down at her watch and says, "We don't have time to wash up, The Closet is going to close in 15 minutes, but you can come here first thing in the morning."

"Sounds like a plan!" I say, excited. I wasn't looking forward to tomorrow but now I am. I could really use a shower, one that I actually take.

We turn to walk out of the bathroom, but someone grabs my hand and spins me around. With my strength just barely back in my legs, I clumsily fall into whoever spun me.

I look up and see Charlie grinning at me. I also notice my hands are touching his bare chest. I quickly step back and see that he's wearing swim shorts and smiling.

"Like what you see?" he asks, flexing his pecs.

"Uhh," is all I can say. I'd never seen a guy without his shirt on in person and Charlie was in great shape, ripped is what the girls from high school would have said. I'm guessing all the guys around here look like him. Washboard abs, huge pecs, enormous biceps, strong broad shoulders, and a strong neck.

"That's what I thought, happy birthday," he says, cockily.

Happy birthday? What's he talking about? And then I get it.

"Oooh, so *you* are my birthday present?" I ask, embarrassed but thankfully the room was dark enough that he hopefully can't see my face turning fifty shades of red.

"Yes, I am," he says stepping closer, placing his hands on my hips. "How about we go for a swim?"

"Uhh," I clear my throat and say, "I can't, I don't have a swimsuit and I'm going with Libby to The Closet."

"We don't need suits, we can skinny dip, it is a bathing pool. No one else is here," he says, looking around and then staring at me with a twinkle in his eye.

"Ummm, no."

"Oh, come on, it'll be fun," he starts to pull me further into the pool room, but I pull back and twist out of his hands.

"No thanks, you go ahead," I say, turning to walk away.

He grabs my hand again and says, "I know you want to swim."

"No, I don't," I say back, pulling on the hand he was holding.

Just then, Shae appears and says, "Back the hell off Charlie, she said no." She knocks his hand away and turns me back towards the tunnel.

I hear Charlie say, "For now."

"Sorry, did I forget to mention that he's an asshole?" Shae says, putting her arm through mine as we start walking down the tunnel.

Five minutes into our walk Libby comes running towards us.

"What happened? I thought you were right behind me but when Max and I got to the Great Room, you weren't there," she says, panting. "I thought you'd fallen or something."

"Charlie was trying to get her to go for a swim," Shae says, shooting Libby a look.

Libby nods ever so slightly at Shae, was I not supposed to notice it?

"He's an ass," she says.

"That's what Shae was telling me," I say back.

"You'll do good to remember it," Libby says, looking behind me. To see if Charlie was coming? Was he really that big of a jerk that they were worried? Well, they didn't need to worry about me, I grew up in New York City, I know how to take care of myself. It was one thing Mom... Nessa... Vanessa had taught me in case we were ever separated, which never happened, but still.

I was just about to tell them that when Ty comes walking up to us.

"Kathryn has information for you. She says we can talk in the Great Room if you'd like. Over in the lounge area," he says.

"Sure, but can I go to The Closet first? I'd like to get some pajamas and bathroom necessities before it's closed," I really didn't want to sleep in these clothes, and I was definitely not sleeping in my underwear and bra with only a sheet for a door. I was actually looking forward to sleeping in pajamas.

"Yeah, that's fine but you guys better hurry, you've got five minutes," he says as he walks away.

"I'll Run ahead and ask Beth if she can stay open just a little bit longer. I'm sure she'll understand," Libby says as she disappears.

"What did she just do?" I ask. Finally hoping to get the answer to this question I've been wanting to ask since I saw Meredith disappear back in the Hospital Wing.

"She Ran. We can run extremely fast," Shae says, laughing at the look on my face.

"That's insanely cool," I say in awe.

We finally get to the Closet and Libby's standing in the doorway.

"Beth says you can go in and get what you need but I have to stay here and keep everybody else out, and that includes you, Shae," she says, rolling her eyes at us.

"But I need-----"

Shae didn't get to finish her sentence because Meredith steps out from behind Libby and says, "And that's why no one else is allowed in except for Emma." She looks at me and says, "Hello Emma, I'm Beth."

I can feel my eyes widen. I figured she'd look like Meredith, but I didn't think they would be *exactly* alike.

Finding my voice, I say, "Hi, it's nice to meet you, Beth."

"Nice to meet you as well. Come on in. I've already grabbed the essentials you'll need but you go ahead and look around at the clothes. You can pick out four bottoms, five tops, a package of underwear, three bras, a pack of socks, a pair of shoes, and a bathing suit. Towels are supplied in the bathroom," Beth explains as we step into her store.

If my mouth could hit the floor, it would be dragging right now. Anything you could possibly want, or need was here. Clothes, shoes, coats, bags, cd's, stereos, books, magazines, I mean anything. Well, except for computers, cell phones, and tablets.

"Wait, how can I afford all of this?" I ask.

"You have some credit but some of your friends

have given some of their credit to you so that you can get what you need, to help you adjust to living here. It can be a bit difficult," she says, smiling kindly at me.

"This place is like a fancy hotel compared to where I was being kept," I say truthfully.

Beth pats my shoulder and walks up to her counter.

I start looking around at the clothes and pick out two pairs of blue jeans, a pair of black sweats and a pair of black shorts with pink stripes down the sides for working out in. I grab two black long sleeve tees, another light blue hoodie like the one I was already wearing, and two royal blue t-shirts. I grab the comfiest looking pack of undies I can find. I pick out two pink sports bras and a pink tank top bra. Since I already have a pair of tennis shoes, I pick out a pair of black slip on boots. I walk over to the swimsuit rack and start looking for something that's my style and of course it's nothing but bikinis. And why not? All the girls here are freaking models.

I grab the least skimpy of them, a pretty royal blue one, and head back to Beth. Before I get to her though, I see the books to the left of her desk. I start looking through them and find three of my all-time favorites.

"How much credit do I need to earn before I can get these?" I ask, placing the books on top of all my clothes that I put on her desk.

"How about you pick your favorite one and I'll give it to you as an early birthday present. The others, it'll take a month's worth of training to get them. I can put them behind my counter to keep them on hold for you, if you'd like?" Beth says, standing up.

"Oh, thank you, that'd be great," I reply. I can't believe how nice everyone is here.

I pick out my favorite of the three books and Beth puts it in one of the bags she's filling with my things. She also had a toothbrush, some toothpaste, shampoo and conditioner, and a brush already bagged and ready for me.

"Since we don't have the sun to tell us what time it is, we all wear watches. That way you know when you're supposed to be somewhere, like training classes, mealtimes, and meetings," Beth hands me a watch that I'd seen on everyone else. It's black and sleek looking.

I start to put it on my right wrist, but Beth says, "Wear it on your left, that way your Mark is fully visible."

"I don't have a Mark," I say, looking at my wrist.

"You will, my dear," Beth winks at me and helps me strap the watch to my left wrist. "Libby, Shae, you girls can come in here and help Emma with her bags."

"Oh no, I can get them," I say, reaching for my things but I see Libby and Shae walking towards us, out of the corner of my eye.

"Girl, you just got your strength back, no need to wear yourself out," Libby says as she grabs a couple of my bags.

I grab a couple bags and then Shae grabs the last two. When we step out of The Closet, Max and Ty are leaning against the wall, talking but stop when they see us.

"Kathryn's ready if you are," Ty says, stepping forward and taking the bags I was holding.

"Okay but I need to run my things to my room," I say, trying to take my bags back. I don't know why I'm stalling on meeting with Kathryn. Maybe it's because I'm afraid of what I'll hear.

Ty gives them to Max and says, "Can you guys take these to her room for her? Kathryn needs to get back to work soon."

"Yeah, no problem," Max says. He and the girls turn and start walking down the tunnel towards my room.

Ty steps back and gestures for me to go first. I start to walk and Ty gets in step beside me. We walk in silence. When we enter the Great Room, it's completely empty except for Kathryn who's sitting over on one of the big fluffy couches. I look at my watch and it says it's 7:45pm.

"Hi Emma, how are you?" she asks as Ty and I get to her.

I sit on the couch across from her and to my surprise, Ty sits next to me.

"I'm okay, how are you, Kathryn?"

"I'm good now that I've found a little information about your parents," she says. She's getting to the point quickly, which is fine with me. Ty did say she needed to get back to work, so the quicker the better, I guess.

"Ty said you need to get back to work, what do you do? If you don't mind me asking," I was curious what she would need to be doing at this time of night.

"I'm a Guardian and I'm a Mentalist. I can read a person's mind but I don't just see what the person is thinking about at that moment, I can see everything they've ever seen or heard in their entire life but I have to be touching them before I can see it all. I can then, remember everything, I have a kind of built in memory board. I have to go into a kind of meditational state so that I can go into my own mind and search for the information I'm needing. I can always find the information, it just sometimes takes a little while before I find it," she takes a steading breath before continuing. "I never had the pleasure of meeting your parents, but I went and found every piece of memory I could that had to do with Vanessa, her family, and a baby. I want to warn you that what I have to tell you might not be something you want to hear. So, you have to decide, do you want *all* of the information or just go with what you know right now?" Kathryn looks at me intently.

"I want to know it all. I have to know who my parents were," I say to her, literally sitting on the edge of my seat.

"Okay. Your parents' names were Ian and Emmalynn Harth. Your mother's maiden name was Jamison.

One of the fascinating things about your parents is that they were born on the same day, same year. This could be why you haven't gotten your Mark yet. No one, as far as we know... as far as I know, no one has ever married and reproduced with someone with the exact same birthdate," Kathryn paused for a second to let this bit of information settle on my mind.

So my last name is actually Harth. I'm Emma Harth. It doesn't sound right. Maybe I'll just stick with Hart. I've lived with it for the past 18 years. I'd have to think about this and figure out what I want to do. My mom's name was Emmalynn. I have that part of her, so I guess that's cool.

I nod at Kathryn and she continues.

"Now for this next part, you need to prepare yourself. Okay?" Kathryn says, looking at me with concern filled eyes.

"Yes," I answer, whether I really was or not didn't matter, I wanted to know more about my parents.

"Your parents, like the rest of us, had twins. We don't know what happened to your mom's brother. He disappeared long before your parents died. We aren't sure if he's alive or dead. But your dad's sister... she's... well, we know where she is now," Kathryn looks down at her hands and then up to me and Ty.

"She's alive?" I ask, getting excited. Maybe we could get word out to her and she could come here, and she could tell me more about my parents.

"She is but listen Emma, this is the part I warned you about," Kathryn says, I bet she could see the excitement on my face. I try to reel it in, but I just can't. I can't help it, I have a real family member out there.

"Don't you see, we can learn all we need to from her. We just need to see if she can come here and talk with us," I say, standing up, starting to pace.

"Emma sit down, please. I can't tell you this while you're standing," Kathryn says a little agitatedly.

Ty reaches out and pulls me back down, gently, but still pulls me back down onto the couch.

"Okay," I say, worry starting to creep into my voice and stomach.

"Your aunt... your dad's sister," Kathryn looks at me and takes a deep breath before she continues. "She's Vanessa, Emma. Vanessa is your aunt."

And nothing, not a single thing could have prepared me for this. I feel instantly sick. I can feel dinner trying to make an escape. No words are forming in my mind to tell Kathryn she has to be wrong.

"I think I'm going to be sick," I finally say. Ty jumps up and is back with a garbage can before I finish talking. I start vomiting the second he puts it in front of me.

"I'll get you some water," Kathryn says, disappearing just like Ty had.

She's back in a flash and hands me a bottle of water and a couple of tissues.

I wipe my nose and start to say, "How...." but have

to clear my throat and take a sip of water before I can continue. "How did no one know this before now? How did no one know who was Vanessa's brother?"

"You have to understand, no one really knew anything about Chris and Vanessa until 20 years ago when they started stealing Talents from other Demi's. We tried to get as much information from them as we could, but no one really knew anything, especially about Vanessa. She never told anyone her maiden name and I never got a chance to get close enough to touch her to get a Reading. I was able to find out that Vanessa, your dad, and your mom weren't from here. They were from Greece, so they would have gone to the institute over there," Kathryn explains, looking sad.

I feel like I'm on the verge of tears again, but I really didn't want to cry in front of Ty, not again. So I close my eyes and take a few deep breaths, trying to keep the tears from spilling over.

"Emma, are you okay?" Ty asks. My eyes fly open and I look at him. Tears, unwillingly, run down my face.

"No, no I'm not. Vanessa was my dad's sister, and she and her husband murdered my parents, her family! And she raised me as her daughter and acted like nothing happened. Then she watched me get beat and tortured every day for the last couple of weeks. What kind of monster is she?" I ask, not able to hold back my tears. I'm actually more pissed off than sad now.

"Vanessa was... is a very jealous person and jealousy

can change the best of us into monsters. She's always wanted what she couldn't have," Kathryn says.

"I just don't understand. I can't imagine murdering someone, let alone a family member, to get what I want," I say as I stand up. "I'm going back to my room."

"I'm sorry, Emma. I know this isn't what you wanted to hear. I'll try to find anything else I can about your parents," Kathryn says, touching my arm as I walk by.

"Thanks," I say. She was right, what she told me is definitely *not* what I had been hoping to hear but knowing the truth is better than living a lie. The woman who raised me is not the woman I thought she was.

When I get back to my room, Libby and Shae are sitting on my bed waiting for me. They had unpacked my bags and put all of my stuff away. They even put some flowers in a vase and a picture of New York City on my bookshelf.

"Hey," is all I can say, sitting down on my bed, leaning my back against the wall.

"Uh oh, what did you find out?" Libby asks, leaning back beside me.

"Yeah, you don't look very happy," Shae adds as she sits down on the floor to face us.

"Definitely not what I was expecting to hear," I say rubbing my eyes.

"What happened?" Libby asks.

"My real parents' names were Ian and Emmalynn

Harth. I guess I just figured they didn't have a twin because I don't have one but apparently, they do. Kathryn
says they don't know what happened to my uncle, Emmalynn's twin. She didn't even know his name," I say,
opening my eyes and looking at Libby and then to Shae.

"And your dad's twin?" Shae asks.

I scream and then say, "It makes me want to be sick
all over again."

"What? Who's his twin?" Libby asks, leaning forward.

"Vanessa," I snarl out her name, biting on my lip to
keep myself from crying and puking all over the place.

"What?" they both say, Libby turning so she can
look at me full on and Shae sitting up straighter.

"Yeah, Vanessa is, was Ian's sister. She's my aunt," I
say putting my head in my hands.

"Oh my gods!" Libby says.

"Holy crap!" Shae blurts out.

"Yeah," I mumble into my hands.

"That's some messed up stuff," Libby says. "Are you
okay?"

I laugh but it's a mad, hysterical laugh. "No, not
even a little bit but I'll figure out a way to deal. It's
just.... I feel like I've had something new thrown at me
every five minutes since I've been here. My head is spinning."

"You have been through so much in the last couple
of days, it's understandable for you to feel like this.

Don't feel like you have to adjust right away. Take some time to let it sink in, digest it," Shae says, getting up on her knees.

"We should let you get some sleep. You'll probably sleep better tonight, these beds are super comfy, way better than that hospital bed you've been sleeping on, and 1,000 times better than the floor you were sleeping on," Libby says. She stands up and then helps Shae up.

"Thanks guy and thanks for setting up my room. You have no idea how much it means to me that you took the time to do that," I say, smiling at them.

"What are friends for?" Shae asks.

"Friends?" I ask back.

"Well yeah, but only if you want to be," Libby says.

"Yes, of course I do. It's just... I've never had friends before now," I say glancing up at them.

"Like, ever?" Shae asks, looking at Libby.

"Vanessa wouldn't let me have friends," I reply, "She said that I had to focus on school."

"What a bitch!!" Shae says, shaking her head.

"I didn't like her to begin with but now the more I learn about her, the more I want to punch her in the throat," Libby says after elbowing Shae in the side.

I laugh a little, "Yeah, me too."

"Alright, we'll see you in the morning," Shae says as she leaves my room.

"Night, Emma," Libby says, giving me a quick hug before she leaves.

Ever since I got here my head has been spinning. I get told crappy news one second and then the next something good happens. I find out my real parents' names but then find out the woman who raised me wasn't just my kidnapper/adopted mom, she is my actual aunt. And now I've got real friends. I could really see Libby and Shae becoming my first best friends I've ever had in my life. To top it all off, tomorrow is my 18th birthday and Doc and Meredith think I will probably be getting my Mark tomorrow. I'm both excited and nervous. Excited because I want to see what it'll look like but nervous because I'm afraid it'll hurt. I've had enough pain to last me the rest of my life.

I put on my new sweatpants and walk down to the tunnel that connects to the bathrooms. I hadn't gotten to see it today but I'm sure it's not that difficult to figure out. The connecting tunnel is short.

When I walk into the bathroom, I walk past the bathing pool, and I go in the side that has a big 'W' on the side of the entrance. There looks to be stalls made out of old doors but no actual doors at the opening, just a sheet. I push aside one of the sheets and see that there's a toilet sitting on the floor. When I look down, I can hear the whoosh of water and see a slight glint from the overhead light on the water. I put my hand just above the toilet bowl and I can feel the warmth from the water. Not bad for makeshift toilets.

I step back out and see more stalls at the end but

there's a pipe running the length of the wall. Every five feet there's a curtain that looks like it can be pulled out and around, to make a complete connection to the pipe on the wall. There are wood 2x4's on the floor and there's a hole on either side, for draining the water out from under the wood, I'm guessing. I glance over to the side wall and see a light about halfway down and there's a lever. I pull it and like the curtains, every five feet water sprays out like a shower. I didn't want or need to go look at the boys' side but I imagine it looks about the same as this side.

There's a big basin, one that I've only seen on western movies that water the horses, but it looks like it's meant to be a sink. I wash my face off and brush my teeth. I would take a shower, but I can feel my body starting to get tired. I'll take a shower in the morning, it'll feel so good.

I get back to my room and I lie down in my bed and pull the string to turn the light off. Before my head hits the pillow, I'm asleep.

CHAPTER 9 - BIRTHDAY

Before I know it, my watch is beeping at me. I'd set it to go off at six o'clock AM. I stretch and yawn but don't open my eyes just yet. I had the best sleep I've had in a long time and I can't believe it's time to wake up already. I could just go back to sleep, but I really want to go take a shower.

Groaning, I push myself up into a sitting position and open my eyes. My room is pitch black, but of course it is, no sun to show that it's morning. I wave my hand back and forth looking for the string to turn on the light and finally, my hand finds it. I click it and I'm instantly blinded. I'll have to remember to close my eyes before I turn it on after waking up from now on.

After the spots go away, I find where Libby and Shae put my bathing suit and change into it. I'm not 100% comfortable with showering completely naked around other people, even if there are curtains. I pull my sweatpants and hoodie back on and slip on my shoes. I look around for a towel but oh right, they'll be in the bathroom.

I grab my shampoo and conditioner, a pair of underwear and a bra. I'll have to find a bag for all my bathroom stuff the next time I go to The Closet. I make my way down the connecting tunnel, my pace picking up, my excitement getting the better of me.

I can feel my strength is back and I don't feel sore. Back to normal. This Demi healing thing is something I can get used to!

When I get to the bathing pool, I'm just as awed as I was yesterday. Man, it's beautiful!

I walk over to where I see the towels and grab one. I walk over to the waterfall first. I really want to check it out. I put my towel and bathroom necessities on the edge of the little pool that was created at the bottom of the waterfall. I slip my shoes, sweats, and hoodie off and place them on top of my stuff. The pool is kind of deep, not real deep but enough that I have to swim over to where the edge of the pool is under the falls. I stand up and let the water fall over me.

I let the warmth and power of the water ease the tension out of my shoulders that I didn't realize I had been carrying until now. It's hard not to relax while this amazing water flows over you.

After a few minutes I swim back over to the other side and get out. I figure since no one is down here yet I can take a swim in the bathing pool. I wade in and find that it's really deep. I climb back out and dive in and swim around for a little bit. It's a tick cooler than the waterfall pool but I like it, if it were a couple degrees cooler it would be perfect.

I start to do some laps, my body taking over the motions that I used to do every weekend. It feels good to do something active. Being on the floor at that place had me cramped up and laying on the hospital bed for the last few days didn't do anything but make me stiff. I knew I missed moving around but I really didn't know how much until now.

I pick up my pace and start swimming faster than I ever have. Before I know it, I feel like I'm having to turn around to go back the other way just as soon as I touch the wall. When I stop to catch my breath, I find that I'm not actually out of breath.

Huh, that's weird.

"You're quite the swimmer," a voice says from above me.

A little yelp escapes my lips before I can stop myself. Of course it would be him.

"Ty, I'm going to have to get you a bell or something and tie it around your neck. You are way too quiet, it's not natural," I say, but I smile up at him. It was nice to see him. "And thanks, I really like swimming."

Ty shakes his head at my comment about a bell but says, "I don't think I've ever seen anyone swim like that. You might have a Water Talent."

Now that he mentions it, he reminds me I should be getting my Mark today. I glance down at my wrist and find nothing.

I shrug as I show him my wrist, "Or maybe I'm just a good swimmer."

"I won't argue with you there."

I look at my watch and see that it's 7:00 already.

"Are you just waking up?" I ask as I get out of the pool.

Ty looks at me weird and then grabs my towel and walks over to me. Are his cheeks red? Nah, must just be a funny reflection from the water and light. I take the towel from him and thank him.

"No, I've been up for a while. I was in the Gym working out. I came here for my post workout cool down," he turns slightly away from me, looking towards the pool but I can see him side glancing at me.

He's acting weird but whatever.

"Breakfast is served at seven o'clock, right?" I ask.

"Yeah, I could smell it when I was coming down here. I think Cooky whipped something up special for today," Ty says, walking over to the towels and grabbing one.

"I'm starving, so I'm going to go shower. Have fun swimming, it feels great, but I thought we weren't really supposed to use it," I mention to him in a mock conspiratorial tone.

"Most everyone showers after breakfast. I like to come down here before everyone so I can use it as a swimming pool, kind of like you did. Don't worry, I won't tell anyone, if you won't," Ty says, smiling at me and then he winks.

With my heart pounding in my chest and my head dizzy, I make my way to the girls' stalls. *What the heck is wrong with me?*

"Hey, Emma," Ty says.

I turn back and say slightly breathlessly, "Yeah?"

"Happy birthday," he says smiling a smile that doesn't make my heart beat faster but makes it stop.

"Thanks," I say back. I watch him take his shirt off and wonder if someone's heart stops beating and then picks up triple the pace, is actually safe for the person's health or not?

My goodness he is.... in great shape. Abs that went on for days, pecks that flex as he moves his arms, and man, those arms! He looks at me and I quickly turn and walk into the girl's stalls. I'm so embarrassed he caught me staring at him, again.

Great, Emma, that was just great. Get a grip.

I take a quick shower. I would have taken a longer one, but my stomach is starting to grumble. Barfing up all my dinner last night after Kathryn told me what she found out, left my stomach empty.

I get dressed and leave the stalls and find the bathing room empty. Ty's post workout cool down must not take very long. When I get halfway down the tunnel, I can smell breakfast and Ty was right, it smells amazing. It smells like, but no, how would they know?

I step out into the Great Room and look over at the table of food. Sure enough, blueberry pancakes, bacon, eggs, fruit salad, and biscuits-n-gravy are lined up on the table.

My stomach growls in excitement! All my favorite breakfast foods!!

I rush over and see who I'm guessing is Cooky, smiling at me.

"Happy birthday Miss Emma!" she says, handing me a plate.

"Thank you! Cooky, right? These are my favorites!!" I say.

"Yes, I'm Cooky. And you are welcome, that's why I made them," she says, winking at me.

"But how did you know?" I ask, I don't remember telling anyone.

"Kathryn did some research and figured out your favorite foods," Cooky answers.

"How did she do research?" I couldn't think of where Kathryn could have gotten any information on my favorite kinds of food.

"She has her ways," is all Cooky says.

"You guys could have asked me, I would have told you," I say, smiling back at her.

"We wanted it to be a surprise. It's your first birthday here at The Pit and we want it to be special," she says, smiling at me.

"Oh, well, thank you," I say again. I can't believe

these people care so much about me, having only just met me.

Cooky winks at me and then fills my plate up with a little of everything. I thank her again and turn to walk over to a table, but I see Libby and Shae sitting at one with a ton of balloons. They are smiling ear to ear at me. I shake my head but can't help but smile back.

"Happy birthday, Emma!!" they say loudly and then pull me into a huge hug.

"Thank you," I say, hugging them back. "How did you get balloons?"

"Beth has everything," Shae says laughing and then shrugs. She sits down on my left side.

"Here, open my present first," Libby says, handing me a medium size present wrapped in shiny purple paper and sits beside me on the right.

"You didn't have to get me anything," I say to her.

"I know I didn't have to, I wanted to. Friends do things like this for other friends," she says back to me.

"I would have been just as happy to spend the day with you guys," I smile at her.

"Whatever, just open it!!" Libby says laughing and rolling her eyes.

I push my plate away and put my present on the table and start to open it. I pull the top of the box off and see beautiful blue fabric. It's the closest color of blue I've seen that matches my eyes. I pull it out and the fabric flows down.

"It's a dress?" I ask.

Libby laughs and says, "Yes, it's a dress."

"It's beautiful, thank you," I really am thankful for it. I've never owned such a beautiful dress, but I can't think of a reason to wear it. We can't go above ground unless we stay in the building.

Libby smiles at me and then Shae hands me a present, "Here now mine!"

Shaking my head, I open up the gift from Shae and find a scarf.

"Oh wow, it matches perfectly! Thank you!" I say, standing up and wrapping the scarf around my neck and holding the dress up.

"You'll look amazing when you wear it," Shae says.

"And when will that be?" I ask.

But before either of them can answer, someone wolf whistles. I look up and see Charlie and Clay walking towards us.

"Hot dress, Emma, it'll look great laying on my bedroom floor," Charlie says, winking at me.

"Grow up, Charlie," Shae says.

I put my gifts back in the box the dress came in and sit down. Instead of saying anything to Charlie, I just start eating. I'm sure what he said was meant as a joke but I don't find it very funny, it actually makes my skin crawl.

Clay hands me a little box wrapped in pink wrapping paper. He says, "Here's a little something from

Charlie and I."

"Hopefully it's something she can actually use because what Charlie gave her yesterday is absolute trash," Shae says. Charlie glares at her and I try to stifle a laugh.

"Well, thank you, it's very thoughtful of you... guys. I hope you know you didn't have to get me anything," I say.

"We know, but 18 is a special birthday," Clay says.

I smile at him and open my present. I take the top off the little box and find a beautiful silver butterfly hair clip inside.

"Oh, that will look so good in your hair," Libby says.

"It's gorgeous, thanks you guys!" I say sincerely to Clay and to Charlie this time.

They both grin and nod their heads. Charlie's chest puffs up a little bit more. I so want to roll my eyes at him, but I resist.

Max comes in and has a box in his hands. He slides it in front of me with a big grin.

"Oh my gosh, you guys! This is really all too much!" I say.

"Hush and open it up!" Libby says, pushing my empty plate out of the way and slides the box closer to me.

I've only ever gotten a present from Vanessa. I was only allowed to have one for my birthday and she always made sure it was something I needed, not something I wanted. If I wanted something, then I needed to do some work around the house to earn money to get it. I was fine with that, but I will admit, there were times I wished I could have gotten something more fun. These gifts that my new friends were giving me, were exactly what I've always wanted. They aren't something that I necessarily need, but I've always wanted a beautiful outfit.

Smiling, I rip open the wrapping paper and pull off the top lid and find a pair of the most gorgeous shoes I've ever laid eyes on. They were silver and they sparkled like they had a million stars stuck to them. If I turned them just right the light bounced off them and made little light dance across everyone's faces.

"Max, I... I don't know what to say... to any of you actually," I look around at them all, tears fill my eyes.

Libby gives me a sideways hug and says, "This is something else you are going to have to get used to."

"What? Getting presents on your birthday? Big deal," I look behind me and see Alysa standing there with her nose in the air.

"No, you spoiled brat, having friends. Not everyone is as superficial as you, dear sister," Shae says causing Alysa to glare down at her.

"Whatever, like getting friends is hard. Well, maybe for some," Alysa says, staring at me for a second before she flips her hair and walks away towards the food table. Malory prancing away beside her.

"She is being such a bitch," Max murmurs.

"More so than usual," Clay adds.

"It's because our tiny friend here is threatening to her. Emma is new and we all like new things," Charlie says, winking at me.

"I am no threat to anyone. Are you kidding me? Look at her and then look at me. Shoot look at all of you! There's no comparison who is more beautiful!" I say back to him.

Libby just shakes her head and says, "Vanessa did a number on you, didn't she? You really have no idea how gorgeous you are?"

"Are you kidding me? Compared to you all, I'm nothing. You all are so tall, and despite there being no sun down here, you all have tan skin. You have beautiful shades of hair color and eyes. I am the complete opposite," I answer back. No way they actually thought I was more beautiful than they were, they were just being nice because it's my birthday. Although, it is true, Vanessa did nothing to really help my self-esteem growing up. She never actually called me ugly, but she never gave me any compliments either.

"Different isn't bad," a whisper from a deep voice comes from behind me. I jump and see Ty walking away.

I look over at Shae and see her grinning at me.

"What?" I ask.

"Nothing," she says back, smiling even bigger.

"Okay, yes, we are all pretty, but we are what everyone looks like around here. We all have tan skin, red or blonde or brown hair, light blue, green, or brown eyes. And yes, we are all tall. But you... you are different from anything we've ever seen. At least for a Demi-god. You aren't the norm. You have gorgeous white, clear skin, and natural wavy, long black hair," Shae says. She purses her lips and continues, "Don't get me started on your eyes. You have eyelashes that look like they could get caught in your perfect eyebrows. And the color? No offense, Charlie and Clay, but your blue eyes are nothing compared to Emma's."

"I totally agree," Charlie says, smiling a crooked smile at me.

I can feel my cheeks getting warmer. I just can't believe Shae actually means what she's saying but it is considerate of her, and the others, to be so nice to me.

"Well, thanks for saying all that. I feel slightly out of place here," I say, smiling back at Shae.

"Then maybe you should go back to where you came from," Alysa says, setting her tray down next to Charlie. He playfully elbows her, but I can see him smiling at her.

"Or maybe you should learn to be nice to others. I know you wouldn't be acting like this if Mom and Dad were here," Shae says, rolling her eyes at her sister.

"Or... Oh hi, Ty!" Alysa says, flipping her hair to

her other shoulder.

"Hey guys," he says, not directly saying hi back to Alysa. He sits on the other side of his sister and Alysa leans over and whispers something into Malory's ear. "What's going on?"

"We were just giving Emma her birthday presents, did you get her anything?" Libby says, giving him a stern look. Ty just shrugs in response.

Libby is about to say something to him, but I say, "No, it's okay. Ty has gone above and beyond for me, he doesn't need to get me a present, ever."

It gets awkwardly quiet now. I look down at my now empty food tray and decide to take it over to the trash and tray rack.

When I start walking back, I can see Libby whispering something to Ty angrily, Ty says something back but when he sees me coming, he gets up and leaves.

"What was that about?" I ask Libby.

"Nothing... don't worry about it. So, are you ready for another surprise?" she says, smiling at me.

"There's more?" I ask.

"Well, aren't you wondering where you get to wear all this fancy-smancy stuff to?" Shae asks, smiling over at Libby.

"Actually, yeah I was," I say, smiling also.

"We talked the Leaders into letting us throw you a birthday party. Cooky is going to make some amazing food and a birthday cake. You get music and dancing.

The decorations are going to be awesome, Beth promised they would be," Libby says, bouncing up and down a little in her seat.

"Seriously?" I can feel myself starting to get excited.

"Of course! It's been a couple years since we've been able to celebrate the "Big" birthday," Libby says leaning into me, bumping me with her shoulder.

"I don't think it's fair that she gets a party when we didn't get one the last two years," Alysa says snottily.

"Do you not remember how extravagant you wanted our 18th birthday to be? That birthday party was worth a lifetime's worth of parties. Give your jealousy a break for today, it's Emma's day, be nice to her," Shae replies.

Alysa gives me a smug look and says, "Oh I remember, no birthday will ever come close to how amazing ours was."

"That's because no one is as materialistic as you are, Alysa. And no one can throw a temper tantrum quite like you either, you can put any toddler to shame with your outbursts," Clay says matter-of-factly.

"Nobody asked you, Clay!" Alysa says sourly. I can see her face turning a little red, which gives me a little satisfaction.

CHAPTER 10 - LESSONS

All of a sudden, all of their watches start to go off.

"Oh crap, we have to get to our classes," Shae says, standing up and hurrying off to put her tray away.

"Wait, what?" I ask.

"We have classes that we go to, to learn how to use and control our Talents. When I first got my Mark, I kept changing into animals, whether I meant to or not. If someone said an animal, I'd change. If I was reading a book, I'd change," Libby says, rubbing her forehead.

"What should I do?" I look down at my wrist and still see blank skin. Since I haven't gotten my Mark yet, I don't know what Talents I have or will have, so I don't know which classes I should be going to.

"You're coming with me," Ty says as he walks back to the table.

"Don't we have class together today?" Alysa asks, walking up to his side, wrapping an arm through his.

"Nope, not today," Ty says, unwrapping himself and stepping away. "Come on, Emma."

"Oh, okay. I guess I'll see you guys later. Thanks for the presents, they mean more than you will ever know!" I say as Shae, Libby, Max, Clay, and Charlie start to walk away. Alysa stands with her arms crossed over her chest, glaring at me. Ignoring her, I gather my boxes and turn towards Ty. "Can I at least take these to my room?"

With a huge sigh, Ty says, "Make it quick, Meredith's waiting for us."

I walk as quickly as I can without dropping any of my boxes and head towards The Quarters. I get to my room fairly quickly. I lay my presents on my bed and decide to change into jeans and a t-shirt real fast. After changing, I head back out into the tunnel.

Just as I notice it's oddly dark, I'm roughly grabbed from behind and thrown into the wall to my right. I hit so hard my head cracks against the hard dirt wall at the same time my shoulder hits. I bounce off and fall to the ground.

Someone is picking me up and shoving me against the wall, holding my shoulders extremely tight.

"I thought I told you to leave Ty alone. He's mine, you stupid little bitch," Alysa's voice says out of the darkness. She slaps me across the face and then grabs my jaw, right where it had been broken and squeezes. Even though I've been Healed, my jaw is still a little sore. I wince and try to turn my head away but Alysa holds my face tighter and slams my left shoulder, the one she's still holding, into the wall.

"I'm not doing anything, Alysa! And it seems to me, he doesn't want to be around you, and that's not my fault. Let go!" I try to push her off with my free arm but she's so much stronger than me, that I barely budge her.

"Malory, turn on the light. I want this little whore to see how serious I am," Alysa says.

Just as the light comes on, I scream, "I AM NOT A WHORE!"

I ball my right fist and swing as hard as I can and connect with Alysa's cheek. She stammers back, dropping my face and shoulder in the process.

I slip down the wall a little and look up. I see pure hate coming from Alysa's eyes. They start to turn red, like red hot, red.

"You're going to pay for that," Alysa snarls out between her teeth.

I duck just in time as fire shoots from her eyes and hits the wall where my head just was, but my move brings me closer to Alysa. She lifts me up and punches me in the stomach. I fall back to the ground on all fours, gasping for air.

"I told you NOT TO MESS WITH TY! THIS WILL BE A REMINDER FOR YOU FROM NOW ON!" Alysa says, whispering at first but ends by screaming.

I feel a searing hot pain on my back-left shoulder, and I can smell my shirt and skin burning. I start to scream.

"Alysa, that's enough! You've proven your point! You could kill her, stop!" I can hear Malory pleading with Alysa, but that just makes the heat intensify.

"ALYSA SHAE! What in the names of the gods are you doing?" Ty screams, running towards us. Instantly, the heat stops but I can still feel the pain from the burn. The damage has already been done.

"I.... She... I just.... I...," Alysa stammers out.

"What's going on? I heard screaming," I hear Cooky say from behind Ty.

"Cooky, go get Meredith, Bill, and Doc," Ty snarls out. Cooky shoots me a concerned look and then Runs away.

"I should get to cla---," Malory starts to say but Ty interrupts her.

"Don't you dare move."

Ty bends down and touches my shoulder, I wince away, whimpering. I can feel myself wanting to pass out, my body's new reaction to pain, but I fight it. I'm tired of always passing out. I have to become stronger than this. I force myself to open my eyes. I feel tears stream down my cheeks, making the floor, next to my face, muddy.

"What the hell were you thinking, Alysa? Do you know how much trouble you're in? And for what? What could Emma have done to make you act like this, to treat her like this? She's one of the nicest people here, one of the nicest people I've ever met. So tell me, what could she have done to you in the short amount of time she's been here, to make you treat her the way you have been?" Ty says, as he put his hand over my throbbing shoulder. I try to relax because I know he's trying to Heal me. As soon as I think the word Heal, I can feel his Healing talent start to pour into me.

I glance up and see Alysa with her head bent down, laying in her hands. Was she crying? There was no way she felt remorse for what she just did to me, she must be embarrassed from getting caught.

"Honestly, Ty, she just got carried away. Her emotions got the better of her," Malory says, wrapping her arms around Alysa.

"Emotions or not Malory, we do not use our Talents against each other. This is supposed to be a safe place for all Demi-gods," Ty says back.

"But is she really a Demi-god? It's her 18th birthday and she still hasn't gotten her Mark," Malory snaps back.

"Yes, my dear, she is. But it does not matter if she is or not, we never use our Talents out of anger," I hear Meredith say.

"What's happened?" Doc says, coming to my other side. He turns my face towards him and he wipes the blood away from my mouth, where Alysa had slapped me. He then places his thumbs next to the corners of my mouth, fingers wrapping up behind my ears. He touches the spot where my head had hit the wall and I wince. He swears under his breath, "Sorry, darlin'." I feel him start to Heal my head, so I lay back and relax more.

Bill stands in front of Alysa, he says, "Miss Shae, why don't you tell us what happened?"

Ty finishes with my shoulder the same time Doc is done with my face and head. They sit me up. I look up at Alysa, waiting to see how she's going to explain what happened.

Alysa drops her hands but keeps her face down and just shrugs.

"Miss Foster, would you like to enlighten us?" Bill asks, going to stand in front of Malory.

Malory just shakes her head, looking terrified to even open her mouth.

"Ty?" Bill looks over at Ty, who's still kneeling beside me.

"All I know is I heard yelling, so I started to come down here. Then I heard a blood curdling scream, so I Ran. When I got here, Emma was on the ground and Alysa was burning her. Malory was trying to get her to stop. She said Alysa had made her point," Ty replies, standing up to his full height as he talks.

"You didn't?" Meredith gasps.

"Well then, maybe the two of you should come to my office and we can continue this conversation there. We can decide what your consequences will be, as well," Bill steps aside and swings his arm out in front of him, motioning for the girls to go first.

"Wait," I say, as I stand up slowly. My head still feels a little dizzy, for some reason they can't fully heal me.

Alysa had just started to walk towards the Great Room but stops in her tracks. Looking over at me, I see she looks sad. Maybe she could feel remorse after all.

"What is it, Miss Hart?" Bill asks.

"I'm fine now. I don't think this will happen again. Please, don't be too harsh on them. I've caused enough trouble as it is, I don't want to be the cause of anymore," I say, wiping dirt off my pants.

"We still have to find out what happened," Bill says.

"It was a misunderstanding, that's all. It won't happen again," I say. I don't know why I'm trying so hard to get Alysa off the hook, but I can't stand her looking like a scared little animal.

"Nevertheless, we have a rule down here. We do not use our Talents against each other out of anger. That's why we have classes, so you kids can learn how to control not only your Talents but also your emotions. Alysa has broken that rule," Meredith says, patting me on the shoulder.

I start to say something but Ty pokes me in the back. I close my mouth and decide to drop it, it doesn't look like they'll listen to me anyways.

"Let's go girls, to my office," Bill says, once again gesturing the girls forward. They walk away with Bill, Doc, and Meredith following behind them.

Ty looks down at me and says, "You might want

to change, I'll wait out here." He steps to my bedroom doorway and holds the sheet to the side for me.

"Thanks," I say as I step in. I throw on another black long sleeve and change into my last pair of clean blue jeans.

When I step back out, Ty's leaning against the wall, facing my room. He looks deep in thought.

"Ready?" I ask.

Ty actually jumps, as I break his concentration.

"Yeah, let's go," he says, running his hand through his gorgeous brown hair.

We're about to the Great Room before Ty says anything again.

"I am curious, why were you trying to get Alysa and Malory out of trouble?" he asks.

"I know she needs to get in trouble, but I don't want it to be because of me, it'll just be one more thing she'll hate me for," I answer back.

"What else does she hate you for?"

I'm a little embarrassed with this question but I answer it honestly, "Well, she thinks I'm doing something to you. Taking your attention away from her. I don't really know. I tried telling her that I haven't been doing anything, but she keeps telling me to stay away from you. So maybe you should tell your girlfriend that there's nothing to worry about. You and I are just... friends? I don't know what we are, we just met."

"First, Alysa is not my girlfriend. After our parents

left to go look for a new place for an institute, Alysa attached herself to me, I guess for some kind of stability. We dated for a few weeks, but I got tired of all her drama. It got to the point where I couldn't hang out with my sister because Alysa thought all of Libby's friends were hitting on me or I was hitting on them. If I wasn't giving her my full attention, one hundred percent of the time, she was unhappy and would make my life miserable. So, I broke up with her about nine months ago. She's been trying to get us back together, but she doesn't get that it's not going to happen."

He walks us through the Great Room which is completely empty now, now that classes are in session. I'm not sure where we're going so I slow down so that he can get ahead of me a little bit. It looks like we're heading down to the Guard Room. Ty continues talking, "And second, even though we just met, I'd say we're friends. Now that you can walk, you aren't quite so annoying." I look up at him shocked but he's smiling and winks at me and my heart skips a beat. I really wish it would stop doing that. He's just a guy.

A guy who is extremely good looking, saved me, and can take my pain away with just a touch. I've got to get a grip!

"Thaaaanks," I say back, smiling a little.

"And lastly, Alysa doesn't like change. You are the first new Demi-god we've had in years. Our little group was the last, that we know of, to be born, and not taken by Rifts. Like they were telling you, there might be some small families out there that have stayed under the Rifts radar but it's highly doubtful. Of course there are Demi-god sanctuaries in different parts of the world but for here, in the US, this is it and this is the biggest. And not only are you new, you are different. I don't mean that in a bad way, but you are. You aren't like anyone we've ever heard about, read about, or seen. And before you start the self-loathing, self-doubting thing, that I know you're about to do, I'm telling you right now, different is not bad! Most of us... well, all of us except for Alysa, are fascinated with you. We want to know everything about you. And that's why Alysa has such a problem with you. She's used to thinking everyone is fascinated with her, now she's realizing that she's just like the rest of us, nothing special."

My mind was still reeling at the thought that he thought I was fascinating and that he wanted to get to know me. In the back of my mind I knew it was just his curiosity and nothing more but the other parts of my mind and body didn't care.

"You guys are special. Take it from me, you walk out those doors and the... Inepties?" It's still weird for me to call normal humans Inepties, I still consider myself just a normal person. "If they saw you, they would think they died and went to Heaven."

"Well I'm not just talking about our looks or your looks. I'm talking about the way you act and think. And who knows, maybe it's the way Vanessa raised you so isolated from everyone or maybe it's just who you are, but most of us aren't quite as selfless or understanding as you have been, especially with all you've been through. You seem to be handling all of this so well. And what you went through before you got here? You don't seem phased by it at all," Ty says.

"I guess I'm just good at internalizing or hiding my feelings. Growing up and then in high school, whenever someone made fun of me about my size, I'd always want to fight back. I would stop myself and think about how it wouldn't really change anything. I couldn't change the way they saw me. I knew they were only picking on me to get a reaction from me, so when they didn't get a reaction, they'd get bored and leave me alone. And that's how I spent my high school years. Walking around invisible," I can't believe I'm telling Ty all of this. I'm not meaning to talk so much, he's just easy to talk to I guess.

"Didn't Vanessa help you?" Ty asks.

"The first day of 6th grade the kids would tell me I was in the wrong building, the wrong class because I looked like a Kindergartner. I cried when I got home and my mom... Vanessa... told me to either fight back or learn to deal with it because she wasn't going to always be around to fight my battles. So I decided to learn to deal with it by ignoring them. I knew I'd always be smaller than most everyone my age, so I had to come to terms with it. What happened to me this last month is something I don't want to think about but I'm going to have to so that I can move on with my life. But I'm not ready to think about it, not yet anyways," this was a much longer answer than what Ty probably expected but I'm really good at over explaining things. It's weird being able to talk to Ty like this because I'm not normally comfortable talking to anyone, especially guys.

"If you ever need someone to talk to, I'm always here," Ty says as he reaches over and puts his hand on my shoulder. A zing of electricity shoots from where his hand is touching throughout my body. He must have felt it too because he removes it quickly.

Ty stops just as we get to the Guard Room.

"What are we doing here?" I ask nervously.

"Oh, we've put some books together for you so that you can learn a little bit about us. So today your class is what I'm calling 'Intro to Demi-gods 101'. Normally you would have learned this from your family but... Anyways, Meredith thought it would be a good idea for you to learn as much as you can while we wait for your Mark to appear," Ty says as he opens the door.

We walk in and the room is empty except for a couple men and women manning the computer screens. On the table are books and a bunch of loose sheets of paper. I walk over and sit in a chair and start my first lesson in 'Intro to Demi-gods 101'. I silently laugh at the name.

"I'll be back in a few. James and Phil are over by the

outside surveillance monitors. Ann and Janet are over by the back screens. If you need any help, just ask one of them," Ty gestures towards the right where two guys wave at me and then turn back around to look at the screen. And then two ladies from the back say hi.

"Ok, sounds good," I say as he walks to the door.

I look over all of the books on the table and pull one off the stack that's in front of me and lay it on the table. It doesn't have a title but it's old leather and smells just like a library smells. I open the book and see yellowing pages. I take a deep breath and start my education into this new world that I apparently belong in and I hope that I can get some answers to some questions I have been holding back.

CHAPTER 11 - DEMI-GODS 101

Having just spent the last six hours reading everything there is to know about Demigods and the gods that bless them, or us, I should say, I feel a bit overwhelmed. I've heard about most of the gods but some of the others, not so much.

I knew about Zeus, god of the sky and Earth; Poseidon, god of the sea; and Hades, god of the underworld. I knew they were known as the Big Three, which means they were the three major Olympian gods. I've heard about the goddess of love, Aphrodite and the goddess of wisdom, Athena. I've also heard about Apollo, god of healing and archery, and Ares, god of war and raw violence. I learned all about their history and how Zeus, Poseidon, and Hades came to be the three major Olympians.

In the fourth and fifth books I read, I was introduced to a god and goddess who were charges of so many things. I learned about Artemis, she's the goddess of the hunt, chastity, virginity, natural environment, and the moon. Hermes is the god of commerce, quick acting, thieves, athletes, and travelers.

The sixth and seventh books I read, I met the last god and last two goddesses. Hephaestus, god of blacksmithing, fire, and volcanos. Hera, is a supreme goddess, she's Zeus wife, she's the goddess of marriage and childbirth. And last but not least, Hestia, goddess of home, hearth, and domestic life.

Somewhere in all the books I read, I learned all of the different Marks. Each god or goddess has a Mark that represents them. Zeus is a Lightning Bolt and Poseidon is a Trident. Hades is called a Dagger, it's a handled dagger with a half circle at the top and inside the half circle is a filled in dot. Aphrodite is a Heart, Hestia is Flames, and Apollo is a Caduceus. Artemis is a Crescent Moon, Athena is an Owl, and Hephaestus is an Anvil. The last three were Hera, Hermes, and Ares. Hera is a Peacock, Hermes is Wings, and Ares is a Sword.

I wonder whose Mark I'll get? I wonder when I'll get it?

I also learned something I had been wondering since they first told me about Demi-gods back in the Hospital Wing. I wondered, what is the purpose of Demi's in the world? Their purpose is to fight demons. Actual demons, one's that escape the Underworld. I'm under the impression that Hades used to let some out when he got bored but was able to draw them back if they caused too much death and carnage. At some point, the demons figured out how to escape and Hades had lost control over them, he couldn't get them to return to the Underworld and they started causing massive havoc in the human world. The gods decided they needed to create something to fight them. That's when Demi-gods were created. They would fight the demons and put them back where they belong.

Hades' boredom and amount of times he let demons out has weakened the Underworlds hold on demons. They get sent there but can return back into the human world after so long. There are Great Demons who are big, bad, beastly kinds. A Great Demon needs multiple Demi's to banish it back to the Underworld. Then there are Minor Demons. These ones can be taken out by a single Demi. Minor Demons can return to the human world quicker than Great Demons. It all seems so surreal.

The door behind me slams shut cutting off my reverie and also causing me to jump. I turn quickly to see Ty standing there wearing a small smirk on his face.

"Did I scare you?" he asks half laughing.

"Yes, don't you always?" I retort.

"Not a few hours ago. You were so into your reading you didn't notice when I came in and by the looks of it, you also didn't notice I had brought you lunch," Ty points to my right.

I turn and see a plate sitting there. It has a sandwich, fruit salad, and a bag of chips resting on it.

"Hmm, guess I was really into what I was reading when you brought that in," I say, a little embarrassed.

"What all did you get read anyways?" Ty walks over to the table, moving some of the books around.

"All of them. Is there more?" I ask.

"You read off of these?" he gestures with his hands out over the table.

"Yeaaaaah, why?" I say, looking at all the books.

"Those are all the books, all the information we have. I don't think anyone has ever gotten through all of them in one day, let alone in six hours. Are you sure you read them all?" he looks at me doubtfully.

I glare at him and reply, "Yes, I'm sure, I had a system. I put all the books on the left and when I got done with one I would put it on the right."

"Wow, that's impressive. Have you always been able to read so fast?" Ty looks at me with his head tilted to the side.

A little embarrassed by his stare, I clear my throat and answer him. "As far as I can remember, yeah. I used to have to pretend to read in class because the teachers thought I wasn't telling the truth when I would tell them I had finished the book. They still wouldn't believe me when I would tell them what the book was about. I got to the point where I'd bring little paperback books and read them after I'd finished whatever I was supposed to have read for class."

"And you retain everything you read?" he's still staring at me.

"Yes."

"Interesting," is all he says in return.

I'm about to ask what's so interesting about me being able to read, yes maybe fast but that didn't seem like something that wonderful, but I'm interrupted by someone else coming into the Guard Room.

"You were supposed to come get her and tell her to get ready, not keep her here longer," it was Libby and she looked irritated.

Ty says, "Right, sorry. Emma, it's time to go get ready for your party."

"Oh, okay. Well, thanks for bringing me down here and letting me read about all this stuff. I feel like I understand everything a little bit better. Oh, and thanks for the lunch," I say as I stand up and walk over to the door where Libby is impatiently waiting.

Ty just nods his head and then walks over to the back screens where Janet and Ann were but aren't anymore. Hmm, I must have been really zoned out, I didn't notice them leave the room either.

"Oh come on!" Libby says exasperatedly. "We have got to get you ready!"

"Okay! Okay!" I laugh, she starts pulling me out the door and into the tunnel.

Before I know it, we're back at my room.

"How did we do that?" I ask, slightly out of breath.

"When we get our Mark, it gives us the ability to run fast. It's not as fast as Jumping but it's a lot faster than walking or running normally," Libby says, pushing aside my curtain to my room.

I look at her with big eyes and ask, "Why didn't we do that yesterday or this morning?"

"Because you had to learn where everything was first and I'm not technically supposed to Run with you yet but Ty didn't send you back when I had asked him to so we're a little behind. Go in and get changed. I'll come in and do your hair."

Laughing slightly and shaking my head, I walk into my room.

I pick up my boxes from this morning and something small falls to the floor. I look down and see it's a little package I hadn't seen earlier. I set the clothes boxes down and pick up the little package and sit on my bed. I unwrap it and find my most favorite book ever. I flip it open and see a note.

It says:

> Emma
>
> I hope this is the right book. I heard you say something about it while you were sleeping. I know you don't have a lot of your own things here, so I hope this helps make this place feel more like home.
>
> Happy birthday!
>
> Ty

I reread the note multiple times just to make sure I'm reading it correctly. Ty had somehow gotten a copy of my favorite book. I was told when I bought mine, that there weren't any more for sale anywhere in the world, which is why I had to use pretty much my entire savings to buy it. Still, how did he get a copy?

I'm again startled out of my reverie when Libby shouts, "Are you ready?"

I jump up and change as fast as I can, "I am now."

She walks in and I'm startled to see that she has also changed. She's wearing a gorgeous green, tight fitting dress, and her hair is up in an elegant bun. She looks me over and I'm about to ask her about her changing so fast, but she interrupts me.

"I think we should keep your hair down but maybe pull the sides up a little bit. You don't need any makeup because you have a beautiful face already. Hmm, maybe this won't take as long as I thought. Thank goodness for your naturally wavy hair. It would have taken me an hour to make it look the way it looks now, well maybe not an hour, I'm getting really good at making curls with my Talent," Libby babbles as she comes to stand in front of me, flipping little pieces of my hair here and there. She uses bobby pins to keep what she's done in place.

"I've got the mirror," comes Shae's voice from the other side of my curtain.

"Perfect timing! I'm just about finished with her hair and putting in the beautiful hair clip Clay and Charlie gave her, and we're all done. Emma just needs to put her shoes on," Libby says, going over to hold the curtain open for Shae.

I bend down and put on my shoes. I stand up and look over at Shae and Libby and see myself in the full-length mirror Shae had brought in. I don't recognize myself. I walk closer to it, eyes wide, mouth slightly gaping open. I don't think I've ever seen my hair look so dark and my eyes so blue. My skin looks like it's glowing but that can't be it, must be from the low lighting down here.

I look over at Libby and she's grinning from ear to ear.

"You look beautiful," she says.

"Stunning," Shae adds. I look over at her and she's got the same look on her face, nothing but smiles. She has already gotten changed too. She's wearing a beautiful yellow dress that shows off her body perfectly and stops just below her butt, I can't imagine being able to pull off a dress like that.

I look back at myself and see that my cheeks turn a light color of red, like I'd just put on a light layer of blush. They were embarrassing me with their compliments. It's hard to believe that girls that look like they do could be so nice. The girls at my old school weren't nice at all.

"By the way, Emma? If my sister doesn't stop her crap with you, I'm going to have Meredith bring my parents back. I can't believe she used her Fire Talent on you like that. I'm glad Bill and Meredith are punishing her

and Malory. They deserve more than what they're getting," Shae says, looking really upset.

"It's fine," I say. "She just lost control."

"It sounds like it's a good thing Ty showed up when
he did," Libby says from behind me. She's double checking my hair, putting a few strays in place.

Not sure what to say, I just shrug.

Libby finally decides my hair is exactly how she
wants it when she places the mirror out of the way,
next to my makeshift door and asks, "Ready?"

"I guess so," I say.

"I'm so excited! We haven't had a good party in
a couple of years! I've been itching to get dressed up!
Thanks for being born today, Emma!" Shae says, nudging me with her elbow.

"Ha. Ha. Oh, you are so welcome!" I say, nudging her
back.

"Remind me to grab the mirror when the party's
over, Alysa will flip her lid if it's not in her room when
she gets back," Shae says.

"That was Alysa's mirror?" I ask, stopping in my
tracks.

"Yeah, she's the only one vain enough to have a full-
length mirror. Most of us just have a little one," Shae replies, looking at me with raised eyebrows.

"She will most definitely freak out if she knows I
was using it," I say.

"Don't worry, she won't find out," Libby says, winking at me. We start walking again.

"I can't wait to see the guys all dressed up," Shae says.

"Will all the guys be going?" I ask.

"Anyone in particular you might want to know about?" Shae giggles, nudging Libby.

Feeling embarrassed, I say, "No, just curious."

"Yeah, whatever," Shae giggles.

"As far as I know, they're all coming," Libby says shaking her head and smiling.

Am I that transparent that they know I'm talking about Ty? I really just wanted to thank him for my book. I love and appreciate all the presents I've gotten today, but that book, that was more personal, and it must have taken him some digging to find.

As we enter the Great Room, there isn't a single person in here. Which is the first time I've never seen anyone eating or lounging around at this time. The Great Room usually has at least ten people milling around. There are balloons everywhere though. As we walk over to the Gym tunnel, I can see a banner hanging from one side to the other.

It says:

HAPPY 18th BIRTHDAY, EMMA!

"Who put this up?" I ask, smiling at it as we walk underneath it.

"That was Meredith and Doc. They did most of the decorations," Libby says, picking up her pace so that Shae and I would walk faster also.

Doc and Meredith had done so much for me already, it seems too much that they did all the decorating for my birthday party. I'm still slightly unsettled by the amount of affection everyone here has shown me. Well, all except for Alysa and Malory, but their attitudes towards me is what I'm used to.

I look up and see we've gotten to the Gym entrance and Shae jumps in front of us and holds out her hands, in a stopping gesture.

"Close your eyes," she says.

"What? Why?" I ask.

"Just do it, we want you to be surprised!" Shae says, looking at me impatiently. Like, I should have guessed they wanted me to close my eyes..

I look up at Libby for some back up, maybe she'd tell Shae to leave me be, but she says, as she grabs my elbow, "It's okay, I'll guide you in."

With a sigh, I close my eyes. I feel Shae jump to my other side and grab my other elbow. They both start walking at the same time.

"Do you feel okay, Emma? You feel kind of warm," Libby states.

"No, I think I feel okay," I answer back.

"She's probably just excited about her party," Shae adds.

I was excited about my party but now that Libby said something and I'm thinking about it, I do feel slightly warm and... off. I can't really explain it. I have never gotten sick before but having heard kids at my school talk about being sick, I guess I kind of feel like how they described it. My body is achy just a little bit, not really bad but enough to notice a difference. That could be from recovering from my injuries, Doc did say I'd take a while to fully recover.

Just as I'm about to say something to Libby about how I feel, Shae shouts, "Okay, look!"

I open my eyes and see nothing at first and then one by one, tiny twinkle lights are turned on. From floor to ceiling, little pinpoints of light start to glow. I follow one line of lights as it starts from the floor and slowly makes its way up the wall, across the ceiling, and then down the other wall, stopping at the floor on the other side of the room.

I look out in front of us and see lights popping on and see that they are on tables. As we walk past a table, I can see that the lights are in little mason jars and around the jars are blue stones, as close to the color of my eyes as they can get.

Standing at the end of the room are hundreds of people. I didn't realize there were that many people down here in The Pit and they were all smiling and looking at me.

Meredith steps out from behind Doc and says,

"Happy birthday, Emma!"

Everyone else says it right after the words have left Meredith's mouth.

All I can do is stare and try not to blink because I know that as soon as I blink, tears will run down my face.

Never in my life have I had so many people wish me a happy birthday, this was all too much.

"What do you think?" Libby asks.

And there it was, a blink. Tears start to stream down my face.

I try to answer her but can't find my voice. I clear my throat and whisper out loud enough that I hope everyone can hear me, "This is the most beautiful thing I've ever seen. Thank you all so much!"

Libby and Shae remove their hands from my elbows and slid them around my shoulders, hugging me. Meredith walks forward and embraces the three of us. Everyone else forms a line behind Doc. He places his hand on Meredith's shoulder and I see that the line behind him follows his lead and places their hand on the right shoulder of the person in front of them. I close my eyes and hug the three women back. I feel a strong sense of peace, acceptance, and affection flow through me.

It feels like we've been standing here for ages when I hear Cooky say, from a few feet away, "Okay, enough of this mushy stuff, let the party begin!"

People start cheering and Meredith steps back. I

can see tears in her eyes as well. I look over at Shae and Libby and see they have tears as well.

"What's the matter?" I ask.

"Did you feel anything?" Libby asks back.

"Feel anything?" I reply.

"Yeah, when we were hugging you," Shae says, wiping a tear away.

"I did, but I thought it was just me. Was that from you guys?" I ask, stunned.

"It was from all of us. As you were getting what we were sending, we could feel the hurt and pain you've endured your entire life," Libby says, sniffing and wiping her nose.

"I have never felt so much sadness in my entire life. What did Vanessa do to you?" Shae asks.

"Nothing," I answer. It was the truth, Vanessa never did anything to me, with me, or for me. She never made me feel unloved though, thinking back now, which seems odd. How can someone not do anything with someone but still make them feel somewhat loved? All I did was go to school and that was about it. That's why the trip to Greece was such an awesome surprise. I had thought that my mother had finally done something nice for me.

Shae and Libby give me another hug and then Shae shakes her whole body and says, "Okay, no more sad stuff. Let's have some fun!"

"Sounds good to me! I'm starving, let's go get some

food!" I say as I look over at the food tables.

Without a word, Libby leads us over to it.

Cooky has outdone herself, once again. Pizzas, burgers, french fries, stuffed bell peppers, salads, fruits, cheese, chips, dips, and a giant birthday cake were just a few of the things that I could see on the table in front of me.

"How did Cooky know these were my favorite foods? I was never allowed to eat them, but at school I'd sneak some if they were serving them for lunch. Vanessa didn't even know I liked any of this," I say.

"Cooky said Kathryn did a little research," Libby says, smiling.

"And thank the gods you like this kind of food. Alysa demanded we have smoked salmon and caesar salad at our birthday. She doesn't even like salmon, she just wanted it to be elegant or something. It was the worst! Thankfully, Cooky had secretly made my favorite food, lasagna, and had a few trays waiting for those of us who didn't eat Alysa's dinner," Shae says, glaring at the table.

I pat her on the arm and then we turn to find a table that no one has sat down at yet and take our seats. We dig in right away and *oh my goodness*, the food was delicious, as always. I look up and see Charlie, Clay, and Max walking towards us. Max sits next to Libby and Charlie sits next to Shae, Clay taking a seat on the other side of Charlie.

"Happy birthday, Emma!" Max says, leaning forward and smiling at me.

"Thanks, Max," I smile back.

"Yeah, happy birthday," Charlie and Clay say at the same time. They look at each other and Clay smiles but Charlie just shakes his head.

"Where's your girlfriend and my lovely sister?" Shae asks Clay.

"She and Alysa have to sit with Meredith and the other Leaders," he replies.

"Great, that'll make her happy and like me even more," I groan and bow my head.

"It's not your fault, Emma. Alysa needs to grow up. I'm half tempted to break up with Malory. She should have stopped Alysa from using her Talents on you and she should have definitely not let her hurt you," Clay says, I can see that he's grinding his teeth.

"She tried, she was telling her to stop," I quickly say. "Please don't break up with her. I'm sure she was torn between doing the right thing and standing by her best friend."

"She could have tried harder and she can always get a new best friend," he says, standing up and walking away.

"Please talk to him, Charlie. Please. I don't want Malory's life getting turned upside down even more because of me," I look over at Charlie, pleading with him with my eyes.

"Fine, but two things first," he says.

Of course he'd want something. I roll my eyes and say, "What is it?"

"One, stop looking at me that way, you make me feel like I should beg him not to do it and I don't beg. Two, you have to save me a dance tonight," Charlie wiggles his eyebrows as he says the last part.

"Fine, whatever. Just talk to him, please," I say.

Charlie smiles and gets up from the table. I see him walk over to his brother and starts talking to him. I hope he talks Clay out of it. I could tell the first time I met Clay and Malory that they really loved each other.

"You don't have to dance with him," Shae says.

"I don't mind, it's just a dance, right? Unless you don't want me to dance with him," I say.

"Oh no, it's not that at all. It's just, with Charlie, it's never 'just' a dance," she replies, wrinkling her nose.

"I'll keep him at arm's length," smiling to reassure her as she gets up and walks over to the drinks table. Charlie set me on edge and I was still unsure if it was good or bad.

CHAPTER 12 - PARTY!

S peaking of being on edge, I haven't seen Ty yet. "Where's Ty?" I ask before I can stop myself.

Libby smiles big and says, "I don't know, but I'm sure he's here somewhere. Max, do you know where he is?"

"Last time I saw him was when I was walking by his room, he was putting on his shoes," he answers back.

"See, he's here somewhere," Libby says, lightly elbowing me.

"I just want to thank him for my birthday gift, that's all," I say, trying to sound nonchalant.

"He got you something?" Libby asks, turning towards me with big eyes.

"Who got her something?" Charlie says, taking Shae's seat and wrapping his arm around my chair, lightly touching my back. Chills run up my spine.

I'm about to say something, anything other than Ty, but loud music saves me from having to say anything.

"Yay! Let's go dance!" Libby says, jumping up and grabbing my hand. "I love this song!"

I let her drag me out to the dance floor, which was where everyone was standing when we first got here. I look around and notice something else too.

"Where is all the stuff that's normally in here?" I ask.

"They moved it," Shae says, coming up to dance with us. I look over at her and see the guys coming up too.

"Where did they move it to?" I ask as Libby grabs my hand and twirls me away from where I was just standing, over to her other side. When I stop spinning I see that Charlie had just came up to stand behind where I was dancing. He glares at Libby, but she acts like she doesn't see him.

We dance for a while and then a slow song comes on. I'm about to go sit down but someone taps me on the shoulder. I turn and see Doc standing there.

"May I have this dance?" he asks, bowing slightly.

I giggle and nod. He places my left hand on his shoulder and holds my right hand firmly in his and we start walking in a circle. I step on his foot.

"Sorry, I've never slow danced before," I say, looking down at our feet.

"It's quite alright, you'll get the hang of it," he says, smiling down at me.

"Thank you so much for everything you and Meredith have done tonight and the last few days. It means more than words can say," I say, squeezing his shoulder and hand, trying to convey how much I really appreciate everything he's done for me.

"Of course," Doc says with a smile.

I glance over his shoulder and see everyone looking at us, smiling. I then see a man standing with his arms crossed, not smiling, just staring.

Doc must have felt me tense because he asks, "What's the matter?"

"There's a man standing behind you, over by the wall. He doesn't look happy to be here," I say, glancing at the man again. He's still staring with his piercing eyes, I quickly look away.

Doc slowly turns me so that he can see who I'm talking about.

"Oh, that's Frank, he's a Guardian, and that's his normal expression. He just got back from a mission. Bill had called all the Guardian's back that were out doing undercover work. He takes his job and life a little too seriously. I had hoped that having a party would have loosened him up a bit, but apparently not," Doc says, looking down at me. "Try and not worry about it."

"Okay," I say. It's none of my business why Frank is so sullen but I am curious. Just as I'm about to look over at him again, I big body blocks my line of sight.

I look up and see Charlie standing in front of me.

"Doc, you mind if I cut in?" he asks.

Doc looks down at me for reassurance that it's okay if he hands me over to Charlie, I just shrug my shoulders. Might as well get my promised dance with him out of the way now.

"Sure, Charlie. If I don't see you two later, have a fun time tonight and again, happy birthday, Emma," Doc says as Charlie steps in.

"Oh, I will, Doc. No worries there," Charlie says. And then, he whispers so that only I can hear, "I'll take real good care of you."

I just shake my head and stomp on his foot.

I say "Thanks, Doc!" Looking at Charlie, I say while giggling, "Oops, sorry!"

"I'm sure you are," Charlie says but he laughs back at me.

"Are you having a good time?" I ask, trying for small talk.

"Yeah, it's a great party. Great food, awesome music, and a gorgeous birthday girl."

I just look up at him shaking my head and roll my eyes. He chuckles under his breath.

Our small talk ends and I start to wonder when the songs going to end when it changes to a fast paced song. People start to swarm the dance floor and I'm about to tell Charlie thanks for the dance when all of a sudden I'm in a room I've never been in before.

Stunned and slightly breathless, I glance around and see tables, a couple pool tables, and then a bar with bar stools. I'm in The Pub. I turn around and see Charlie standing behind me with a smirk on his face.

"What the hell did you just do?" I ask, not quite yelling, I haven't gotten my breath back yet.

"I thought we could use some alone time," and then he's kissing me. It's hard, aggressive, and really wet. And my very first kiss.

I push him away but he holds me tight against him so my chest is pressed against his stomach. Catching my breath, I look up and see he's got a cocky look on his face.

"I can feel your heart pounding, I can turn it up a notch," he says, leaning in towards me.

I reach up and slug him, hoping to knock the look right off of his stupid face. Surprised, Charlie let's go of me, and puts a hand to his cheek.

"What is wrong with you?" I scream, wiping my mouth off, finally being able to take a few steps back.

"I can tell you like me, your heartbeat doesn't lie," he says, smiling at me.

"I don't know how I feel about you except that you scare me because you are so intense, extremely flirty, and crude!" I say haughtily. "Your intensity level is a ten, you need to bring it down to a five, at the highest. We just met, for crying out loud! You don't need to be acting the way you're acting."

"I thought all girls like to be shown how much they're wanted?" Charlie says, sounding slightly embarrassed.

"Not all girls, at least not me," I say, crossing my arms in front of myself.

"I'm sorry, I... I just... I really like you," he says.

"You hardly know me. I'm just new, that's all," I snap back. He's about to say something else but I interrupt him and say, "Charlie, just go back to the party. I'll be there in a few minutes. I need some time to calm down."

I can tell by the look on his face that he wants to say something dirty but then his expression changes and he says, "I'm really sorry." For a second his face is a light pink color and then he's gone. Him and his Jumping talent. I shake my head and go sit down at one of the tables.

There is no way that Charlie actually likes me, it's only because I'm new, like I told him. My novelty will wear off and he'll leave me alone. But, do I want him to leave me alone? I know I had some kind of reaction to his kiss, but it was so sudden and rough. I know my heart was racing but that was more out of shock, right?

Could I like someone like Charlie? If I didn't have to listen to his vulgar talk and could just look at him all day, yes.

Eeesh, when did you become so shallow? I ask myself. He is gorgeous but the personality that I see right now isn't very attractive. Maybe that's not how he really is, but the way it sounds from Shae, he really is, the way he is.

I take a deep breath, ready to sigh when I get a whiff of something that's haunted me for the last month.

MINT!!

I whirl around in my chair and scan the room. I can't see anyone, but I can smell mint like I'd just walked into a mint field and I know The Pub didn't smell like this before now.

"Who... who's there?" I ask out loud, my voice shaking.

"Only me, Darlin'."

That voice! It's Mint-man! I jump from my chair and back away from where I'd heard his voice. It had come from over by the door. As far as I can tell by looking around the room, it's the only door in or out of The Pub

"Wha... what are you doing here? What do you want?" I ask, stumbling further back.

"What I've wanted from the beginning. What Tim stopped me from having... your death," he whispers the last word.

My heart racing, I turn and sprint for the back of The Pub, hoping for a back door or a storage room that I can lock the door and hopefully wait for someone to come find me and hope he doesn't break it down.

I get behind the bar and see nothing but a wall of shelves full of liquor.

I hear a ghostly laugh come from the middle of the

room. "Nowhere to run to Darlin'. It's just me and you. Rest of the party goers will be busy entertaining themselves back in the Gym, we've got quite a few hours to ourselves."

I turn around slowly, my heart is about to jump out of my chest, and then it stops completely when I see the man, not 10 feet away. It's Frank, who I'd just seen while dancing with Doc.

"You? But... No, you're in the Guard. Doc just told me. How can you be in the Guard but work for Vanessa?" I ask, my eyes wide.

"I am a Guardian, or I was. I was sent to be a spy for the Leaders, but Vanessa figured me out and she offered me a deal that I couldn't refuse. Something I knew the Leaders would never give me in a million years," Frank says.

"What was the deal?" I ask, not sure I really want to know.

He just looks at me and says, "I could help torture you and then be the one to finally end your life."

I get that feeling you get when you've taken a step thinking you've reached the last stair and you fall, that pit in your stomach feeling. My mom, no... my aunt... said that this creepy man could be the one to kill me if he joined forces with her? I feel like I'm going to be sick.

I shake my head and I look around, hoping to find something to use as a weapon. Nothing, except for bottles of booze. I reach for one behind my back and hold it ready to throw when I need it.

"So you turned your back on your people?" I ask. I really don't want to talk to him or hear anything more he has to say but I'm trying to buy me more time, I'm still hoping someone will come. Maybe Charlie will come back to check on me or Libby and Shae coming to find me.

"Like I said, she offered me a deal I couldn't refuse," he says and then takes a step towards me.

I chuck the bottle, which connects with his head in a loud thud. I turn and run towards the other end of the bar, bringing me closer to the door. When I get to the end of it, I turn, and sprint as fast as I can to the door. But then the floor beneath me heaves and I fly into the air. Hitting the ceiling and then crashing to the floor.

I roll to my back, stunned, and trying to catch the breath that has just been knocked out of me.

"You really shouldn't have done that, Darlin'. I don't think I'm going to be as nice as I was going to be," Frank says from a few feet away.

Just as I'm getting air back into my lungs, I see him looming over me. He kicks me hard in the side, making me roll to my other side, clutching my ribs that he, for sure, has just re-broken.

He takes his foot and rolls me over to my back and continues to roll me until I'm on my side he has just kicked so that I'm facing him. He says, "That was for the bottle." He kicks me again, this time in the face. I can feel pain radiating from my nose, all the way to the back of my head. "And that's for making me rethink my plan. I only wanted to hurt you, feel your last breath leave your body. That's where I get my joy but now that I've seen you in this dress, I may change my plans now."

I roll myself to my back while pressing my hands to my face, trying to stop the bleeding and to stop the pain. Through watery eyes I can see Frank standing beside me. He steps over me so he's got a foot on either side of my hips.

He bends down so that he's straddling me and starts to touch my face.

"You shouldn't have done that Darlin', now you've gone and messed up your pretty face," he pulls my hands away from my face, holding them in one hand above my head. He slaps me hard and kisses me roughly. I bite his lip which causes him to yelp and pull back.

"Don't touch be," I say, my 'M's sound like 'B's because of my, now, re-broken nose.

"Or what, Darlin'? What are you going to do about it?" Frank asks, slapping me again. He puts his free hand around my throat and starts to squeeze. Dots start to appear in my vision as it gets harder to breathe. His hand closes tighter and tighter. I start to thrash around, to get away from him, to get some air into my lungs, but he just sits on me harder.

When he releases my throat and I take a deep breath, he punches me in my side, the side with broken ribs. I whimper in pain. He grabs my chin and holds my face still, staring at me.

"Yeah, I think I'll take my time. You really aren't my type but you'll do," he says. Using his free hand, he reaches down, groping my breast, ripping my dress down to my stomach. Before he can do anything else, he's interrupted by The Pub door crashing open.

"WHAT THE HELL?" I hear someone yell. I hear running footsteps and then the weight of Frank is lifted off of me and I hear a crash from a few feet away. I roll to my side and curl my knees as close to my chest as I can, and I watch the fight that's unfolding before me.

I see two shapes wrestling on the floor. I can hear thuds as fists connect with body parts, grunts coming from both people. One of them stands up and I can tell it's a man, it's not Frank though. The mystery man reaches down and grabs Frank by the shirt, he lifts him up and tosses him a few feet away from me. The man runs after Frank, picks him up again, and slams him into the wall, where the mystery man starts to throttle him over and over with his fists.

After a few long minutes, the mystery man stops, and Frank slides to the floor in a heap. The mystery man stands there for a minute to make sure Frank's really knocked out and then he runs over to me. My reflexes have me flinching away from him, scared he might hurt me also.

"I'm not going to hurt you," he says softly.

It sounds like Ty.

"Ty?"

"I'm here, Emma," Ty says as he takes his jacket off and wraps it around me.

I hear gasps from the direction of the door and running footsteps coming towards us. I jump as I see two people standing over me and Ty.

"What the hell?" Shae exclaims.

"Oh my gods! Emma.... oh my gods!" Libby is all but in tears.

"What happened?" Shae asks Ty.

"Well, when you guys came to see if I'd seen Emma, I Tracked her here. Not knowing why she'd be in The Pub, I came and found that piece of shi... about to..... Everything went red for a second. I pulled him off of her and I beat the living hell out of him. She's hurt pretty bad. Shae, Run back and get Doc, Meredith, and Bill. But be discreet, she doesn't need an audience here. Libby, help me Heal her."

I feel a breeze as Shae Runs away. Libby kneels down beside me, across from Ty. She tries to place her hand on my forehead, but I flinch away.

"Emma, I'm not going to hurt you. Ty and I want to help you. We want to Heal you. Please let us," Libby pleads softly to me.

I can feel myself start to shake. It starts in my chest and then spreads out to my arms, up to my head, then down my stomach all the way down to my toes.

"Why is she shaking?" Libby asks, sounding extremely concerned.

"Shock?" Ty suggests, in a questioning tone.

I can tell it's not from shock. It feels different. I can feel something happening. My body is starting to heat up. I try to say something but all that comes out is a gurgle.

"What's wrong?" Ty and Libby say at the same time.

"I'm... so... hot...," I whisper out. Libby puts her hand on my forehead and pulls it back immediately.

"Ty, she has a fever of well over 110 degrees! We have to get her to the Bathing Room," Libby says, standing up.

Ty puts his hand on my head and I feel the pressure of it leave instantly. His hand, and Libby's for that matter, should have felt cold. If I have a temperature of over 110 degrees, anything under that should feel cooler but their hands didn't feel like anything, only a slight pressure.

"Is she glowing?" Libby asks, really panicking now. "Ty, is she?"

"Uhh yeah, she is! What the hell?!"

My eyes start to get blurry so I blink them rapidly and my ears start to ring. Through the ringing I hear people running towards us.

"Shae told us what happened. Is she..." Meredith is about to ask something but she stops and then says,

"Jim, leave Frank, come over here, quickly!"

I hear Doc hurry over from where Frank was still lying and when he gets over to me, I hear him gasp.

Bill says from the other side of the room, "Why would Frank do this?"

"I don't know, Bill, but take him to a cell. Hold him there until we can all have a chat with him. Libby, Shae, go get Emma a change of clothes, hurry," Meredith orders.

"I'm not leaving her!" Shae and Libby say together.

"Girls, please!" Meredith pleads.

"No, Meredith, we aren't leaving her!" Shae says stubbornly.

"Fine but you sit over there and be quiet!" Meredith demands. "You too, Ty!"

"But I can help, I want to help," Ty says.

"You can help her by going over and sitting by your sister," Meredith says sternly.

After a minute of hesitation, Ty gets up and lets go of my hand, I hadn't realized he was holding it until the pressure of his grip disappeared. As I feel the air stir as he leaves, my body temperature spikes, and I let out a moan which turns into a scream as I now feel like I've been thrown into a pit of fire.

"What's wrong with her?" I hear Shae ask from across the room.

"Why is she shinning?" Libby asks before Meredith or Doc can answer Shae's question.

"Have you ever seen anyone shine like this before?" Meredith asks Doc.

"No, never," Doc answers sounding dumbfounded.

"What's happening?" Shae and Ty ask at the same time.

"It's the Change. We need to get her to the Hospital Wing before she transitions into it fully, I have all the supplies there that we might need," Doc states.

"I've got her," Ty says and then I feel his arms underneath me, lifting me up, but as soon as I'm fully in his arms, pain radiates from my chest throughout my body.

I scream.

"Emma, what hurts?" Doc asks next to my head.

"Ev...ery...thing!" I pant out.

"Doc, she's getting warmer. If I'm going to carrier her and not get burned, we have to go now," Ty says sounding beyond concerned.

"Let's go!" Doc says.

"Wait!" Meredith yells.

"We don't have time, we need to get there now!" Doc insists.

"Ty, do not Run with her. I don't know what will happen if you do. You can run normally but that's it," Meredith instructs just as I start to scream again from the increase of scorching fire starting to burn its way through my limbs.

"Okay, fine, I won't," Ty says sounding annoyed.

"We'll Run ahead and get everything set up," Doc says and with a slight breeze, they are gone.

"Hang on, Emma, I'll get you to the Hospital Wing and then we'll make you comfortable. This won't be so bad. Just hang on, okay!?" Ty pleads with me.

"Ty, thank you... for... thank... you...," and then all thought disappears and I'm thrown into fiery darkness.

CHAPTER 13 - TY

B y the time I get to the Hospital Wing, Emma is so hot that I can barely stand to hold her. It takes all my willpower not to chuck her onto the bed Doc, Sara, and Libby have setup for her. They have ice packs and tubs of water with rags in them on one side of the bed and trays of bandages on the other.

"What's going to happen?" I ask, as I lay her down, eyeing the tray.

Meredith looks at Doc and then at me and says, "We aren't sure. We've never seen a Change like this before."

Of course Emma would have to have some kind of strange Change, she definitely isn't normal. I look down at her and the shining light that's emitting from her pulses and then gets brighter. It's like the sun is trying to burst out of her.

"What do you mean? Aren't all Changes the same?" Shae asks, coming from the entrance, holding some of Emma's clothes.

"Usually," Doc says, reaching down to touch Emma's arm but wincing away before his hand can get within six inches of her. "We need to leave the room," he abruptly says, grabbing me and pulling me towards the door.

"No, I'm staying with her," I say as I try to pull away but Doc, as gentle as he is, is one of the strongest people I've ever met.

"Me, too!" Libby and Shae say together. Libby runs over and links arms with Shae, to show solidarity, I'm sure.

"Girls, we don't know what's going to happen, it might not be safe for anyone to be in here with her. Out!" Sara says, pointing towards the door. They still don't move. I have to give it to my sister, she sure can be stubborn when she wants to be.

Meredith walks over and touches both their shoulders, "I know you're worried about her, we all are but right now we have to keep you guys safe. We don't know what's going to happen. We should be safe outside the door, but we have to go now."

Just as the girls start to move, Emma's light pulses again and this time she screams in agony, and the light gets brighter. Doc pushes me towards the door and Sara and Meredith each grab one of the other girls and Run to the door.

Doc swings the doors open and we all jump out of the way as he starts to shut one of them. I grab the other and as I start to shut it, I look one more time at Emma. Her back is arching and she is shaking so bad, she looks like she's vibrating. Her light is pulsing faster and faster. I can feel the heat coming off of her all the way over here by the doors. The water in the tubs by her bed are steaming from the heat.

I shut the door and Doc locks them with a bar, and he says, "No one goes in unless I say so." We all nod in agreement, knowing not to cross him.

I can hear Emma screaming.

Libby grabs onto Doc's arm and asks while crying, "Can't we do anything for her?"

"I wish I knew but it's too dangerous. Her light, her heat, could scorch us. We have to wait for whatever is happening to stop," Doc says, patting Libby's hand.

Just then, Max and Bill show up and Libby falls into Max's arms, sobbing. Shae slides to the floor and covers her ears with her hands, trying to keep herself from hearing Emma's cries of pain.

"What's happening?" Bill asks.

"Emma's changing but it's... different," Doc says, glancing around at all of us. "Where's Frank?"

Hearing Frank's name brings the furry I felt earlier to the forefront of my mind. It's a welcomed distraction from having to listen to Emma screaming in pain and not being able to do anything.

"Yeah, where is he?" I ask, my hands balling into fists.

"Nowhere where you can talk to him right now, he's still out cold, you did a number on him," Bill says sternly but also with a hint of pride.

"I can't just stand here and listen to her, I'm going for a walk," I say. As I walk past my sister, she reaches out and touches my arm.

"She's going to be okay," she says. I shake her off and keep walking.

So, what does it matter to me if she's okay or not? I just met Emma a few days ago. I'm only feeling this way because I feel responsible for her, right? I don't have actual feelings for her, do I? No, I can't, I just met her.

She is fun to talk to though, I don't think I've ever wanted someone to keep talking as much as I did when we were walking to her class today. That seems like a dorky thing to say but it's true, her voice is somehow soothing and I find myself fascinated with her. Every time I find something new out about her, it draws me to her even more.

She's smart and funny. Shy, but seems to be able to stick up for herself. Some girls pretend to act like they don't know how beautiful they are, which is really annoying, but I really think Emma has no idea how gorgeous she really is. Sure, she's got a rockin' tiny body but her personality is what makes me think she's the most beautiful girl I've ever met. That and her eyes. I could stare into them all day long and still find them mesmerizing. Not to mention the shock of electricity I get when I hold or touch her. It's something I've never felt. It's not the shock from static electricity, it's deeper down than that, down in the very core of my being.

Dude... get a grip! I internally yell at myself. I'm half-way down the tunnel to the Great Room when Charlie walks into view.

"What the hell, man?" he yells.

"What?" I grumble back.

"Kathryn said she saw you running by, like actually Ineptie running, with Emma in your arms and she said she was glowing or something? What's going on?" Charlie belts out.

I'm finally to him and we both stop.

"She's Changing but it's not a normal Change, at least that's what Doc, Sara, and Meredith say," I answer. I need to keep walking. I can feel something trying to pull me back to the Hospital Wing. Probably Libby, worrying about me.

"She was fine when I left her," Charlie says, running a hand through his hair.

"When you left her?" I ask, confused. "Where did you leave her?"

Embarrassment crosses Charlies face and he bows his head, "I took her to The Pub. I thought I was getting a vibe from her, so I took her there for some privacy. I kissed her and---," before he could finish what he was saying I had him slammed up against the tunnel wall.

"You what?" I snarl.

"Hey man, let go," Charlie says, trying to pull my hands away from him. I'm a lot stronger than him so he was trying pretty hard.

"What did you do?" I growl louder.

"I kissed her and then she punched me. I thought she wanted me to kiss her," he says still trying to pry my hands out of his shirt. "Dude, what's your problem?"

"Have you heard her talking about Mint-man?" I ask through my teeth.

"Yeah, so? What does that have to do with me?"

"He's Frank and Frank followed you guys there and when you left her, he attacked her," I punch the wall right beside his head, leaving a huge hole when I pull my fist out.

"What the hell, man? I didn't know he was following us, let alone Mint-man. Had I known, you know I wouldn't have left her alone. I'm going to kill that asshole. How hurt is she?" he says as he tries to push my hands away. "Dude, let go of my shirt!"

Shaking my head, I let him go, and I say, "He hurt her pretty good but her Change is doing more damage than he did."

"How?" he asks, looking down the tunnel towards the Hospital Wing.

"I don't know man, but it's weird. She was glowing, like a light was shining from her and it started to pulse, like her heartbeat or something. And she was hot. Think of the hottest day you've ever felt but add a few 20-30 degrees," I run my hand through my hair, looking down at the ground and then up at Charlie. The only reason I got so mad is because he left her in The Pub, not because he had kissed her. Right? No... damn it... I'm pretty sure I just experienced my first bout of jealousy.

"Damn," is all Charlie can say. He looks up and stares at my arm and asks, "What did you do?"

I look down at my right arm and it has blisters. I look at my left arm and it's the same. Both hands also. I only now realize that they hurt.

"Must have happened while I was carrying Emma. I'll Heal it in the bathing pool, water always makes burns feel better. I'll see ya later," I say as I walk away.

"Yeah, okay, see ya," Charlie says but then he reaches out and stops me, "Hey, Ty?"

"What?" I grumble out. The need to go back to the Hospital Wing is growing more intense. Why can't my sister just stop worrying about me? She has enough to worry about with Emma.

"I didn't know man," Charlie says, shrugging.

"I know, none of us did," I say back. How could any of us know Frank was the guy Emma had nightmares about. I have never liked the guy. He always stared at the girls in a creepy, intense kind of way but I didn't think he was capable of doing what he had done to Emma and what I caught him about to do.

"No, dude, how you feel about Emma," Charlie says, smirking.

"I don't know what you're talking about," I say back, glaring at him.

"Sure Ty, sure. Go take care of your arms, they look painful," Charlie says, quietly laughing as he walks away.

Uhh... I don't have feelings for Emma, other than protective ones.

Who am I kidding? I don't think I've ever felt this way towards anyone. It's not just a physical attraction but it feels deeper down than that and I don't know how I feel about it. I just met her for heavens sake.

I shake my head again and Run to my room. I grab a pair of swim shorts, changing quickly, and then Run to the bathing pool. Everyone is probably still at the party, hopefully Kathryn didn't tell too many people about what she saw. She's not normally a gossip spreader so she probably only told Charlie because she knows he and I are best friends.

But I could punch him, the weasel. I can't believe he kissed her but if I'm totally honest with myself, it's not too surprising. Charlie has always been one to go for what he wants, I just wish it wasn't Emma he wanted. But if Emma really did punch him, maybe she doesn't have any interest in him and that would be the first time, ever, that a girl has turned down Charlie's advances. It's good for his ego to get shut down, if only once in his life

I laugh a little as I sit down on the edge of the pool. I always thought I had some sort of Water Talent but it's nothing dominate. I'm fairly good at swimming and the water calms me more than anything else I've found but Professor Densmore has given me every Water Talent test there is known to us and I can't do any of them. She thinks I might have an affinity for it which is why it probably calms me but it's not enough to give me a real Talent.

I slide myself into the water and dive under. I swim all the way to the bottom and sit. Forcing myself to stay under for as long as possible. I know I can stay under for as long as it takes to Heal my arms so I start healing them. I let the sensation flow through my hands and over my arms.

When you're a Healer and you Heal someone, your hands tingle like when an appendage has fallen asleep. It's not the pins and needles, that hurt feeling, but the feeling right after that, just before all the blood returns to whatever had fallen asleep. It's more difficult to Heal oneself but it's one of the things I've been practicing with Sara. I could probably let myself Heal the 'normal' Demi way but since I'm a Healer, why not speed up the process?

All of a sudden, someone dives into the pool and swims towards me. I swim up to the surface and head over to the edge. I catch my breath, waiting for whomever dived in, to surface.

I feel someone down by my feet and then Alysa's face is right in front of me. She wraps her hands around my neck and pushes herself against me. I can feel that she doesn't have a top on.

"Hi," she says, all sultry like.

"What do you want, Alysa? I'm not in the mood for your games and I'm not all that happy with you," I say, pulling her hands away from my neck and pull her over to the side of the pool.

She pouts and says, "What did I do?"

"You know what you did. Why do you have to treat Emma so bad?" I ask. I already know the answer. It's because she's a spoiled rotten girl and thinks she can have whatever she wants, whenever she wants.

"Why do you care so much? You have no more obligations to her, she's all better," she says, rolling her eyes.

"No thanks to you. You could have really hurt her, you did really hurt her. You're lucky they didn't put you in a cell for a day or two for that. You know we don't use our Talents against other Demi's," I say, my voice getting louder as I talk.

"I know, I know. Bill already told me. If she hadn't spoken up, I would have spent the night in a cell and missed the party. I do feel bad. I just got so upset. I thought she was trying to take you away from me," Alysa says as she runs a hand down my chest to the top of my shorts and tries to pull me closer to her.

I push her hand away and get out of the pool.

"Ooooh, back to my room then?" she asks as she pulls herself out after me.

She only has on a skimpy piece of fabric that supposedly passes as underwear. I'd be lying if I said she didn't turn me on, but just thinking about how she treats people shuts that down real fast.

"For crying out loud, Alysa, put some clothes on," I say, grabbing a towel and handing it to her.

"Don't pretend you don't like what you see," she says, grabbing the towel but stepping closer to me. "I vividly remember some spicy nights we've shared. I know I turn you on," she runs a finger down my chest.

"Being turned on and liking someone are two different things," I say as I walk over to grab me a new towel.

"What's that supposed to mean? You don't like me?" Alysa says, sounding actually hurt and close to tears.

I sigh and walk back to her.

"I like you just fine, Alysa. It's just not the way you want me to like you. We've had this talk before, nothing has changed," I say, pulling her into a hug. I can't stand it when a girl cries.

Alysa turns into me, and as fast as a cobra, she's kissing me, her tongue spasming around in my mouth. She pulls my towel away from me and pushes her half... or basically naked body against mine. I can feel her breasts pushing up against my lower chest. One hand is holding my neck, while the other is reaching into my swim shorts.

I pull away and grab her hand, "Alysa, enough,

STOP!" I growl.

She's not that much shorter than me but short enough she has to be up on the tips of her toes, and she slowly lowers herself down to stand. She bends down to grab her towel and as she does, she drags a finger down my stomach, my thigh, and then back up when she stands up.

"You'll be mine again, Ty, I promise you, you will," she says and then she Runs away.

With a sigh of relief, I grab my towel and head to take a shower. She's never going to get it. I don't know what else I have to say or do for her to understand that there is nothing between us.

I look at my arms and hands and see that all there is left to show for the burns, is a little pinkness. New skin forming, I was completely healed. I can't imagine how strange this must be for Emma. Having grown up in a house where Talents were used and what we are, was talked about daily, it's probably the same as Inepties talking about the weather. For Emma to find out she's completely different than what she always thought, it's got to be so confusing. Not to mention what that bitch of an aunt put her through, it's a miracle she survived as long as she did.

I take a few calming breaths, just thinking of Vanessa gets my blood boiling. I decide to walk back to my room and take the long way, back to the Great Room and then down the tunnel to The Quarters.

Just as I'm stepping into the Great Room, I feel a rush of warm air. I look around and see that everyone else has felt it too. I look towards the Hospital Wing tunnel and see a bright orange light coming towards us. It looks like the sun starting to rise, sending rays of light everywhere, it's brighter somehow. It's coming towards the Great Room fast. I look to the tunnel leading to the Guard Room and it's lit up like normal.

"What the---," is all I can get out before the light gets to the Great Room and I'm knocked to the ground. My head slams to the floor. I hear other people hitting the floor or wall or crashing into tables, and people yelling in surprise. And then everything goes black.

CHAPTER 14 - CHANGED

L *et me die... Let me die... Oh please just let me die...*
Let me die... Is all I've been thinking for the last... who knows how long? It feels like forever.

I would gladly go back to the hell hole I was in before the Guardians saved me. I would gladly take getting my ass kicked by Tobacco Man, whose name is Tim, and Alcohol Man, because nothing could be worse than what I am feeling right now.

I feel like my body has been torn in half. My arms and legs feel like they've been torn away at the joints. Every last one of my bones must be a pile of dust because they feel like they've been smashed to smithereens. Even my fingernails and toenails hurt, not just the tips of them, which hurt also, but my actual nails. My head feels like it's about to explode, also.

How can my hair feel like it keeps getting torn away from my scalp?

I'd imagine getting hit by a train might feel like this but that probably wouldn't hurt as bad. At least one would die, hopefully instantaneously, after being struck by a train.

And to top it off, to make it all so much worse, I feel like I keep getting set on fire. Someone puts the fire out and then I get lit up again. Over and over, until I lose track of how many times it's been extinguished and then relit. The most painful spot is on my right wrist, it burns like someone is holding a red-hot branding iron there and there is never a relief. It is constant and it doesn't feel like it's ever going to stop.

I try to open my eyes but searing pain shoots from my eyes to the back of my head, making the exploding feeling inside my head, feel like a very real possibility. It feels like it's cracking.

I try to think around the pain. Think of anything that might take my mind off of how awful this is but every time something or someone enters my mind, the pain blasts it away. Why can't I go and wait out this torture in my dark place?

Again, I'm not sure how much time has passed but I start to feel a change.

My bones don't feel quite so crushed. My limbs and body feel like they've joined at their proper areas. My head doesn't feel like it's going to explode as often as before and my hair feels like it's permanently placed back on my head. Everything feels better, except the burning. I still feel like I'm on fire, then a cool reprieve, and then burning fire again. I do notice that my wrist isn't burning anymore.

My whole body feels like it's vibrating within the burning fire. I'm not sure how much more I can take of this, when all of a sudden I feel like I'm floating. Floating in a burning hell fire, but floating, nonetheless.

Then coolness spreads from my back to my front and I feel like I'm finally floating in a cool cloud. I wait in fear for the fire to come back but it doesn't.

I finally slip into peaceful darkness.

I feel myself slip out of my dark place and I wait for the burn to hit me but it doesn't come. I wait to feel if anything else will start to hurt again but there's nothing. I feel myself relax and that's when I finally feel something.

A bed, pillow, and blankets.

At first, I'm afraid to open my eyes because last time I did, agony greeted me, but maybe just like everything else, there won't be any pain. I slowly open my eyes and a sigh of relief escapes my lips. No pain.

There's a rustle to my right and a really cute guy comes into view. I stare at him, trying to figure out why he looks so familiar. I can see every shiny, honey, highlight strand of his hair. The flecks of gold in his emerald green eyes.

Hmmm, I never noticed the gold in his eyes before. Ty really does have beautiful eyes.

TY!

All my memories flood back to me at once.

I reach up and pull him down into a hug.

"I'm alive or is this heaven? Or is this a dream?" I ask.

"You are alive and you are awake," Ty says into my hair, rubbing my back. He leans back and I look up at him. He doesn't look like he has slept much. I tilt my head to the side and try to look closer, when all of a sudden my vision zooms into his face like a camera would zoom in on a flower.

Startled I close my eyes and when I open them again, my vision is back to normal.

"What the heck was that?" I whisper.

"What? What happened?" concern fills Ty's face.

"I was looking at your face and I tried to look closer, metaphorically, when all of a sudden I felt like you'd moved right in front of my face, only you hadn't, my eyes had just zoomed in on you," I say, still stunned.

"I've never heard of that, I'll go get Doc," Ty says. He gets up and Runs out of the room. He and Doc are back in a flash. Before, I wouldn't have been able to have seen them enter the room, but it was like I could slow down time and watch them enter. It was so bizarre! They looked like they were running but in slow motion.

"Good to see you're back with us," Doc says, patting my arm.

"Thanks," I say. "It's good to be back?" I didn't mean to make it sound like a question but it came out like one.

"I sure hope so," Doc smiles. "So how do you feel? Tell me everything."

"I feel like a noodle, honestly. Or like jello. But I'm not in any pain," I say. I flex all my muscles and I'm pleased with how strong they feel.

"What do you mean by pain?" Ty asks, looking over at Doc.

"While I was... out, I was in hell. Every inch of me felt like I was torn and broken but the worst part was the fire. I felt like I was burning alive," I say, shivering at the memories.

"You shouldn't remember how it felt," Ty says. "Should she? I don't remember it. I know Libby doesn't either."

"Wait, what?" I ask, but Doc ignores me and answers Ty.

"No one, as far as I know, has ever shown signs of remembering the pain. The only reason we know of the pain, is because of the Healers who watch over the Changlings while they are Changing," Doc explains.

"Changlings? Change? What are you guys talking about?" I ask. I can feel my patience disappearing.

"When you receive your Mark, you go through the

Change," Doc says. "Since the Mark gives you so much power, your body has to Change to be able to absorb your Talents."

"Why didn't anyone tell me about the Change?" I ask. I think back, wondering if someone had told me and sure enough, I can't think of anyone saying anything about a change.

"We didn't want to stress you out even more about getting your Mark. You were already worried about if you'd get it or not. Plus, you weren't supposed to remember," Libby says from the doors.

I look behind Doc and see Libby and Shae standing there. They've got red puffy eyes and look like they haven't slept in days, either.

"LIBBY!! SHAE!!" I squeal, sitting up too fast and being rewarded with a sharp pain in my head.

"Try to relax. Come on in girls," Doc says.

They rush over and they each take hold of one of my feet. Smiling a huge grin and crying. Shae says, "I am so glad you're okay."

"Well, why wouldn't I be? I mean, you all went through the Change and came out fine," I say, still confused why they all seem so worried.

"Your Change was far different than anything we've ever seen or heard of," Doc says, sitting down beside me.

"How so?" I ask.

They all look at each other.

"How so?" I ask again.

"You had an extremely high temperature. Normally, one's temperature would only reach 105 degrees during their Change but yours got up to 136, that would have killed a normal person, Demi-god and definitely an Ineptie," Doc states.

That explains my fire from Hell.

"You were also shaking," Libby says.

"No, you were vibrating," Shae corrects her.

"Vibrating?" I ask.

"Yeah, you were shaking so fast and hard that you were vibrating. You only stopped doing that yesterday," Doc explains.

Maybe that explains the feeling of my broken bones and body being torn apart.

"Is that normal?" I ask.

"A little shaking yes but what you were doing, no. That wasn't really normal," Doc says.

Why was my Change so different? Nothing's making sense.

"Anything else?" I ask, might as well find out everything.

And they again all look at each other.

"What?" I'm nervous of what it could be now.

Ty clears his throat and says, "You were shining."

A startled laugh escapes me before I ask, "Shining?"

"Yeah, it was like the sun was shining through you. A bright, golden, orange color. Then it would pulse like lightning was striking inside of you, we could see the flash from it, and then it would go back to shining like the sun. It would switch back and forth about every six hours," Ty says looking down at me and his eyes trailed down my blanket covered body to my toes and then back up until they were staring into my eyes.

"The first burst was the most powerful. A heat wave went throughout The Pit, followed by a flash of light which knocked everyone out," Doc says and then seeing my concerned look he hurriedly says, "Don't worry, no one got seriously injured, just some bumps and bruises."

"Umm, I'm afraid to ask and I'm sure I already know but, is *that* normal?"

"Nope, not one bit," Shae says, patting my foot.

I close my eyes and breath in deeply. What is going on?

"Anything else? How long was I out for?"

It's Libby's turn to clear her throat, I look at her and she grimaces and says, "Nine days."

"And I take it that's not normal either? What's the normal time a normal person takes to go through their Change?" I inquire.

"A day, two days tops depending on the Talents they are receiving," Doc answers.

"Great... why am I going through such a strange Change?" I ask.

"Maybe having a look at your Mark will give us that

answer. It might give us a hint at what Talent or Talents you might have now," Doc suggests happily.

"About that, right before you came in, I kind of zoomed in on Ty's face," I sheepishly say.

"Zoomed in?" Doc asks.

"Yeah like a camera or something. One second I'm looking at him and the next I'm thinking about looking at him closer and BAM! his face is not one inch away from me but neither one of us had moved. My vision just zoomed in," I answer, looking from Doc over to Ty. Ty nods in agreement.

"Well, that's something, isn't it," Doc says, scratching his head.

"Let's see your Mark," Libby says.

"Yeah, can we see it?" Shae asks.

"You guys haven't looked at it yet?" I ask back.

"Someone's Mark is something very personal, very special for that person. It's only right they get to see if first. We'd never look at it if we can help it. Sometimes, the way the arm is lying, it's unavoidable to see it but 95% of the time, the Changeling will get to see it first," Doc states.

"Changeling?" I ask, momentarily sidetracked by a name I've never heard.

"It's just something we call Demi-gods who have just recently gone through the Change," Libby says matter-of-factly.

Well that makes sense. New Demi-god wouldn't be

accurate because we are Demi-gods whether we have our Talents or not.

I look down at my right arm and see it laying nicely by my side. I pull it up slowly to my chest and close my eyes.

I sigh, open my eyes, and turn my arm so that I can see my wrist.

"Huh... that's weird," I say.

"What?" they all say together.

"It's just... I don't think I read... Well, just look," I turn my wrist out so that they can all see it.

Nothing. Not a sound. Nobody says a thing. It doesn't even sound like any of them are breathing. They are just staring at my wrist and then at me and then back at my Mark.

I can't take it anymore, so I say, "Well, what!?

That startled them out of their thoughts.

"Have any of you seen this Mark before?" I ask quietly.

They all look at each other and then one by one, they shake their head no.

I pull my arm back towards me and I stare at my Mark.

Why was I given a Mark they didn't recognize? Does this explain my Change? What's going to happen now?

As if reading my thoughts, Doc says, "It's all going to be okay. I'm going to go get Meredith and Kathryn. Maybe they've heard of a Mark like this." And just like

CHAPTER 14 - CHANGED   201

before, I see him start to flash out of the room, and just like before, I see him in slow motion.

"That's so cool," I say out loud.

"What's that?" Ty asks.

"Oh you know, how you can slow down someone Running and see them. It looks cool. Like in a movie, how you can pause it and then slowly play it so it's in slow motion," I say.

With a dumbfounded look, Ty looks at the girls, and says, "We can't do that. Can we?"

"Not that I know of," Libby says, looking over at Shae.

"I know I can't. Maybe it's one of your Talents. Maybe it has something to do with your eyes," Shae says, looking like she's trying to be more reassuring than how she feels.

In a gust of air, Meredith, Doc, and Kathryn are standing behind Shae and Libby.

"It's so good to see you awake," Meredith says, beaming at me.

"Doc filled us in, may I see your Mark?" Kathryn says. I like her. She gets right to the point, right to business.

My arm is resting on my lap so I just flip it over.

"I thought you were pulling our legs, Jim. How fascinating!" Meredith says.

"So, have either of you seen or heard of anything like this?" I ask.

Meredith shakes her head and says, "No, I haven't. Kathryn?"

"I haven't either. I'll go back to my library and search all the ancient writings and see what I can come up with. How are you feeling, Emma?" Kathryn asks suddenly.

"I feel fine, confused, but fine."

Kathryn smiles at me kindly and then Runs out.

"Emma has just told us another one of her Talents," Shae says, looking over at Meredith.

It's Doc who asks first, "Oh really? What is it?"

"I can slow down time, I guess. I figured it out when you and Ty first Ran in here. I could see you guys Running, only I could slow you down. And I could do it again when you left to go get Meredith and Kathryn," I say.

"Really?" Doc and Meredith say together.

"Yup," is all I can think to say.

"How interesting!" Meredith says.

"Have either of you heard of this?" Libby asks them.

"No, I haven't," they say together.

Great! So not only was my Change not normal, my Mark isn't normal, *and* my Talents aren't either. Why can't I just be a normal Demi?

"Being special isn't a bad thing, Emma," Ty says.

"Huh? Can you read my mind?" I ask him, that was weirdly coincidental that he says that as I'd just thought about being normal. "Umm, no. You just said you wished you were normal," Ty looks at me with a little concern.

"Oh, I didn't realize I had said it out loud," okay, maybe not a coincidence. I'm losing my mind. I don't know when I'm saying things out loud or when I'm thinking them.

"Maybe you should rest a bit more, we'll be back in to visit with you in a little while," Doc says. He and Meredith say goodbye and leave.

"While you're resting, we'll go get your birthday presents so you can open them when you wake up," Shae says.

"Birthday presents?" I ask, I thought I'd already opened them.

"Oh yeah, everyone that was at your party left a present for you," Libby says, beaming.

"They didn't have to do that," I say a little exasperated.

"They know they didn't have to, they wanted to," she says, smiling even more.

I shake my head but can't help but smile back, her smile is contagious. Speaking of presents.

"Oh... Ty, I never did get to thank you for my book. That must have been really hard to find," I say, turning to look at Ty.

"A book? He got you a book?" Shae says in disgust and rolls her eyes.

"It wasn't too hard," he says.

"Of course it wasn't, Ty loves books. You should see his room, Emma, it's like a little library," Libby says, smiling at me even more. Ty just shrugs.

"Well thank you, it's perfect. And while I'm at it, thank you for coming to my rescue, once again. I don't want to think about what Frank would have done if you hadn't came in when you had, so thank you," I say, reaching over and grabbing Ty's hand and give it a little squeeze. With that little contact, my heart starts to hammer against my ribcage from the jolt of electricity that went from our hands to my heart.

"No problem," is all he says. I slowly pull my hand away, turning bright red.

Shae clears her throat and says, "We're gonna go but we'll bring you some of your birthday cake. Cooky saved a big chunk for you."

I had to laugh a little at that. Of course Cooky would think to save me some cake, she would know that I love cake. Shae and Libby leave, skipping.

"They are so relieved you're okay. We all are. You had us pretty scared," Ty says.

I look over at him and see him blushing a little.

"Even you?" I ask and instantly regret it. I can feel myself turning bright red. My brain must have gotten a little fried, I don't ask boys questions like that.

"Yes, even me," he says, looking down at his hands.

"Why?" I ask, again, not something I would normally ask but apparently all normalcy for me has gone out the window.

Ty looks up and I see something cross his face. I'm not sure what it is but it's gone. He says, "Since the day I found you and my guys and I brought you back here, I've felt like it was my duty to protect you. I wasn't able to completely stop Frank when… when he hurt you… and then he was… he tried to…"

"So you feel obligated to be here?" I ask, hurt coloring my tone.

"No, I mean, at first but now…" he trails off.

"Now what?" I ask.

"I don't know," and there's that look again, but it's gone just as quickly as it had appeared. He continues by saying, nonchalantly, "I feel like it's my job to protect you."

"Well, then. I'll fix that. You are from here on out, relieved of your duty, job, obligation, or whatever else you want to call it. You don't have to worry about me anymore," I say, a little angrily.

"No, that's not what I meant. I don't mind… It's not that I don't want to do it," Ty stammers out.

"It's fine, Ty. You can go… you look like you haven't slept for days. That's probably my fault. You were just doing your job," I say, laying my head down on the pillow.

"Emma, I---"

"Ty, it's fine. I'm fine but I'm actually really tired.

Do you mind if I go to sleep?" I am most definitely not fine and I need Ty to leave before I start crying. I mean ugly crying, not just a couple tears, I can feel a good sob coming on.

"Well... okay... sure," Ty says, standing up.

"I'll see you later," I hope he can't hear the hitch in my voice.

"Umm, okay," Ty walks over to the door. I roll over to my side, facing away from him and the door, and let the first tear slide down my cheek.

"Emma?"

"Yeah," I try to sound like I'm not choking on something.

"I really am glad you're okay and I did mean what I said about being special," he says softly.

"Okay, thank you," I say back, now trying with all my strength not to cry.

"See you later," he says and then I hear the door close.

I let out a small whimper and all my tears flood out of me. I guess I liked him more than I thought. If I didn't, then him telling me he felt like I was his obligation wouldn't hurt so bad. I thought that maybe it was irritating him, to have to cart me around all the time, but I didn't know that he felt the way he did. I had allowed myself to fall for him before I even knew him.

CHAPTER 15 - THE MARK

!

I must have really snotted on myself hard core before I fell asleep because I wake up and my pillow is soaked with tears and gross snot. I don't cry, I've never been a crier but when I do, I do it big. Sighing, I roll to my back and stretch my arms above my head. I reach over onto the table and grab a washcloth and wipe my face off, I take my pillowcase off and toss it over to the dirty laundry hamper.

I sit up and look down at my Mark again.

It really is something. Three circles kind of making a triangle, with one on top and two on the bottom, all interlocked with each other. It has what looks like wings coming out of the sides of it and something resembling an infinity sign inside the circles. It wasn't like any of the other Marks. They all represent a god or goddess. I wonder what, or who, this Mark represents and which god gave me my Talents? I run my finger over it and I can't feel a difference in the skin. Strange. It's like I was born with it.

The door to the Hospital Wing bangs open and

Libby and Shae walk in.

"Oh good, you're awake!" Libby says.

"We were hoping you would be. It's been four hours," Shae says.

"Wow, I was more tired than I thought," I yawn.

"We brought food. Are you hungry?" Libby asks, coming to sit on the foot of my bed.

My stomach growls and we all laugh.

"I guess that answers that question," Libby says.

She pulls out fried chicken, mashed potatoes, green beans, and biscuits. Shae hands me a plate, plastic fork, and a bottle of lemonade. We all dish up and eat in silence. When we're done with the chicken and sides, Shae jumps up and grabs a plastic box and brings it over to me. I open it up and see the most delicious looking cake I have ever seen.

"Chocolate cake with strawberry glaze topping?" I ask in amazement.

"It's Cooky's most popular cake. She thought you'd like it," Libby says, smiling.

"Of course she did," I laugh.

Instead of using plates, we just grab our forks and dig in. It's amazing! I am definitely going to have to fig-ure out a way to get Cooky to make this even if there isn't a special occasion happening.

"Oh man, I'm stuffed!" I say, as we scoop out the last bites of cake.

"Me too!" Libby and Shae say together.

I laugh, "You two act more like twins than you do with your actual twin."

They laugh and Libby says, "She's my sister from another mister."

"Damn straight!" Shae says.

"And apparently, that mister was a potty mouth," Libby says, laughing.

"Better believe it!" Shae says back, looking proud.

I shake my head and close the lid to the cake box. I look up and see Libby and Shae staring at me with smiles.

"What?" I ask with uncertainty.

"Wanna open some presents?" Shae asks, clapping her hands.

I groan, "No, not really. Maybe when I get back to my room."

Libby starts laughing and says, "I told you she wouldn't want too! Don't worry Emma, all your presents are waiting for you in your room."

"Thank you!" I say. I look at Shae and see her rolling her eyes, obviously upset I wasn't up for presents.

"Okay, fine, if no presents then tell us what happened before your Change, before Meredith and Doc come back and kick us out!" Shae says.

"Shae, she doesn't have to tell us anything about that. Ignore her, Emma," Libby says, giving Shae a look that said to knock it off.

"Emma, you're going to have to tell Meredith, Doc,

and most likely Bill about what happened. You might as well tell us to get the emotional aspect out of the way. We're your friends, we're here for you," Shae says, grabbing my hand.

"Shae, enough," Libby says sternly.

"No, it's okay. She's right. If I tell you guys what happened before I tell The Leaders, maybe it won't be as hard to talk about it when they want me to tell them. At least you guys won't judge me too harshly if I cry, I'm not a very pretty crier," I glance at Libby and then at Shae.

"Who is?" Shae asks, smiling encouragingly.

"I bet your sister isn't an ugly crier," I say, rolling my eyes this time and then laughing.

"Actually, she is the ugliest crier I've ever seen. All that makeup just runs down her face. I don't know why she wears it all, she doesn't need to. None of us do, our skin is flawless," Shae says, framing her face with her hands and then she sticks her tongue out at us, laughing.

"Okay, well here's what happened," I go on to tell Libby and Shae about everything that happened. Starting with my dance with Doc, seeing Frank for the first time but not knowing who he was and then Charlie cutting in on Doc's dance. Then Charlie Jumping us to The Pub and what happened there between us.

"What a sleaze ball! Good for you for putting him in his place!" Shae says, looking perturbed.

"That's why he looked so upset when I saw him standing over by the guys. By the time we got over to them to ask if they'd seen you, he had disappeared," Libby says, looking at Shae.

"Wonder where he went?" Shae asks.

I had started to wonder the same thing. If Charlie really did like me, like he said he did, why hasn't he been in to check on me? I'm sure the news about what happened, has already spread around The Pit like gossip in high school. I shake myself inwardly, what do I care if Charlie has or hasn't been here? I don't like him... or do I?

Bringing me out of my reverie, Shae asks, "Okay, so Charlie Jumped you to The Pub and got handsy, you shot him down, and then what happened?"

I take a deep breath and let it out slowly. I can feel my heart starting to pound. This was the part of the story that I was most nervous to tell. Frank scared, scratch that, scares the living crap out of me and what he did and could have done will give me nightmares for who knows how long.

"It's alright, Emma, you're safe, he can't get to you," Libby says, taking my hand.

I smile at her, take a steadying breath, I jump back into my story, ending with me first waking up from the Change.

"Oh... my..." Libby starts to say.

"Gods," Shae finishes.

They both have stunned faces that turn quickly to grimaces and then to pissed off.

"I'm going to kill that creepy, pervy, nasty man!" Shae snarls.

"I'll bring the shovel!" Libby says, flaring her nostrils.

Hearing their response and seeing their angry faces, has me laughing hysterically, for some reason I'll never know.

"What's so funny? We're serious," Shae says, putting her hands on her hips, which causes me to laugh even harder.

Libby starts laughing too and shortly after, so does Shae. We laugh until we're all crying.

"No, but seriously Emma, that's messed up," Shae says.

"I know," I can't think of anything else to say about what happened the night of my birthday. So, I ask something that's been on my mind all day, "What do you guys think my Mark means?"

Libby instantly turns towards me, and Shae sits up straighter. They look at each other and then at me.

"I honestly don't know," Libby says, looking down at my arm. She takes it into her hand and looks at it closer.

"I don't know either. It's not anything anyone has ever seen. Kathryn doesn't even have a Record of anyone having a Mark that's different than the twelve original Marks," Shae says leaning in closer to look.

"It's really cool though. It's definitely unique." Libby says, smiling at me and putting my arm back down on my lap.

I turn my arm over and look at it. It's quite beautiful. It's definitely not a simple Mark. I can't help but be excited and admittedly, scared. If no one knows anything about this Mark, how am I going to know what it means? Trial and error? That doesn't sound like much fun.

"Don't worry, Emma, The Leaders are going to be meeting with you and you guys can all figure this out together," Libby says as she wraps an arm around my shoulder and hugs me.

"Oh, you haven't told us about what you and Ty talked about after we left," Shae says, scooting closer like she was excited to hear a great story.

Blah, I don't want to talk to them about this, especially, Libby. Being Ty's sister, she might be a little biased in the brother front. But if I couldn't talk to these girls about it, who could I talk to? They were my friends, best friends really. And for once, I have boy issues and best friends to talk to about it. Hopefully Libby wouldn't be too one sided.

With a sigh I say, "Well, he told me he was happy I was okay, that *all* of you were happy I was okay," Shae grins and Libby smiles big and is about to say something but I cut her off and continue by saying, "And then he pretty much told me he was relieved I was okay because he felt bad he wasn't there to protect me because he feels like it's his job or that he's obligated to keep me safe. He said from the moment he brought me here, he's felt like that. So I fired him."

"You what?" Shae says. I look over at Libby, she's chewing on her lip and fiddling with her fingers, NOT looking at me. So I look back at Shae and answer her.

"I fired him," she looks at me dumbfounded so I say, "From his job of being my protector. He doesn't have to feel obligated to keep me safe anymore, now that I've gone through the Change."

"Emma, I doubt he felt like it was his job. Or if he did feel like that, he doesn't feel like that anymore," Libby says.

"I don't know, he seemed pretty sure about it," I say, trying not to sound annoyed.

"He gave you a present for your birthday," she says back to me.

"So?" I ask slightly confused.

"So, he doesn't give anyone gifts, for anything, not even me. He says he doesn't like giving people gifts because most of the time, people don't really like what they've been given. They only say they like it to be polite. He also says that the only reason someone actually does like the gift is because they specifically told people to get them that gift. But he gave *you* a gift. His favorite book, in fact. Didn't you notice how worn out it was?" Libby asks.

"I did but I thought it was just from being an amazing book, from the previous owner reading it over and over," I say, looking down at my hands.

"That owner was Ty and he read that book at least once a month. It is, or was, his go to book. And the fact that he gave it to you, that tells me more than anything he could ever say. I think he likes you, Emma, but he doesn't know what to do with those feelings. His first and last relationship was with Alysa and it was more out of her demanding to be together rather than mutual feelings. Don't get me wrong, I'm sure he liked her but he also couldn't stand her. Her personality ruined it for him," Libby says.

"Her personality ruins it for everyone," Shae says, winking at me.

"Why, then, would he say all that? Why not just tell me he likes me?" I ask.

"Because he's a dude. They don't know how to talk about their feelings. They are either a Charlie, who shows you in the least gentlemanly way or they are a Ty, who can't talk about or show you the way they feel," Shae says pursing her lips.

"That's not true, Max talks to me about how he feels. He's really good at communicating about things," Libby says.

"That's because Max is beyond his years in maturity," Shae says laughing.

Libby and I join in and laugh. It's so easy to laugh with these girls. I have never felt so comfortable with two people in my life.

Libby takes my hand and squeezes, "Let Ty figure out his feelings. Maybe he just wants to get to know you better and you get to know him better, before he proclaims his love for you."

I giggle and say, "I honestly don't know how I feel about him either. I mean, I know I have some strong feelings going on but like you said, we need to get to know each other a little better first. I do enjoy the way he looks though."

"Eww, gross," Libby says, pretending to vomit.

"Mmmm hmmm, that boy has definitely got it goin' on." Shae says, wagging her eyebrows at me.

"Double eww," Libby says, plugging her ears.

Shae and I laugh and just as I'm about to say something the Hospital Wing doors open and Doc walks in.

"I'm happy to see you laughing, Emma. You must be feeling better?" he asks.

"I am, thank you," I reply.

"Meredith and the other Leaders have asked that I bring you to the Guard Room but only if you are feeling up to it," Doc says as he walks over. Shae and Libby hop off my bed and start clearing up our lunch mess.

I slide my feet out from under the blankets and try to stand and find that I'm not dizzy or anything. I feel more myself than I have in a long time. Actually, I feel better than I can ever remember feeling. I have never felt comfortable in my body but right now, something feels different, but a good different.

"How do you feel?" Doc asks, turning my shoulders so that I'm standing directly in front of him.

"Different?" I say it like a question.

"How so?" he counters.

"Well, I feel normal but I don't. I feel more like myself than I ever have in my entire life. Like something finally clicked into place," I say, looking down at my hands. I see my Mark and I say, "It's because of the Change and my Mark, isn't it?"

"Yes. The Change doesn't necessarily change us into a different person, it changes us into who we are meant to be. So it's natural for you to feel normal but not the normal you are used to feeling," Doc says smiling at me. "Anything else?"

"No, everything else is fine. I was expecting my face and ribs to hurt but they don't. Did you guys Heal me while I was out?" I ask.

"Actually, we didn't. When you stopped," Doc pauses for a second and then continues to say, "Well, when you stopped shining, your injuries were healed all by themselves. I've never seen anything like it. Even Demi's who come out of the Change with the Healing Talent, can't Heal themselves until they've learned how. For instance, take me for example, when I went through the Change, I fell and hit my head. When I came to, I had a gash and a huge goose egg. It took me a couple classes until I was able to fully Heal myself."

This is unexpected news, I had somehow Healed myself. Maybe I'd have the Healing Talent to go along with my weird 'zooming in and slow motion' sight.

"So, I guess since you're feeling well, we will have to head to the Guard Room," Doc says, walking towards the door.

"Umm, could I change first?" I ask, looking down at my hospital gown, wondering who had changed me.

"Oh, I'm sorry, of course. Libby and Shae brought you some clothes while you were Changing. I'll step out and when you're ready, just come on out to the tunnel," Doc says, stepping out through the door.

Shae runs over with a pair of jeans, one of my black long sleeve shirts, and my undergarments.

"Thank you," I say. I turn around and start to change into my nice, comfy clothes. With a sigh, I realize I'm still the same ol' Emma. I'm happy to see my bust size has stayed the same. It is the only thing I have going for me. I am, however, disappointed to see I'm still short.

Get used to it, Hart!

The girls and I head to the door and as we walk out Libby says, "Come to your room when you're done, we'll wait for you there."

"Okay, see you later," I say and then they Run away.

"Before we go, I just want you to be prepared. You'll

be meeting *all* of The Leaders," Doc says, looking at me seriously.

"So not just you, Bill, and Meredith will be there?" I ask.

"No, we've called all The Leaders in to talk to you and ask you their questions," he says.

"Should I be nervous? I'm starting to feel really nervous," I say.

"Just keep an open mind and remember, we are all on the same team," Doc says, half smiling at me.

"What does that mean?" I ask.

"You'll see," he says and then asks, "Are you ready?'

"Sure, I guess," I say trying to sound like I'm not scared but my voice gives me away by shaking.

"Since you've Changed, we can Run, if you'd like?" Doc suggests

"I'd love too!" this is something I've been excited to try on my own since the first time I'd seen Meredith disappear.

"All you have to do is think of where the Guard Room is and how to get there and then start to run, once you hit your Ineptie top speed, you'll Run. I'll hold onto your arm just to make sure you stay on track and don't get hurt," Doc says, smiling at me.

"Okay," I say, feeling my heart rate pickup in anticipation.

Doc grabs my arm, just above my elbow, and I concentrate on the door to the Guard Room. We take one step forward and all of a sudden we are at the door. I look over at Doc and he's looking around us and then looks at me, shock crossing his face.

"Well, that was fast," I say, giggling.

"We didn't Run. We were Jumped here," Doc says, as he places his hand on the wall for support.

"I didn't know you were a Jumper," I say and then see how slightly pale he is and I ask, "Hey, are you okay?"

"I'm not a Jumper. I didn't Jump us here, you did. And I'll be okay, I don't handle being Jumped very well," he says, grimacing.

"I Jumped us?" I ask.

"Yes, it looks as if you have the Jumper Talent," he laughs. "And it's advanced. Normally, after you've Changed and you have the Jumper Talent, it takes quite a bit of training before you can Jump yourself, let alone another person."

Huh, so I have the crazy Vision Talent, Healing Talent, and now this Talent. This is all so bizarre. Maybe after talking with The Leaders, I'll get answers to the many questions that I have overloading my brain.

"Ready to go in?" Doc asks. I look over and see that his color is back to normal and he's not leaning against the wall anymore.

"Yeah, I guess so," I say, not sure if I am or not.

Doc opens the door and walks in, I follow just behind him. I look up and see Meredith and Bill standing there talking to a man and a woman whose backs are turned towards us. When Meredith looks up and smiles, the two unknown people turn around and I get my first glimpse at them.

I don't think I've ever seen any one person look as perfect as they do. Demi's were gorgeous, don't get me wrong, but these two people were even more beautiful than what I've seen of Demi's. Their skin is so clear, not a blemish to be seen. As I get closer, I can see that their eyes are different shades of brown, but they both have a shine to them. They are just as tall as everyone else in here and their bodies are just as perfect. Although, just noticeably thinner than Demi's.

When Doc and I stop in front of them the man sticks his hand out for me to shake.

"Hello, you must be Emma, my name is Dom Michaels," the strangely beautiful man says as I take his hand. I'm shocked to find his skin is cool to the touch. Not quite freezing but about what it feels like when I used to hold onto a cold drink for too long.

The woman steps forward and offers her hand to me as well.

"My name is Jenna Michaels, Dom's other half," she says, shaking my hand and I find that her skin is the same coolness as Dom's.

"Nice to meet you both," I say.

"Let's take our seats," Bill says from the other side of Dom. Everyone turns and takes a seat around the table. I sit next to Meredith and Jenna sits next to me.

Meredith stands up and says, "I would like to welcome you all here. We've been needing to have a meeting for a while now. I'd like to introduce to you, Emma Hart, she is quite special to us. We know you have some questions and we'll get to them but first we need to talk to Emma about what happened to her a little over a week ago and we need to decide what to do. However, before we get to that, I'd like for those who haven't met Emma yet, to introduce themselves now, and to tell her a little bit about your group."

Embarrassed, I wave at those who are saying hello. A man sitting directly across from me stands up, he's very muscular but shorter than any Demi man I've seen. He's still taller than me, though. He's got a short, dark beard, long dark hair pulled back into a ponytail, and dark, but kind eyes. He places his right first over his heart and introduces himself.

"I'm Bane Woods, this is my wife, Maisie," he gestures to the woman to his left, she nods and smiles at me. She's just a few inches shorter than him, with really long dark brown hair like him but hers is braided into a side braid. She also has the same kind, dark eyes. He interrupts my staring by saying, "We are the North American Werewolf Pack Leaders."

CHAPTER 16 - WEREWOLVES, FAE, & VAMPIRES

I try to greet them but I can't find the words. Did he just say werewolf pack leaders? I look around the room, waiting for someone to say just kidding but no one is looking at me in a joking way. I look back and smile.

"I'm sorry," I clear my throat. "Did you say werewolf pack leaders?"

"Yes, that's right," Bane says.

"Huh, okay," I say, trying to wrap my head around this new information.

"Why don't you tell her your history?" Meredith says to him.

"Okay," he says. Bane leans back in his seat, puts his left arm behind Maisie's back, resting it on her chair, and says, "I was one of the very first Demi-gods to be made by the Big Three. I was a Shifter, Tracker, and Healer. Four top fighters and I were sent to fight a demon called the Werebeast. It was hiding in a cave in a mountain range, what is now known as the Pindus

Mountain Range in North-Western Greece. It was killing so many people, village after village, so the Big Three sent us to send it back to the Underworld. Since there were no survivors, we didn't know what we were looking for at first. We knew we had found it when we found human bones strewn all over the forest floor, leading to a cave."

Bane takes a breath, maybe letting what he has said so far sink in but he continues after a minute. "We knew we didn't want to fight it inside so we drew it out to us. When it stepped outside of its cave, I swear you could hear all of our hearts stop beating. It was enormous, the size of a house. The beast was a cross between a bear, wolf, and lion. It had the body of a bear, head and coloring like a wolf, and had the mane and tail of a lion. It instantly killed two fighters, it was as fast as lightning. I yelled for my comrades to fall back so that we could form a better attack plan, but they were already in the middle of fighting it. It had one fighter in its mouth in a matter of seconds and another under its huge paw, crushing him to death. I rushed it since I was the fastest of the group. I was able to move around so that it would lift its paw up off the one it was crushing. I was able to get him out of its reach. I went back, my Magikida drawn, and I sliced it a few good times before it whipped its tail around and caught me by surprise. I flew into the air and hit the top opening of the cave. Before I could stand up fully, it was on me. As I brought my Magikida around, driving it into its underbelly to the hilt, it's large canine tooth sliced my shoulder. It reared in pain just as I stumbled back in my own pain. I instantly knew it had venom, I could feel it spreading through my body. It ran off, abandoning its home. I crawled over to my comrade, finding he had died of his injuries. The last thing I remember is my body spasming so bad my muscles were locked into place."

Maisie looks at me and says, "Are you doing okay?"

"Yes," I cough to clear my crackly voice. "Please, keep going."

Bane smiles and continues on with his story, "When I came to, I had Transformed into an animal form. I suppose it was the closest my body could make to resemble the Werebeast that had infected me. My body had chosen the look of the wolf, only it was five times the size of the biggest wolf I had ever seen. I found that I could change back to my human form but when I tried to Shift into a bird to fly back to Mt Olympus to report back, I found that I couldn't Shift. I tried the wolf form and was able to Shift with ease. I tried other forms but couldn't make them work. I was stuck with my human or wolf form. Before I went back to Mt Olympus, I tried to track the Werebeast but I couldn't find it. I didn't know if it had died or fled to heal itself. Villagers saw me running in my wolf form and started calling me 'The Werewolf', so that's where the name originated. When I finally got back to report what happened, the Leaders at the time, held me in quarantine to make sure I wasn't going to be a danger to others. Once they realized I could control my Shifting, I was free to come and go as I wished. I was relieved of my duties and they sent me on my way. I traveled around with no real idea of where I wanted to go. I decided to track down the Werebeast that had infected me, killing any demons I came across in the process. I never did find it. I finally migrated to the US in the early 1800's. I met Maisie in 1826. She was walking down the street and I saw a minor demon stalking her, it was in man form. It jumped her---,"

Maisie jumps in and says, "It jumped me and dragged me into an alley, covering my mouth so I couldn't scream. But no sooner had it got me, Bane was there, running his Magikida through its back, all the way through to the front of it. As soon as I made eye contact with Bane, I knew I was his."

"She said to me, 'I've been waiting for you.' It took me by surprise. I thought she'd start to scream after what had happened but she was as calm as the night air. I said, 'Excuse me, Miss?' and she repeated what she had said, 'I've been waiting for you.' I thought maybe she had hit her head so I checked her out. She just stared up at me with her big brown eyes. I asked where she lived and she told me, so I took her home. I tried to forget about her but that proved to be another battle I would lose. Whether goddess of love, Athena, had her hand in it or not, I don't know, but I kept running into Maisie everywhere I went. I couldn't leave town, I was drawn to the place. If I got further than five miles out, my stomach would cramp up so bad, I'd vomit. It was probably good that I did stay, the city was being overrun by minor demons. I tried to distract myself with vanquishing them all but my mind kept returning to Maisie. I never had an issue avoiding women before this, I never had a desire to befriend anyone I met. And I wasn't 100% sure what would happen if I were to get together with someone. But again, my mind kept going to Maisie and needing to find her. About three months after saving her, I gave in, and Tracked her down. I told her what I was and what had happened to me and she said---" this time Bane looks over at Maisie and nods at her, smiling.

"I said, 'You are who you are and I know that you are a good man, I've been waiting for you.' I brought him home that night and introduced him to my momma and papa," Maisie says, reaching over and taking Bane's hand.

"I courted her for almost a year and we got married exactly a year after our first meeting. Maisie had asked me to try to change her so she could help me with vanquishing demons, one had killed her youngest sister. I was hesitant and told her I wasn't sure if it would change her or kill her. I kept putting it off. Our wedding night was when I realized I could turn humans.

During our love making, I had accidentally grazed her lip with my teeth and she instantly started screaming. I held her, praying to the gods she wouldn't die. Two days later, I woke up to a wolf lying on the bed. I Shifted and found that we could telecommunicate with each other, I walked her through how to Shift back to her human form. Our bodies run about 15 degrees warmer and our hearts beat quite a bit faster than humans and Demi's for that matter. We found out four months later that we could reproduce. Because of how our bodies are different, Maisie was only pregnant for five months. She gave birth to a perfect, fully developed baby girl. We had a son the next year, another son three years after our daughter was born, and two more daughters the next two years. When our oldest daughter was eight, we had twin boys, our last born children. That was in 1835. We had no way of knowing if our children were infected so we kept an eye on our oldest for the first five years, nothing ever happened. But when she was 12 and she hit puberty, she changed. It wasn't as painful as the change Maisie and I went through and it only lasted 24 hours. They all changed when they entered puberty, at the age of 12. When our oldest daughter fell in love with the neighbor boy, they got married after their 18th birthdays, and we found out that our children could turn human's as well and all their children changed at the same time of puberty. All of our children, except for one of the twins, Xander, met and fell in love with a human, married and then changed them. We have 36 grandchildren and a couple million great grandchildren. Our first born great grandchild is well into her 100's. Our oldest great, great, great, great, great, great, great grandchild just turned 12. We have a big family," Bane says laughing quietly.

"So do you all live here in the United States?" I ask, my mind feeling like goo from trying to comprehend everything they're telling me.

"Maisie and I live in the US with Sub-Packs spread out all over North America, but we have a daughter or son who run the packs on the other Continents. On each Continent, there are Sub-Packs in every country," Bane answers, in deep thought.

"How does that all work? Are they all pretty loyal to you or is there discord quite a bit?" I ask but I'm instantly embarrassed. I don't know if these are the types of things I'm supposed to ask.

Maisie smiles reassuringly and says, "Every single werewolf is 100% loyal to Bane. If he tells them something, they willingly do it. There are rumbles every once in a while but that's normal for any big family and we have a huge family. Every Sub-Pack listens to their Pack Leader without hesitation. We visit often but we haven't had a real family reunion in 100's of years, you can imagine why."

"Do you still track down demons?" I ask, totally intrigued. "Yes, we do. I've made sure that we keep the Demi code of trying to keep the Inepties safe from demon infestation," Bane says proudly.

"Can I ask you a couple more questions?"

"Go right ahead, it's why we're here," he says, smiling at me.

"They might be silly but I am curious. All the werewolf myths, are any of them true?"

"Like what?" Bane asks.

"Does silver hurt you?" I ask, turning red.

Bane laughs and says, "No, silver doesn't hurt us. For werewolves to be killed, they have to be dismembered, each piece of our body, and then set on fire, otherwise we can reform. I think it comes from my Healing Talent I had as a Demi. We also stop aging at the age of 25, just like Demi's."

"You can change at will, so the full moon doesn't bother you?" I ask.

"No, we enjoy the full moon, it's easier to hunt demons during that time but it doesn't affect us," Bane says, laughing.

"What other Talents transferred with you when you changed?"

"Strength, Speed, and Super Hearing and Vision," Bane answers.

"Ummm, what do you eat?" I ask, not sure if I want to know the answer.

Bane and Maisie both just laugh and Maisie says, "We still eat what you eat only three times as much."

"Oh okay, wow, I'm just... blown away," I say, trying to comprehend everything I just learned. Werewolves are real, how crazy. And the way they were created, even crazier.

As I'm mentally digesting what Maisie and Bane have just told me, I look over next to Maisie, and see a small, petite and very beautiful girl, she looks to be my age, 18. As she stands up, I see she has long very wavy light blonde hair. It's so light, it's almost white, which makes the headband made out of real white daisies she's wearing actually stand out. Her skin is a pretty brown. Her eyes look like the color of green grass in late spring. She's wearing a silver cloak that shimmers when she moves. She bows her head and introduces herself.

"I am Queen Talia, Queen of the Fairy Folk, or Fae as we like to be called," she says, smiling kindly at me.

"Hi," I say.

"Would you please explain to Emma, your history?" Meredith asks Queen Talia, bowing her head at her.

"Of course," Queen Talia says. She turns towards me and begins her story. "We are magical beings. Artemis, goddess of natural environment, persuaded Poseidon to help create us to help take care of all plant life and living creatures on land. Once Demi-gods were made, the gods made it possible for us to change into a bigger size to help the Demi's defeat demons. It's also easier for Demi's and Fae to communicate when we are in our larger forms. We are three inches tall in our original form. We live a very long time and we can reproduce. The Royal Fae family are the only ones that rule our kind. We reside in the rainforest and forests around the world but because of our magical powers, we travel from continent to continent through water or flying, but water is faster, almost like how you Demi's can Jump. We submerge ourselves in water, say where we want to go, and the water transfers us there instantly. We don't have to breath air to live, so being underwater isn't deadly to us. We die from old age and are the only known beings, between Vampires, Werewolves, Merfians, and Demi's to actually age and die from being old."

"Wait, Vampires? Merfians? What are Merfians?" I ask, interrupting Queen Talia.

"We'll get to that later," Meredith says, patting me on the shoulder and then inclining her head towards Queen Talia, encouraging her to continue.

"We can be killed as we do not heal as well as the others but it's unlikely for us to die any other way than old age unless there is a battle. We live for 100's of years. The oldest known Fae was 326 years old before she died. Also, it's the Queen that is ruler, not the King. In fact, Queen's aren't required to have a King, they can have as many suitors as they wish. If the Queen finds someone she wants to spend her life with, she can marry him, otherwise, she does as she wishes. The Queen's subjects are very loyal and do as the Queen asks of them. Her subjects can live their lives but any major decision has to be asked of the Queen. A Queen only has one child in her life, a girl. When the Queen reaches 150 years old, the Princess becomes the new Queen, allowing her mother the chance to live the rest of her life exploring and enjoying herself. If the Queen dies unexpectedly, of course the Princess becomes Queen, no matter the age. All Fae children are born during Full Moons. That's where our wings get the translucent look, frim the moon light."

"The Princess is required to serve in our military, to learn how to protect herself against any type of attack we may encounter. She is also required to help take care of all the living things we are in trusted to care for, along with our elderly Fae. She is born in secret, only the Queen, the father, and the royal medical staff knows she's the Princess. Nobody else knows who the Princess is until the Queen decides it's time for her to start her Queen training. That way the Princess doesn't get any special treatment. The Queen can feel when there is a need for the Fae to take action. To pass time, some of us like to play tricks on humans. Nothing too serious, just misplacing something while they are at the park, or getting confused out in the forest. If we come across a human trying to cause unjust harm to nature, animal or plant, we tend to confuse them enough that they get lost in the woods. Unlike Vampires and Werewolves, we cannot change a human into a Fae. If one of us falls for a human, we can permanently change into a human. We however, can never change back. The Princess is not allowed to fraternize with humans as it is too dangerous if she were to fall for a human man. The Queen, after she's been retired, may seek out humans if she wishes, but usually she has already chosen your life partner and spends her remaining years with him."

"This handsome man is Ragnor, my personal guard," she says, as the giant of a man stands up beside her. He may have just looked huge because he's standing next to her but he's also standing next to Bill, who hasn't taken a seat yet. Ragnor was making him look a little small. Ragnor bows his head as well and sits only after Queen Talia has seated herself back down.

I am dumbfounded. What the what? Werewolves? Fae? Vampires? And what in the frack are Merfians?

Bill clears his throat and says, "And you've met Dom and Jenna Michaels, North America's Vampire Coven Leaders."

Startled, I glance over at Jenna and I must have a surprised look on my face because she says, "Oh, sorry, I didn't mention that earlier, did I?"

I shake my head quickly and look over to Meredith, whose smiling at me. I take a deep breath and try to calm my heart and my breathing. They can't be dangerous if Meredith and Doc have let them come here. No wonder their skin felt so much colder. A shiver runs down my spine which causes me to shake myself.

"Shall I tell our story?" Jenna asks, looking over me to Meredith.

"Please do," Meredith says, placing her hand back on my shoulder, calming me more.

"Our story is much the same as Bane's. The year was 1764. I was a Demi-god and I was tasked with the job of Tracking a monster that had been killing humans that crossed it's path. It was a ginormous snake called Vanpyreth. I was a young, foolish Demi and once I Tracked it to its den, I thought I could handle taking it down. I was bitten by the Vanpyreth but I was able to kill it with my Magikida before I passed out. Much the same as Bane, I was infected with the Vanpyreth's venom. When I came to, I had been changed in what I called a monster. I was thirsty and hungry but no amount of water or fruit or foliage I found satiated me. I came across the scent of a man hunting in the forest nearby. His scent drove me mad, I basically flew to him in a blacked out state. When I came out of my blackout, I had drained him of all his blood. I wanted to die. I couldn't believe I had done that to an Ineptie. I tried all sorts of ways to kill myself, even running myself through with my Magikida. But nothing worked. I barricaded myself in a cave for years but when a hunting party passed by, I attacked in a hungry frenzy yet again. I decided I couldn't allow myself to kill innocent Inepties anymore so I set out to hunt evil Inepties. Inepties that had done inhumane things to their fellow beings. The murderers, rapists, abusers, and those equally as awful. I found that if I did this, the other Inepties were safe from my hunger outbursts. I told myself I was doing the right thing but I could still feel myself falling deeper into a depression with every Ineptie I drained. I also became extremely angry with every Ineptie I drained, my anger kept rising. I found that the blood from Inepties was highly addictive and soon I was hunting evil Inepties just to get my fix, whether I was hungry or not."

"30 years after I was transformed, I came across a human man, Ian Thomas. I was in a fit of hunger and I was about to attack him but he was cunning enough to talk me out of it. He became my companion. I hadn't had any human contact like that in so long that I fell in love with him. During a hunt of an absolute disgusting excuse of a man, Ian got in the way and I accidentally bit him. I thought I had killed him but he woke up three days later, changed. We got married and continued our hunt for evil Inepties. For the first 100 or so years, I thought Inepties were my only form of food. I believe the gods didn't send Demi's after me and Ian because we were hunting demons and evil Inepties. Had we started to go on rampages and killing Innocents, I have no doubt we would have been hunted down like the monsters Demi's hunted. It wasn't until we were in the deep woods, tracking a serial killer when we first found another form of sustenance. I was beyond hungry when we came upon a cougar and her kill, an elk. The smell of the elk's blood wasn't as appetizing as that of an Ineptie, but it still smelled appealing. I fought the cougar and obviously won, I finished draining the elk of his blood but found I was still hungry. I decided to try the cougar and found her equally as tasty as the elk. My mind was instantly cleared. I no longer had the anger inside of me and my depression I had been living in for so long was gone. We found a nearby elk and Ian drained it, coming to feel the same as I had. We found the serial killer and disposed of him but I had no desire to take his blood. I could tell Ian wanted to but he withstood the urge. We swore to ourselves that we would not kill another Ineptie if we could help it. We would turn them over to the Ineptie authorities if we ever came into contact with the evil scum. We started hunting demons and monsters full-time. My life was once again, happy. We also figured out that I was stronger after drinking animal blood and it lasted longer. We also found that sick, weak, or old animals were just as strengthening as the healthy, young ones. I decided we would only hunt the sick, weak, or old so we weren't hurting the animal population. We were only having feed twice a month on animal blood, rather than two or three times a week when we were feeding on Ineptie blood," she takes a breath and looks at me. I can feel my eyes bulging wide and my mouth hanging slightly open. I snap it shut and blink wildly for a second.

"I have so many questions, but please continue," I say, my heart beating fast.

"Now that I've told you how I was made, let me tell you a little bit about me, as a Vampire. I decided to call myself a Vampire since I was made from the venom of the Vanpyreth monster. I have a heartbeat but unlike Bane's, my heartbeat is very, very slow. For every one of my heart beats, an Inpetie's or Demi's heart beats 10 times. I have blood in my veins but because of my slow heartbeat, it's colder than usual, which is why I feel cooler to the touch. Vampires can reproduce but we carry our unborn child for 12 months, due to our slow body. Once the baby is born, they are a Vampire, there is no change they go through. We can also turn Inepties with a bite. Unlike Bane, I can turn Demi's into Vampire's. However, other Vampires cannot turn them. It's highly unlikely to find a Demi who wants to be changed but there are a few that have Tracked me and asked to be changed. The venom is in our DNA, just like Bane's but I think since I am the original Vampire, it is more potent in me, which is why I can change Demi's. Most everything Ineptie's think they know about Vampires, are myths we let them believe are true about us. For instance sunlight doesn't hurt us, we can go out in the middle of the day. Wooden stakes can't kill us but a stake through the heart will stop our hearts but once removed, we heal, but slowly. We can feel pain but only slightly. We will heal eventually. Garlic has no effect on us. We can eat food but only need to eat once a day. Drinking blood twice a month like I stated before and the food once a day sustains us enough."

"Ian and I moved to America in 1883. Ian and I were happily married for 155 years, or so I thought. We had 64 children over the course of those 155 years, our last being born in 1922. The last 10 years of our marriage I could tell something was wrong with him. He wasn't outwardly upset but little things were starting to come to my attention. I would walk into a room where he and a group of our adult children would be talking but they'd quickly quiet when I'd walk in. He started asking about hunting evil humans again, he never called them Inepties. Then in 1944, while we were at our home, doing some research on a demon in Boston, Massachusetts, Ian walked in and put a stake through my heart."

I gasp. Meredith pats my shoulder she's still holding and Jenna continues, "I was instantly immobile. He explained that he was tired of surviving on animal blood and hunting demons. He wanted to go back home to Italy and finally become what he was meant to be, the Vampire that Inepties thought we really were, bloodthirsty monsters. 20 of our children that had stayed home while the other 44 had gone out doing some recon on the Boston Demon, their intentions were becoming clear. They were a mixture of some of our oldest children and some of our youngest and they wanted to follow him, return to Italy and begin hunting evil humans. They left, leaving me lying there with a stake in my heart. If it weren't for my oldest coming home to check in sooner than we had been expecting him, I don't know how long I would have stayed in that situation. I was able to heal and tell him what had happened. He called his other brothers and sisters home and we regrouped. I was heartbroken. My remaining children reassured me that they were on my side and understood why I refused to drink human blood. We knew when Ian and the others made it back to Italy. There were stories of mass disappearances and murders. We came to understand that he thought me and our children that stayed with me, would track them down so he was trying to build his numbers. Dom, and 17 of the Vampires that Ian and the others created, came to us in 1951. Dom had heard some of my children talking about the difference of blood and how they felt since drinking human blood for the first time. Dom and the 17 tried drinking animal blood and realized they preferred that way much better than drinking human blood. When they showed up at my home in Kansas City, our suspicions of Ian's plans were confirmed. Dom said he had a group of 36 vampires, but some would leave, not wanting to be a part of his coven. I had learned not to fall too fast for a man I had feelings for but something about Dom had me thinking he was meant for me. In 1960, we married. We have been together ever since and share the same views on the world. Not only do we hunt demons but we hunt down Ian and his coven, we call them Rogues. They don't just kill evil Inepties, they kill whoever they want, whenever they want. And change whoever they feel would make a good Vampire. I won't change and won't allow anyone to change an Ineptie unless they are wanting to be changed. For the most part, Ian and his coven stay over in Europe, Africa, and Asia. I have covens on every continent, consisting of 20-30 Vampires, a daughter or son leading them. None in our group have ever shown signs of deflecting like Ian and the others but I am always on the watch for it. They all understand they are free to do as they wish but they must follow my law, no killing humans or changing a human unless the human wants to be changed. After Dom and the 17 left, Ian has forced his coven members to stay with him. If they leave, he and the others track them down and kill them. Some have escaped and made it over here but more often than not, Ian finds them. We are slowly making way on his numbers but they move around so much, it's hard to know where he is exactly. As far as we know, he hasn't changed anyone in 12 years."

I just stare at her in disbelief. I don't know if my brain is just shutting down from the overload of information I'm getting or if I'm just accepting all this as is, no questions asked. Well not entirely no questions asked.

"Wow…," I say, I hear a laugh go around the room.

"If you have any questions, now would be the time to ask them," Doc says, peaking around Meredith's shoulder.

"Oh, ummm...," I dumbly say. Where do I even begin? "You were a Demi when you were changed, what Talents did you have and what Talents transferred with you when you transformed into a Vampire?"

"I was a Protector, so Super Strength, Speed, Super Eyesight and Hearing, all transferred, and also transferred to my children and all Inepties that become Vampires. I was an Earth Mover and that Talent transferred as well but not to any of the others," Jenna says, smiling at me.

"Oh, okay," I say. I seriously had so many questions for her earlier but now I can't think of any more interesting than what her Talents were... are, now that she's a Vampire.

"If that's all, I'd like to introduce you to one more set of Leaders before we continue on with the meeting," Bill says looking at me expectantly.

"I'm done for now. Thank you, Jenna," I say, smiling at her. She places her hand on my shoulder and I can feel the coolness from it. A chill runs down my spine, maybe just my instincts telling me she's dangerous in nature but in reality she's very nice.

"Then I'd like you to meet, Merfian Leaders, Merking Keanos and Merqueen Lassa," Bill says, gesturing towards a gorgeous couple sitting on the other side of himself. Merking Keanos has long, wavy, dark black hair. His eyes are the color of an angry, gray, stormy day and dark tan skin. Merqueen Lassa has dirty blonde hair that's braided to the side and goes well past her hips. Her eyes are a deep blue and she also has dark tan skin.

"I'm sorry to sound ridiculous, but what are Merfian's?" I ask, I couldn't help it. For the life of me, I can't figure out what or who they are supposed to be.

"Merfian's are what humans call Mermaids," Merking Keanos says in a very deep, melodic voice. It is very soothing to hear.

"Mermaids?" I ask, I'm in total disbelief mode now.

CHAPTER 17 - AND
MERFIANS TOO!

"Yes, but Merfian is the correct term in which we prefer to be called. Much to the same creation of the Fae, we were created by Poseidon himself. He created us to help protect the ocean, seas, and all that live in them. As you can see, we don't have to stay in water and we also do not have tail fins. Breathing air is just as natural to us as breathing underwater. We have little gills behind our ears to help when we are underwater," Merking Keanos states as he turns his head to the side, allowing me to see the gills behind his ear. They were indeed quite small. Had he not pointed them out, I probably wouldn't have noticed them. "We are ruled by one royal family, my family. The eldest of the family becomes ruler. I was the oldest in my family, so therefore I became King when my father stepped down. There is no age at which we have to step down, we can rule as long as we wish. Most step down around 65 so that we have plenty of years to enjoy our retirement. Past Merking and Merqueens serve on the Mercouncil for the residing Merking and Merqueen. The merpeople live in mercities and mertowns throughout all the ocean and sea waters. We are protected from humans by a Jump Force Poseidon put around all of our inhabited areas. If a submarine, or divers, or any type of human submerged water vehicle were to come close to one, they'd be Jumped to the other side, not realizing it, they'd think they had continued on with their travel as usual. The Royal Region is all of the South Pacific Ocean, our home mercity is Atlantida Vasileio. There are six governing families in the other oceans, they are Merlords and Merladies with children either Merdukes or Merduchesses, and they help run their regions, reporting back to the Merking and Merqueen. The North Atlantic Region is governed by Merlord Tyfon and Merlady Koralli. The North Pacific Region is governed by Merlord Nero and Merlady Ilios. The South Atlantic is governed by Merlord Pani and Merlady Fargida. The Arctic Region is governed by Merlord Falain and Merlady Selino. The Southern Region is governed by Merlord Pagetone and Merlady Anthi. The Indian Region is governed by Merlord Fyrain and Merlady Kyma."

Letting this sink in, I just stare back at Merking Keanos. Glancing over at Merqueen Lassa, I see her smiling at me.

"I think my brain is on overdrive right now," I say shyly.

"That is understandable," Merqueen Lassa replies and her voice is very pleasing to the ear also, kind of like the softest of singing voices. "Do you have any questions for us?"

"A couple," I quietly laugh. "What happens if the ruling Merking or Merqueen dies? Who becomes the ruler?"

"The ruler is of royal bloodline. So for example, when our eldest, Merprince Dynami, becomes Merking, if he chooses to marry, his wife will become Merqueen but if he were to die while ruling, his eldest child will become ruler. If they do not have any children at the time of his death, Dynami's sister, Merprincess Omorfia would become ruling Merqueen. Dynami's wife would then serve on the Mercouncil," Merqueen Lassa answers.

"What happens to the Merprinces and Merprincesses who don't become Merking or Merqueen?" I ask.

"They marry one of the governing families sons or daughters. They can choose to stay in the Royal Region or move elsewhere. The Merprinces and Merprincesses are required to serve in the Stratos, which is what we call our Guardians. All mermen are to join at adult age, which in our world is the age of 17 and they must serve 10 years. After that they may choose to stay in the Stratos or move on to something else. We believe it makes for a better ruler if the Merprinceses and Merprincesses have fought along side their people, not just sitting in the rulers chair passing judgement. The Merprincesses and merwomen are to help take care of the young, old, and sick in their regions. Merprincesses and merwomen are trained for battle in case their home regions are ever attacked and they need to protect themselves. A lot of the Stratos warriors help around their regions caring for the young, old, and sick also. We all have our duties but we are willing to step in where there's a need," Merqueen Lassa says.

"Oh wow, that's cool," I say. "What do you eat?"

"We eat what you call seafood, we just call it food," Merking Keanos laughs. "We can also eat land food but if we can find a place that has seafood on the menu, we prefer to eat it, whether cooked or raw, it makes no difference to us. We also eat sea plants."

"I thought so but I didn't want to assume anything," I say blushing a little.

It's quiet for some time, me trying to think of what to say, and everyone else just looking at me.

"I think that will do for Emma's 'Other Beings' lesson for now," Bill says, smiling down at me.

"I think you've met everyone else, Emma. So, let's get this meeting started. First we need to talk to you about what happened with Frank. Are you okay with that?" Meredith says, putting a hand back on my shoulder. This brings me back to reality fast.

"Yes," I croak out.

"When you're ready," she says, placing her hands on

the table, intertwining her fingers.

I take another steadying breath and tell them, all of the details, about what happened the night of my birthday, from the first time I saw Frank all the way until I passed out. No one said a thing until I was down talking.

"So Frank is 'Mint-man'?" Doc asks.

"Yes," I say.

"I didn't get a sign of him lying to me when I debriefed him. If I would have, I wouldn't have let him go to the party. He would have been kept in a cell until we could find out what he was hiding from us. I'm sorry, Emma. My Talent has never failed me before," Bill says, running his hand over his face.

"It's okay, it's not your fault. I bet Vanessa gave him some kind of Talent to be able to keep his thoughts silent. Or something so that he can lie. Is there a Talent like that?" I ask, looking at Meredith.

"Not that I know of," Meredith says, looking around the room. "Anyone else?"

"Maybe a Shield. The Lie Detector Talent has to do with being able to read minds or get a sense in the purity of the person's thoughts. He could have gotten a strong Shield Talent from Vanessa," Vince, a Guardian, suggests.

"That could be it. We'll have to get all the Lie Detectors we have and have a conversation with him. If he's told Vanessa where we are, we could be in danger."

Meredith says.

They all start to murmur with one another. I look around the room and see Ragnor staring at me. Meredith looks at him then at me and then back at Ragnor.

"What is it?" Meredith asks him.

Ragnor looks at her, then at me, and then at Queen Talia. She looks at me and then nods.

"How do we know that she isn't a spy?" Ragnor asks.

I look behind me, thinking he must mean someone other than me, but there isn't anyone behind me. I look around and see everyone staring at me. Bill has his head cocked to the side, looking as if he's considering it. I quickly look to Meredith and she's staring at me also.

"She was raised by Vanessa," Bane says, almost snarling at me.

"Yeah, she could have been training her just right all these years so that we could trust her," Maisie says, crossing her arms over her chest.

Finally finding my voice I say, "I am not a spy. My mother," I shake my head, I have got to get over the fact that Vanessa is not and never was my mother. "Vanessa wasn't training me for anything except how to not have a life. Having spent time with people who actually show me kindness and affection, I have come to realize Vanessa never treated me like a daughter, she treated me like something she *had* to take care of rather than a daughter she *wanted*. She was only waiting for me to come of age to see if I was 'The One' and to see what Talent or Talents I would have. She also sat back and watched me get tortured for a month. And while I was in that hell hole, Frank tried to kill me, but some other guy named Tim stopped him, and Vanessa was probably there for that too. She doesn't care about me."

At the mention of the name Tim, Bill looks quickly at Meredith but neither says anything about it.

"But do you care for her?" Bane asks.

"Not after everything she's done to me," I say back. After everything I've gone through because of her greed, I know it's the truth.

"If we were to capture her and found that death was her penalty, you'd be okay with watching her die?" Dom asks from the other side of Jenna.

"Watch her die? No. I don't want to watch anyone die. I don't want any more of our people dying. Hasn't Vanessa caused enough death?" this was the first time I have said 'our people' rather than 'your people'. It feels right, not strange or anything like that.

"You'd want her what? To be put in a cell? A cell wouldn't be able to hold her for long. She'd get out and start this nonsense all over again but with a fiery vengeance," Queen Talia says.

"If... no, when... when we catch her, death will be her only option," Bane says. Glaring at me and then he asks, "Are you okay with that?"

"If you, the Leaders and Elders, decide that is

what's best for our World," I say, looking around the room. "Then who am I to disagree. She's killed count-less children, and who knows how many adults, for her selfishness. Maybe death is what she deserves but I'm not okay with anyone dying, nobody should be. Can't we... I don't know... strip her of her Talents somehow?"

Not a single person says a thing. I look over at Bane and Maisie and see them smiling at me. Smiling? They are strange but Queen Talia is smiling at me too and she bows her head and Ragnor does the same, minus the smile. Meredith puts an arm around my shoulder and squeezes.

Jenna pats my arm with her chilly hand and Dom leans forward and says, "Good girl."

"Uuuh?" is all I can, brilliantly, say.

"As a rule, we do not choose death for another liv-ing soul lightly, so we wanted to see how you would react to the suggestion that Vanessa would be put to death if she's ever caught. And you answered just as those who have gotten to know you in the short time you've been here, thought you'd answer. Actually, even better than we thought," Bill says, answering my award winning question. His smile lights up his face, and makes him look less intimidating.

"So she won't die when she's caught?" I ask.

"We'll have a vote and convene with the Elders about it, if and when that time comes. Although, the odds are not in her favor. She has done some heinous atrocities and will be punished accordingly. And to answer your question about stripping her of her Talents, it's not something that has ever been done but it's definitely something we will talk about and figure out how to accomplish if we decide to go that route," Meredith says matter-of-factly.

I guess I can see their point. If they can't strip her Talents, Vanessa probably could break out of a cell faster than anyone, and who knows what she would do for revenge. I can't say I hope she's caught and killed soon but I do hope she's stopped soon.

"Now that we've determined that Emma is not a spy, what are we going to do about Frank? Bill have you heard from Tim?" Meredith asks in her serious tone of voice.

"No, not yet. I'm starting to get concerned. I can't imagine him turning against us but I thought the same about Frank. I might have to take my Unit out and see what information we can find. In the meantime, we should try to locate one of the Seekers and see if they've found a new place for us," Bill answers.

"Bane and Maisie, could you pass a message on through your ranks, that we're looking for our Seekers and if they're found, have them come home as soon as possible, please? You also, Jenna and Dom?" Meredith says glancing at the Werewolves and Vampires. Then she looks at Queen Talia and Merking Keanos. "Would the Fae and Merfians be willing to send word out for us?"

"Absolutely, as soon as we get above ground, I'll send my warriors that I've brought, ahead of me to gather what we can spare and send them out. Same message?" Queen Talia asks.

"We will do our part as well," Merking Keanos says.

"Yes, thank you," Meredith says. She looks over at me and says, "You can go now, Emma."

I get up to go but Jenna grabs my arm and says, "Wait, we haven't heard about her Change."

"It's still too soon to know, she does have some remarkable Talents showing through already but we really won't know for a while. We will have another meeting once she's had time to adjust and we will hopefully have more of an idea of how she's doing," Doc says, coming to stand behind me, placing his hands on my shoulders.

Jenna releases my arm and says, "Sorry about that, it's just been awhile since we have had a Changling in our midst."

"Umm, that's okay," I say. I'm not sure how I feel about her. She seems nice but she also makes me feel uncomfortable.

"You can go, Emma," Doc says, gently nudging me towards the door. "Oh and you probably shouldn't go the way we came."

I look up at him and he nods ever so slightly. He doesn't want me Jumping. That's understandable. I'm not sure if I'd be able to do it again without an older Demi there to help me, even though Doc didn't help me last time, I still didn't want to chance it. I nod and leave the Guard Room.

I can't Jump myself but maybe I can Run. I start out walking fast and then into a normal run and then, before I know it, I'm Running. I was expecting everything to be blurry from the speed but it's not. I can still see everything, it just looks like it's in slow motion.

Not a second goes by and I'm in the Great Hall and I see Alysa and Malory walking towards the Gym. I have a half second thought to mess with them but I decide against it. I'm trying to get on their good side, they'd probably guess it was me, and they'd hate me even more.

When I get to my room another second later, I find Libby and Shae sitting on my bed, presents taking up every empty space in here.

My mouth drops open and they laugh at me.

"What in the world?" I ask.

"We told you, you had some presents to open," Libby says, scooting over on my bed to make room for me to sit down.

"This is not 'some'," I say, shaking my head.

"Open this one, it's from John. He's a Guardian," Shae says handing me a box wrapped in purple.

I open it and find a soft blue sweater.

"Oh this is great!" I say, feeling how soft it is with

my hands.

"This one is from Carla, she helps Cooky in the kitchen," Libby says.

I open a similar box as the last and find a blue hoodie.

"Again, this is great! They must know I need more clothes," I laugh.

"Well, looking at most of these, I think you're right. Here, this one looks different," Libby says, handing me a box that feels slightly heavier.

I look at the tag and it says it's from Kathryn. I open it and find a couple of books. I turn one over and see that it says, '*Jamison Family Volume 3*', on it. I hastily put it down and turn the next one over, '*Jamison Family Volume 2*', and the last one says, '*Jamison Family Volume 1*'. I look up at Libby and Shae with big eyes and a huge smile.

"What?" they say together.

I hold up the first volume and show them.

"Jamison? Wasn't that your mom's maiden name?" Shae asks.

"Yeah, that's what Kathryn said but that's all she knew about my mom's side of the family," I say, turning the book over in my hand.

"Oh my gods! Who's that from?" Libby asks.

"Kathryn! She must have found some new information," I say back. "Give me a second, I want to read these real quick."

Libby and Shae look at each other and then back at me.

"Yeah I can read fast, always have been able to," I say, shrugging. I open the first volume and start reading. I'm done with it within five minutes. "Oh, my mom's brothers name is Richard but it says he goes by Rick," I say excitedly as I reach for the second book and put the first one down.

"Do you mind?" I hear Shae asks and out of my peripheral vision I see her pick the book up.

"No, go ahead," I reply. I read the second book and grab the third one and start to read it. About halfway through I come across something that might just be something of use. "Oh my gosh!"

I jump up and Run from my room. I distantly hear the girls ask what's going on before I'm at the door of the Guard Room. I knock and wait, bouncing on my toes.

Doc opens the door and looks at me in surprise.

"What's the matter, Emma?" he asks.

"I think I've found something. Can I come in?"

He steps aside and lets me enter. Everyone in the room looks up and stares at me.

"What's going on?" Meredith asks, standing up from her seat, looking concerned.

I smile and say, "Ask Kathryn."

Everyone turns their stares to Kathryn, who stands up.

"Ask me what?" she says, looking stunned.

"You gave me the books, don't you know?" I ask.

"Oh, no, I have no idea. I got ahold of a friend of mine who works for the Elder's and asked him to see if he could find anything on your mom and dad. He found the books in the Elder's storage warehouse. I didn't read them. They are your family's books after all," Kathryn says.

"What did you find out?" Meredith asks, walking over to me.

"I think I know where we can go, where we can move to," I say, holding out my book. "My mother's family owned a huge estate, actually it's an island. But I guess there's a huge house and all sorts of other stuff on it."

"I haven't heard about this," Meredith says, taking my book and looking at the page where I'd found the information about my family's island. Island? That sounds so weird, no way it's a big island.

"That's probably because my mom's family kept it a secret and only a Jamison can get to it and only a Jamison can give other people permission to come to the island. It has some kind of super protection on it or something," I say to Meredith. Turning to Kathryn I say, "And in the first book it says that my uncles name is Rick, well Richard, but he goes by Rick. Do you think you could use that to maybe find more information about him?"

"Yes, I believe I can," Kathryn says smiling over at me.

Meredith puts a hand on my shoulder and says, "I see what you mean about the protection on the island but this could be the answer to our prayers. We'll have to send some Guardians there to see if it's safe. Could you give Bill and a few of the others permission to get on the island?" Meredith asks, smiling as she hands me back my book.

"Of course," I answer excitedly.

"We are just about finished here. Come back in about an hour, they should be ready to leave by then. Oh Emma, this could be our chance!" Meredith says, hugging me.

I turn and leave the Guard Room and Run back to my room. Libby and Shae are still there but pacing now.

"What the hell was that all about?" Shae asks, walking over to me, looking upset.

"Sorry, I got excited and just Ran. I think I found a place for us to move to. An actual place where we can go outside whenever we want," I say.

"Are you serious? Where? How?" Libby asks.

I show them my mother's book, my book. "In here. My mom, Emmalynn, her family owned an estate, an island. Some Guardians are going to go check it out and make sure it's safe. But supposedly only a Jamison can get to it and give permission for anyone else to get to it. So it should be okay if that's the case. I also read that the protections can tell if the permission given was given freely or forced. So if someone forced a Jamison to give them permission to get to the estate, they wouldn't be able to get there."

An island? Really?" Shae asks. "Damn girl, you're rich!"

"I doubt it's big and I'm not rich, it was my mom's family. I don't know what they'll find when they get there. It might be run down and in need of a ton of TLC," I say, slightly embarrassed.

"But it's a place above ground, where we could be free and safe again," Libby says, giving me a hug. "When are the Guardians leaving?"

"I think in about an hour. That's when I have to go back and tell them where to go and give them permission. They were still in their Leader's meeting when I got back there," I answer her, hugging her back.

We settle back down and the two of them pick up the third Jamison book and start to read it. I grab the first one and reread what had been written. In it, not only did I find out my uncle's name but it says he and Emmalynn and their family are from Katerini, a city about five miles from the Thermaic Gulf.

I put the book down and spend the next 45 minutes opening the rest of my presents, not because I want to but because Shae suggests it would be a good way to pass the time before I have to go back to the Guard Room. I ended up getting 20 new pairs of pants (holy cow, right!), a couple new pairs of shoes, 10 pairs of black workout outfits, 15 hoodies that were a different shade of blue or plain black, 10 white long sleeve shirts, a ton of different colors of tank tops and t-shirts, and a ton of socks, underwear, and bras. Libby said I really needed to start getting some different colors in my wardrobe but I told her blue, black, and white were my favorite colors. I also got a couple of nice blankets. I feel really spoiled.

I look at my watch and see that it's time for me to go back to the Guard Room.

"I'll be back in a few minutes. This shouldn't take too long," I say as I get ready to leave.

"We'll be here," the girls say, once again, at the same time.

I Run to the Guard Room and knock on the door. Bill answers the door this time and steps back for me to enter. I walk in and see the Leaders are all gone. It's just Bill, Ty, Charlie, Clay, and Max. Nobody else, no one at the monitors and no one sitting at the table.

"Hi Princess," Charlie says.

I shoot him a look and he says, "Sorry, old habits die hard."

"We're ready when you are," Bill says before anyone else can say anything.

"Okay. Well, as far as I can tell, the island is halfway between Los Angeles and Hawaii, out in the Pacific," I say.

"I've been to Hawaii, there's no island between there and Los Angeles," Charlie says.

"That's because you didn't have permission to see it," I say. "At least that's how I think it works. If you don't have permission to be on the island, you can't even see it."

"Well, it's worth a look if it means we can get out of here," Max says.

"Do you give Clay, Max, Charlie, Ty, and myself permission to access your island?" Bill asks.

"Yes!"

"We'll take the jet and see what we can find," Bill says. "Get your gear boys, let's go."

"Be safe, you guys," I say.

"Can I talk to you?" Charlie asks.

"Sure," I say.

The others nod as they walk out of the room. Ty stops and acts like he's about to say something but decides against it and just says bye.

"How are you?" Charlie asks.

"Fine."

"I came to visit you but you were still Changing. I wanted to apologize, again, about how I behaved. It's my fault you were in The Pub and Frank getting you alone," he bows his head in shame.

"It's fine. You're forgiven," I didn't want another one of the guys feeling obligated to protect me.

"I better go, bye," Charlie says.

I wave goodbye as he walks out of the door.

Now all there is to do is wait.

CHAPTER 18 - THE ESTATE

I t's been three days since Bill, Ty, and the guys left for the island. I keep wanting to ask Meredith if maybe she's heard from them but I know if she had, she would have told us already. I've been spending the last few days in the Gym, working out, and learning combat moves, trying to pass the time as best I can.

Also, I've been trying to avoid, well everyone. Everyone, except Libby and Shae. Ever since I got my Mark, my weird Talents, and found out about the island, everyone has gone back to staring at me and whispering whenever I walk by. I can see them trying to catch a glimpse of my Mark when I'm eating or just walking around, so I try to stay away from large crowds if I can help it.

Doc said they'd start testing me in four days, on Monday, to see what I might have for other Talents.

I'm standing in line, waiting my turn to get some food when Libby Runs up to me and says, "They're back! I was just in there asking Meredith if she'd heard anything when they showed up. Let's go find Shae and go see what they found out!"

"She's in her room, let's go!" I say.

"Are you sure? I thought she'd be in the Gym," Libby says, helping me put my tray, plate, and silverware back where I'd gotten them.

"I can't explain it but I just have a feeling she's in her room," I say, shrugging. Shae could possibly be in the Gym but something was telling me she wasn't, that she was in fact, in her room.

"Maybe you have a Tracker Talent. Let's go check her room," Libby says, looking at me with bright eyes.

I think about Shae's room and wrap one of my arms around Libby's and go to step away but when I look up, we're in Shae's room.

"Whoa! Did you just Jump us?" Libby asks looking a little dizzy but she's handling it way better than Doc.

"Crap! Sorry, I didn't mean to do that. I guess if I concentrate on a place to hard and start to walk or Run to it, I automatically Jump there. Are you okay?" I ask.

"Oh yeah, I'm fine. I just wasn't expecting it. You've done it before?" Libby asks back, lightly shaking her head.

"Yeah, once before with Doc. He doesn't want me to do it until I've had training because he doesn't want me to hurt myself or anyone else. He was really surprised that I was able to Jump him and myself," I answer sheepishly.

"Well, you did it perfectly and I feel fine. You've got

quite the Talents, Em's!" Libby says, smiling.

Remembering what we were doing, we look around, and see that Shae is lying on her bed, on her stomach, with headphones in her ears.

"You were right," Libby says laughing. She then jumps on the bed making Shae bounce and jump up swearing.

"What the fuuuuu... oh it's you! You are such a brat!" Shae says, putting her hand over her heart. "You scared the hell out of me!"

"HAHA, sorry, but we thought maybe you'd want to come with us and talk to Ty and the guys. They just got back," Libby says while she sits up.

"Hell yeah I do!" Shae says. "Let's go!"

She looks like she's about to Run out of the room but Libby grabs her arm and stops her.

"Emma, you wanna take us? It'll be faster," Libby says, holding out her hand.

"I don't know if I should. I don't want to hurt you guys and Doc said not to do it," I say, holding my hands behind my back.

"Have her what?" Shae asks.

"We won't tell him and I don't think you'll hurt us," Libby says, walking towards me while pulling Shae with her.

"Again, I ask, have her do what?" Shae asks, impatiently.

Libby smiles at her and says, "Emma Jumped us

here from the Great Room. I think she should Jump us to the Guard Room."

"Hell yeah you should! Come on, I wanna try! We won't tell Doc and it'll be good practice for you," Shae says, offering me her hand too.

Easily convinced, I say, "Alright, just hang on tight."

"Don't Jump us right into the room, take us to the door," Libby suggests.

I take their hands and concentrate on the door to the Guard Room. I close my eyes to help me focus better and I take a step forward. I open my eyes and see the Guard Room door.

"Awesome!" Shae says excitedly.

"Great job, Emma! And I'm not even dizzy this time, but then again, I was expecting it," Libby says.

Their smiles are contagious and I can't help smiling back.

"Shall we?" I ask, raising my hand to knock.

They nod so I knock three times. The door opens and Doc is standing there.

"I should have figured you girls would know they were back. Come on in," he says, smiling.

We walk in and see the guys sitting at the table. Libby runs over to Max and just about knocks him over as he stands up to give her a hug. She gives him a kiss and then turns, and pats Ty on the shoulder.

"Good to have you guys back!" she says looking at them all.

"Yes, it's so good to see you guys all back and in one piece," I say. I fight the urge to rush Ty. I look at Charlie to distract myself and find I'd like to hug him too.

"Welcome back," Shae says, pounding Charlie on the shoulder as she walks by to grab a seat.

"What? No kiss?" he says to her.

"You wish," she says back.

I walk by and Charlie says to me, "What about you?" while puckering his lips.

"Umm, no thanks," I stammer out.

"That was quick, Libby. I didn't think you ladies would be back quite this fast," Meredith says, looking at Libby, then Shae, and then finally at me.

"We hurried," Shae says quickly.

Meredith raises an eyebrow at her and Doc looks at me, tilts his head to the side, and then smiles. He knows what I have done but he doesn't seem too upset. I'm sure he'll talk to me after this meeting is over though.

"Bill, why don't you tell us what you guys found," Meredith says.

Bill stands up and points a little remote to the wall to the right of the room. It turns out to be a huge screen and a map of the World pops up. He does something with the remote and the map changes to just off the West coast of the United States. It slowly moves to where we can see Los Angeles and Hawaii.

"Right here," Bill pushes a button and a red laser dot shows up on the map and he's making circles in the space right in the middle of the ocean between Los Angeles and Hawaii. "Right about here is where the island is, Emma was right. We were able to land without any problems. There's a nice landing strip there, really easy to spot from the air. From there, we followed a road about two miles until we came to the Estate."

At this point, he stops and smiles at his Guardians. I look at them and see they are smiling too, even Ty. And man, I gotta say, his smile is amazing. I shake my head and look back at Bill.

"We walked through the gates and did a perimeter sweep and found nothing dangerous waiting for us. When we got back to the entrance, we walked down the lane, which is about half a mile long before we got to the...... house," Bill says, making a face. I can't tell what that facial expression means because it's a mixture of amusement, shock, and disbelief. Does that mean the house is a wreck?

I hear Charlie snicker. I look over at him and he whispers into Clay's ear, "Yeah right, a house."

Clay tries to hide his amusement too but Doc catches him. Doc clears his throat causing Clay and Charlie to straighten up in their chairs.

So the house is a wreck. Hopefully not so far gone that we can't fix it up. I'm sure everyone would pitch in and fix it up, if it meant getting out of The Pit. I guess I had let my hopes get too high because I can feel myself becoming disappointed.

"Did you guys run into any problems?" Meredith asks.

"No, Ma'am. We combed the entire island and... house, which is why it took us three days. We just finished the last part of the... house, this morning," Bill answers.

Meredith smiles and says, "That's wonderful. Now, why don't you let the girls in on the secret."

Libby, Shae, and I all look at Meredith but all she does is smile and laugh.

"What secret?" Shae asks.

"Is it about the house? You've been pausing every time you're about to say the word," Libby states.

"Very observant," Bill says, smiling. "Yes, it's about the house. It's not really a house. It's more like a mansion, no more like a castle. There's well over 200 rooms, each with their own bathroom. There's a huge kitchen that Cooky will most likely hyperventilate over when she sees it. There's a whole wing that would be perfect for a Gym and another one for your hospital, Doc. It's set up perfectly for us. It's almost like Emma's family knew we'd one day need it," he looks at me and smiles the biggest smile I've ever seen him express.

"If I may," Ty says. "The island is a perfect diamond shape. Even though we won't need to, what with Emma's family's protection, I've been thinking that it would still be a good idea to put Guard towers on each point. That way we can keep an eye out for any intruders that may come to the island. Strictly precautionary."

"I don't know if that will be necessary. That protection is strong, we might not need to have any type of surveillance at all, since we will have Emma there," Charlie says, looking to the other guys for agreement and then looking at me.

I clear my throat and say, "I think that's putting too much faith into the protection and me. I understand it's been working for many years because the island isn't on any maps and nobody has ever mentioned seeing it. What if something happens and it stops working. What if Vanessa figures out a way to get me to give her permission to get on the island? I'm not willing to risk everyone's life. I think it would be a really good idea to have Guard Towers, like Ty said. It's just being smart and extra careful and when it comes to Vanessa, you can't be too careful, right?"

Everyone murmurs in agreement and Meredith is smiling down on me with such pride, that I have to look away before I turn bright red.

"Exactly right!" Meredith says.

"Wait, back up. The house is a castle?" Shae asks.

"Yeah, it's huge," Clay says.

"There's an outside pool AND an inside pool," Max says, smiling. He loves to swim but he would have been happy with just having the ocean to swim in.

"It needs a little TLC, mostly dusting and cleaning

but other than that, everything is pretty dang close to perfect. We will need to bring in furniture and what not but that won't be a problem. The only issue is there is no electricity. Every room has a fireplace for warmth and candlelight was the only source of light at night," Bill says, smiling.

"I'm sure we will be able to make do," Meredith says.

"Are you serious?" Libby and Shae say together.

"We're going to move into a castle?" Shae asks, bouncing up and down.

"Only if Emma says it's okay," Meredith says.

Every pair of eyes in the room looks at me.

"Oh, I don't know, a castle all to myself? That sounds pretty nice," I pause for only a second and then I continue saying, "Just kidding! Of course we can move into it! My mother's family must have known we'd need it someday, it sounds like it's perfect for us. When can we go?" I turn towards Meredith as I ask.

"We'll have to change our message to the Seekers from sending one back to having them all return back to The Pit immediately. Why don't we go spread the word that I have an announcement and I'll give it after dinner tonight? That way everyone will be in the Great Room so we don't have to interrupt your trainings or classes," Meredith says, looking around the room.

"Ummm, Ma'am, it's dinner time right now," Bill says, looking at his watch.

"Oh, so it is," she says as she looks at her watch. "Right, let's get in there and tell everyone the good news."

We all get up and walk towards the door.

"Emma, would you do the honors? Just to the entrance of the Great Room. We don't want to run into anyone," Doc says. I looked up at him and see him smiling and he nods at me.

"Are you sure?" I ask.

"I am. Do you think you can do all of us?" he asks me back.

I look around and see the guys looking at me with questioning looks and I see Meredith, Shae, and Libby smiling at me. Meredith already knows what we're going to do because of her Mind Reading Talent.

"Uh, yeah, I think so," I say.

"Okay, then. Everyone get in a line. Place your hand on the shoulder in front of you. Emma is going to Jump us," Doc says.

"All of us?" Bill asks doubtfully, but when he sees me looking at him he says, "Sorry, Emma, but there are nine of us, ten counting you. That's quite a few people to Jump for a Changeling."

"It's okay, Bill. I know I can do it," I turn towards Doc who steps behind me and places his hand on my shoulder. "Everyone ready?"

I hear a lot of yeses, so I close my eyes and concentrate on the opening to the Great Room and take a step there. All of a sudden, I hear the buzz of a lot of chatter and eating utensils hitting plates. I turn and look at everyone in the tunnel.

"Is everyone okay?" I ask.

"That was awesome!" Max says, stepping out from behind Clay, holding Libby's hand.

"She's amazing," Libby said.

"Pretty cool, kid," Bill says, stepping forward and patting my shoulder as he walks by.

"Alright, everyone, go get some food and I'll make sure everyone's here before I get the announcement started," Meredith says.

We all walk over to see what Cooky has prepared for us tonight. Burgers and fries. It smells amazing.

"What's going on?" a snotty voice asks from behind us.

"Go sit down and you'll find out," Shae says to her sister.

"No, I want to know now," Alysa says. I turn to see her with her hands on her hips. I hold back a giggle, she looks like a two year old that isn't getting her way.

"How does it feel to want? Meredith is going to tell everyone in a minute. She's just making sure everyone's here," Shae says, walking past her.

"It has to do with your family's house, doesn't it?" Alysa asks me. "I bet it's just a little shack out on a crappy little island and it wasn't even worth the Guardians time to go out and check it out, right?"

"Yeah, something like that," Ty answers her and then discreetly winks at me.

That little gesture sends my heart into overdrive. Does he not know what he does to girls when he does that?

Alysa gives me a pleased look and walks away. Libby and I burst into laughter and follow our group over to a table and sit down. Just as we're digging into our food, Meredith steps up on a stand and clears her throat. Someone whistles to help get everyone's attention to quiet down.

"Good evening, everyone. Please excuse my interruption. I feel like this announcement cannot wait. As you know, we recently came across some information about a possible location for us to move to," Meredith pauses for a moment, making sure she has everyone's attention. A lot of people turned and glanced at me before returning their eyes back to Meredith. "Our Guardians have returned this evening. We just got out of a meeting with them where they divulged what they found. The island and house are secure and big enough for us to move into. They say the place needs a little TLC but that is nothing we can't handle. If everyone will pitch in and help, I'm sure we can get everything packed and The Pit cleaned within a few days."

Dead silence fills the room for about ten seconds. I think everyone is waiting for a "just kidding" because slowly people begin laughing and then more people start cheering, until the whole room is nothing but shouts of joy and cries of excitement.

"Look at Alysa's face," Shae says, laughing.

I look around until I find her and see her standing over by Malory and Clay and some other people I haven't met yet. Her expression was a mixture between extreme happiness and disbelief. She sees us looking at her and shoots us the dirtiest look I've ever seen on anyone's face.

We all turn and laugh. Then join in on the cheering. I can't believe we'll be leaving The Pit. We'll be able to go outside. It's been so long since I have gotten to walk around in the sunlight.

All of a sudden, I don't feel right. I sit down quickly, trying to get my thoughts to quit running together. I feel like I am in two places or at least my head is, I can see everyone down here in The Pit but I can see the Dry Cleaners upstairs.

"Emma, what's wrong?" Libby asks, bending down in front of me.

"I don't know. Something's wrong... I think someone is here... I need to get to Meredith... NOW!" I scream the last part.

Ty is by my side in a second and scoops me up and Runs me up to Meredith. She looks down and sees me and is instantly by my side.

"What's wrong?" she asks and waves Doc over.

The room goes silent.

"Something's wrong. I think someone is here, up above, in the Dry Cleaners. Mr. Fitzgerald is trying to get them to leave but they're insisting on checking the place out," I say, trying to See more. "Oh... my... gods! It's Vanessa! I see Vanessa and she has a ton of people with her."

A hush goes through the crowd, deadly quiet.

Someone yells, "What do we do?"

I snap my thoughts back to down into The Pit and look up at Meredith. She has gone white as a ghost and she's staring into Doc's eyes.

A plan starts to form in my mind and I don't know how, but I know it'll work.

"Meredith, I have a plan. Do you trust me?" I ask. She looks down at me and then around at everyone else. I could sense everyone staring at me.

"Yes, I do," she says taking Doc's hand. "What's your plan?"

"Get anyone who can Jump to move the couches and comfy chairs into the Gym. Get everyone to stand at the back wall, where Cooky's food table is, as far back as possible, away from the tunnel that Vanessa and the Rifts will come down. Make sure they are tightly together," I say, looking at her. She's just standing here. "Meredith, we need to move now!"

"Right, sorry," she says to me and then yells to everyone else. "All Jumpers to me, everyone else, back by Cooky, as close together as possible."

It was chaos for a minute but then everyone but fifteen people were standing at the back wall. "We need all the furniture that isn't a table or folding chair moved to the Gym. Go, now!" she says to the Jumpers.

"What now?" Doc asks.

"Go get with the group. I'm going to do something and I need to have everyone in one spot. Hurry," I say. I take a few deep breaths and turn. Ty, Libby, Shae, and Max are still standing by me. "I need you guys to go stand over there too. I'll be there in just a second," they all Run over to stand by Meredith and Doc.

I look over and see Charlie and the other Jumpers have worked fast, the comfy furniture has all been moved. I take a deep breath, close my eyes, and concentrate on all the folding chairs. I visualize all of them being stacked against the wall over where all the comfy furniture used to be. I hear startled yelps from some people and I know it's worked. I open my eyes and see the chairs where I had wanted them to go. I concentrate on the tables and stack them the best I can over by the chairs too. It was amazing to watch. One minute they were in front of me and the next, they're on the other side of the room. I make all of the tunnel openings look like part of the dirt walls, except for the one Vanessa will come out of, and I turn the tunnel connecting the Guard Room and the one she'll come down, into a smooth wall also.

I run over to the crowd and find Cooky. "Cooky, I'm

sorry about this but I'm going to have to move your food," I say, looking at her with sad eyes.

"Whatever you need, sweetie," she says, her eyes are very wide.

Since I've never been to the kitchen I can't send the food there so I guess I'll send it to the Guard Room, there's enough tables to hold it all.

I close my eyes and concentrate on what's going on above us.

"They're in the elevator, they're coming down. I need everyone to stay right here, stay together. Don't make a sound and try not to move. I'm going to need to focus like I've never focused before."

"What's your plan?" Libby asks.

"I'm going to make us invisible," I say, not looking at her directly in the eye.

"You're what?" Shae sputters out.

"Can you do that?" Max asks.

"I think so. I've never tried it but with everything else, I have a feeling that I can but I need to concentrate. I need a connection with the group, so everyone has to be touching and then someone needs to touch me," a big hand instantly drapes over my shoulder. I don't need to look to see whose hand it is, the zing tells me who but I look back and see Ty standing behind me. I look around behind him and see everyone holding hands with the person beside them.

I look forward and concentrate on everyone disappearing, on everyone being silent and not being able to be heard. I can feel a tingle flow through me, it's the same feeling like when a limb falls asleep, and the blood is flowing back into it. I hear Ty take a shaky breath in and his hand tightens on my shoulder. That must mean he can feel it too? I hope so anyways.

"Nobody freak out but I'm going to turn the lights off. It has to look like no one has been down here," I say loud enough so that everyone can hear me. I think in my head that I want the lights off and instantly, the lights go out. Even with the warning someone yelps from the sudden darkness.

It's eerie being in complete darkness. Even though the lights were just on not seconds ago, my mind starts playing tricks on me about scary monsters roaming the room. I shake that thought from my head and return my focus on keeping everyone invisible and from anyone hearing us.

We are all so quiet that we can hear the footsteps from the tunnel echoing down to us before we can hear the voices.

"What's down here?" a voice so familiar to me that it almost makes me cry. Vanessa.

Mr. Fitzgerald stammers and when he can't think of anything to say, I whisper out, "Storage. We cleared it out for storage," and to my surprise, he says my exact words.

We can hear them at the mouth of the tunnel now.

I can hear everyone taking deep breaths, probably to hold it in, in anticipation for what was going to happen next. This was do or die time, either they could see us or not.

"Be a dear and turn the lights on please, Mr. Fitzgerald," Vanessa says in a fake sweet tone.

"Uhh, yes Ma'am, let me just find it really quick," he stammers out.

I can sense him searching in the wrong direction, so I send him the other way. He finds the switch and flips it on.

Light burst on, making me squint for a second before focusing on the people in front of us. Not a breath is made. We all just stand frozen, staring at Mr. Fitzgerald, Vanessa, and her group of Rifts.

"Well then," she says. I try to see what her face looks like but she is too far away. I think about how I had wanted a closer look at Ty, that day I had woken up from the Change, and all of a sudden I can see Vanessa as if she were a foot away. She had a fake smile on her face. So could she see us?

Ty's hand tightens on my shoulder, I'm not sure what it means. Is he about to do something stupid?

"Wait," I whisper to him. His hand freezes on my shoulder, squeezing a little too tightly but I ignore it.

"What do you use the tables and chairs for?" Vanessa asks, looking over at Mr. Fitzgerald.

I focus on Mr. Fitzgerald and whisper, "If we run

out of space upstairs for mending and folding, we come down here. In the heat of the summer, it stays nice and cool."

He repeats my words.

Vanessa starts to walk into the room, looking around. Three of her biggest men follow her.

"I see. Is there anything else down here we should look at?" Vanessa sneers, glancing around the room.

"Umm, no Ma'am," I whisper, for Mr. Fitzgerald. Followed by, "This is it."

"What does the floor above have on it? We didn't stop to check it out," she asks. She's now getting extremely close to me, about five feet away. Ty's grip tightens even more.

"The kitchen, Ma'am," I whisper. Mr. Fitzgerald repeats my words louder from back by the entrance. Vanessa is now just a foot away from me. It looks as if she's looking at everyone behind me.

"And why would a dry cleaner have a kitchen that takes up a whole floor?" Vanessa asks. She turns and her stare lands on me. I feel like she's staring me in the face. Ty rubs his thumb against my shoulder, never relaxing his hold.

Mr. Fitzgerald doesn't answer. So I send out the words using my mind.

"It's not just a kitchen, Ma'am. There's a sitting area that has enough seating to seat my employees and their families for when we have special occasions. We also use it for our break room."

Vanessa glares, it looks like she's glaring at me, but then she turns and walks back towards Mr. Fitzgerald and the rest of the Rifts.

"Very well, let's go," she says, shortly and with annoyance.

One of the bigger guys that came walking out into the Great Room with her says, "Are you sure Ma'am? We can search the whole building."

"No, they aren't here. We've wasted our time. When Frank shows back up from whatever rock he's crawled under, we'll have a talk with him," she says, still walking away from us.

"Are you sure they aren't here?" the same guys asks.

Vanessa turns and shoots the guy the most evil look I've ever seen, "You doubt me?"

The guy starts to make a choking sound and falls to his knees. He squeaks out, "No, no Ma'am. I'm sorry... I'm sorry..."

Vanessa shoots him another glare before she turns and walks away. The guy takes a big gulp of air and tries to catch his breath before he stands up. His buddies help him. They follow Vanessa and the rest of the Rifts out of the Great Room and down the tunnel.

Mr. Fitzgerald looks around the room. Finally letting shock show on his face and just before he turns, I whisper to him, "Mr. Fitzgerald. Come back down here once they've left. But make sure they are gone before you do."

With a startled jump, Mr. Fitzgerald turns and looks around the room. When he doesn't see anything, he turns and quickly walks down the tunnel.

I can feel Ty start to relax his arm and I can feel the tension start to leave the room.

"Wait, nobody move," I whisper out for the crowd to hear.

As soon as the words are out of my mouth, one of Vanessa's minions walks back into the room. He looks around and puts his hand on the wall. He pulls his hand away and wipes it on his pants. I see a dirty handprint.

He shakes his head and says, "Frank, you fool." And then he turns and jogs into the tunnel.

Not a single person makes a sound for what feels like an eternity. Ty leans forward and says, "Are they gone?"

"I can't tell," I say, I start to sway. I feel really tired all of a sudden.

"Hey! Emma, are you okay?" Ty asks, using his hand to help me stay up right.

Just then Mr. Fitzgerald comes back into the room and looks around.

"Ummm, they're gone," he says, looking around.

With a sigh of relief, I fall into Ty. As I do Mr. Fitzgerald lets out a startled scream and jumps back.

"Oh my heavens! How did you... Never mind," he shakes his head and then continues to say, "Oh Mrs.

Riserson, I was so afraid. I didn't know what to do. She threatened to kill everyone if I didn't bring her down here. I'm so sorry," Mr. Fitzgerald says, running towards us.

"No worries, my dear friend. You did the right thing. We were just lucky to have our Emma with us," Meredith says looking over at me. And then worry crosses her face "Emma? Emma! What's wrong?"

"I'm just really tired and I feel kind of sick. My head is starting to hurt really bad too," I say through gritted teeth. I can feel my burger trying to make its way back up and my head feels like it could burst in half.

Apparently not loud enough because Meredith says, "What did she say, Ty?"

"She's not feeling well at all, she should go lie down," he paraphrases.

"Take her to the Hospital Wing," Doc says.

"No! Please, no. I've spent enough time there. Just take me to my room," I say. I peek out from under my eyelashes at Doc to see what he says and he just nods at Ty. He carefully swings me up into his arms and carries me to my room.

He lays me down carefully and feels my forehead.

"You're burning up, Emma. I'll be right back," he says, disappearing from sight.

Libby and Shae walk in and sit at the foot of my bed.

"That was amazing," Libby says in awe.

"Totally. I've never seen anything like it," Shae says, grabbing my foot.

Ty comes back in my room holding a wet wash-cloth and comes over to put it on my forehead.

"It really was," he says.

All I can do is smile and close my eyes. I'm getting so tired. I try to open my eyes but it feels like someone has glued them shut. I try to say something but my lips feel like they've been filled with sand.

I hear laughter and someone tells me to go to sleep, they'll keep an eye out on things. I smile, or at least I think I'm smiling, and I fall peacefully asleep.

CHAPTER 19 - WATER FIGHT

I wake up with a jolt. I'm alone in my room. I jump out of bed and run down the tunnel, checking the rooms as I make my way to the bathrooms. I can't find a single person. I Run to the Gym and find no one. They are all gone. No one is left in The Pit.

I walk into the Great Room and with a sigh of relief, I see everyone. They're all sleeping... in strange places. On the tables, on the floor, the chairs and couches. I walk over to were Shae and Libby are lying down, next to Ty and Max. As I get closer, I see that something isn't right. I run to them and shake Shae. She just flops around. She's cold. Something isn't right.

"Shae!" I scream but she doesn't respond. I turn her over and she stares blankly back.

"Libby?" I say, about to burst into tears. I shake her and she feels the same. Cold. I roll her over and she has the same look on her face.

I touch Ty on the shoulder and he's cold, also. I can't bring myself to turn him over. I wouldn't be able to handle seeing his face the way I know it will look.

What's happened? I think to myself.

I reach down and check Shae and Libby for a pulse. Nothing.

Covering my mouth so I wont scream, I feel tears running down my face.

Looking around I see faces staring off in different directions but with the same blank look. I don't need to check everyone to know, they are all dead.

"NOOOOOO!" I scream. "NOOOOO! Help me!" I fall to the ground and start to sob.

I feel a hand on my shoulder and I look up and see Vanessa standing over me, smiling an absolutely evil smile.

"Foolish Emma, did you really think you could trick me?" she says, brushing my hair away from my face.

I slink away from her and whisper, "You've killed them. All of them. Why?"

"Why not?" she replies. "They have something of mine, I'm merely taking it back."

"What was so important to you that you had to kill all these people? They didn't do anything to you," I say, trying not to cry.

"You. They were hiding you. You are mine. I raised you. I knew you were The One. They were keeping you from me, so I did what needed to be done. And I also wanted some of their Talents, but that was more of a bonus," Vanessa says, while glancing around the room.

"You truly are evil," I spit out.

"No my dear, I just know what I want and I get what I want, always. Now get up, we're leaving," she reaches down and grabs my arm and pulls me to my feet.

"No! I'm not going with you. Let go of me!" I scream and I pull back on my arm

Her hold tightens and she heaves me towards her.

"Do not test me, Emma!" she growls.

I pull my arm as hard as I can and free myself.

"I said no!" I yell, taking a step away from her.

She takes a step towards me and I step away but fall over something and land on my side. I look over and see that somehow Ty has gotten from the table to the floor. I look into his face and see what I didn't want to see.

The light in his eyes are gone. The stern, hard lines of his face are gone. He's just staring at me but there's nothing behind his eyes.

"No!" I close my eyes and start to cry. I can hear myself screaming no over and over.

Vanessa is shaking me. Her grip gets harder and the shakes get faster.

"No, leave me alone! Don't touch me! Vanessa, I swear, if you don't let me go, I will kill you!" I scream. I open my eyes and see Libby standing beside my bed, she's got ahold of my shoulders.

I jump away from her and pull my blankets up to my chin.

"What the---?" I start to ask, crying.

"I was just going to ask the same thing," Shae says. She's at the foot of my bed.

I glance between the two of them, back and forth.

"You're alive?" I ask. They look at each other with questioning glances.

"Yes?" Libby says but it's more of a question.

I spring up onto my knees and pull them both into a hug, still crying. They're warm and I can feel their hearts beating against my cheeks.

"Emma, what's the matter?" Libby asks.

"Yeah, what the hell man?" Shae says.

I take a deep breath and explain, "I had the worst dream. No, nightmare. I woke up and I was alone. So I went looking for everyone but couldn't find anyone. I looked everywhere and when I got to the Great Room, everyone, you all, were in there but dead. Then Vanessa was there and she said she killed you all because you were hiding me and she knew I was The One. She also said something about taking everyone's Talents. Then she tried to make me go with her but I wouldn't go. I pulled away and tripped over Ty. That's when I started to scream and she grabbed me."

"I was grabbing you, Emma," Libby says. "You started moaning in your sleep so I tried to wake you up but you wouldn't wake up, Shae was just about to go get Doc. And then you started screaming and then you said something about killing Vanessa."

I blush, "She wouldn't let go, so I told her if she

wouldn't let me go, I was going to kill her."

"That's reasonable," Shae says, shrugging.

Libby gives her a look, "Do you think you could? I mean, kill Vanessa if you had to?"

"No... I don't know... I don't think so. I don't think I could kill anyone but I was so mad at her. Seeing you all dead, it made me feel... I don't know. Scary. It scared me how angry I was at her," I say. I shake myself a little. The feelings in my dream of seeing them dead, and the feelings I had toward Vanessa, they feel, felt so real.

"Hopefully you'll never have to feel that again," Libby says, patting me on the back.

"So how *are* you feeling?" Shae asks.

I sit down on the bed and stare at her. "Umm fine, still a little shaky. That dream felt so real."

"No, I mean from last night. You kind of passed out on us," she says.

"I feel... okay. My body and head feel kind of like jello. Like someone stretched me out and then I slowly pulled myself together, like I'm really loose feeling. And I have a dull headache, nothing that won't go away after a while," I say.

"Do you want to go have Doc check you out?" Libby asks.

"No, I'll be fine. I think I just need something to eat," I answer her in a haste and realize just how hungry I am.

"Okay, get dressed and we'll go get some lunch,"

Shae says walking towards my door.

"Lunch?" I ask.

"It's after one o'clock, so yeah, lunch," Shae says, pausing to look back at me.

"Man, how long was I out for?" I ask, looking at Libby.

"About 17 hours. Doc said if you were still sleeping by dinner time, he was going to come check on you," Libby says.

"I don't think I've ever slept that much, all at once, without waking up, other than from being hurt or during the Change," I say.

They both laugh and Shae says, "I don't think anyone has either. What you did? Nobody has ever seen that before now. No one has ever made themselves and hundreds of people invisible. And not only invisible, but Vanessa and her people couldn't even hear us, Sense us, or anything."

"Nobody can do that?" I ask.

"There are some Demi's that can turn themselves, and if they touch something, invisible. And the way you were able to talk to Mr. Fitzgerald, it takes a lot of training to be able to do that. Meredith has only been able to do that for the last 20 years," Libby says, looking from Shae to me.

Shae just shrugs and says, "You're pretty badass, Emma. Let's go get you some food."

Libby laughs under her breath and heads to the

door, "We'll wait for you to change."

I jump out of bed and put on a clean pair of underwear and socks, a bra, and jeans. I decide to wear a black tank top, I'm feeling a little warm. I slip on my shoes and walk out the door.

"Ready," I say.

"Let's go!" Shae says. "Feel like Running?"

"Sure," I answer while smiling.

We start off jogging and before I know it, I'm in the Great Room. I look behind me and I don't see Libby and Shae. I look around and I'm completely alone. For a second my feelings from my dream come back to me and I'm on the verge of panicking when all of a sudden Shae and Libby are in front of me.

"You've gotten faster," Libby says.

"I didn't know that was possible," Shae says, shaking her head.

"Is anything I do normal?" I ask.

Libby puts both hands on my shoulders and looks down at me, reminding me again how much taller she is than me, "Emma, none of us are normal but I have a feeling nothing about you is going to be our normal and that's okay. Embrace it."

I shrug my shoulders and turn to walk over to the food table. Cooky has left things to make sandwiches and an amazing fruit salad.

"Where is everyone?" I ask.

"Getting everything cleaned and organized to be

sent to your island," Shae answers while scooping a big pile of salad onto her plate.

"Please don't call it that. Just call it our new home or something," I say, blushing.

"But it is your island. If it weren't for you, your mom, and her family, we wouldn't have a place to go," she says back, with a mouth full of melon.

"You've got fruit juice running down your chin," Libby says, handing her a napkin while shaking her head. "She's right though, we'd be in a pretty big mess right now if you hadn't offered your place. I'm excited to see it."

"Well, we need a place to go and it sounds like it's big enough for us all. It would be pretty selfish to keep it a secret. I want to do something to help us all," I say, scooping some fruit onto my plate.

"You did that last night," Shae says. "You still haven't told us how you did it."

We sit down at the closest table and before I answer I take a couple of bites of my sandwich.

Mmmmm it's so good.

I take a deep breath and put my sandwich down.

"I honestly don't know how I knew it would work, I just knew it would. I don't know how I knew how to do it, I just knew I could and what to do. It was all subconscious. I was trying to think of something to do to protect us and then all of a sudden, I just knew. I wasn't 100% sure it would work but I was pretty certain it would. I didn't know for sure if Mr. Fitzgerald would be able to hear me but again, I was pretty sure he would be able to. I just knew that if we were all connected, I'd be able to make us invisible and silent. It obviously took a lot of energy for me to do it because I slept for so long and I'm starving but I would do it all over again in a heartbeat. I'd do anything to keep us safe from Vanessa and her goons," I take another deep breath and then take a bite of my fruit salad.

"It'll get easier once you start your classes, all though I don't know how you're going to get all of them in. You have a ton of different Talents and each Talent usually has a day's worth of classes we go to, to learn how to control and use that Talent," Libby says.

"Yeah, and some of your Talents, no one has ever seen or heard of, so there probably isn't a class for it yet," Shae says while walking over to the trash can to throw her plate away and put her tray up.

"So I've got to figure it all out alone?" I ask.

"Of course not, we'll help you. Doc and Meredith will help you. It just might take some time to figure out the best way to do that. But we've got time. We've got to get moved to The Island and then get settled in. By then, I'm sure we all will have thought of something," Libby says smiling over at me.

I finish my second sandwich and third helping of fruit before I feel full.

"Come on, let's go help get things done so we can

get out of this place. Now that Vanessa has been here, it gives me the creeps," Shae says.

Libby and I stand up and walk our stuff over to the trash can and table. As we're about to walk out the door, Meredith comes into the Great Room with Bill and six other people.

"I'm so glad to see you up and about, Emma," Meredith says, patting my shoulder.

"Thanks," I awkwardly say.

"Emma, these are the Jumpers that will be starting to take stuff to your island, do you give them permission to access it?" Bill asks, getting straight to the point.

"Yes," I say as I look at each of the Jumpers in front of me, nodding to each of them.

"Great, thank you. See you girls later," Bill says as he leads the Jumpers out of the Great Room.

"I have to go meet with Jim, will you girls be joining the cleaning efforts?" Meredith asks.

"Yes, Ma'am, we were just on our way," Shae says.

"Good," Meredith says, smiling at us and then she Runs out of the room.

We turn to start walking towards the Gym but Ty comes into the Great Room.

"There you guys are, I was sent by Doc to find out if you, Emma, were awake yet. If you've eaten and feeling up to it, it's time to clean the floors," he says, walking up to us.

"I feel fine," I say, trying to not sound like an idiot.

"Let's go," Ty says as he turns and walks back out the way he came.

To my delight, we clean manually, not with our Talents. I can tell that the others aren't too thrilled about not being able to use theirs but ever since I got mine, for some reason, I try to do as much "normally" as I can. I don't want to become solely reliant on my Talents to get me through life.

Some of us have buckets with soap and water with sponge type mops and the others have hoses. I notice the little round drain holes in the floor and I'm thankful that all this water and soap has a place to go, I was starting to wonder if we were supposed to dry the floors as well.

We have one room left to do. The Gym, the biggest room, I hear the older group saying they had to get to a meeting, which left us younger ones to finish. As I'm dipping my mop into my bucket, I get sprayed with water from behind. I yelp in surprise and turn and see Charlie standing there laughing.

"Sorry about that Emma, I didn't see you there," he says and then turns back around to spray the other direction.

I glare at him but then get back to scrubbing the floor. I wasn't going to tell him this, but it actually felt good. I was getting pretty warm from all the work, I only yelled because I wasn't expecting the cold water to hit me in the back.

"Hey, Emma?" Charlie calls again and as I turn, I get sprayed in the face and as I'm backing up quickly to try to get away from the stream of water. I fall over my bucket and I land butt first in it. Then me and the bucket topple over backwards until I'm lying on my back with soapy water running all around me.

I can hear everyone laughing and I start to laugh too. I hear Libby yell, "Water fight!!!"

I roll over to my side and see buckets of water being thrown, tugs of war over hoses being fought, and people running for cover. Alysa and Malory go screeching from the room, yelling something about their outfits and hair. I see a hose lying on the ground over by the back of the room and I run for it. Just as I'm wrapping my hands around it, I feel a tug. I look up and see Ty holding on to it too.

He smiles a crooked smile and says, "You might as well just give it to me, Emma, I'm stronger than you."

I was momentarily stunned by the way he had said my name but then his words sink in and I'm really annoyed.

"Don't misjudge me, I'm pretty strong too," I say, trying to sound brave but my voice quivers a little at the end.

Ty pulls on the hose just enough to make me take two steps towards him, now we're only about a foot away from each other. He smiles down at me and says,

"You were saying?"

I try to pull back and take myself a little further away from him. Being this close to him is making me want to do things I really shouldn't do. Like run my hands through his wet hair and then kiss him. I shake my head and try to pull again but the hose doesn't budge. I glare up at him, which only makes his smile widen.

"We aren't supposed to use our Talents," I say, glaring even more.

"I'm not but if you want too, you can use yours," he says.

"I'm not a cheater," I say, tugging again but with no success.

"I'll give you a five second head start before I soak you even more than you already are," Ty says and then he looks at me, from head to toe, raising an eyebrow as he does.

What was that look? I think to myself.

Just as I'm about to let go, I see Ty realize what I'm going to do so he loosens his grip on the hose, I'm about to pull on it when I'm pulled into him and the hose slips through my fingers and Ty's. He catches me before I can actually fall into him and we both turn and see Libby standing about 10 feet away with the hose we'd been fighting over.

"Guess I'm stronger than both of you," she starts to laugh and turns the hose on us. Ty turns us and shields me from the blast of water and then he's pulling me into a run. He doesn't stop until we are in the back corner, away from all the flying water because we've wiggled our way through the maze of stacked Gym equipment and other stuff. I can hear Libby laughing.

Ty is kind of pushing me against the wall with his hands on my shoulders but I'm leaning back awkwardly because there's something by my feet. I look down and see it's a bunch of flat weights, so I step up on them and when I look up, I see that I'm not looking at Ty's chest anymore but his mouth is right at my line of sight.

Those lips.. man they look so kissable. I think before I can stop myself. I bite my lip before I can act on my thoughts. I look away for a minute but then I look back at his lips and notice that the bottom one is a little bit bigger than the top one, it doesn't look weird, it looks perfect. Totally kissable. I look down and away before I really do something stupid.

All of a sudden, Ty slides his hands down my arms and puts them on my hips. I look up at him in surprise and see him looking back over his shoulder, totally oblivious to what he's doing.

"We should be out of the line of fire for now. Libby will get distracted with someone else and then we can run for the Bathroom tunnel," he looks at me when he's done talking and has a look of surprise on his face. "You're taller."

"I'm standing on the weights I was falling over," I

whisper out, my voice doesn't seem to be able to go any higher than that.

Ty looks down at our feet and notices his hands, he squeezes them slightly. He looks up at me through his long eyelashes and he's about to say something but before I know what I'm doing, I lean in and kiss him. My brain catches up with my actions and I pull back, covering my mouth with my hands.

"Oh my gosh, Ty! I'm sorry, I didn't... I don't know... I just wanted..., " I mumble out from behind my hands. I cover my face completely before he can really see how ridiculous I am. I feel his hands leave my hips and wrap around my wrists, pulling my hands away from my face, and he puts them down by my side. Lifting a hand to my chin, he tilts it up.

"Wanted what?" he asks, his voice is low. I just shake my head and close my eyes. "Emma, please look at me. You wanted what?"

I open my eyes and see he's just inches away from me. I look down at his lips and then back up to his eyes and I say, "I wanted to kiss you." I bite my lip again, for a couple of reasons; I didn't want to say anything more, I was about to cry, and I really wanted to kiss him again.

All he says is, "Oh."

He moves his hand away from my chin and to my surprise, places both of them on my hips, again. He steps into me and I place my hands on his chest. I look up into his eyes and see the wall that he has had up since the very first time I met him, melt away. I can feel his pecks rising with every breath he takes.

CHAPTER 20 - KISS, KISSES, KISSING

"I'd like to kiss you," he whispers.

"Ooookay," I breathlessly stammer out.

He leans in and softly kisses me on the lips. Electric energy starts to flow through me. My heart starts beating so fast it feels like it's going to fly out of my chest. I can feel his chest start to rise and fall faster with his breathing picking up pace.

I slide my hands up higher and wrap them behind his neck. He takes a step closer to me so that now our bodies are touching. Our kiss deepens and I raise my hands to his hair and run them through it like I had been fantasizing about earlier. When I get to the back of his head, I pull it even closer to mine, and a sigh escapes my mouth.

I hear and feel Ty moan and he slides his hands around my back. I feel his hands on the little bit of skin that's showing from my tank being stuck up my back from the water. With his feet straddling the weights, he presses his body into mine so that I am now pinned between him and the wall. He parts my lips with his and his warm tongue searches my mouth for mine.

When they touch, the most intense shock rocks through me and I feel my heart stop but then it picks up speed double time. I gasp in surprise and I hear Ty do the same. We start to kiss even more passionately, and I wrap my arms completely around his neck, holding him tighter to me. He runs a hand around to my hip and draws his thumb over my hip bone while his other hand slides up the back of my shirt, warming my skin as it goes. When he reaches my bra strap, his hand stops, and slides back down to my hip.

I don't know how long we've been kissing like this but soon, all too soon, our kissing slows. He slowly pulls away, giving sweet, soft kisses as he does.

I look up and see Ty staring at me with something blazing from behind his eyes. I feel like that's how my eyes look, also. I want more, I don't want our kissing to stop. I lean in and kiss him again. He doesn't pull back, he leans into me too but just as we're about to really get into it again, I hear Libby from somewhere on the other side of the stuff we are using as a shield.

"Guys, the water fights over. You can come out now," she yells, while trying not to laugh.

I can feel my face start to turn into a pout and I look up and see Ty smiling.

"We can continue this later, if you want?" he whispers with his crooked smile and a raised eyebrow.

I try to answer back but my voice gets caught in my throat. I clear it with a little cough and finally whisper out, "Okay."

Ty kisses me on the nose and says, "Okay", smiling as he steps back.

He gives me his hand as I step down from my, oh so wonderful, makeshift stepping stool. I expect him to let my hand go but he just intertwines our fingers as we walk through the maze of equipment.

As we come out, Libby's eyes instantly lock on our hands, and then she looks at us smugly.

"Have fun?" she asks her brother. He lets go of my hand and grabs her in a headlock.

"Did you?" Ty asks her back while messing with her hair.

"Stop Ty!" Libby squeals and pushes away from him. "Max is getting us some towels and we're supposed to meet him in the Great Room. Let's go, I'm starving."

Ty shrugs and starts to walk away. Libby skips to my side and puts her arm through mine.

"Tell me everything later," she whispers while giggling.

I turn red instantly and smile back.

We meet Max in the Great Room and he hands us towels. Libby and I sit down with the rest of our group and dry our hair. Max and Ty head straight for the food table. Everyone else has their food, it's pizza.

I get up to head over to get me a slice, when Ty

comes back with a couple plates full and a couple bottles of water

"I wasn't sure what kind you like, so I got a slice of each," he says.

"Oh, um thanks," I say, turning pink. I sit back down next to Libby, Ty sits next to me.

I glance over and see Max laying a plate with two slices of Hawaiian in front of Libby.

"Thank you," she says leaning in and giving him a big kiss.

I instantly look down and my mind goes back to 10 minutes ago when Ty and I were kissing. I bite my lip again and wish we were still in our hiding place.

"Quit biting your lip, it's driving me crazy," Ty discreetly whispers in my ear as he leans over to grab a napkin from the pile Max brought over.

I instantly turn a bright red and take a quick drink of water and start coughing, hopefully to pass off my red face as if I had just swallowed my drink wrong.

"You okay?" Libby asks as she pats my back.

"Yeah, wrong pipe," I say. I can see Ty in the corner of my eye and see him crack a half smile, the kind that makes my heart skip a beat.

How can he already have this kind of effect on me? It's pathetic, I'm pathetic. But man, that kissing. That electricity that flowed through us, WOOOW. Nothing has ever made me feel like that. Does all kissing feel like this or is it just because it was Ty? I didn't feel like this after Charlie kissed me or Frank. No, it's definitely because of Ty.

We eat our pizza in silence but every so often, Ty's leg rubs up against mine. How can an innocent action cause so much havoc on me?

I hear someone clear their throat, followed by a whistle. I look up and see Meredith standing in front of the room, announcement time.

"Good evening everyone, I have some wonderful news," she says, glancing around the room and waits for everyone to be quiet. "We have gotten just about everything moved out of The Pit, except for the Gym equipment but we will do that tomorrow. The Seekers will be back tonight and then we will leave the day after tomorrow. Let's get to bed so we can get an early start in the morning. We, well, Emma, fooled Vanessa but she might send some Rifts back to double check. I'd like us to be long gone before that happens. Now, off to bed."

Everyone starts to get up and make their way to the Quarters, throwing their plates and cups away as they go. I stand up and Ty stands also. He looks down at me like he's about to say something but Bill comes up and interrupts whatever he is about to say.

"Guard Room, now. We're going to redo the patrol schedule so we can make sure Vanessa or her Rifts don't catch us off guard again. Get the rest of the guys and meet me there," he says and then storms off.

I look up at Ty and he's watching Bill walk away. He

then looks down and says, "Good night, Emma. I'll see you in the morning."

"Okay, sounds good," I say back.

Ty hesitates for a minute but then nods at me and takes off towards Charlie, Max, and Clay. They are hovering around the food table, grabbing as many slices of pizza as they can before Cooky gets the platters gathered up.

Libby, Shae, and I walk to our rooms. My mind will not stop going back to Ty and I kissing. I can't stop thinking about it. The kiss Charlie and I shared was okay but it wasn't anything like what happened between Ty and me. And Frank forcing his kiss on me was definitely nothing like Ty and me kissing. There has to be something between us, to make it feel like that. He had to have felt it too, I could tell he had the same reaction as me.

Before I know it, the girls and I are standing outside my room and they are staring down at me. Libby smiling and Shae tilting her head to the side in wonderment.

"What's the matter?" she asks.

"She had some fun during the water fight," Libby answers.

"Oh shut up," I say, turning bright red and rushing into my room.

"Do tell!" Shae shrieks.

"Nothing, nothing happened," I say, trying my best

to be nonchalant about it.

"Bull-butter! Something happened. If you could see your face..." Shae says, laughing.

"Yeah, if nothing happened, why was my brother holding your hand when you guys came out from your hiding place?" Libby asks, raising one eyebrow.

"He was just helping me out, my feet kept getting tangled in everything on the floor. I about fell multiple times," I say.

Yeah that could work, I'm clumsy. I think to myself.

Libby narrows her eyes at me and says, "I don't believe you, that wasn't a 'helpful' hand hold."

"Well, that's what happened," I say. I don't know why I don't want to talk to them about it. Maybe because it just happened, I want to keep it personal just a little while longer. I also have a feeling that Ty is very personal and doesn't like his business gossiped about. Even though it's my business too and Shae and Libby are fast becoming my best-friends. I just don't think he'd want me to be talking about it, at least not yet.

"If you say so," Libby says, smiling at me. She really doesn't believe me but she's respectful enough to not push the issue. Another reason I really like her.

"Like Ty would do anything with her," a snarky voice says from my doorway.

I look up and see Alysa standing there. She's got her arms crossed and an all and knowing look on her face.

"What makes you think that? Just because he

wouldn't do anything with you doesn't mean he wouldn't do anything with Emma," Shae says, walking over to her sister.

"You don't know what Ty and I did while we were dating. Should I go into detail?" Alysa says, sneering at me.

"Please don't," Libby says. "I really don't want to hear anything that has to do with you and my brother."

"Well, just know it's far more juicier than just holding hands. How nice for you, I'm sure Emma, for a man to actually touch you. Maybe once you've graduated Kindergarten, you'll get your first kiss," she flips her hair and walks out of the room.

"What. A. Bitch," Shae says. "I really don't understand why she's acting like that."

"Hey, don't listen to her," Libby says. "I doubt Ty and her did anything. And she's just jealous of how gorgeous you are. THAT is why she's so nasty to you."

"No, she's just a bitch," Shae says, nudging me.

I give her a small smile and fake a yawn.

"Shae? Is that you?" a girl's voice I'm not familiar with comes from just outside my makeshift door.

"Yeah," Shae answers.

A girl with almond shaped eyes and tan skin, pokes her head in and she looks around the room, pausing a second on me before talking to Shae again.

"Your parents are back, I thought you would like to know," she says, grinning.

"Yeah, thanks Amber!" Shae says excitedly. "Come on, I want you to meet my parents. I can't wait to see them!"

We all Run to the Great Room and find several sets of parents have gotten back. Shae runs to a beautiful woman who has the same color of red hair as her but light green eyes, the woman could be Shae's and Alysa's triplet. A man standing next to her has dark brown hair and Shae's brown eyes.

"Oh sweetie, there you are!" the woman says, wrapping Shae in a big hug.

The man puts his arms around both of them and says, "Oh Malysa, we've missed you!"

"Daddy!" I hear Alysa's voice from back at the Quarter's tunnel entrance. She Runs over and joins in on the family hug.

"Mom, Dad, this is Emma Hart," Shae says, finally detaching herself from her parents' hugs. I see Alysa roll her eyes.

"It's nice to meet you Mr. and Mrs. Shae," I say, sticking my hand out to shake theirs.

"Please, call me Helen," Helen says as she pulls me into a hug. "Meredith has told us all about you. We are so happy to meet you and so thankful for what you've done for us."

Mr. Shae shakes my hand and then gives me a hug also, "You can call me Robert. Helen is right, we are so thankful. We've been gone for so long without any luck on finding anywhere safe enough for us to move too. We were starting to lose hope in ever getting out of The Pit."

"I'm just glad Kathryn sent word to her friend at The Elder's and he was able to find the books and send them to her. I wouldn't have known anything about the place," I say, smiling back at them.

"Daddy, Daddy!" Alysa says, trying to get her dad's attention.

"Yes, Darling?" he asks, looking as if Alysa is the sweetest thing he's ever seen.

"Alysa, we need to have a chat with you about what's been going on here since we left," Helen says, narrowing her eyes at her daughter.

"We don't have to do that just yet do we, Hun? Let's enjoy this reunion just a little bit longer," Robert says, giving Alysa a big hug and then pulling her off to the side to have a conversation with her.

"You'll have to excuse Robert, he's always spoiled that girl," Helen says a little harshly.

"Tell us everything, Mom," Shae says, sitting down on a couch, pulling her mom down beside her. I sit in one of the seats across from them, Libby squeezing in beside me.

After about two hours, I start to feel tired.

"I'm sorry to say but I need to go get some rest, I'm beat," I say. Libby looks at me like she'd like to say something but she just grins. This girl intuition is too good sometimes.

"It was so nice to meet you, Emma. I'm sure we'll have plenty of time to visit later," Helen says, standing up and giving me another hug.

I say good night to everyone and start walking back to my room, too tired to Run.

I get about 10 feet from my room when I feel a hand on my shoulder. I stifle a scream, a flashback from when Alysa attacked me races through my mind but I register the zap I got from the hand and when I turn, I see Ty standing here.

"I'm sorry, I really don't mean to sneak up on you all the time," he says, smiling that half crooked smile that lights a fire in my stomach.

"It's okay, I wasn't paying too much attention to my surroundings," I say a little too breathlessly.

"Are you really tired or do you want some company?" he asks as we get to my room, leaning against the doorway.

I clear my throat and say, "No, I'm not that tired."

"Good," he growls. He puts his hands on my waist and pulls me to him, lifting me easily so I'm at his height. I wrap my arms around his neck and he presses himself into me, pinning me to the wall so I can't slide down and then he's kissing me. There's instant fire in my stomach and electricity flowing throughout my body.

After a few minutes, he slowly lowers me down so

my feet are touching the ground. He slows our kissing and pulls back. I look up into his eyes and see the fire is back in them.

"Why'd you stop?" I ask, breathless again.

"I thought maybe we could step inside so we aren't out here for all the world to see," he says, kissing my forehead, my temple, my cheek, and then he kisses me softly on my lips.

"Yes, yes come in," I say stepping back into my room, pulling him by the shirt. He stops at the door and slides my curtain shut.

I sit on my bed and he walks over and stands in front of me. I get up on my knees which doesn't make me much taller than if I were standing but tall enough that I'm looking at his gorgeous lips again. I look up and see him staring at me.

"Emma, I---" he starts to say but I interrupt him by putting my finger on his lips and grabbing his shirt, I pull him towards me, lying myself down on my back as I bring him closer. He uses his strong arms to catch himself so he doesn't fall on me.

We scoot up to where my head is on my pillow and then I pull him to me until he's laying half on me and half on my bed. I run my hands through his hair and he sighs. He leans in and kisses me softly. He slides his lips to my cheek and then to my neck. He softly kisses up to my ear, back down my neck. He pulls my tank top and bra straps away from my shoulder and kisses down to my collarbone and shoulder.

"You're driving me crazy," I whisper. I grab his face in my hands and pull him up to my face. He chuckles under his breath before I'm kissing him passionately.

I run my hands through his extremely soft hair again and then down his strong shoulders. I run them down his back until I find the bottom of his shirt. I trace my fingers on his soft skin that's showing just above his pants line. I feel him shiver. I grab the hem of his shirt and start to lift it. Sensing what I want, Ty stops kissing me, reaches behind his head with one hand and pulls his t-shirt up over his head, and tosses it to the floor. I sit and admire him for a second. He's got muscles that go on for days. As he leans back down to me, I can feel his shoulder muscles working.

We kiss like this for some time. I run my hands over his back, and around to the front, running the back of my hand on his stomach. I trace his collar bones, up to the back of his neck and back down his spine. He's warm and soft skin are a contradiction to his hard muscles.

I decide to try what he had and pull my lips to the side, kissing him on the cheek. I kiss his neck up to his ear, and back down to his collarbone.

He groans out, "Now I'm the one going crazy."

I let a little giggle escape before he's kissing me, running his hand up my arm and back down again, sending goosebumps all over where his hands were just touching. He trails his hands down my ribs, stopping at my waist. My shirt has lifted a little, showing more of my skin than before. His thumb glances across my hip bone as his fingers dig into my lower back. He slides his hand down the side of my leg, grabbing my knee and hiking it up over his hip.

A gasp comes from me and he pulls back, "Is this okay?" he asks.

"Yes," I breathe out, pulling him to me again. He slides his hand back up my leg to my stomach where he lays his hand, palm down, flexing his fingers slightly. I don't want the kissing to stop, ever. With every kiss and every touch, the electricity inside me intensifies.

"Tell me if you want me to stop or if I go too far," he whispers into my lips, I nod.

He slides his hand up slowly, giving me time to tell him to stop but I don't. His hand gets to the top of my rib cage and his fingers wrapping around to my back so that his thumb is just under my bra. Our kissing deepens even more, both our tongues doing a sort of wrestling match with each other. He slowly rubs his thumb on the lower part of my bra cup, again, giving me a chance to tell him to stop but again, I don't, I just keep kissing him.

He slides his hand all the way up until it's covering my bra covered breast. Sighing, I pull him closer to me. He slides his hand back down to my stomach and pulls it out from under my tank top and grabs the bottom of it. Ty pulls back and I open my eyes to see him staring at me in a questioning way.

"Just my tank top," I say as I sit up and let him pull my tank over my head, he tosses it in the same direction as his shirt.

"Okay," he says softly.

I lie back down but he doesn't. He just stares at me. Looking at my face then my chest, my stomach, and then back up to my face.

"You are the most beautiful woman I have ever met, Emma. I don't mean just in looks either. You are the nicest, sweets, most caring person too," he says, slowly leaning into me. Before I can say anything back, Ty's kissing me again.

He slides his hand up to my neck and holds me to him for a second or two, making our kiss even deeper than before. He slowly slides his hand down, over my collar bone, to my shoulder and then to the side of my bra covered breast. He starts to kiss over to my neck again but instead of going up, he kisses down to my collar bone, over to my shoulder, and then back to my collar bone. He cups my breast again and he slowly kisses down to the top of my breast, where my bra begins. He kisses to the middle of my chest, over to my other breast, and then up to my neck on that side. Every place his lips touch, it feels like fire is lighting my skin up. The fire in my stomach is all but fully engulfed now.

He makes his way back to my mouth and I passionately welcome his lips back to mine. His hand slides back down to my stomach, down my leg, and then to the back of my knee again. This time though, he rolls until I'm on top of him. He runs his hands up the back of my legs, over my butt, and then rests them on my back, just below my bra strap. His fingers rubbing softly from side to side in slow, short movements.

We lay like this for a while, kissing. Every once in a while, Ty's hands slide down to the top of my pants, his fingers resting on my butt, but then he moves them back up to the middle of my back again.

I slide my left hand out from behind his neck where both of mine have been since we rolled and I run it down his chest, to his stomach. Mentally marveling at the ridges his muscles make. I can feel him quiver every time my hand touches a new place on him. I run it down to the top of his pants and slide it behind his back, running my pinky finger through his belt loop, my thumb resting on his hip bone.

What feels like too soon, Ty's alarm on his watch starts going off. He slowly pulls away from me as he slides his hand up my back and looks at the time.

"Crap, it's time for my Guard patrol," he says, looking down at me.

"If you *have* to go," I say as I pucker my lips in a pouty type of way and slowly move off of him, letting my hand slide over his hard abed stomach.

"I have a few more minutes," Ty says, rolling us

again until he's on top of me.

I giggle out, "Okay but I don't want you to be late."

He's kissing me on the neck when he says, "I won't be."

We get another five good minutes of kissing in before his watch is going off again.

"Damn it," he growls. "I really have to go now."

He kisses me deeply one more time then slows our kissing and pulls back, his arms straightening. He kisses me on the nose and in one movement he's standing up. I lay here watching him find his shirt and admire how his muscles move as he pulls it on.

"Do you want yours?" he asks, trying not to ogle my breasts but he fails miserably.

"No, that's okay, I'll just change into pajamas," I say and I see him visibly gulp as his stare snaps to my face. I inwardly laugh at that.

"My shift ends right after breakfast, maybe we can go do something when I'm done," Ty says as he reaches for my hands and he pulls me up into a kneeling position on my bed.

"I'd like that," I say, running my hands over his shoulders.

He kisses me one more time and then says, "Ugh, I really have to go. Good night, Emma."

"Good night, Ty," I whisper into his ear. He shivers, kisses me quickly and then steps out of my doorway.

"Hey, what are you doing?" I hear Libby say.

Shoot! I inwardly shout as I jump up and pull on my tank top.

"Just talking with Emma," I hear Ty say but from the tone of his voice, I can tell he's smiling.

"Mmmm hmmm, I'm sure," Shae says.

"Bye girls," Ty says.

There's a soft thud just outside my curtain, the only sound a knock can make.

"Emma?" Libby asks.

"Yeah, come on in," I say, hurriedly running my fingers through my hair, hoping it doesn't look like I've just spent who knows how long, making out.

Shae and Libby walk in with eyebrows raised and they're trying to keep a straight face.

"What's up?" I ask.

"From the looks of it, Ty's---," Shae starts to say but Libby interrupts her.

"Shae! Don't say that!" Libby says but then busts out laughing. "What was that all about?"

I just shrug, trying to hang on to the feelings the last hour or so brought on.

"Yeah, you left like two hours ago saying you were tired," Shae says, taking a seat at the foot of my bed. I sit at the head, grabbing my pillow and hugging it tightly. It smells like Ty.

"I was tired... I am tired," I say, correcting myself.

"I'm sure you are now," Shae says, wagging her eyebrows at me.

"Nothing like that happened," I say. "I swear."

"We believe you, Shae is just teasing. I can tell you don't want to talk about it but just know we're here if you do. As much as I don't want to hear about my brother's business, I can tell you're happy and I can tell he's happy. Happier than I've seen him in a very long time," Libby says.

I yawn for real this time, laying my head back.

"You do seem pretty tired," Shae says.

"I am," I say, yawning again.

"Okay, we'll see you in the morning. Night, Em," Shae says, leaving my room.

"Night, Shae," I holler after her.

"Night Em," Libby says, winking at me as she leaves.

"I....." I start to say but I don't really know what to say so I just say good night. I get in my comfy pajamas and climb into bed, breathing in Ty's scent on my pillow. Today hasn't been that long of a day because I slept so much but I feel exhausted. I drift off to sleep with ease, eager for tomorrow to come.

CHAPTER 21 - ONE LAST SWIM

I wake up smiling. I dreamt of Ty. All we did was walk around holding hands, stopping once in a while to kiss and then continued on with our walk. I don't want to wake up but knowing I'll get to see Ty again, helps immensely.

I look at my watch and see it's only 5:00 AM. Ugh, I'd only slept four hours but I feel like it's some of the best sleep I've gotten since before I was kidnapped.

I decide to go for a swim before everyone else gets up. It would be good to burn off some of this energy flying around inside of me. I don't want to be bouncing off the wall when I meet up with anyone, especially when I meet up with Ty.

As I expected, I have the pool to myself. I time myself, trying to beat my time with each lap. Holding my breath has gotten easier. I can go two laps without needing to take a breath. That must be some kind of Talent. It sounds conceited thinking this and I really don't mean it to but, is there anything I can't do? I've always wanted to be able to do something special but even with the most special people I've ever met, I stand out. And with people like Alysa and Malory around, standing out isn't something I really want to do.

I take a quick shower and head back to my room. I change out of my pajamas and put on a t-shirt and jeans. Looking at my watch, it shows 6:45AM. Cooky might have breakfast out so I head on down to the Great Room.

There are a few early birds meandering around. Cooky does have food out; french toast, eggs, and sausage links. Going over and getting a plate, I head over to a table we've been sitting at recently. I eat slowly, hoping Shae and Libby might be coming in soon. Or maybe even Ty, but probably not, he said after breakfast and since it's not even seven o'clock yet, I bet he still has an hour or two left on Guard duty.

I'm just finishing my plate when Shae and Libby appear at the table, they Ran here.

"We stopped by your room and you weren't there. We were wondering if you'd still be in here," Shae says. She runs over to the food table and dishes herself up some food. I stand up and walk over with Libby.

"We weren't sure if you had plans with someone else this morning or not," Libby says, smiling at me. "Still don't want to talk about it?"

"I kind of do have plans but not until a little later and I do want to talk about it, just not yet," I say, hip bumping Libby, hopefully letting her know I desperately wanted to talk to her.

"I get it and like I said, we're here when you're ready," Libby says, hip bumping me back.

I get another plate of food and walk back over to the table with Libby and Shae.

"I don't think I've ever been able to eat this much," I say, looking down at my heaping pile of second helpings.

"Late night shenanigans will do that to you," Shae says rolling her body suggestively while a sausage link sticks out from between her lips.

"Shae! Shhh… I told you last night, nothing like that happened," I say in a rushed whisper.

"Okay, okay, but you're turning red so something happened last night," she says, eyeing me expectantly.

"And she'll tell us when she's ready, stop teasing her and badgering her for information. You know how that feels. Remember Alysa doing that to you about---," but Shae cuts Libby off before she can finish.

"Okay, okay! Yes, I remember. I'm sorry Emma, it's not nice and I'll stop," Shae says, shoving the sausage into her mouth.

I'm about to say something to her but I feel a tap on my shoulder. I look behind me and see Ty. My heart stops and then about flies out of my chest.

"Good morning," he says as he sits down beside me.

"Good morning," I reply, staring at him.

We stare at each other for a minute and then Libby

says, "Good morning, brother!"

We both jump in startlement, I momentarily forgot there was anyone else in the room with us. Shaking my head, I look down at my plate of food. Last nights, to say it like Shae, shenanigans, rush to mind. My face gets warm and the embers from that fire in my stomach start to flare up.

"Good morning, sister," Ty says as he leans forward to look at Libby. "And good morning to you too, Shae."

"Mornin'," she says with a mouth full of french toast.

"Did you sleep well?" Ty asks me.

"Mmmm hmmm," is all I can think to say, my face getting even warmer. I take a bite of my food to try to distract from the fact that my face is turning bright red.

"Me too," he whispers into my ear. Chills run down the right side of me, where his breath leaves goosebumps down my neck, to my arm.

Smiling, I start to eagerly eat my food. Today was going to be a good day.

Max and Clay show up, carrying two plates of food each.

"Man, I'm starving," Max says, sitting down beside Libby. He kisses her on the top of the head. "Good morning, Lib."

"Morning," she says, leaning over and giving him a kiss on the cheek.

"You guys want to play a game of basketball before

they finish taking everything from the Gym to the new place?" Clay asks, shoveling an entire piece of french toast into his mouth.

"OOh yeah, I love basketball!" I exclaim.

"Sure, sounds fun," Ty says, bumping his leg into mine. I glance over at him and he winks at me. My heart gives a little squeeze.

Everyone agrees it would be fun to play. So we finish eating and all go back to our rooms to change. I've just finished putting my sports bra and shorts on, getting ready to put my tank top on when there's a knock on my door frame.

"Just a second," I say as I hastily pull my tank top on. "Come on in."

Ty steps inside, pulling the curtain shut behind him, and says, "Hi."

"Hi," I bashfully say back.

He steps towards me and pulls me into a hug.

"I've missed you," he whispers into my ear.

"I've missed you, too."

I turn my head just a little to the left and find his lips. Shock from the electricity causes a gasp to escape my lips. Ty's hug tightens and he kisses me harder. He slides his hands up to my hair and holds my head tightly, pulling my face as close to his as possible.

After a few minutes, he pulls back, "We should probably get to the Gym."

"Mmmm, yeah, maybe," I say breathlessly, pulling

him back to me and began kissing him again.

Another few minutes pass by and finally I pull back, reluctantly, "Okay, we definitely should go before they come looking for us. Libby and Shae are already asking questions."

"What did you say?" Ty asks as he steps away from me but grabs my hand as he does.

"I haven't said anything. I wasn't sure what you'd want me to say and I was wanting to keep it to us for just a little while longer."

"I usually keep things to myself too but my sister has a way of knowing things, she's got an amazing ability to read people."

"Is that a Talent or just how she is?"

"Just how she is."

"So should we act like nothing is happening for now?"

"For now, just until we get to your new place."

"Our new place," I correct him.

We step out of my room and start walking towards the Great Room, still holding hands.

"Wanna Run?" Ty asks.

"Yeah, I'll race you!" I say back.

"Okay, you're on!" Ty says as he gets in the runner's pose, we let our hands fall apart.

"Ready... Set... GO!" I say. We both take off but we're only Running for a second before I'm at the Gym entrance. Ty comes up behind me a second later.

"You're fast! Faster than Demi fast!" he exclaims. "Did you Jump?"

"I don't think so, it didn't feel like it does when I've Jumped before," I say.

"You're incredible," he says, kissing me on the top of the head.

"We better get inside before we get too carried away," I say.

Ty looks down at me like he wanted to do nothing but get carried away. He steps aside from the entrance and motions me in first.

Clay, Max, Libby, and Shae are all inside, shooting around but so is Charlie, Alysa, and Malory.

Libby skips up to us and says, "Charlie overheard Max and Clay talking about our plans and insisted on coming, he brought along the other two, also."

"It's about time," Shae says walking over.

Malory tosses me the basketball and says, "Let's see what you got?"

I dribble it a couple times and then take a step towards the three-point line and take my shot.

SWOOSH!

Everyone stares at me.

"I thought you said you weren't allowed to play sports?" Max says, dumbfounded.

"I wasn't allowed to play on any teams but I did have to take P.E. just like everyone else," I say laughing at their expressions.

"I'm not going to play, I just did my nails," Malory says, sitting down on the floor next to the entrance.

"What are the teams?" Alysa says, walking over to Ty and putting her arm through his. Ty pulls his arm free and steps away from her, moving closer to Max and Shae.

"Shoot for them?" Max suggests.

"So that all the good shooters are on a team? I don't think so," Alysa says snottily.

"Boy vs girls?" Clay suggests.

"Talk about unfair advantage," Libby says.

"You guys have Emma now, it'll be pretty well even," Max says. "She can shoot as good, if not better than Ty and he's the best player The Pit has."

I look at Ty and he winks at me. Out of the corner of my eye I see Alysa stiffen and then she throws a glare at me.

"Boys vs girls sounds good to me," Alysa says. "I'll take Ty."

Inwardly growling, I look anywhere other than at her.

"Of course you will but I think Ty and Emma should guard each other since they're the better players of the bunch," Libby says as she walks by me and hip bumps me.

"Skins vs shirts?" Charlie asks, walking up to me. "Girls are skins."

"Ha... ha... ha... in your dreams," Shae says.

"Oh, you have no idea what I dream about, Shae," Charlie says, putting his arm around me but I slide out from under his arm and grab the ball from Max.

"Emma, take a shot. You make it, girls get the ball first and you keep your points. You miss, we get the ball," Clay says, walking over to stand next to Shae.

I dribble once and take a step to the line, take my aim, and shoot.

SWOOSH!

"Three to zip," Shae says, high fiving me.

Max rebounds the ball and passes back to me. I check it to Ty and he passes it back. I pass to Libby before I cut to the middle and back out to the side. Libby passes it to Alysa who tries to take a shot where I had but misses. Clay rebounds and passes it out to Ty who dribbles to the top of the three point line.

I get down in my defensive stance and stay with him. Wherever he goes, I'm there too. Charlie comes up and sets a screen.

"Switch," Alysa giggles. She puts her hands on Ty's butt as he tries to dribble around her.

Ty passes the ball to Max who shoots and makes it.

"Three to two," Shae says, getting the ball and passes it to Libby.

"Switch back," Ty says to Charlie as he walks over to me. Charlie sends a look at me and then to Ty but reluctantly walks over to Alysa who is shooting daggers at me.

Libby passes me the ball but Alysa runs into me, catching the ball and causing me to go flying. I land on the floor with a loud thud.

"Ooops, sorry," Alysa says. "Didn't see you there."

"The hell you didn't," Shae says, walking up to her sister. "Knock it off, now, Alysa."

"What? I didn't do it on purpose," she says, but I see her smile over at Malory who's silently laughing where she's sitting.

"No more of that or we aren't playing anymore," Ty says, walking over and giving me hand up.

I wipe myself off and say, "I'm fine. Let's keep playing."

Shae grabs the ball from Alysa and tosses it to me. The game starts up again and that one incident with Alysa only happened that one time. The game goes on for a couple of hours. It finally ends when I make another three pointer just as our alarms on our watches go off telling us it's lunch time.

"48-42, girls win!" Shae says, running over to me and hugging me tightly.

"There's a first time for everything," Clay says laughing.

"You're really good," Libby says, walking over to where Shae and I are standing. "Nobody has ever been able to keep Ty below ten points."

"Too bad your mom... err, aunt, didn't let you play on a team. You would have been the MVP," Max says, as he walks up to Libby and takes her hand.

The mention of Vanessa kind of kills the mood for me, until Ty says, "She's the star of the team here."

I glance up at him and he's smiling his dazzling smile, my happy mood is restored. I bend down to re-tie my shoe for what feels like the 100th time and see everyone waiting for me.

"You guys go ahead, I'll catch up," I say, tying my shoe.

When I'm finished, I stand up and see Ty standing here waiting for me. Everyone else was out of the gym, except Malory, Clay, Charlie, and Alysa who were just walking out. Ty offers me his hand and I stand up.

"Thanks," I say.

"You're welcome."

He steps towards me, pulls me into his arms, and is kissing me once again. Swooning, I sway a little.

"Are you okay?" he asks, slightly out of breath himself.

"Yes, I just forgot to breathe for a second," I laugh out and laugh even louder when I hear my stomach growl.

"Let's get some food," Ty says, bending down and kissing me again.

"Food smood," I say when he steps back away from me. I catch a flash of red from the entrance and look over but nothing is there. Must have been a trick of the light.

He grabs my hand and we start walking out of the Gym.

"Wanna race again?" I ask.

"And have you beat me yet again today?" Ty counter asks.

I laugh, "Well if you want to look at it that way...." I trail off.

"Winner gets to choose what we do this afternoon?" Ty suggests.

"Deal!" I say eagerly.

"Ready... Set... GO!" Ty shouts.

I make it to the Great Room in a blink of an eye, Ty coming up two seconds later.

"If it's possible, I think you've gotten faster in the last couple of hours," he says, brushing his hand across my back as he walks by, sending electric shocks down my spine.

When I look around the room, I see Alysa talking with Charlie over in a corner, she looks pissed. Charlie looks like he's trying to calm her down, but she stomps her foot and storms away.

Huh, I wonder what they were arguing about?

We get some sandwiches and veggies, then head to the table were our friends are sitting. I love that I can say that now. It's an amazing feeling, to have friends. It makes me a little sad that I never got to experience this in school.

"What's everyone doing after lunch?" Clay asks.

"Basketball rematch?"

"No dude, don't you remember Bill asking if you and I could help get things moved from the Gym to Emma's place?" Max says. "Charlie is supposed to help Jump it all to the airport and then we're supposed to load the jet with the remaining stuff. Everyone else is on patrol."

"Oh man, I forgot about that. I need to find Mal and tell her I can't help her pack her stuff this afternoon," Clay says, scanning the room for Malory.

"She'll love that," Shae says under her breath so that only Libby and I can hear her. We both stifle a laugh.

"What does Bill have you doing, Ty?" Clay asks as he takes half of his sandwich in one bite.

"He gave me the rest of the day off since I'll be pulling a double tonight into the morning, just before we leave," Ty says, bumping my leg with his, a hint that we'd get the afternoon together.

Clay spots Malory across the rooms and jumps up and runs over to her. She puts her hands on hips and gets a pouty look on her face but in the end, she nods her head and gives Clay a hug and a kiss before she turns and leaves the Great Room.

Clay walks back over to our table and taps Max's shoulder, "Let's go, so we can get this over with. Where's Charlie?"

"He was over there," I say pointing towards the corner of the room opposite of us.

"Let's go find him," Max says, standing up but bending down and giving Libby a deep kiss before he leaves.

"Come find me when you guys are done," Libby says, kissing him one more time.

"You know I will," he says.

"What are you guys up too?" I ask Libby and Shae.

"Doc asked us to help finish cleaning the Hospital Wing. They got it all moved yesterday but he'd like it to be deep cleaned before we leave," Libby says. "He didn't ask you because he wants you to relax. He's still worried you might have overexerted yourself the other night."

"Oh," is all I can cleverly say.

Libby and Shae stand up and take their lunch stuff to the trash cans, on their way back over Shae says, "Enjoy your afternoon, we'll see you after a bit."

"Bye Em, bye Ty," Libby says as she walks by and then they Run from the room.

"So, what are we doing this afternoon?" Ty asks, turning towards me, his knees bumping into my thighs, sending zaps of tingly goodness up to my stomach.

"I don't know, what do you want to do?" I ask back.

"You won the race, you get to decide," he laughs.

"Hmmm, wanna go for a swim? A farewell swim since we'll be leaving tomorrow?" I suggest.

"Sounds good to me," Ty says standing up. "I'll meet you at the bathing pool in 10 minutes."

As he Runs out of the room, I stand, smiling like an idiot. But I'm instantly nervous, I'd have to wear my swimsuit and it has less coverage than anything I've ever worn.

When I get to my room, I take my clothes off and with shaking hands, pull my swimsuit on. I pull a black t-shirt over the top and pull on a pair of blue shorts. I take my hair out of the ponytail I threw it up in to play basketball and French-braid it, hoping it'll stay out of my face as we swim.

I Run to the bathing pool, thinking Ty would already be here, but he's not. I feel a little bit better about taking my shirt and shorts off without him staring at me. I strip them off and jump in, and I'm still awed at the temperature.

I do a couple laps before I hear someone clearing their throat. I stop in the middle of the pool, treading water, and look towards the entrance.

"I could watch you swim all day," Ty says. "You look like you belong in water."

Laughing, I swim slowly over to the side, closest to where he's standing. He takes his shirt off, tossing it to my pile of clothes, and jumps in over the top of me, splashing me with water when he lands.

He's under for just a second before his head pops up a few feet in front of me. He swims slowly over to me, not taking his eyes off of mine.

"Feels good, huh?" I say.

"It does," he says as he gets to my side.

We tread water for a minute, just staring at each other. The electric tension between us rising. I look down at the water, expecting to see currents flowing between us, but of course there isn't, it's all inside.

"Wanna swim over to the waterfall?" he asks.

"Sure."

We kick off and swim to the back of the bathing pool, where the waterfall thunders down at us. The water is a little shallower back here, I can stand and the water hits me just a little higher than mid stomach. When Ty stands, it hits just below his swim shorts hemline.

He grabs my hands and steps into the flow of the waterfall. He slides his hands up my arms until their on either side of my neck. He bends down and kisses me. The flow of water and his kissing sends me into overdrive, all my senses are on the edge of exploding.

I suddenly step into him, pushing my body into his. This surprises him, and me for that matter, and he falls backwards out of the waterfall flow, landing on his butt, the water coming up to his shoulders. I fall on top of him. We both laugh and he readjusts me so that I'm straddling his lap.

"Sorry about that," I say nervously.

"I don't mind," Ty says, running his hands up my back.

I bend my head down to his and kiss him. His hands

freeze in the middle of my back, his fingers gently digging into me. I run my hands behind his head, intertwining them in his hair, pulling his face closer to mine.

After what feels like hours of kissing like this, I
slowly pull away.

"Maybe we should talk for a little bit," I say. "I feel
like I hardly know anything about you and that seems
weird since we've had a couple make-out sessions."

He laughs and says, "Sounds good to me."

I go to slide off of him but he pulls me to him, wrapping his arms around my waist. He pushes off the pool
floor with his feet and glides out to the middle of the
pool where it's deepest. I gently push away, giving him a
small smile as I do.

"It's hard to concentrate on anything but kissing
you when I'm touching you," I admit embarrassingly,
my face flushing.

"Don't be embarrassed, I feel the same way," he
says, circling me as he treads water.

Trying to think of something to say, I dip the lower
half of my face into the water, so that only my nose and
eyes are visible. Ty continues to slowly circle me.

"Where did you guys live before coming to The
Pit?" I finally ask.

"Mission Hills, Kansas," Ty says, stopping his circling and just treads water in front of me. "We were some
of the first to get to The Pit. My parents are some of
the best Seekers and Rifts were hell bent on Tracking

them down. The Rifts were taking every kid they could get their hands on and my parents being who they are, they thought for sure Libby and I would be taken soon. Luckily, Beth was able to put the Untraceable Shield on the Dry Cleaners, The Pit, and everyone inside of it. We think that's why she can't put a Defensive Shield up for very long, because she's already Shielding."

"So you guys have been here for 10 years?" I ask.

"Yeah. Once the Elders bought the building and the Leaders put the Dry Cleaners in, we got started on the work for The Pit. Libby and I were only 10 but we helped wherever we could."

"That's crazy."

"What about you, where are you from?"

"New York City."

"OH wow, how was that growing up?"

"Noisy."

Ty laughs and says, "Yeah, I bet."

"Can I ask you a personal question?" I ask slightly embarrassed.

"Sure, you can ask me anything," Ty says swimming to get closer to me.

"Have you ever... Did you and Alysa ever... Are you still a...?" I can't seem to ask. "Never mind forget it."

"Have I ever had sex? Did Alysa and I ever have sex? Am I still a virgin?" Ty asks, swimming closer to me.

"Yeah, but never mind. You don't have to answer, it's too personal," I say sheepishly.

"It's not too personal. It's definitely something to ask when you're getting to know someone, especially when you feel a certain way for a person," Ty says. "To answer, no I've never had sex. No, Alysa and I never had sex. And yes, I'm still a virgin."

"How come? I mean, she's really pretty and you're really good looking too."

"Just because your body reacts to someone a certain way, doesn't mean your mind and heart want to follow those impulses, or that you have to act on those feelings. Was I attracted to Alysa? Sure, but her personality and the way she treats others is a total turn off. It's what ultimately made me breakup with her. I know most guys would have told themselves to get over it and just do it because sex is such a big deal when we're young or whatever but for me, it has to be with the right person. Alysa was not the right person."

"And no other girls have ever caught your eye and made you think maybe they could be your first?"

"Not until recently," Ty says swimming closer to me, our hands touching every so often as we move them to tread water.

I turn a little red at his comment, could he be talking about me?

"Can I ask you a personal question?" Ty asks, copying how I said it.

I laugh and mimic him, "Sure, you can ask me anything."

"Same question just minus the Alysa one, but I guess the two remaining are basically the same."

"I've never had sex," I say, ducking my head down again so that only my nose and eyes are above the water.

"Have you done anything sexual?"

I shake my head, causing the water to splash around my head.

"You never wanted to or never had someone you wanted to do anything with?"

Sighing, I pick my head up and say, "I never had anyone I wanted to do anything with in that way. Even if my... even if Vanessa would have let me date, I don't think I would have done anything. I always told myself I wanted to be out of high school before I had sex. I felt like I would be a little bit more mature at 18 to make that choice... decision... whatever you want to call it."

"And what about now?" Ty asks, grabbing one of my hands and pulling me towards him.

I'm about to answer him but we hear someone laughing, coming up the tunnel towards the bathing pool.

"Should we let people see us?" Ty whispers.

"I don't know. Are you ready for all the questions?" I ask.

"Are you?" he counters.

"Not really, I've liked keeping it just us, keeping it personal," I say.

"Me too, I'll hop out and go into the bathroom. We'll finish this conversation later," he says but before he swims to the side to get out, he pulls me closer so we're touching, and kisses me passionately.

Leaving me dizzy, he swims quickly to the side where our clothes are, picks his shirt and shoes up and Runs for the bathroom. I start doing laps, pretending that's what I've been doing the whole time.

Three girls come in. I've seen them around but have never met them to know their names.

"Oh, sorry, we didn't think anyone would be in here," one of them says.

"It's okay, I was just finishing up, it's all yours," I say as I climb out, grab a towel and start drying off. The girls jump in and swim towards the waterfall.

I feel a rush of air and look behind me, towards the entrance, and see Ty Running out, gotta love this Time Freezing Talent. Smiling I put my shirt and shorts on and head out the door.

The last question Ty asked me is still bouncing around in my head. I definitely have strong feelings for Ty and he certainly causes the fire in my stomach to flare every time he touches or kisses me. I don't think I'm ready for sex yet but maybe other things. Things that test the waters so to speak. Just thinking about doing some more things with Ty has that little flame inside me flaring up.

Shaking my head, I try to think of something else.

When I get to the Great Room, I find the perfect distraction. It's dinner time and Shae and Libby are sitting on a couch talking with Shae's parents. I swing by the food table and grab a plate of food and head over to where they're sitting.

"Hi Emma," Helen says.

"Hi Helen, hi Robert," I say smiling at them both. "Hey Lib, hey Shae."

"Hi," Robert, Shae, and Libby all say together.

"What have you been up to all afternoon?" Shae asks with a hint of suggestive intuition.

"Swimming. I wanted one more soak before we leave," I answer truthfully.

"Oh," Shae says a little disappointed. Libby looks at me, not convinced. Luckily, she's an amazing friend and doesn't ask for clarification.

We spend the next couple of hours talking to Helen and Robert. They told us all the stories they had accumulated over the last couple of years doing the Seekers jobs. They told me how Seeking was different before they all had to go into hiding. Libby and Shae filled them in on what had been happening here at The Pit. The Shae's asked me the same questions I have been asked before. How I grew up, how I feel about the woman I thought was my mother, things like that.

At about a quarter past eleven, Helen yawns and says, "We better get to bed, we've got a big day tomorrow."

We all get up and head to our rooms. I had thought I'd see Ty before going to bed but he never came in for dinner. He did say he had Guard patrol tonight, that's probably where he was, I couldn't, wouldn't, become one of those girls that got all butt hurt if the guy she likes didn't spend all his time with her.

Breathe. Relax. You'll see him tomorrow.

I climb into bed and think about the last couple of days. It's amazing how one thing can change things so completely. Had we not gotten into a water fight, would Ty and I have kissed anytime soon? The answer is no, I don't think we would have. It put us in a situation where we were completely hidden from everyone, close to each other, and the electricity between us was forced to connect. I will forever be thankful of that water fight.

I laugh quietly to myself as I fall asleep.

CHAPTER 22 - JAMISON ISLAND

I wake up happier than I had yesterday and had anyone told me I could have woken up any happier than I felt yesterday morning, I would have told them they were crazy. But here I lie on my bed, smiling like an idiot.

I still have to pack up my room. I haven't been here for very long but this little room has felt more like a home than the huge house I lived in for 17 years ever felt. The Pit has even felt more like a home. As dark as it is down here, the people, well most of the people, make it feel bright and happy. I have missed the sun and going outside though. It will be nice to be able to go out whenever we want to. I am really anxious to get to the Island and see what all the excitement is about.

Someone, probably Beth, delivered duffle bags sometime during the night. I'm guessing everyone got them to pack their clothes and personal belongings. It doesn't take long to get all my things packed, it does take all five big bags though. I use the one small bag to pack a day's worth of clothes, my toiletries, and the books I've been given since I've been here. Except I keep out the book that Ty gave me and start to read the first couple of chapters. It's only half past six o'clock, I'll head to breakfast in a little bit.

A little bit into my reading, there's a soft tap just outside my door.

"Come in," I say as I put my book in my bag, my heart racing. I haven't seen Ty since last night and I'm anxious to see him.

When I turn to see him, I'm surprised to see Libby standing in the doorway.

"Oh, hi Libby," I say, sounding a little too disappointed.

"I was sent to see if you were okay."

"Yeah, I'm fine."

"Well, we're ready to go, just waiting for you. Doc thought maybe you needed a little extra sleep but he thought you'd be to the Great Room by now. Cooky has cleaned everything up but I saved you a plate. If we go now, you'll have time to eat before we leave," Libby says, grabbing three of my bags.

"Ummm, yeah, sorry, let's go," I say, a little bit sadder than I wanted to sound.

"Were you waiting for someone?"

"No, not really, I thought maybe... but... anyways. I got caught up reading a book."

"And you still don't want to talk about what happened during the water fight? Or when he was here the other night? Or swimming yesterday?" Libby asks, grinning at me.

"Not yet, maybe later," I say, smiling back at her.

"I'll hold you to it. Not that I want to hear every detail about my brother but you seem to be really happy, and I want to hear about that," Libby hip bumps me and waits for me to pick up my last big bag and the little one off my bed.

As we enter the Great Room I can see that everyone is here. I see a lot more older people than before, the Seekers. I follow Libby over to a table where a man and woman are sitting. Ty and Libby have the exact same hair color as the man.

"Mom, Dad, this is Emma Hart. Emma, my parents," Libby says, sitting down next to her mom.

"Mr. and Mrs. Conner, it's nice to meet you," I say shaking Mr. Conner's hand first and then Mrs. Conner's.

Mrs. Conner stands up, gives me a hug, and says, "It's so nice to meet you Emma, and please, call me Maggie. Libby has told us so much about you."

I hug her back as Mr. Conner stands up, takes me from Maggie, and hugs me too.

"You can call me Michael and it is so nice to finally meet you, Emma," he says. He releases me and steps back. It's a little weird getting a hug from someone that looks like an older Ty but having no feelings for him. Now that Maggie and Michael are standing, I can see that Ty has his mom's eyes and Libby has her dad's.

"Thank you, it's nice meeting you guys as well. When did you guys get here?" I ask.

"Late last night," Maggie says as she sits back down next to Michael.

"Sit, eat. We're about to leave," Libby says as she hands me a plate of eggs and bacon. Turning to her parent's she asks, "Have you guys seen Ty yet?"

"Not yet, Meredith says he's been on Guard patrol and helping move things. He should be in here shortly," Maggie says to her.

I try not to show too much interest so I ask, "How are we all getting to the Island, anyways?"

"Since we can't Jump, we are going to an airport and there are some jets waiting for us. You will have to grant each jet and all its passengers permission to the Island. Then we will fly there. We'll be on the first jet and we'll lead everyone there," Michael says.

"Won't it look suspicious for so many jets to leave at once?" I ask, I take my last bite of my breakfast and Libby takes my plate and runs over to throw it away.

"We're leaving from a private airport, so no. Once we get up in the air, the jets will become invisible," Maggie says.

"How is that possible?" I ask.

"Each jet will have a Demi that has a Talent for Invisibility. They can touch something to make it go Invisible," Maggie answers, smiling at me.

"I thought no one could do that," I say.

"They can only do one thing but everything inside it will become invisible, too. No one can do what you can do. Make a hundred people and things invisible? It's not something we've ever seen before. It'll be fun to see how you develop and what other Talents you have," says Michael, smiling over at me.

"Oh, okay. When do we leave?" I ask, drinking the last of my juice.

"Now," Michael says.

"Oh," I stand up and look around. Everyone is heading for the tunnel that leads us to the elevator. I look at my watch, it's 8:30 AM. I still haven't seen Ty yet, so I ask, "Where are the Guardians?"

"They are securing our route to the airport. Seekers who are part of the Guard are helping as well," Michael says, walking beside me.

"So we have to drive?" I ask. I'm getting a little nervous. Vanessa could have Rifts watching and we wouldn't even know.

"Yes," Maggie says.

"I don't think that's a good idea. Why can't we just Jump to the airport? It's private, right? So if we all appear, it won't be that big of a deal," I say, looking at Libby and then her parents.

Maggie and Michael look at each other and then at me.

Right when Michael is about to say something, Meredith's voice comes out of nowhere, like it's coming out of the walls.

"We have just been informed that Vanessa, Chris, and all of the Rifts are heading this way. Do. Not. Panic. As long as we keep moving at a safe and steady pace, we will get out of here before they arrive. I just want to let you all know what's happening, do not dilly-dally," Meredith's voice says.

"We have to hurry, why won't they let me Jump everyone?" I ask.

"Doc doesn't want to overexert you, so he didn't ask you to try," Libby says.

"I want to, it's safer and faster if I do it," I reply. I hurry past them and Run to the front of the queue of people. I find Doc and Meredith standing there talking to some other adults I can only guess to be Seekers.

"Emma, hello," Meredith says a little surprised.

"Hi. So can I just Jump us to the airport instead of us driving. I don't even want to know how many cars we have to take to get all of us there. We have what, 150 people to get there?" I say, looking back over my shoulder.

"177 and that is too many for one person to Jump. You haven't been to the airport either, so it would be difficult for you to concentrate on it to get us there," Doc states.

"You two have been there, correct?" I ask.

"Yes, but we have time to get there. Chris and Vanessa aren't in the city yet," Meredith says.

"Take my hand," I say to both Doc and Meredith. "Take my hand and think of the airport."

"Emma, you don't have to do this," Doc says sternly.

"Doc, it will get us where we need to go quicker and safer, please let me try. If I can't do this many people, what will happen?" I ask.

"Nothing to us but it could knock you out," he says.

"I can do this. Just take my hand and think about where the airport is and what it looks like," I stick my hands out for them to take. Meredith takes my hand and nods at Doc. He reluctantly takes my hand.

I close my eyes and focus on quieting everything in the tunnel. I can hear everyone talking and then silence. I focus on Doc's and Meredith's breathing. As I focus, I get a picture in my head. It starts off with a bird's eye view of fields, and then big shop buildings, and then airplanes. I look around and I can see which direction the city is and I know where the airport is located. I open my eyes and smile at Doc.

"I can do this. I just need everyone to be touching again," I say, looking from Doc to Meredith.

"Are you sure? Last time you passed out right after," Doc says, looking at me with concern.

"Yes, I'm sure. I can do this and I won't pass out this time," I say. I'm not 100% sure if I will pass out or not but I feel like I can keep myself from doing so.

"Okay, Emma. I'll tell the Guards to head to the

airport now," Meredith whispers something under her breath and then she looks down the tunnel and touches her throat. "I need everyone to place their hand on the shoulder in front of them. Hold on tight and don't let go until I say so. Do it now," she has made her voice sound extremely loud.

I look down the tunnel and see everyone following her instructions. Doc stands in front of the person at the front of the line, the man places his hand on Doc's shoulder and then Doc grabs Meredith's hand. Meredith then grabs my hand and says, "Good luck."

I nod at her and count to 30, giving everyone a couple extra seconds to do what needs to be done.

"OH shoot, before I forget," I say, I close my eyes, think of the airport, and snap my fingers. When I open my eyes, all of the bags that were by everyone's feet, are gone.

"Did you just send everyone's stuff to the airport?" Doc asks, eyes wide.

"I did... or I think I did. We'll find out when we get there," I say, laughing nervously. "Okay, ready?"

"Whenever you are," Meredith says.

I take a deep breath, close my eyes, and think about the airport again. I concentrate on the feel of Meredith's hand and through her I can feel Doc holding her hand. I let my mind flow through him into the guy that's holding his shoulder, and so on throughout the line until I come to Libby and her parents. Michael is the last in line.

I focus on the airport, take another deep breath and take a step forward. I feel a slight tug from Meredith but I hold tight and keep focusing. Instantly I feel a breeze on my face. I open my eyes and we have arrived, all of us, at the airport.

"Incredible!" Doc exclaims.

"Well done Emma!" Meredith says, hugging me.

I look around and see the Guardians standing by nine identical jets. They look super-fast. I sway a little and see Doc reach for me.

"Emma... Emma, look at me," Doc says, turning my head so he can look me in the eyes.

"I'm okay. Really, I am," I say. I feel a little wobbly but nothing that won't pass in a few minutes.

Meredith does the weird throat touch thing and tells everyone to board the jets, starting with the second one, 20 people to a jet. Everyone starts making their way to the jets, but as they pass, they place their right hands over their hearts in fists and bow their heads as they go by.

"They know what you've done for all of us, again," Meredith says, smiling proudly at me.

"I'm just glad to help," I say, swaying again.

"Emma, are you sure you're okay?" she asks, putting her arm around my shoulder.

"Yeah, I just need to sit down. I'm okay, though," I say, my head was starting to throb a little, not as bad as it did the other morning, though.

"Doc, Bill, take her to the jets. Have her touch each one and ask her if she gives it and its occupants permission to land on the Island," Meredith says as she starts for the first jet.

"Come on Emma," Doc says, putting his arm around my shoulders. Bill walks us to the last jet.

He places my hand on the landing gear and asks, "Do you give this jet and all its passengers permission to access your island?"

"I do," I answer.

We do this to the next seven jets. When we get to the 1st and last one that I have to grant permission to, Bill leads us up the stairs and has me sit down.

"Do you give this jet and all its passengers permission to access your island?" Bill asks one last time.

"I do," I answer, sighing with relief.

I swivel my chair and see Libby and Shae sitting behind me. Libby's parents are on the other side of the aisle, facing one another talking. They look over at me and smile, then they place their fisted hand over their heart, and they nod. I nod back.

"That was pretty cool, everyone is talking about how amazing you are. There's no denying it now, you're The One," Libby states, giving me a high five.

I shake my head and say, "No, I just have odd Talents."

"Whatever you say," Shae says, rolling her eyes at

me and laughs.

I look down the aisle and see Alysa staring at me, smiling. No, it looks like she's gloating or something. As I'm watching her, she gets up and goes over and sits on a couch on the other side of the aisle. Sitting next to her is Ty. She reaches over and pulls him into a deep kiss and he kisses her back.

My mouth drops open and I'm staring in shock.

"What is it?" Libby asks, turning quickly.

"What the...?" Shae asks. She's about to get up when Meredith comes over the loudspeaker.

"Please remain seated and fasten your seat belts, we're going to take off," I can hear her but it sounds like she's talking from down a tunnel.

"Emma? Emma?" Libby is calling my name but I can hardly hear her. I can't take my eyes away from Alysa and Ty kissing.

Alysa pulls away and looks me straight in the face and mouths the words 'he's mine'.

Ty looks up and towards me, he looks slightly dazed. When he sees me looking at him, he shakes his head slightly, and then looks at Alysa. She looks back at him and they start making out again.

I can hear my heart pounding in my ears. It's so loud. I can feel a tightness in my chest. Something is tickling my face so I put my hand to it and when I pull it away, it's wet. I'm crying. I finally look at Libby and she's mouthing my name and saying something else. I look back down at my hand and then everything goes black.

When I come to, the jet is empty, except for Shae, Doc, Libby, and her parents.

"Emma?" Libby says, coming over to me. "Are you okay?"

I still feel like I could sleep for days but I force my eyes to stay open.

"Yes, I'm fine. I don't know what happened," I say. I try to think back to what had happened before we took off but my mind is blank.

"I think you held off blacking out until we had taken off just to make sure you did all you could... to get us all here," Doc says, looking a little sterner than I've seen him.

"But I felt fine. Before I felt tired and then blacked out. I don't remember feeling like that," I say. "Wait, did you say here? Are we on the island already?" That's a stupid question. If we weren't here yet, the jet would have more people on it and we'd be moving.

"Yes, we're here, everyone made it safely, thanks to you," Michael says, smiling down at me.

"You are remarkable," Maggie says, taking my hand. "Are you feeling well enough to go to your Estate?"

"Yes, I feel fine. Just a little hungry. And please, call

it The Estate, not mine," I say. Libby reaches into a bag and pulls out a sandwich.

"I thought you might get hungry so I had Cooky make a sandwich for you before she closed up her kitchen," she says as she hands me the little baggy.

"Thank you," I say. Roast beef and cheddar cheese, my favorite. How does Cooky know exactly what to make?

"Alright let's go. We have a vehicle waiting outside for us," Doc says, standing up.

Libby and Shae help me stand.

"Are you sure you're okay?" Libby asks.

"Yes, why?" I reply.

"Because of what happened just before---" Shae starts to say but Libby cuts her off.

"You Jumped 177 people, that would be enough to knock anyone out," Libby says while giving Shae a look.

They aren't telling me something.

"What's going on?" I ask.

"Nothing, we'll talk about it when we get to your... I mean... The Estate," Libby says.

"Right, let's get there. I want to see what it looks like," Shae says, smiling at me but the smile doesn't reach her eyes.

They really are hiding something from me. Something to do with something happening before we took off? What happened? I try to think about it but my brain is fighting against me to remember.

I'll worry about it later. We get outside and I stand with my face towards the sun and just let it warm me. It feels so good. Sun warmth is different from any kind of heat I've ever felt. Well, except for the fire I felt when I changed. *Nothing* can compare to that.

I look over and see that there's a Suburban waiting for us.

"How did this get here?" I ask.

"After Bill and the Guardians got all the Pit stuff Jumped, they started Jumping extra stuff over too," Michael says as he opens the door for us.

Thinking of Ty brings instant sadness. What the heck? I think harder and get a glimpse of Alysa's gloating face as it flashes in my mind. My brain shuts the thought down and there's nothing. I shake my head. Something weird is going on.

Michael gets in the driver's seat and pulls us away from the jet. As we drive, I can see the ocean. It's gorgeous. We drive into a dense forest of palm trees and other tropical plants. The drive is only five minutes and then he's slowing down.

"I don't believe it," he exclaims.

I lean forward and stare out the front windshield and see The Estate for the first time. It doesn't have huge towers like a castle from fairytales have but it is huge and it's so beautiful.

The main entrance is made of huge double doors. There are four large windows on both sides of the doors. Next to the furthest windows out, on both sides, it looks like six, maybe seven, windows make up huge bay windows. Extending out from the bay windows, are six more large windows, ending with bigger bay windows.

It's six stories high. The sixth floor goes from the closest bay window on the right of the entrance, to other the closest bay window on the left side of the entrance. It also has steep pitches, making it look as if it's made up of a bunch of little towers. The mansion is made from beautiful gray stone with white window shutters.

As we drive up to the double doors, the last of the first SUV's is driving away. As we pull up, I can see where the flower beds once were and I can imagine how beautiful it will look once flowers are there again. There are trees spaced throughout the ginormous lawn so that there is shade just about anywhere a person would want to sit. I'm actually surprised to see some of the trees. I wouldn't have expected to see Weeping Willows or Maple trees here but that's what most of the trees are made up of, or at least those are the only ones I know the names of.

I can't see what's to the side of the mansion or what's behind it. I'll have to go for a walk later and see what the rest of the place looks like. I'm sure the pool is out back, that's where I would have put it.

Michael pulls to a stop and everyone opens their

doors to get out. I slide from sitting in the middle and step out onto the gravel that makes up the driveway. I look up and I really have to tilt my head back to see all the way up to the top floor.

"Shall we go in?" Doc asks, looking at me.

"Yes, please," I say.

We walk up the white stone steps, to the huge double doors. Doc and Michael pull them open and we can hear people cheering and laughing from inside. Once they notice the doors opening, they slowly quiet down. Meredith is waiting for us just inside the door

I step inside and look at the foyer that most everyone is standing in. The ceiling seems to go on forever. The wood banister that follows the stairs upward, is a beautiful dark brown. The floor is made out of marble, it looks like one solid slab of it.

As I step closer into the room, people start making a path for me, well for us. Shae, Libby, Doc, Meredith, Michael, and Maggie are walking with me.

The natural light from all the windows makes the room look so bright and happy. I spin around and see doors leading to the left, doors leading to the right, and doors on either side of the staircase.

Before I can decide which way to go first, people start to clap. Soon everyone is clapping and yelling their thanks to me. Then everyone starts to try and get closer to me, to pat me on the back or give me a hug. Soon my little group of friends are pushed out of the way and I can't see Shae or Libby anymore. Doc and Meredith are gone from sight, as well as Michael and Maggie. I can hear them calling my name but I can't see any of them.

In a blink of an eye, Charlie is standing beside me and he bends down and says, "Would you like to get out of here?"

I wasn't sure about going anywhere with him but it would be better than getting smothered to death by all these people. So I say, "Yes, please."

Charlie grabs my hand and the next second, we're in an empty bedroom. It's been dusted and cleaned. I can smell the fragrance of fresh laundry detergent.

I put my hands on my hips and glare at Charlie.

He smiles and puts his hands up, "Hey, I'm not hinting at anything bringing you here. This is your suite, I thought this would be the best place to bring you right now. You can rest while all your fans calm down a little."

I breathe a sigh of relief but also roll my eyes at him and say, "I don't have fans, they're just excited to be out of The Pit, that's all."

"Sure, Emma, whatever you say," Charlie smirks back.

I look around the room and see that it is in fact more of an apartment than just a bedroom.

"Are all the rooms this size?" I ask.

"No, the other rooms are set up more like hotel

rooms. They have a bedroom and a bathroom. We all voted and thought you should get this suite though. It is your family's estate after all. And before you start to argue, we already voted. It's yours, so just deal with it," Charlie says, looking around.

I look around and see that my bags are sitting on the couch to the right of the room. I don't care what Charlie says, I am not staying here. I'll talk to Meredith as soon as everything calms down a bit.

I walk over to the couch and look out one of the many, enormous, windows that's in the room. I can see forever from up here. This apartment must be at the very top of the mansion. Looking over to the left of the room, I see a kitchen. Why would there be a kitchen, wouldn't they think I'd want to eat with everyone else? I shake the idea of being completely secluded away from everyone out of my head and walk straight ahead to the door. I open it and see a room that's about 20 times the size of our rooms back at The Pit, and triple the size of the big living room I just came from, it's huge. It's beyond huge. The bed looks like someone slapped five king size beds together and called it good. It's way too big for just one person. One of the walls is nothing but windows. I bet the sky would look beautiful from here.

I go to the door to the left of the bedroom and find a bathroom. Everything in here is just so extravagant and big. The tub could fit ten people easily, it's more of a small pool than a tub. Shaking my head I close the door and go back out to the living room.

I thought Charlie had followed me but I find him sitting on one of the chairs when I come in, his eyes are closed.

"What's the matter?" I ask.

"Oh nothing, just tired. We worked through the night to get things set up here. Have you noticed? We have electricity," he says, waving his hands in the air.

I look around and sure enough, there are light fixtures where I had been expecting to see candelabras.

"How?" is all I can cleverly ask.

"It was Meredith and Doc's idea. They thought it would be better to figure out how to get electricity here so that we, the younger generation, wouldn't have to suffer from lack of technology. Of course Alysa was all for it," Charlie says, rolling his eyes.

Hearing Alysa's name brought to mind a scene I'd witnessed on the jet, just before I passed out. Ty and Alysa making out. I, all of a sudden, feel dizzy and sick, I sway just a little before catching myself on the arm of a chair I'm standing next to.

Charlie runs over and grabs me before I can fully fall to the floor.

"What's the matter?" he asks. "Should I go get Doc?"

"No, I'm fine," I say. "Charlie, answer a question for me? Truthfully, please."

"I'll do my best," he says, eyeing me carefully.

I sit down and put my face in my hands before I say, "Were Ty and Alysa kissing on the jet or did I just imagine that?"

Charlie looks at me and shrugs, then says, "They were. None of us could figure out what was going on. I guess Alysa finally talked him into it."

Trying to keep my breathing even, all I can say is, "Oh."

"To be honest, I thought he had a thing for you. You like him too, don't you?" Charlie asks, sitting down in the chair next to me.

"I thought so, but it doesn't matter now if he's with Alysa," I say, wiping a tear away as it falls down my cheek. I should not have let myself grow such strong feelings for Ty, it was stupid of me.

"Can I ask you something?" Charlie says, standing up and offering me his hand.

I'm not sure what he's going to do or ask, so I hesitantly take his hand.

"Sure," I say, looking up into his blue eyes.

"Can I kiss you? This time the right way?" he says, shyly.

I didn't think Charlie could ever sound shy or unsure of himself, but here he was, blushing and looking down at his feet, not at me.

Back at The Pit, Charlie was so intense, he scared me. Right now, however, I can see a more vulnerable side to him. It was a pleasant surprise but I wasn't ready for anyone to kiss me again, especially having Ty's kisses still fresh on my mind.

"Not today, not right now," I say back.

"Did I royally screw my chance with you?" he asks, searching my eyes for an answer.

"No, you didn't but I was serious when I said you needed to ease up on the intensity. I'm not used to the attention you are or were giving me and it scared me. Why don't we hangout a little, get to know each other better and see where it goes from there, sound like a deal?" I ask, smiling at him.

For the first time since I met Charlie, he actually smiles. It looks like his true smile, not the cocky smile I'd come to expect on his face. I have to admit, it makes him look good.

"Sounds good to me," he says, hugging me but then he pulls away and says "Sorry." Then offers me his hand to shake.

I take it and shake hands with him, laughing, "Hugging is okay, friends hug."

He laughs and says, "Good to know. I'll leave you to unpack. Come down in a few when you're ready. Just follow the hall and it will lead you to the stairs."

He walks to the door and waves bye, I wave back.

I let out a huge sigh and sit down on the couch my bags are on. I push them off onto the floor and lie down.

I'll take a quick nap and then I'll go find Libby and Shae. Then we can go find Meredith and talk to her about this suite situation. I think to myself. I close my eyes and drift off to sleep.

CHAPTER 23 - TOUR
OF THE ESTATE

I wake up to someone knocking on my door. I glance out the window and see the sun starting to set. I was more tired than I thought. I get up and go to the door and open it. Libby and Shae are all but bouncing to get in.

"Charlie told us about your place, can we come in and see?" Shae asks, peering around me.

"Actually, I was going to come find you guys and then go find Meredith. I don't want to live here. I'd rather she and Doc take it. I want to be in a normal room close to you guys," I say, glancing behind me at the living room.

"I told them you'd say that," Libby says. "But they didn't believe me. They figured once you saw the place, you would change your mind."

"Uh, no. Definitely did not change my mind," I say. I step out into the hall and shut the door behind me.

Shae pouts and says, "You won't even let us check it out?"

I laugh a little and say, "No, because I'm afraid you'll talk me into keeping it and I don't want it."

Libby says, "She has a point. You're pretty good at talking people into things."

"Oh, whatever," Shae says, rolling her eyes.

Libby and I laugh, as we turn to walk away, Libby puts her arm through my right arm and Shae grabs my other. I am so very thankful to have these two!

"Do either of you know where Meredith is?" I ask.

"Last I knew, she and Doc were finishing up the final touches to the Hospital Wing. Sara had everything pretty much in place but Doc was finalizing a lot of the stuff," Libby answers.

"Have you guys toured the place yet?" I ask as I look up to the ceiling and see nothing but skylights.

"No, we've been waiting for you. We thought it would be fun to check it out together," Libby says, nudging me with her hip.

"Thanks for waiting for me, I honestly didn't think I'd sleep so long but I guess I was more tired than I thought," I say, yawning and then laughing at the fact I just yawned after sleeping most of the day away.

"Well, you did Jump, how many of us? 175... 180... to the airport," Shae says, in awe.

"Yeah, about the airport, what I saw on the jet?" I say. "When did that start?"

"I'm sorry Emma, I have no idea. I didn't see Ty all morning until we got on the jet and he was lip locked with Alysa," Libby says, looking sad.

"I think my sister did something to him, to be honest. He's been very adamant about not wanting a relationship with her and then all of a sudden their making out, it just doesn't feel right," Shae says.

"I was going to say the same thing," Libby says, nodding in agreement.

Is it possible that she has?

"What could she have done?" I ask.

"I don't know, but I'll find out," Shae says, narrowing her eyes.

We finally get to the stairs and start making our way down. There are pictures of different places around the world with different types of people and creatures in each picture. One had unicorns that looked like they were dancing with Fairies.

"Are unicorns real?" I blurt out before I can stop myself.

Libby and Shae laugh, and Libby says, "Yes, they're real. The Fae have been protecting them for thousands of years. The humans used to kill them for their horns. They didn't use them for anything, they just like having them. The Fae decided that they needed to step in before there were no unicorns left, so they made it so humans can't seem them or if they do, they look like a regular horse before they disappear."

"I met Queen Talia, she seemed nice. It was all very surreal to meet all the Leaders," I say, thinking back to a week or so ago when I met them all. I never put much thought into if Vampires or Werewolves were real. I loved reading fantasy fiction stories that had them in them but I never went further into thinking about them than their books. And I never thought Fairies, or I mean, Fae people or Mermaids, no, Merfians, were real. How amazing is it that they all do exist! I wonder what other magical creatures are real that I thought were just a myth?

"I met a werewolf once, she was pretty cool," Libby says, looking deep in thought.

"I'm sure they're all mostly nice but just like any species, they have their assholes," Shae says, laughing slightly.

Libby just shakes her head but then says, "I guess you're right. We do have our fair share. Charlie for instance."

"Oh, I don't know. He's not as bad as I thought. He brought me up to the suite when everyone was trying to get to me, down in the foyer. That was nice of him. He also didn't try anything while we were there either. Although he did ask if he could kiss me, the right way," I say, blushing.

"What?!" Shae and Libby says together.

"What did you tell him?' Libby asks, coming to a halt on the landing between one of the floors, I'd lost count. I think we were between floors two and three.

"I told him I'd like to get to know him better and

that we could hangout more if he wanted to," I said, blushing even more.

"Ems, I'm telling you, he's bad news," Shae says, grinding her teeth.

"I'm going to keep my guard up around him, I just want to give him a chance to show me if he's any different than what I saw back at The Pit, so far he's shown me he can be better," I say.

Shae just grunts but Libby says, "I think that's a nice thing to do, just remember that we've known Charlie most of our lives, we know how he is but if he's willing to change, then I think that's great."

"We'll see," Shae says, and she starts walking again, pulling us along with her.

"Oh! This is our floor, the first floor. Well technically the second floor but the first floor with bedrooms. Let's show Emma," Libby says, stopping at the door on the landing.

"And then we find Meredith?" I ask.

"Yes, then we'll find Meredith," Libby says laughing.

She opens the door and we step into a small square room with a door on either side and one in front of us. Shae opens the door to the right and we step in. There are four pool tables, two foosball tables, arcade video games along the walls, and then tables with board games all over them.

"Oh this will be fun, I love playing games," I say.

We walk back out and go through the door across from the Game Room. It's the same as the other, only slightly smaller but all the same games are here and it's set up the same way.

"With 68 rooms on one floor, having two Game Rooms is a must," Shae says, laughing.

We walk back out and go through the door that's directly across from the door leading out to the staircase.

She opens the door and we step into a huge living room area. There's a wall that is one big TV. All over the room there are couches, fluffy chairs, reclining chairs, oversized bean bag chairs, and those banana looking chairs that someone can lay down in and it kind of rocks back.

"This is the TV Room. Each floor has one. Actually, every floor that has bedrooms is the same. Well, except for your floor," Shae says, laughing slightly embarrassed.

"Not my floor for long," I say.

Shae just rolls her eyes and leads us to the right where there's a door. She opens it and we step into a room with more comfy looking seating areas.

"We're calling this the Sitting Room. There's one on the other side of the TV Room too," Libby says and then adds as she plops down into an oversized chair. "Doesn't this chair look comfy?"

"Yes, it does," I say, sitting down beside her. It was

big enough Shae could have sat down with us and there still would have been room for another person.

"Yes, yes, it's comfy. Come on, we've got more to see," Shae says, grabbing our hands and pulling us up. Libby and I laugh as we bump into her.

We walk through the other door and into a hallway where there's eight doors, four on each side. Each one is decorated in a different way.

"These are bedrooms?" I ask.

"Yes," is all Libby says.

"This is my room," Shae says. Pointing to the second door on the left. It has what looks like waves painted on it.

She opens the door and lets me in. She has her stuff unpacked and the room decorated. Charlie was right, it's set up almost identical to a big hotel room. There's a desk, mini fridge, and the bathroom has a shower and tub and nice big sink. Unlike hotel rooms, it feels homier.

"This is awesome," I say. I turn and look back at Shae and Libby, smiling at them. "I'm definitely changing rooms.

Shae rolls her eyes and says, "Whatever. Come on, let's keep going."

We go back out to the hallway and Shae shuts her door.

"And this is my room," Libby says, pointing to the door next to Shae's, the third one down. It's got all shapes and sizes of animals painted on it, along with caduceus' spread out amongst them.

"So the doors get decorated with our Talents?" I ask.

"Yeah, pretty much. We can decorate it however we want but most everyone is doing something with their Talents," Shae says.

Libby opens her door and I peak inside. It's set up just like Shae's only decorated differently.

"Whose room is this?" I ask, pointing to the door next to Libby's, it's decorated with caduceus' and scales with a gavel across them.

"Meredith's and Doc's," Libby says.

"So hopefully mine once we switch," I say, smiling.

The girls just laugh at me and we walk the last couple of feet down to the end of the hall were there's a double door. Shae opens them and my mouth pops open.

"Wooooow!", is all I can say. The room is circular so I'm guessing we've finally made it down to the side of the mansion, but that's not why I'm blown away. I'm blown away because it's a Library. Filled with books from floor to ceiling. The room is double the size of the TV and Sitting Rooms.

"Every floor has a Library?" I ask. There's a big wooden sign that says '**LIBRARY 3**' up on the wall over the doors we just came through.

"Two, actually. One on each end. All have different

books and as far as I've seen, they're by subject. This one is on all animals from the sea and land. As well as all plants, insects, birds. Basically everything in nature," Libby says. "The other one, '**LIBRARY 4**', on this floor, is about Vampires, Werewolves, Merfians, and Fae. Plus animals and other beings of our world. Inepties call them Mythical Creatures.

"This is amazing!" I say.

"We thought you'd like it," Shae says nudging me.

We walk to the right where there's another door. We find another hallway with more doors decorated for the individual that will be living inside the rooms and two closets as we step into the hallway, on both sides. This hallway has six doors on the left side and only one on the right side. Halfway down the right side is a plain door. At the end of the hall is another closet on the left, by the door that looks like it leads outside.

We walk out that door and enter some type of garden oasis. It's beautiful here. Lots of benches to sit on and grassy areas to lie down on. Looking back at the mansion I can see the rooms on this side, all have balconies, with little gates connecting with their neighbor's balcony.

"Do your rooms have balconies?" I ask Shae and Libby.

"Yeah, they do. It's pretty cool. This side of the mansion and the side our rooms are on, are the only rooms that have them. A lot of people missed out on getting a balcony room because they wanted to tour The Estate first," Shae says laughing.

"Luckily for us, we waited for you before we took a tour," Libby says, smiling at me.

We walk back through the door that brought us out here and go to the door now leading to the left.

I open it and step into another hallway. This one is longer than the other two. As we walk, I count eleven doors on the left and eight on the right. At the end of the hall, there's another door. We open it and we're back at the staircase.

"Oh cool, so it just kind of loops around," I state.

"Yeah, and like we've mentioned, the other side is identical to this. You walk through the same TV Room, then go through a Sitting Room, eight rooms, Library, seven rooms, and then another 19 rooms just like the hallway we just walked down," Libby says, starting to walk down the stairs.

We come to a sort of walkway, that's high above what looks like a huge dining room. At the end of the walkway, there are two spiral staircases, one on the right and one on the left. There's also an archway straight ahead.

"We can either go straight and go to the foyer or go down one of these and be in the Dining Hall," Libby says, gesturing towards the spiral staircases.

"Let's go straight," I say.

We make it down to the foyer and we all stop and

look around. It's empty and I can really take in how big it is in here.

"Where to?" Libby asks.

"Have you guys looked around down here yet?" I ask.

"No, we unpacked and decorated our rooms, checked out our floor, and then waited for you," Shae says, looping her arm through mine.

"Yup, we wanted to explore with you," Libby says, taking my other arm. "Which way, Em?"

"Let's go to the left," I say.

We walk over to the doors to the left of the foyer and walk into what looks like a study room. Chairs, desks, and tables are on both sides of us. Basically, what you'd find in a library just minus all the books. We walk straight and go through some more doors and there's a long hallway and halfway down the hallway, there's a door on either side. On the door on the right, a plaque says, '**Classroom 1 - Professor Densmore - Mentalist 1**'. The door across from this one says, '**Classroom 2 - Professor Moris - Mentalist 2**'.

"We have actual classrooms!" Libby exclaims.

"Nerd," Shae says but she looks just as excited.

We continue walking and walk through the double doors just like the ones upstairs and we find another library. As we walk through it to the door to the left, I glance at some books. There were some that had to do with the Mentalist talents and some about Healing.

"Who wrote these books?" I ask.

"Demi-gods who have pretty much perfected their Talents," Shae says.

"Every Talent is just a little different with each person but these are the basics," Libby says.

"That's cool," I reply.

We walk through the door and find the offices of the professors and Doc. Continuing down the hallway we come to two big, swinging doors that have caduceus on each of them.

We walk in and find the Hospital Wing. Doc is walking around putting brand new linens on the beds, Sara is doing the same on the other side of the room. This Hospital Wing is easily three times the size as the one back at the Pit. All the equipment looks brand new and shiny.

Doc looks up from placing a pillow on a bed and says, "Hi girls! Taking a tour?"

"Yeah, thought we'd check things out," Libby says. "This is amazing!"

"Pretty neat, huh! Through there is Professor Moris' and my classroom. It's so great we have all this space. Someone in your family must have been a Psychic, Emma, for them to have made sure we had all of this," Doc says, sweeping his hand around the room.

I smile back at him and nod. It's so weird to think of my family having Talents. It also makes me sad thinking that I'll never know them. Knowing what my own

378 EMMA HART AND THE DEMI-GODS

aunt did to me and is doing to others, makes me even more sad and angry.

"If you go back the way you came, the door to the right will take you to the kitchen," Sara says. "I bet Cooky will have something started for dinner."

We say goodbye and head back down the way we came. Just outside the Hospital Wing door is a door to the right, just like Sara said there would be. We walk through it and smell the most amazing smell ever, BBQ!

"Cooky!" Shae hollers, "It smells amazing in here!"

Cooky comes out of a room to the left of us, holding a large box of corn on the cob. She puts them on the center island where she's already put 10 other boxes and looks over at us.

"There are six BBQ's and Traeger's outside. Everything I could have ever asked for in my dream kitchen is here. I thought it would be nice to have a BBQ and eat outside for our first dinner here. We can enjoy the night sky since we've gone without it for so long," she walks over and hugs me. "Thank you so much, Emma. This truly is the answer to our prayers."

Embarrassed, I hug her back and turn beet red.

"The Dining Hall is through there, doors on the left-hand side will take you back to the Foyer or doors to the right will take you outside. I'd go check out the other side of the mansion before you go outside. Once you're out there, you won't want to come back in. I'm sure you guys have already seen the walkway," Cooky laughs as she starts to shuck the corn.

We go into the Dining Hall and find three extremely long tables. There are small round tables in each corner. The spiral staircases are over to the left, on either side of all the drinks area. It's pretty awesome. There's every type of drink a person could think of; soda-pop, juices, water, Gatorade, iced tea, lemonade, everything.

We take Cooky's suggestion and go through the door on the left and walk through the foyer over to the other side. We find another study room and through the next door, two more classrooms. The room on the left says, '**Classroom 4 - Professor P. Burnette - Body 1**' and the room on the right says, '**Classroom 5 - Professor M. Burnette - Body 2**'. At the end of the hallway, another Library. This one is full of books about the body, fighting techniques, and the elements.

When we walk through the door to the right, we walk into the Gym. It's quite a bit bigger than the Gym back at The Pit. There were a ton of people here working out, playing basketball, or doing Yoga. We walk through, saying hi to those who say hi to us. People are being a bit nicer to me, not just staring, but saying hi, also.

I glance over to the right and see a Men's locker room and a Women's locker room. To the right of the Women's locker room is a door that has "**POOL**" painted onto it.

"Oh the pool!" I exclaim. Shae and Libby look over and we take a detour over to it.

When we walk in we stop dead in our tracks. It's an Olympic size swimming pool. There's two water slides and two diving boards. There are people messing around and doing laps, plenty of room for everyone to have a good time.

"Incredible!" Shae whispers.

"Way better than the pool at the Pit, that's for sure," Libby says, laughing.

We walk back out to the Gym and keep walking towards the other end. We come to another classroom and the sign on the door says, '**Classroom 6 - Professor Densmore – Elements**'. There's a door to the left and right of the classroom door so we go out the left-hand side door.

We emerge into a clearing that's rimmed with trees. We walk to the right, around the Elements classroom and find an outdoor swimming pool twice the size as the one inside.

"Holy crap!" Shae exclaims.

"My thoughts exactly," I agree, laughing in disbelief.

This looks like where the majority of everyone is, lounging around the pool. It was still warm enough outside that being wet wouldn't have made a person too cold.

Looking over towards the castle we see a bunch of

picnic tables. Some that will seat six people and big ones that could seat about 20. Sitting at one table, I see Max, Charlie, Clay, Malory, Alysa, and Ty. My heart stops and my throat feels like it's closing up.

Libby comes up beside me and says, "We don't have to go over there." Except as she says this, Max waves us over.

"No, it's okay," I say as I clear my throat. After all, Ty and I hadn't been anything official.

We walk over and Max scoots over for us to sit beside him.

"Pretty great, isn't it?" he asks, kissing Libby on the cheek.

"It's amazing," Libby answers him.

"Soooo amazing," Alysa says in a fake happy voice, getting up and sitting on Ty's lap, basically shoving her chest into his face. "Don't you think, Emmmmma?" she over pronounces my name, making it sound like there were more than two 'M's in it.

"Yeah, it's pretty great," I say, looking away from her, looking at Clay and Charlie sitting across from us.

I could feel Shae tensing, like she was about to say something, but I reach under the table and squeeze her knee, hopefully conveying she didn't need to. I felt her relax, only just slightly.

"Well, I'm bored now babe, wanna walk me to my room? I need some help with something," Alysa says, getting up and running her hand down Ty's chest. I look down.

Stop looking at them. I tell myself.

Out of the corner of my eye, I can see that Ty doesn't automatically stand up. I'm going to kick myself for this but I look over at him. He's staring at me. He's slightly tilting his head to the left, and then to the right, and blinking a little too fast, too much for a normal person.

"Dude, are you okay?" Max asks, looking concerned for his best-friend.

"He's fine. He's just tired. He was up late," Alysa says, with a hint of something in her voice. She pulls him up to his feet and guides him away, towards the castle. Malory and Clay get up and follow, Clay a little reluctantly.

"There is something seriously wrong with him," Max says.

"I'm going to go talk to Meredith, see if she can talk to him," Shae says. She jumps up and Runs to the mansion.

Shortly after Shae leaves, Cooky comes out to the tables and tells us food is ready. We all walk over to the table she's set up by the Dining Hall doors and find everything a person could possibly want BBQed laying on the table. I grab two corn on the cobs, some ribs, chicken drumsticks, watermelon, and walk back over to our table.

We eat in silence and just enjoy being outside.

There are some birds in the trees, singing the night life into the evening. I look up and get a glance at the night sky in I don't know how long.

"Wow, it's beautiful," I whisper.

"It sure is," Charlie says. I look over at him and he's staring at me. I feel my face turn red and I quickly look back at the sky.

Can Charlie really change? Can he really not be how Libby and Shae says he is? I feel like once someone is his age, he's pretty much who he's going to be. I mean, I know people can change but I feel like he'd have to change his personality. A person's personality can't really be changed, can it?

When I finish eating, I get up and take my stuff over to the trash bin. When I turn, I see Charlie has followed me over.

"Wanna go for a walk?" he asks.

My first instinct is to say no and go back to the group but a very small voice tells me to give him a chance.

"Ummm, sure," I say. I see Libby and Shae start to stand up but I wave at them, letting them know it's okay.

We walk around the right of the mansion, over by the Hospital Wing. We find a quiet little sitting area with benches surrounding a water fountain. Charlie motions for me to sit, so I do.

"So how do you like your place?" he asks.

"Our place," I correct him, "is great. Quite a bit bigger than I had expected but I guess to house all of us, it needs to be."

"Yeah, it's pretty great. All the professors I've talked to, have said the place has everything they could have asked for. It's amazing," Charlie says, scooting a little closer to me. I'm not 100% sure if it was intentional or out of habit.

"That's great," I say. I look around, trying to find something to talk about.

"So where exactly did you grow up?" Charlie asks.

"Umm, New York City," I say.

"Oh, I've been there quite a few times. Not too many Rifts. I wonder if that's because Vanessa lived there and she didn't want to draw attention to herself," he states.

"Maybe," I say and then change the subject away from Vanessa, it's still not easy for me to talk about her. "Where are you originally from?"

"Clay and I are from Los Angeles. My parents ran a Demi-god Housing there," he must have seen my questioning look because he says, "A Demi-god Housing is basically a hotel for Demi-gods and other Leaders visiting the area. We had a lot of Internationals stay with us when there was a Gathering in Los Angeles. or if they were just flying in and had a layover, or they were heading somewhere else."

"Gatherings?" I ask.

"Well, Conferences is another word for it. It's when all the Leaders get together and discuss important happenings in their region. Internationals is pretty self-explanatory, people from different continents," he says. I nod, I figured that one out.

"When did you move to The Pit?" I ask.

"Eight years ago. It was starting to be apparent that Vanessa and the Rifts were getting stronger. Meredith had sent out all the Seekers to bring us all in when 75% of the kids started to disappear. All the Demi-god Housings closed and Internationals found other ways to communicate with each other so that traveling wasn't necessary," Charlie says, looking down at his hands.

"Eight years? That's a long time. But being a Guardian, you must have been able to get out quite a bit?"

"Yeah, that helped a lot. I felt bad for Shae and Libby, and the other girls. They didn't really get to go out much," he says, running his hand through his hair. He's really quite handsome when he's not being a tool.

"So girls can't be in the Guard?"

"Oh no, they can. Just the girls you know don't have a Talent that allows them to be in the Guard right now. Libby could be because she's a Shifter and Healer. We have taken her with us on a couple missions when we thought we'd found some kids the Rifts had taken because she's so good with kids. More times than not, though, it turned out to be false information. We could tell each time we didn't find anyone, it hurt her deeply, so we try not to take her if we can help it."

"She is a very sweet person. I can see how she'd be a good one to take when it comes to kids," I say.

"When you lived in New York, what did you do for fun?" Charlie asks, turning towards me so that he's sitting with one leg bent on the bench.

"Well, I wasn't allowed out except to go swimming on the weekends and even then, the community pool was empty when we'd go. I read a lot of books and watched a lot of movies. I'd draw or paint when I didn't have anything to read or watch," I answer, trying not to think too much about my time with Vanessa.

"You weren't even allowed to go to the mall or anything?" Charlie asks sounding doubtful.

"Nope, Vanessa didn't let me go anywhere except to school. She even went grocery shopping alone. She always went to get me new clothes when I needed them. I didn't get things because I wanted them, I got them because they were a necessity. Luckily for her and unluckily for me, I didn't grow much after the 7th grade. The clothes I got from The Closet, are the newest clothes I've gotten in five years," I say matter-of-factly.

"You're kidding"? Charlie asks, mouth hanging open and then his eyes travel down to my chest. One eyebrow raises and with a smirk, he says, "Well, I know you've grown a little since the 7th grade."

I cross my arms over my chest and tilt my head in a disbelieving way.

"Sorry, that was crude," he says.

"You think?"

"Sorry," he says, sounding embarrassed but then he asks again. "You really didn't go anywhere?"

Looking down at my hands I answer, "Nope."

"That didn't seem odd to you?" he asks.

"No, not at all. I didn't know any different. I didn't go to the mall or grocery store, so I didn't see teenagers there, walking around by themselves. I assumed all parents went out and did the shopping alone. I did think it was strange she never let me go to friends' houses when they invited me over when I was in elementary school but she always had a good excuse as to why I couldn't go. After 5th grade, people stopped asking me over," I shrug.

Charlie just shakes his head.

CHAPTER 24 - ANIMA GEMELLA

C harlie has been asking me questions for about two hours. He hasn't really given me a chance to ask him any, he just keeps firing one after another at me. He has just asked me what my favorite time of year is when Shae, Libby, and Max walk around the corner of the Hospital Wing.

"There you are," Libby says, sounding relieved. She looks over at Charlie and sizes him up. "Have you been behaving yourself?"

"Yes, Mom, I have," Charlie says, a little bit too snarkily.

"Good, I was afraid I'd have to kick your ass," Shae says, walking over and sitting between us.

"I'm always ready for a rumble, Shae!" Charlie says, wrapping his arm around her shoulders and then removes it quickly. He peeks behind her and winks at me.

"What's up?" I ask.

"We were trying to find you to see if you wanted to look for Meredith and Doc, to talk to them about switching rooms. It's almost 11," Shae says. She nudges me and adds, "Unless you've changed your mind and you're wanting to keep the Suite?"

"No, no I haven't," I answer. I look at Charlie and say, "Thank you for hanging out with me. I'm sorry I didn't get a chance to ask you many questions."

"You aren't keeping the Suite?" Charlie asks. "It's a pretty awesome place."

"It's too much for one person. Plus, Meredith and Doc deserve it more than I do. I'll be happier in a regular room down with everyone else," I say.

"Too much maybe for you. If you don't want it, I'll take it," Alysa says, walking up the path from the front of the mansion.

"Nobody is offering it to you," Shae says. "And did you hear her say, 'deserves'. You don't deserve anything."

"Whatever," Alysa says snottily to her sister.

"Where's my brother?" Libby asks.

"Oh, I put him to bed," Alysa says, eyeing me with a look.

"What have you done to him?" Shae asks. "We all know he wouldn't be hanging around you if you hadn't done something to him."

"I haven't done anything to him that he hasn't wanted done. He's just realized that he wants a real woman, not a little girl," Alysa says, glaring at me.

I get up and walk away. I feel like I could explode. If it's true, that she has done something to Ty, I'll......

I don't know what I'll do but my thoughts aren't good right now. I can hear Alysa saying something but I don't know what. I hear Shae yelling at her but again, I'm too far away to hear what she's saying, also.

"Hey, wait," Charlie says from behind me.

I take a deep breath and stop, calming myself before I turn around.

Charlie steps in front of me and asks, "You okay?"

"Yeah, I'm fine. I just want to find Meredith and Doc and get our rooms switched. I'm getting tired again," I say.

"You don't have to lie. I know you're upset about Ty and Alysa," he says, coming closer to me. "Do you want a hug?"

I shrug. Charlie steps even closer and pulls me into a big bear hug. My face presses into his chest, he smells like a fresh, rainy day.

"Emma?" Charlie whispers my name as a question.

"Yeah," I say, looking up at him.

"Can I kiss you?" he asks huskily.

"I...." I don't get my answer out before he's bending his head down and kissing me softly on the lips. It's not electric like kissing Ty.

I guess since I didn't stop him, he steps closer to me, and kisses me deeper. I don't kiss him back. I keep my hands on his chest, but he wraps his arms around my waist. After another minute, I break away, and pull back.

"Sorry, you were saying?" Charlie asks, smiling down at me.

"I was going to say 'I don't know' but..." I answer, not sure if I'm annoyed with him for kissing me again without me actually saying yes or if I'm still annoyed with Alysa.

"I'm sorry, I know I said I'd wait until you said I could but I have been wanting to kiss you like that since the first time I met you. I know that last time, the first time I kissed you, wasn't all that nice, and I truly am sorry about that. This should have been our first kiss," Charlie says, he grabs a strand of my hair and puts it behind my ear.

"The problem is Charlie, I don't know how I feel about you. Yes, I have... had, feelings for Ty but I don't know how I feel about him now and even those feelings, I don't understand them. You just kissing me like that, it confuses me," I say, stepping back away from him.

"I can work with confusing," he says, smiling at me.

"I'm serious," I say, annoyance rearing its head.

"I am, too. If you didn't like me, you wouldn't be confused. I think you're confused because you like Ty but you also like me," he says crossing his arms over his chest, stubbornly.

I put my head in my hands and try to think. Is he right? Do I like him? Every time I think about him, Ty bursts through my thoughts.

"I'm sorry, Charlie, I really don't know how I feel

about you. Like I said before, you're pretty intense for me. I've... I've never had a boyfriend before, so I've never...... you know," I turn bright red. I'm not ashamed to still be a virgin but it's still embarrassing telling a cute guy, who just kissed me, that I'm still a virgin.

"Now I don't believe that!" Charlie says surprised.

"Remember, I never got to go out. I never got to have friends over or go over to their houses. How was I supposed to have a boyfriend if I couldn't see him?"

"You never sneaked? Were there any guys from your school that you were even interested in?"

"No, I never sneaked. That never crossed my mind. I wanted to please my mom, I mean, my aunt. There was a guy or two from my school I thought was cute but none of them ever really talked to me. Like here, there were mean girls, and no one went against them. The girls didn't like me, so the guys didn't like me," I say, wrapping my arms around myself.

"I know why the girls didn't like you," he says. "They were jealous."

"Of what?" I ask, shocked he'd even think that.

He's about to answer when Shae and Libby catch up to us.

"I'm so sorry about her, Em, she really is such a bitch. We'll figure out what's going on with Ty," Shae says, coming to stand next to me.

"Max went to go see if Meredith and Doc are in the Hospital Wing, I told him we'd meet him in the Dining

Hall," Libby says.

"What floor are you guys on?" Charlie asks Libby and Shae.

"The 2nd floor," they answer at the same time.

"I'm on the 4th. Come and get me when it's time to move her stuff, I'll help," Charlie says, he stoops down and kisses me on the cheek. He winks at me when he stands up and leaves. Little butterflies flutter in my stomach. Nothing like with Ty but a little flutter.

"What... was that?" Shae asks.

"Nothing," I say. I really don't want to get into it with them.

"Didn't look like nothing," Libby says, staring at Charlie's back as he walks away.

"It was a kiss on the cheek, it's nothing," I say. "Let's go, I'm getting tired again."

As I start walking, I see Libby and Shae give each other meaningful looks. I appreciate them looking out for me but I'm starting to think Charlie really is changing. He's a totally different guy here than how he was at The Pit.

I pretend I didn't notice their look and keep walking. When I round the Hospital Wing and head towards the Dining Hall, the girls catch up to me and link our arms together.

"I'm just going to say one thing and then I'll leave it alone," Libby says, "Just be careful."

"I will," I say. "Thanks." I truly do mean it. It feels

good to have people worry about me. I mean, really, worry about me. The people here, aside from Alysa and Malory, treat me a great deal better than Vanessa ever did.

When we walk into the Dining Hall, Max, Doc, and Meredith are waiting for us.

"Emma, Max said you were looking for us?" Meredith says in a questioning tone.

"Yeah, I am. I wanted to see if we could switch rooms. I really, really don't want the Suite. I would be much happier having a regular room. Will you two please switch rooms with me?" I ask.

"Emma, that room is for you. We don't want to take it from you," Doc says, putting a hand on my shoulder, in a fatherly way.

"You aren't taking it from me, I'm giving it to you," I say, smiling at him and Meredith.

They look at each other and I plead, "Please? Your room is right by Shae's and Libby's. It's meant to be."

"Alright, if you're sure?" Meredith says.

"Oh, I am, I totally am!" I say, clapping my hands together.

"Well, we've got some things to move," Doc says, laughing as he starts to walk back through the Dining Hall.

"Actually, I think I can make the process easy. Let's go to your room, I mean my room," I say, laughing. "I've seen all my stuff, I just need to see yours and I can transfer them to the other rooms for us. They won't be where you want them but at least we won't have to make 100 trips up and down the stairs."

"You'll wear yourself out again," Doc says sternly.

"This will be nothing compared to earlier today. Plus, I'm already tired and ready to go to bed, so being a little bit more tired isn't going to hurt me," I say, patting Doc's shoulder.

"I don't think---" Doc starts to say but Meredith cuts him off.

"She's already proven she can do more than what we think, if she wants to do it, I think we should let her," she says. Doc looks at her and then at me. I can see him warring with himself on me being a Changeling and me already being advanced in my Jumping talent.

"Alright but you have to promise me no more until we do more practicing, simple practicing," Doc says, raising an eyebrow at me.

"I promise," I say.

We make it up to the 2nd floor using the spiral staircases and go to Meredith and Doc's room. I walk in and look around. Everyone follows me in.

"Okay, I think to do this I need everyone to be out, just so I don't accidentally hit anyone with anything," I say as I turn towards the door. They all hurriedly step back out into the hallway.

Closing my eyes, I concentrate on the stuff in this room. I visualize it going from here, all the way up to the Suite. I, then, think about all of my stuff, still in my bags, being placed in this room. I take a deep breath and open my eyes. Doc's and Meredith's things are gone and my bags are sitting on the bed, my bed.

"That was awesome!" I hear Libby say from the doorway. I look over and see them all staring at me.

"We are going to have to get you into some classes and see what you can really do," Meredith says, sounding awed.

"We'll leave you to your room but get some rest," Doc says sternly but then smiles at me.

Libby and Shae hop out of the way so they can leave.

The girls help me unpack and organize my room. I don't have a lot of decorations, but I can go to The Closet and find some things tomorrow. Wait, The Closet?

"Hey, I didn't see The Closet anywhere. Does Beth have her store here?" I ask.

"Uh, I don't remember seeing it either. We'll have to ask tomorrow. I saw her eating dinner, so she's here," Libby says.

By the time we get done unpacking and talking, it's a quarter after one in the morning.

Shae yawns and says, "Alright, I'm done for the day. See you in the morning." She stands up and heads to the door.

"I'm tired too. Night, Emma," Libby says, giving me

a hug and heading out the door behind Shae.

"Night, Shae. Night, Libby," I say, yawning.

I lay back and pull out a book to read. It happens to be the one Ty had given me for my birthday. I put it back and pull out another, but I don't feel like reading it either. Sitting up, I walk over to my sliding glass door and step out onto my balcony. I take a few deep breaths and concentrate on relaxing. I feel tired but my mind won't stop turning.

Coming back into my room, I lay on my bed and try not to think. I toss and turn for another hour before I get up and walk downstairs. I want to get a couple books on Menatlist and Healing in Library 2.

When I get down to the foyer, I think I hear something coming from the Dining Hall but it's probably just Cooky. I go into Library 2 and start looking for books about spells, or whatever they're called, that people can put on another person's mind. I find a couple and go sit by the big window. I don't turn on any lights, the moon is bright enough outside that I can see just fine. Also, my eyesight in the dark has sharpened. Another side effect from the Change, no doubt.

I take my time reading, let it all really soak in. I've gone through four books and haven't really found anything that could help me. I put the book I just finished, down and lie back, grab one of the huge pillows and hug it to me.

My mind starts to wonder and it comes back to Ty

and Alysa.

Ty and Alysa. It sure seems like something is going on there, something Alysa has done to Ty but how do we prove it. I don't want to figure it out just because I would like to be with Ty. I want to figure it out because if she is doing something to him, it's not right and she needs to be stopped.

What about Charlie? I feel like I could like him, but he scares me. And it's not how he thinks of it. I feel like he wants more than what I'm capable of giving him. He seems like a very sexual guy and I am not ready for that with him.

My eyes feel really heavy and I can tell I'm close to falling asleep. I shut my eyes and try to shut my mind off. I'm just on the edge of sleep when I hear someone come into the library.

"Shh, no one is up, it's fine," a female voice says... of course it's Alysa.

"I thought you and Ty..." a male voice trails off, it's Charlie's voice.

"We are but he's still adjusting, so it's difficult to do anything right now and I need a little something to hold me over," Alysa says.

"I really don't think I should, I'm finally getting somewhere with Emma. You don't want me to ruin that, do you?" Charlie asks.

"Don't worry, she won't find out. I won't tell her, will you?" Alysa asks in a very seductive voice.

"Hell no, I won't," Charlie says.

I hear kissing and then unzipping of pants. Just as I hear a small giggle, I fall deeper into asleep.

❖ ❖ ❖

I wake up to early morning sunlight streaming in and birds chirping in the trees outside the window, that tells me the sun must have just started to come up. I glance at my watch and see it's just after five o'clock. I must have only been asleep for an hour or so. I stretch and look around the library, it looks the same as it did when I first got here.

A memory from what I had heard right before falling asleep comes to me in a rush. Did Charlie and Alysa really come in here and fool around or had I just dreamt it since I was thinking of them and Ty right before sleep took me?

Shaking my head, I stand up and head to my room. I can smell breakfast being cooked in the kitchen as I make my way over the walkway above the dining hall. Cooky is making Cinnamon Rolls!

I get to my room and turn on my shower. It's been well over a month since I last showered in an actual shower, the pool and showers at The Pit cleaned me enough but there's just something about standing in a shower that makes my heart smile.

I strip my clothes off and put them in a basket in

the corner of my room. Stepping into the hot shower instantly relaxes me. Libby had put all my shower necessities in here last night, all lined up in order of what gets used first. Shampoo, conditioner, razer, and then body soap. I take a little bit longer than I usually would, just enjoying the fact that I have my own bathroom. I decide to shave my legs, I think I want to check out the beach today. Now that could really make my heart smile.

I step out of the bathroom, wrapped in a towel, and make my way to my closet. I pick out a blue tank and grab a light hoodie to take just in case it gets chilly. My dresser has my shorts and undergarments in it. I decide to put my swimsuit on, I can always come back up here to change if I go for a swim. I throw my suit on, black shorts, and my tank top, no way am I walking around with a bikini top and shorts. I'm proud of my chest size but not brave enough to show it off.

I look at the clock on my desk and its half past six o'clock. Cooky usually has breakfast ready at seven o'clock, so I'll go get Libby and Shae before heading down, see if they want to go down to the beach with me after we eat.

As I'm leaving my room, I see a key on a blue lanyard hanging next to my door. I hadn't noticed it last night. There's a note under it.

It says:

This is to lock your door when you leave. Not that anyone would dare to steal anything, it's just for peace of mind. Doc

I grab the key and notice it has ELH engraved on it, my initials. I step outside my door and lock it. Shoving the key into my pocket, I step next door to Libby's room and knock. I can hear her moving around in her room and then her door opens.

Smiling, Libby says, "Good morning, Emma! Did you sleep well?" She steps aside and waves me in.

As I'm walking in I reply, "Morning, Libby. I couldn't really sleep so I went down to Library 2 and read some books about Mentalists. I couldn't really find anything in the books I had read but I know there's a ton more books to go through. I fell asleep on the couch in there and slept for a couple hours. But I think I had a weird dream. I thought maybe we could go down to the beach and check it out after we eat breakfast. Smells like Cooky is making Cinnamon Rolls."

"I love Cinnamon Rolls. And I was hoping we'd get a chance to go to the beach soon, I've been dying to go. What was your dream about?" Libby says, as she rummages around in her closet.

I tell her what I think I dreamt about, "But I don't know if it was real or not. I was just about to fall asleep when it all happened. That's why I don't know if it was real or a dream."

"It does sound like something Charlie and Alysa would do but if you think he's trying to change for you, maybe you did dream it. You said you were thinking about them right before you fell asleep?" Libby asks as she starts to change, not shy at all.

"Yeah, I was. I was thinking about how awful it would be if Alysa was doing something to Ty and how we would need to do something about it. I was also thinking about how I'm not sure how I feel about Charlie," I say, sitting down cross legged on her bed. Just then, there is a knock at the door.

"Would you get that? It's probably Shae," Libby says as she walks into the bathroom.

I get up and answer the door. Sure enough, it's Shae.

She gives me a big hug and says, "Morning Emma, Libby ready yet?"

"Hi Shae, she's almost ready," I answer, shutting the door behind her and going back to sit on the bed. Shae sits in the desk chair.

"I was hoping we'd go to the beach today," Shae says, pulling at her bikini string sticking out under her white tank top.

I laugh and say, "Yeah, we were hoping too."

Libby walks out of the bathroom and greets Shae. She sits on the bed and turns to me.

"Will you tell me now about what happened between you and my brother?" Libby asks, looking at me with her face in her hands, her elbows resting on her knees.

"Yeah, you still haven't told us what happened during the water fight back at The Pit," Shae says, wiggling her eyebrows at me.

"Or when he was in your room and I know he went swimming with you," Libby adds.

Sighing and turning a little pink in the face, I say, "We just kissed."

"Just kissed?" They both say at the same time. We all laugh, they really do act more like twins than they do with their actual twins.

"Okay, well maybe it was really, really good kissing," I say, turning downright red now.

"Who initiated the first kiss?" Libby says, looking serious, as she stares at me.

Putting my hands over my face, embarrassed, I mumble, "Me."

"What did Ty do when you kissed him?" she asks.

I decide to tell them everything that happened. From the moment Libby started spraying us with water until we were walking out of our hiding place, holding hands. When Ty was in my room and when we went swimming.

"Oh my lanta," Libby breaths.

"Yeah, that's more than just a kiss. You really felt all that electricity when you guys were kissing?" Shae asks.

"I did, I don't know about Ty. It was pretty intense but a good intense, you know," I say.

"That's how it feels when Max and I kiss. It's getting easier to function while it's going on but it definitely hasn't lessened and we've been together for two years now," Libby says, looking dreamily at the far wall of her room.

"Function as in fu---" Shae starts to say but Libby cuts her off.

"SHAE!" Libby shouts, "No, that is not what I mean."

"You mean you guys haven't consummated your relationship yet?" Shae asks, looking surprised.

"I would have told you if we had. We both want to wait until we are absolutely sure we are Anima Gemella," Libby says, her cheeks turning a light pink.

"Anima Gemella? What's that?" I ask.

"It means 'Soulmate' in Italian. It's what we call it when we, Demi-gods, find our one true love, our soulmate, our partner for eternity," Libby answers, smiling at me.

"And if what you say you've felt, you've both found your Anima Gemella. Your description of what it feels like when you join, even if just kissing, is exactly what the Elder's wrote it would feel like," Shae says, looking slightly upset.

"What's the matter?" I ask.

"Oh it's nothing," Shae says, standing up and walking over to the sliding glass door.

"Don't lie, tell her," Libby says.

"Ugh, I don't want to, you tell her," Shae says, opening the door and stepping out on the balcony.

"Tell me what?" I ask looking from where Shae was just standing to Libby sitting next to me.

Libby takes a deep breath and says, "Shae had, has, these same feelings for someone. When she asked him about it, he said he also felt the same way but wasn't ready to be, I quote, 'stuck with the same person for the rest of my life, we're too young for that type of commitment.' He dumped her and started going after any girl that would have him, which is most girls."

"Don't tell me it's Charlie? Why didn't you guys tell me?" I say, getting a knot in my stomach.

I hadn't heard Shae come back in from the balcony but she's standing just inside the curtain.

"Yeah, it's Charlie. Unfortunately, we didn't have the Anima Gemella talk until after we had sex. He confessed to feeling the exact same way I was feeling but as Libby said, he didn't want to have that type of commitment as we were only 17 at the time. We hadn't even went through the Change yet but all the Change did was make our feelings stronger. Doc thinks if Demi-gods don't commit to their Anima Gemella when they've found them, the feelings can intensify until they can't stand it anymore. It's why I can't stand him touching me. The feeling of being shocked from my head to my toes and knowing I can't do anything about it, doesn't feel good. It just about brings me to my knees," Shae says, wrapping her arms around her chest. "I've had three years to practice staying out of Charlie's touch but every once in a while we'll connect and those damn feelings rear up. I've tried dating other guys and I like them but it's nothing like when I'm with Charlie."

"I think he dates or is with so many girls so he can drown out the feelings he has for Shae. It's pretty immature but it's how Charlie deals with it, until he comes to his senses and comes back to Shae," Libby says, standing up and giving Shae a sideways hug.

"In his dreams," Shae says but I can tell she doesn't mean it.

"So your saying that Ty is my Anima Gemella? We just met, how can that be right?" I ask.

"It doesn't matter if you've just met or have known each other your entire lives, if you are Anima Gemella, you have been from the beginning of time," Libby says.

"The beginning of time?" I ask, doubtfully.

"Yeah, every time a Demi-god dies, a little bit of their soul is reattached when we are born again. We can't remember our past lives but our Anima Gemella is the same soul," Libby says.

"We are supposed to be strongest with our Anima Gemella, it gives our Talents a supercharge," Shae says half laughing, half scathingly.

"But how can you be sure that the feelings you have for someone is 100% the feelings the Elder's said they'd be? Can't someone just be really, really attracted to someone?" I ask. Being told that Ty and I might be Anima Gomella's has me freaking out a little bit. Not that I wouldn't mind, Ty seems like an amazing guy, but it's just that I did, in fact, just meet him. I'm just now getting used to the idea of being a Demi-god, now they're telling me I've found my soulmate?

"Because being attracted to someone and having the Anima Gemella feelings are completely different. How do you feel when Charlie touches you?" Libby says, side glancing at Shae.

I don't even have to think about it, "It doesn't feel like anything compared to when Ty has touched me. Even when I was in the Hospital Wing, at The Pit, when he'd touch my foot, I'd get a zap."

"What about when other guys have touched you? And I don't mean in a sexual way but in a hug, or a brush of a shoulder, or when they shake your hand? Any type of contact," Shae asks.

"Same, nowhere near how it feels when Ty touches me," I say, lowering my head into my hands.

After a few minutes of silence, Libby says, "I guess we've found the way to break the spell Alysa put on Ty," I look up and she's beaming at me.

"How?" I ask.

"You have to kiss him," Shae says. "Sooner the better. Knowing my sister, she's probably put some kind of strong Love Hold on him. The longer it stays on him, the harder it will be to break it, even for his Anima Gemella."

I can feel my face pale.

"I have to kiss him?" I stammer out.

"You said you've kissed him before," Libby says.

I stand up and say, "Yeah but that was in a secluded place."

"I don't think you'll have a choice on finding him alone, I bet my sister will be by his side from here on out, she has to stay in contact with him when you're around, until the hold has really taken root," Shae says.

"So when you see him today, you have to walk right up to him and kiss him. It doesn't have to be Rated R, just a 1-2-3 kiss, long enough for it to register in his brain you're kissing but not long enough you'll need to get a room," Libby says laughing.

"This is going to be humiliating," I say.

"No, it won't. You're saving him from Alysa, you just happen to have to break the Hold a different way than what we normally would have to," Libby says.

"What did Meredith say when you asked her about it?" I asked Shae, grasping at straws that didn't lead me to kissing the hottest guy here in front of everyone standing around at the time.

"She said she'd look into it but she said it did sound like a Hold. So far, Alysa hasn't stuck around long enough when Doc and Meredith have been around, for them to Read her. Malory has kind of been a watchdog for her, alerting her when Doc and Meredith come into a room. Which is why I know she's done something to him," Shae says, grinding her teeth together.

"Like Shae said, the sooner the better. It's already been a couple of days since he started acting funny. We can't let it go much longer," Libby says, taking my arm in hers as she walks towards the door. "Let's go have breakfast. We can go to the beach and enjoy the morning but if we see them after that, you need to make your move."

"OOOkay," I stammer out, not at all excited at the thought. "But what if we truly aren't Anima Gemella. Me kissing him won't do anything and Alysa will be pissed"

"I know you two are Anima Gemella and we'll be there to ward off Alysa," Shae says, slightly laughing at the thought.

CHAPTER 25 - LOVE
HOLD BROKEN

We walk down to the Dining Hall and find barely anyone here yet. Sure enough, Cooky was making Cinnamon Rolls. She's laid out platters of fruits, eggs, bacon, and sausage. A whole table by itself has the Cinnamon Rolls on it.

We all load our plates up and head to a spot to sit at one of the huge dining tables. We're halfway done eating when Charlie, Clay, and Max show up. After loading their plates to the point of overflowing, they come over and sit by us. I notice Shae, scoot a little further away from Charlie when he sits next to her. He sits by her not even noticing what he's doing as he's talking to Clay, like his subconscious led him there. Max walks around the table and sits next to Libby, who I see relaxes quite a bit as soon as he sits down.

Hmm, I'll have to pay more attention to other couples and see if they all have the same reaction when their partner shows up. Might be an Anima Gemella thing or it might just be a Max and Libby thing.

Looking back at Charlie, I get another flash from last night. He and Alysa fooling around. I wish I knew if that was real or not. Or maybe I don't want to know. It would be horrible for them to mess around, especially now that I know about him and Shae.

Max interrupts my thoughts and asks Libby, "Since it's Saturday and we don't have any classes, what are we doing today?"

"Shae, Emma, and I were thinking about going to the beach to check it out, you guys want to come?" she says, smiling.

"Yeah, sounds fun. We haven't had a chance to go check it out for enjoyment purposes," Max says, holding a strawberry up for Libby to bite. I look away, it seems a little too intimate for onlookers.

"Definitely!" Charlie whoops, "Babes and the beach, what more can a guy ask for?"

"A brain," Shae says as she stands up and takes her plate to the table.

"Good one, Shae," Charlie says mock laughing at her. He then looks at me and asks, "Hey, Emma, you get moved into your new room? You guys never came and got me to help."

"That's because Emma Jumped all of her stuff and Meredith's and Doc's stuff. It only took about five seconds and then another hour or so to organize her room," Libby says, smiling proudly over at me, like a big sister.

"She could give you some lessons on Jumping," Clay says, laughing at his brother.

"Emma can give me all the lessons she wants," Charlie says, wagging his eyebrows at me and then winks. After finding out about him and Shae, that little flirtation annoys me.

I roll my eyes at him, stand up and take my plate over to the table. Shae is talking to Cooky when I get to her.

"Great breakfast, as usual," Shae is saying to Cooky.

"Yeah, thank you so much. I can't remember the last time I had a homemade Cinnamon Roll," I say.

"Glad you liked it. Meredith told me last night, after this weekend, she wants hearty, healthy, meals as classes and trainings will be starting back up on Monday. She's going to make sure everyone is working as hard as possible, now that there are plenty of rooms for classes," Cooky says, smiling at us.

"No more Cinnamon Rolls?" Shae asks sounding like a little kid being told they can't have any more candy.

"I'm afraid not, not unless it's a special occasion," Cooky says, patting Shae's shoulder as she walks back towards the kitchen doors.

Libby walks up to us and says, "I told the guys they can meet us down at the beach. We could wait for them but I want to check it out before their craziness shows up."

"Good thinking," Shae says.

We walk out to the foyer and out the main doors. I hadn't noticed the signs that resemble street signs standing in the grass. If we were to walk straight, it would take us to the landing strip which is called East Beach. If we went right, we'd go to South Beach and left would be North Beach. If we walked around the side of the castle and walked on the path through the trees, we'd come to West Beach.

"Who came up with these names?" Shae asked.

"The Guardians," Libby says, laughing. "It's what happens when a bunch of guys decide to name something. Simple and logical"

"Maybe we can figure out better names for them once we get there," I say.

We decide to go to East Beach, the sun would still be low enough the view would be amazing. We follow the path and make our way through a small patch of palm trees. It only takes 20 minutes before we can really start to hear the waves.

"I love that sound," Shae says, looking dreamily up the path.

"Well, you do have the Water Talent. I bet it'll feel amazing to be in the ocean," Libby says, touching Shae's arm.

"You betcha," Shae says, smiling over at her.

We walk another 15 yards and then we're walking on sand with the ocean spread out in front of us. We just stop and stare.

It's a good ten minutes before we talk. Shae breaks the silence.

"It's the most beautiful thing I have ever seen," she says, walking forward.

"Same here," Libby and I say at the same time. We giggle, it's the first time we've ever done that.

We get about five feet from where the sand starts to get wet, before we stop and take our shorts and tank tops off. Shae's the first to run to the water. She takes a graceful leap and then dives into the water, popping up about 20 yards away from us.

"The water feels amazing, get in here!" Shae shouts at us before diving back under the water.

Libby and I run to the water and dive into the wave coming at us. Shae's right, the water feels absolutely amazing! It's not as warm as the Pool back at The Pit but it's not too warm that it feels like we're taking a bath. Also, not so cool that we're cold. It's the perfect temperature.

I swim to the surface and see Libby beside me, Shae swims up to us.

"This is the best I've felt in years," Shae says, lying back, floating with her arms and legs outstretched.

"You haven't been in open water in far too long. I bet how you feel is how a fish would feel getting back in the water, maybe not that bad but the relief would be close enough," Libby says, lying back like Shae.

I do the same and we float around for who knows how long.

All of a sudden something has me around the waist and is pulling me down. I hear Shae's and Libby's shouts of surprise but then I can feel Libby being pulled down also. I faintly hear Shae shout some curse words and then I can't hear anything but the deafening sound of silence from the water.

I roll my body so I'm facing whatever is holding me and I kick out. I would have figured I would have had to fight more but one push off and I'm free. I swim back a few feet, open my eyes, I peer into the water, trying to see what had a hold of me.

I once again find that I am not in desperate need of air yet. I move my hands in half circles to keep my body in the same spot. I can see quite a ways in front of me but can't seem to find what had ahold of me.

Whoosh!!!

Something swims in front me fast. I take after it, swimming as fast as I can. I reach out and grab a foot. A foot? It's a human foot. I pull back with one fast tug and Charlie crashes into me.

I go flipping backwards a little ways until I can stop myself. I look over at him and he looks like he's laughing but then points up.

Once we break the surface, he's laughing hysterically.

"You're pretty strong, Em! You must have a Water Talent," Charlie says between laughs and spitting water out of his mouth that has splashed in with the little waves we made as we came up.

"Where's Libby?" I look around, she, Shae, and Max are a good 50 yards away from us. "Did Max pull her down?"

"Yeah, we saw you gals out here. We thought we'd see if we could scare you. I think we scared Shae more than anyone. You didn't seem scared at all," Charlie says, swimming over to me.

Now that I know he and Shae are Anima Gemella, I feel uncomfortable being this close to him. I push off of him with my hands and swim towards the others I beat Charlie by quite a bit.

"You were under for so long, Charlie came back up for air and went down to find you, I'm glad he did. Are you okay?" Libby asks, swimming over to me.

"I'm fine, water doesn't bother me," I say matter-of-factly.

"I'm pretty sure she has a Water Talent," Charlie says and then adds, "She's extremely strong and fast."

"Let's go back to shore," I say, as Charlie swims closer to me.

We all start making our way back to shore. We went further out in the ocean from the boys' sneak attack than we probably would have had they just swam up to us.

I make it back before anyone else. They are breathing pretty heavily, except Shae, by the time they get to shore.

"You are fast," Shae says. "I was swimming as fast as I could and you still beat me back."

"Can we not swim like we Run?" I ask.

"Only those who have a Water Talent," Libby says, lying down on a towel Max must have brought her. I look around and see that they brought a whole pile of them.

Clay's lying beside it with his eyes closed. I walk over and he reaches out, grabs a towel, and hands it to me.

"Thank you," I say.

"You're welcome," he says, still with his eyes closed.

Remembering he's a Mentalist, I ask him, "Did you know I was coming? Could you read my thoughts?"

"No, I could feel someone walking this way, I assumed it was for a towel," Clay says, opening his eyes and smiling at me.

"Oh," is all I can cleverly come up with to say.

I turn around, drying my hair with a towel, and walk back over to where Shae and Libby are now lying in the sand on their towels. Charlie is lounging next to Max. Charlie looks up and ogles me from toe to head and back down again. His eyes go slower on the way back down, stopping at my chest, my stomach, and then makes his way back down my legs. A small smile spreads across his face. I stop drying my hair and wrap my towel around me, tightly. I go and sit on the other side of everyone, next to Shae.

We lay here for a while, enjoying the warmth from the sun, and the sound of the waves. It's very relaxing. But all too soon, someone steps into my sunlight. I open my eyes and see an outline of a large man standing in front of me.

"Mind if I lay here?" Charlie asks and once again, doesn't wait for a reply.

"Sure, but I'm going for a swim, I'm hot," I say, just needing an excuse to leave.

"That you are," I hear Charlie whisper under his breath. I look back but it doesn't look like anyone else has heard, or if they have, they aren't acting like they did. I pretend I didn't hear either.

I dive into the water and swim down and out for quite a ways. Coming up to swim on my back. Floating out here is just as relaxing as lying down back on shore. I hear a laugh that's becoming an all too familiar sound. I sit up so that my legs are submerged in the water and look back at the beach, Alysa and Ty have shown up.

Just seeing Ty makes my heart skip a beat. What if he truly is my Anima Gemella? I don't want to think about it and what I'm going to have to do once I get back to shore so I lie back down and float some more.

Sometime later I hear shouts from shore. I sit up

again and look over, I'm now 70-75 yards away. They're all shouting and pointing towards me. I look down at myself and see nothing. I look back up and see them pointing again but it looks like they're pointing behind me. I look over my shoulder and freeze. A ginormous fin is coming my way. Not just any old fine, a great white shark fin, and it's no less than 20 yards from me.

I dive. It's the only thing I can think of doing. As I dive, I look over my shoulder to see the huge shark diving further under water than it had been, so that it's fin is completely submerged. I kick out and swim as fast as I can, going down deeper, and deeper. The temperature of the water slowly gets cooler.

Over to my right, I see the continental slope, I swim towards it. I'll be closer to shore if I'm next to it and maybe I can find somewhere to hide. I glance behind me and see the shark has gotten closer but not by much. I push harder.

I'm to the slope in seconds, my hands going over the sand and rocks and other objects, trying to find some place I can squeeze into. There is nowhere, it's just one big slab of wall.

I turn around and find the shark feet away, opening its mouth, getting ready to bite me.

I throw out my hands and mentally shout, *STOP!*

To my utter surprise, the shark stops.

HUNGRY, I hear in my head, it's a rough but female sounding voice.

You're hungry? I ask. Am I really talking to a shark?

The shark swims up and down, yes? Does that mean yes?

I'm not food.

Not food? Smell like food.

No, I'm not food, I'm a person. Your food is in the other direction, a long, long ways away. Go out there, go!

The shark turns and starts swimming away.

I stay there with my hands out, making sure she's not going to turn back around. After what feels like hours but most likely only minutes, I, somehow, can sense that she's gone, miles away.

Using the continental shelf, I kick out and up and propel myself towards the surface. Swimming as fast as I can. When I break the surface, I'm now only 30 yards from shore, and the sight I see confuses me. Max is holding on to Libby and Clay is holding Shae back from the water, while Alysa and Charlie are both trying, with all their strength, to hold Ty back. I can see that Shae and Libby are crying. Ty looks half insane, half confused. The instant they see me swimming towards them, Shae and Libby fall to the sand. Ty stops struggling against Alysa and Charlie. Alysa looks at Charlie with a questioning look and I see him shrug slightly.

When I get to where I can stand, I start to walk towards them, not at all exhausted from swimming or lack of air but the fear from the shark chasing me has left me shaking. I've never stayed under water that long. I feel like I could have stayed longer but I wanted to get to shore. I don't want to test my luck with any other sea creatures. Max and Clay run out and grab my arms, helping me make it the rest of the way.

They sit me on the warm sand and Shae and Libby run up and throw themselves on top of me.

"Are you okay?" Libby sobs.

"What happened?" Shae asks at the same time. They're both hiccupping from crying so hard.

"Shark," I whisper out through chattering teeth.

"We saw, but what happened? We saw you dive and you were under for at least 20 minutes," Max says, rubbing Libby's back. She stands up and hugs him.

"I saw it coming so I dove. I swam down and then I saw the continental shelf so I swam to it, thinking I could find somewhere to hide but I couldn't. The shark was on me, about to have me for lunch when I yelled for it to stop, with my mind. She said she was hungry and I explained that I wasn't food and that she had to go back out to sea to find her food, so she turned around and swam away. Then I swam up here," I say with my eyes closed, shaking a little as I think back about how close I was to being shark chow.

Nobody says a thing. I open my eyes and see them all staring at me, except for Alysa, she's trying to get Ty's attention but he hasn't taken his confused eyes off of me.

"But it takes years before someone with a Talent

to talk with animals to be good enough to communicate with them. It starts off by being able to sense
them, sense their moods, but to actually communicate
with words? Years!" Max exclaims. "I can barely understand when I've Shifted into an animal and I've been
practicing for two years now."

"We need to get back to the mansion and tell Meredith," Clay says, standing up and says to Charlie, "Come
with me so you can confirm what I tell them, that way
they can have some kind of idea by the time Emma
makes it back."

Charlie bends down and says, "Are you sure you're
okay?"

"Yes, I'm fine. Go with Clay," I say, still not liking
him being this close with Shae hugging me.

Charlie looks at me for one more second, stands up
but before he leaves, he looks over at Alysa. I see her nod
her head ever so slightly before he turns and he and Clay
Run to The Estate. What was that about?

"Let's start our way back, I'm starving," I say.

"We were just talking about going back for lunch
when that shark showed up," Libby says, sniffling a little.

I get up and hug her. She hugs me back, tightly. She
jerks up straight and when I look at her, she's looking
behind me.

I glance over and see Ty doing something weird.
He takes a step towards me and then a step back. Like

he's dancing but not really. I see Alysa is touching his bare back and mumbling something under her breath, her eyes closed.

I look at Libby and she whispers, "Are you up for it?"

I take a deep breath and nod at her. Shae jumps to her feet and walks over nonchalantly towards her sister.

I walk over, looking at only Ty. Staring into his eyes. He tilts his head to the right and then to the left, like he's trying to figure something out.

Once I reach him, close enough to touch him, Libby and Shae grab Alysa and pull her away from Ty. I reach up and touch Ty's face, he closes his eyes and almost relaxes.

"NO!! Stay away from him you BITCH!" Alysa screams at me. "Let me go!" I hear Libby shout in pain but then she stops instantly. I glance over and see Shae drenching the three of them in water. Alysa is trying to send fire at Shae and Libby and at me but it just gets surrounded by water before it can really leave her hands.

I look back at Ty, his eyes are still shut. I stretch up on my tiptoes and kiss his lips. The instant our lips touch, electricity shoots from them to where my hands are touching his face, down to my heart, to my stomach, all the way down to my toes. I feel like my entire inside is nothing but a lightning bolt. It doesn't make us jump apart, it makes us draw closer. Ty opens his lips a little, mine mimicking his. He tilts his head to his right, I tilt mine to my right. When our tongues touch, it's like an explosion. He wraps his arms around my waist, picks me up, and pulls me into his body.

I can faintly hear something that sounds like a siren going off and then Shae is yelling in pain and shouting, "Alysa, NO! Stop! Don't! Emma, look out!"

I turn my head just in time to see Alysa's ball of fire throw Shae and Libby to the ground. I nudge Ty and he lowers me. Just as my feet hit the ground, Alysa's focus is on me.

Shae is Throwing water at Libby and every time she Throws it at Alysa, it evaporates before it can get close to her. Alysa. Is. Mad!

I stand in front of Ty and wait for Alysa to Throw her fire. She rolls her hands together and just as she's about to Throw it, Shae screams for her to stop, but she doesn't. Alysa Throws the ball of fire as hard as she can. It's not just a ball, it's a ball followed by a torch. It's a torch that's never ending, coming from her hands.

I throw my arms out like I had with the shark and feel the warmth as it hits my hands. I slowly split my hands and move them to my sides, making the fire arch around me and Ty. To Alysa, Shae, Max and Libby, it probably looks like we're being engulfed. I look behind me at Ty, to make sure he's okay, and find him just staring down at me in awe.

I can hear Libby and Shae screaming at Alysa

to stop. She doesn't. I bring my hands back together quickly, clapping them, and intertwining my fingers. A second later, I open them, palms facing her, and force the fire back towards her. I see, and feel, the fire race back to her and she's thrown into the air, falling on to her back.

Libby and Shae race over to me and Ty, crying again. Max on their heels.

"Are you guys okay?" Libby asks, turning me and then Ty, checking us for burns.

"We're fine," I say. "Are you guys okay?"

"I was able to put the Fire out before it got us too bad, but it was enough to let her through to you guys. I'm so sorry, she's totally lost her mind," Shae says, walking back to her sister, who is lying motionless on the sand, breathing slowly.

"We'll take her to Bill, I'm afraid she's really crossed the line this time. Thank goodness you did what you did," Max says looking at me in shock.

"Yeah, how did you do that?" Shae asks.

"I don't know. It's like everything else, I don't know how I do it or did it, I just let my instincts take over," I answer, half hysterical, and shaking slightly.

"Absolutely amazing," Libby says, smiling at me. She then looks behind me and Runs to her brother.

I turn just as Ty falls to the ground, his head in his hands.

"Ty? Ty what's the matter?" Libby asks, touching

his arm.

"My head... it feels like it's about to split open. What did Alysa do to me?" he asks.

"We'll get you to Doc and Sara, we have to be really careful how we Heal you after you've had a Hold on you," Libby says.

Max goes and picks Alysa up while Libby and I put a shoulder under Ty's arms and help him stand. Shae walks beside Max, staring alarmingly at her sister. Ty seems dizzy and wobbly on his feet. We walk slowly up the path, back to the mansion.

CHAPTER 26 - DUPED

Meredith and Doc meet us halfway between the beach and the mansion.

"Oh good heavens!" Meredith exclaims. "What's happened to Alysa?"

"She got what was coming to her," Shae says nastily.

Libby explains what happened from what they could see, that it looked like Alysa was burning Ty and me alive. I explain what I had done.

Doc checks Alysa out first since she's passed out, "She'll be okay. Better take her down to one of the cells, Max."

"Cells?" Libby, Shae, and I say at the same time.

"There's a lower level, below the main floor. It's where the Guardians have set up their headquarters. There are cells down there and it's where the parking garage is at also. Beth has set up The Closet down there for now, too," Meredith explains, as she watches Max walk away with Alysa. "We are going to have to do something about her. This is unacceptable behavior and we've given her plenty of chances to control herself."

"We'll figure it out," Doc says. He's checking Ty out now. "How do you feel?"

"My head is killing me and I'm really dizzy. Very confused," Ty answers, rubbing his temples with his thumbs. "I can remember the last few days but they seem more like dreams than anything, like I had no control over anything I was doing or saying."

"Let's get you to the Hospital Wing, you might have to stay there for a day or two," Doc says, taking Ty out Libby's and my hands.

Before they can take too many steps away, Ty turns and says to me, "Come to the Hospital Wing in a few hours, I really want to talk to you."

"Okay," I say in a small voice.

Meredith steps to Ty's other side and helps Doc walk him the rest of the way to the mansion. Shae, Libby, and I just stand quietly for a few minutes.

Shae finally breaks the silence and says, "I'm going to go find my parents and tell them what Alysa has done. They need to make sure Meredith knows she has their support in whatever they decide her punishment will be."

She Runs away, up towards the mansion.

"Will Ty be okay?" I ask.

"Yeah, he'll be back to normal in a day or two. Holds grow stronger the longer they're on someone.

The older the Demi, the stronger the Hold will be because they'll have more experience with their Talents so therefore more power. Holds can cause permanent damage but since it was only on Ty for a couple of days and done by a fairly young Demi, it won't have any lasting effects on him, I don't think anyways. Alysa kept her Hold Talent a secret. I don't think anyone knew she had it," Libby says.

"Oh," I say as we come into view of the mansion. "Will she be in trouble for hiding it?"

"Not for hiding it but for using it against Ty, yes. She's in big trouble. I'm going to go shower and then I'll go check on Ty."

"I'm going to shower also but I'll wait a bit before I go down to talk to him. Give him a chance to feel better."

We walk into the foyer and silently make our way up the stairs. Crossing the walkway over the dining hall reminds me of how hungry I am.

"I think I'm going to eat now, I'm starving," I say.

"Sounds good, I'll see you later."

I watch Libby walk the rest of the way down the walkway before I turn around. I walk back towards the spiral stairs and make my way down. I grab a couple sandwiches, some fruit, and a couple glasses of water and find a seat.

"Mind if I join you?" someone asks, but I recognize his voice instantly.

"Sure, Charlie, go ahead," I say, sliding down the bench a little ways.

We eat in silence for a few minutes before he asks, "Is everything okay?

I snort out my nose, in a disbelieving type of way, and say "Is everything okay? No, it's not. You've probably heard by now about what happened at the beach. I can't believe Alysa did that to Ty. I can't believe she tried to fry me and him alive. What's wrong with her?"

"She's just jealous. She wants what you and Ty apparently have," he says before taking a bite.

"So that makes it okay? She's jealous, so we should just shrug it off? I'm tired of everyone using that as an excuse. It's a bunch of crap," I can feel my face turning red as my anger starts to rise.

"No, no, no, that's not what I meant. But I can see where she's coming from."

"What? You can? Why? How?" I say, dropping my sandwich and turning to face Charlie.

"Well, you know how I feel about you, and I can see how Ty feels about you. I guess I'm jealous too, of the fact that you seem to feel the same way about him. You broke the Love Hold, that takes something powerful to do that."

"I don't think you feel about me the way you think you do."

"I do, I know how I feel."

"What about you and Shae?"

With that question, Charlie slowly looks up at me. "What do you mean?"

"You know what I mean. I know about you and Shae being Anima Gemella. How can you say you have such strong feelings about me, when you have that with her? Nothing compares to that, what are you afraid of?"

"I'm not afraid, I'm just not ready for it."

"That statement right there just proves my point, you only *want* me. You're trying to force your feelings about Shae down by chasing lust, not love. Once you allow yourself to feel the full force of the love you have for Shae, nothing will ever be the same again."

"You can't tell me how I feel, I know how I feel about you," with that, Charlie gets up and walks away, slamming his leftover lunch into the garbage before he storms out the doors leading outside.

Shaking my head, I stand up, my appetite is gone. I wrap my sandwiches in a paper towel and put my tray on the pile next to the garbage can. I make my way up the spiral staircase and before I know it, my room door is in front of me.

It's amazing how in only 24 hours, this room has started to feel like home.

I step out of my semi-wet, sandy clothes, and take a long hot shower. This day is only halfway over, and it feels like it's been two whole days. I decide to take a relaxing bath once I'm down showering, so I let the tub fill, and then lie down in the water.

I don't know how long I've been soaking but the water is significantly cooler when I hear a knock on my door. I step out of the tub and wrap a towel around myself. I holler out, "Just a minute."

When I get to the door I ask, "Who is it?"

"It's Charlie, I came to apologize to you," Charlie's voice says from the other side.

I open the door and see Charlie standing there with concern all over his face.

"Hi," is all I can say.

"Hey," he runs a hand through his hair. "I'm sorry I talked to you that way."

"I know it's a touchy subject for you but I think you need to talk to someone about it."

"I don't really want to talk about it now though. Let's talk about how you're feeling after this morning's ordeal. Are you okay?"

"Yeah, I'm fine. I just feel a little drained, nothing a nap won't fix."

I step to the side and let him in. I shut the door, walk over to my desk, and I see myself in my mirror. I forgot I was only in a towel.

"Shoot, just a minute, I need to change," I say, turning bright red.

"I don't mind," Charlie says, his eyes roaming over me from head to toe.

I roll my eyes at him. I go to step around him, my dresser is behind him, but he steps in front of me, blocking my way.

"What are you doing?" I ask, really annoyed now.

"I just…" Charlie starts to say, but then he grabs me by the shoulders and starts kissing me.

I cling onto my towel with one hand, willing it to not fall off. With my other hand, I push him back.

"Stop it, Charlie!" I holler.

"Come on Em, I know you want me. I can feel your heart pounding," he says as he pulls me closer to him. He steps towards the wall, squashing me between it and him.

"My heart pounding has nothing to do with you, Charlie, stop it," I push at him again, harder this time.

He staggers back a few steps. I take the space between us and go to walk around him. He grabs my arm and swings me around, wrapping his other arm around my waist and makes us fall onto my bed, him on top of me.

He starts kissing me, running his hands all over my towel covered body, he stops kissing me and whispers into my ear, "Oh Emma, I knew you wanted this. I'm going to make you feel so good, you'll never think of Ty again."

"Like hell you are!" I scream. Just as he's about to pull my towel away, I ball my hands up in front of my chest and then open them fast. Charlie goes flying off of me and hits the wall on the other side of the room.

"What the hell, Emma?" he screams.

I stand up, making sure my towel is snug and tight around me with my left hand. With my right, I hold it, palm out, towards Charlie. I can feel the energy pulsing out of it, pushing Charlie up against the wall.

"I am not going to let another asshole think he can do whatever he wants to me because he's deluded himself into thinking I want him or that I'm his. I don't know what's going on with you, Charlie, but you need help. We just talked about you and Shae. What is wrong with you?" I scream, pushing the energy out towards him harder.

At the mention of Shae's name, Charlie's eyes get wide.

There's a bang on my bedroom door and Libby yells, "Emma, are you okay? I heard shouting... Emma?... Open up!"

Before I can answer, Charlie disappears. He must have Jumped somewhere.

I run to the door and open it, Libby rushes inside.

"What's going on?" she asks, looking around the room. The stuff on the wall that Charlie flew into, has fallen to the ground.

"Charlie," I say, shaking a little.

"He was in here? What happened?"

I tell her what happened and she gasps.

"You guys warned me about him but he totally duped me into thinking he was changing. After I found out about Shae and him, I wasn't going to have anything to do with him except be his friend. I'm such an idiot to think he was changing," I say.

"It's not your fault. There's something wrong with him. Are you hurt?"

"My wrist hurts a little where he grabbed me but it's nothing."

"We need to go tell Meredith and Bill what's happened. We can't have him running around thinking it's okay he can treat you or anyone else like that," Libby says, sounding really mad.

"Let me get dressed and then we can go tell them," I say. Just one day, just one, I'd like to have nothing crazy happen.

When we get to the Hospital Wing, Shae and Max come Running up to us just as we're about to walk in.

"You won't believe what just happened!" Shae says. She has scratches on her neck.

I look over at Max and see he's got a cut lip.

"What happened?" Libby says, touching his face, turning it to the right and left.

"Let's get in here so we don't have to tell it twice," Max says, wiping his lip on his shirt sleeve.

When we walk into the Hospital Wing, Ty is lying on a bed with an ice pack on his forehead. Doc is looking into his eyes with a flashlight and Sara has her hands on Ty's head.

When they look over and see the state of Shae and Max, they all ask at once, "Now what's happened?"

Before Libby or I can say anything, Max says, "Charlie jumped to the Cells. He hit me across the face, knocking me to the floor, and let Alysa out of her cell. Shae tried to get her back inside but Alysa started fighting her. Charlie grabbed Shae and tossed her into Alysa's cell and before I could get up, Charlie Jumped himself and Alysa out."

"Why would Charlie do that?" Meredith asks.

"Tell them," Libby says, nudging me.

Slightly embarrassed, I tell them what had happened back in my room.

As I'm telling them, Ty jumps out of bed and says, "Where the hell did he go? I'm going to rip his heart out!"

The amount of energy it took for Ty to do this, has him turning pale and swaying where he stands. I rush over to him and put my shoulder under his arm.

"Calm down, I'm fine. I didn't let him hurt me. You need to lie back down," I say, trying to ease him back down onto the bed. He resists but when I place my hand on his chest, that all too familiar electrical current zaps my fingers. I look at him pleadingly in the eyes and he sits. He then lets me push him back so he's lying down again. I grab the ice pack from the floor and put it back on his forehead. I hear a sigh of relief escape his lips.

I hear Meredith whisper, "Bill."

Sara says, "I'm finished with Ty's head, he doesn't have the Hold on him anymore, Emma took care of it.

Have you Healed what you can?"

"He doesn't have any lasting injuries but he'll have a headache for a day or two. Nothing we can do about it, it's a side effect from the Hold," Doc says.

Bill bursts through the doors with five men behind him and we all jump.

"What's going on?" he exclaims.

"We have to find Alysa and Charlie," Meredith says as she walks towards Bill and the Guardians. "I'll explain along the way. You girls stay here with Ty. Max, come with us."

As they leave, Shae crumples into a chair and starts to sob. Libby goes to her and puts her arms around her.

"It's okay Shae. They'll find them," Libby says, rubbing her back.

"I just don't understand. What was Charlie thinking? What was Alysa thinking?" Shae sobs into Libby's shoulder.

"Jealousy can make a person do things they normally wouldn't do and Alysa is extremely jealous of Emma. And for Charlie? I don't know, I'd like to have him checked for a Hold, he's been acting weird the last few days," Libby says looking thoughtful.

Shae scoffs at her and says, "You are 110 percent right about my sister but as far as Charlie? Dead wrong. He's been acting like a tool for the last three years."

Shae starts to cry again, Libby just holds her and rubs her back, telling her it would all be okay.

"Are you sure you're okay?" Ty whispers from beside me.

I look down at him and have to swallow hard before I can answer. It's ridiculous to say but him looking so vulnerable makes him even more attractive.

"I'm really okay. I Pushed him off of me and threw him across the room before he could do anything. I was seriously pissed," I whisper back.

Ty reaches for my hand and pulls me down so that I'm sitting next to him.

"The thought of someone hurting you, let alone a friend of mine, makes me insane with rage," Ty whispers out, his voice shaking a little with his anger.

"I've got Talents now, no one will ever hurt me again," I say, trying to ease his anger.

"We need to get you into some Classes and Trainings so you know exactly what Talents you have," Ty says.

"That would be nice. So far just following my instincts have shown me what I can do but *knowing* what I can do would be a lot better," I say, squeezing his hand. He squeezes my hand and smiles.

"Emma, are you hungry?" Libby says, still consoling Shae.

"Yeah, I barely ate earlier," I reply.

"Ty? You feel up to eating?" she asks her brother.

"Yeah, I could eat," Ty says, scooting over a little so that I can sit beside him more comfortably.

"Shae and I will go get some food and bring it back," Libby says. She grabs Shae's hand and pulls her from the room.

Ty and I just sit for a minute, not saying anything. I don't know what to say. I can't imagine how he feels, it makes me dizzy just thinking about the whirlwind from the last couple of days.

"So, about the Hold," Ty says, clearing his throat.

"You don't have to say anything."

"The last thing I remember consciously doing, was taking a box from the kitchen up to one of the SUV's we were using to drive loads of stuff to the airport. I had just loaded the box in when I turned around and Alysa was there. I was about to ask her what she wanted when she grabbed my arm and everything went fuzzy. I just want you to know that nothing I said or did was me. It felt like Novocain had been injected into my brain, I felt mentally numb. Except when you were around. Every time I saw you or heard your voice, I felt like I was about to wake up. I'd get so confused. I couldn't figure out why I was holding Alysa's hand when all I wanted to do was to be over with you but as soon as she'd tighten her grip or make contact with me, the numbness would take over again. When I saw that shark go after you, it was like someone had thrown a bucket of cold water on me. It took all of Alysa's and Charlie's strength to keep me there. Had my head not felt like it was going to split in half, I would have gone in after you. And when you kissed me, the zap of electricity that flew through my veins was enough to clear all the foggy, numbness away."

"So you feel it too?" I ask.

Ty turns a little red but he says, "Yes, I feel it too. I've never felt like this about anyone and I don't think I'll feel this way about anyone other than you. Have you heard about Anime---"

"I don't think that's a good idea Shae. They'll find her and Charlie and bring them back," Libby says to Shae as they come back into the Hospital Wing, holding trays of food. She interrupted what Ty was about to say. He was going to ask if I knew about Anima Gemella. Does this mean he thinks that's what we are?

Libby puts a tray of food on Ty's lap and hands me one as well.

"Thank you," Ty and I say at the same time. I giggle and he just looks at me, smiling.

"Don't you think I should go after Alysa and Charlie?" Shae asks Ty and me.

"Do you know where they went?" Ty asks back.

"No but---"

Ty interrupts her and says, "Then no, I don't think you should. I think we need to know where they're at before we go off looking for them. Nobody wants them found more than I do, for what Alysa did to me and what Charlie did to Emma. I want them found now but it won't do anyone any good to go out looking blindly, especially when Chris and Vanessa are out there."

Shae slumps into a chair and starts to cry again. "I'm so sorry you guys."

"It's not your fault," I say, getting up and walking over to her. I give her a sideways hug and she starts crying harder. "Shae, listen. It's not your fault. You can't control or change a person, they have to want to change themselves. I honestly don't know what Charlie was thinking. Once we find them, he can explain himself. Alysa needs a reality check. She needs to realize she can't have something or someone just because *she* wants it."

"Emma's right," Ty says. "Alysa and Charlie have always thought they could have whatever they wanted and now that Emma is here, they're starting to realize it's not the case. It's not your fault, Shae, it's all of ours. I should have been a better friend to Charlie and told him when he was being a dick. I tried to tell Alysa over and over again that we were done but maybe I was doing something that kept leading her to think there was still a chance for me and her to get back together."

"She knew you were done with her, why else would she put a Hold on you?" Shae asks sounding a little better.

"I think the point Ty is trying to make, is that we all should have done more to make Alysa and Charlie realize that they aren't entitled to everything they want just because they want it. They have to own up to their actions and accept the punishment that Meredith and Bill decide they deserve because in the end, they chose to make those awful decisions," Libby says, grabbing the trays off of the bed Ty is lying on.

Doc comes through the door and says, "Bill has your unit getting ready to go search the island for Alysa and Charlie. They should be back in a few hours, hopefully they find them. If they've left the island, it might be awhile before they're found, if they're found at all."

Ty leans back and sighs, "I wish I could go and help look for them."

"You need to rest, your brain has been through an ordeal," Doc says, walking over and looking into Ty's eyes. "Your eyes are looking better, more focused than they were earlier."

I walk back over to Ty's bed and sit next to him, he grabs my hand instantly. Doc's eyes flash to our intertwined fingers and a small grin appears on his face.

Ty whispers into my ear, "You have no idea how good it feels to hold your hand, it honestly takes the ache away."

"I know exactly how it feels. It's what happened when you were touching my foot while I was in the Hospital Wing back in The Pit," I say, smiling at him.

"Shae, let's go get you cleaned up. I bet a shower will make you feel better, maybe a nap as well," Libby says, standing up and extending her hand out to Shae.

Shae takes her hand and wipes her face with her

other hand, she looks at me and asks, "Will you let me know if Bill finds anything?"

"I'll come straight to your room if they get back before you're back down here," I smile over at her.

Libby and Shae walk out of the room. Ty yawns and leans back further onto the bed.

"You really should rest, take a nap, it would be good for you," I say, situating myself so I can stand up.

Ty squeezes my hand and asks, "Will you stay here with me?"

"I will if you want me to," I answer, smiling like an idiot.

"I want you to," Ty says, smiling as his eyes close.

I scoot myself back onto the hospital bed and Ty pulls me into him so that I'm lying in his arms. I tuck my arm underneath myself, place my other hand on his stomach, and my head on his chest. I can hear his heart pounding, it sounds like he's been running a race.

"Do you feel okay?" I ask, looking up at him.

"I feel great, why?"

"Oh, it's just... your heart is beating really fast."

"Oh," is all Ty says as his face turns red. "I guess it's just from me being happy your here."

I smile and kiss him on the cheek, "I'm happy I'm here, too. Now get some sleep."

He kisses the top of my head and then I feel him relax and his breathing slows. He's fallen asleep faster than anyone I've ever met. Listening to his breathing is making me drowsy as well. I might as well take a nap, it's been a very long half of a day.

CHAPTER 27 - VISION

Ty and I are startled awake by the sound of the Hospital Wing doors banging open and Libby shouting our names.

"Emma! Ty! I need help... Emma! Ty! Wake up!"

We bolt out of the bed and rush over to her, she's supporting Shae as if she's been hurt.

"What's wrong with her?" Ty asks, grabbing Shae from Libby and sitting her down on the bed closest to where we're standing.

"She's having a Vision. I could hear her yelling from my room. She comes to just long enough to say what she's seen and then she goes back to being half unconscious. It's something to do with Charlie and Alysa," Libby says, running to the sink to get a wet washcloth.

"Where's Meredith and Doc? Our parents?" Ty asks.

"Nobody knows, Bill's gone too. They might still be out searching the island but from what Shae says, Charlie and Alysa aren't on the island anymore. She went back under before she could tell me anything other than Charlie and Alysa are in danger," Libby says as she puts the washcloth on Shae's forehead.

"How long were we asleep?" I ask, looking out the window, it's dark outside.

"Eight hours."

"Eight!?" Ty and I exclaim together.

"I kept coming in every two or so hours to check on you guys but you were both sound asleep. Around four o'clock, I told Shae to go rest, she kept pacing and worrying about where Charlie and Alysa were hiding. I fell asleep around a quarter after six o'clock and got woken up a couple hours later to her screaming," Libby says.

"Emma?" Shae says in a hoarse voice.

"I'm right here," I say, moving in closer to her.

"We have to go get them," Shae says as she tries to sit up but Libby pushes her back down.

"Get who from where?" Ty asks.

"Charlie and Alysa. They're at the Pit and they're in danger. I can't see why yet but..." Shae slumps back limply and her eyes roll to the back of her head.

"Shae!" I scream, reaching for her.

"She's okay, she has just went back under," Libby says. She reaches out and closes her eyelids so it looks like she's sleeping.

"I'll go get the guys and bring them here. I'll try to find Bill on my way," Ty kisses me quickly on the forehead.

"Are you sure you should be out of bed? I ask him.

"I'm fine, you've helped Heal me the rest of the way," he answers and then Runs from the room.

"No... No... No... Not her... Not them... NO!" Shae screams.

"Shae, breath... Take a deep breath and just breathe... What did you See?" Libby asks, pulling Shae by the shoulders until she's sitting up straight.

"Charlie... Alysa... The Pit... Vanessa and Chris... They're all there... Charlie and... and Alysa... they... they...," but Shae doesn't finish what she's saying she just bursts into tears. I'm not sure if I want to know what happens to Charlie and Alysa but I do know we have to get to them right now!

"When does this all happen?" I ask.

"Could be now, could be hours from now," Libby says.

The doors bang open again and Ty, Max, Clay, and Malory file into the room.

"What's she doing here?" Shae spits out between her teeth.

"She overheard me talking to Clay and Max but she's NOT going," Ty says, glaring over at Malory.

"Alysa is my best-friend and if she's in danger, I'm going with you to help. I know she's messed up but she doesn't deserve to..." she doesn't finish her sentence.

"Vanessa and Chris and all the Rifts show up at The Pit, that's the danger they're in," Libby says.

"I figured as much," Ty says. "Alright, Max, go start

up one of the jets, grab as many guys as you can. We're heading out."

"I'm coming too," Libby and I say at the same time.

"You are not, this is going to be way more dangerous than any mission you've ever been on," Max states matter-of-factly before he takes a step to leave.

"I'm still coming," Libby says stubbornly.

"We're all going," Malory says.

"I hate to agree with her, but she's right, we all are," Shae says.

I can tell Clay is about to start arguing with us too, so I cut him off and say, "Listen, we can stand here and argue until we all turn blue in the face and pass out or I can Jump us to The Pit and get Charlie and Alysa out of there. Hopefully Vanessa hasn't gotten there yet. But the longer we sit here and fight with each other, the closer she gets."

"It's up to you, Ty. You're in charge since Bill isn't here," Max says.

Ty looks at me and then at his sister, "Fine you guys can come but be careful. Go change and be back down here in five minutes."

Nodding, we Run from the Hospital Wing to our rooms. I throw open my drawers, looking for something to wear. My door flies open and Libby is standing beside me.

She's wearing black, tight, fierce looking clothes. I look in my drawer for my black long sleeve shirt and a pair of jeans.

"Here, wear these. They were my first set of battle gear, they're too small for me now but they should fit you. Ty is grabbing you a pair of boots and he'll pick out a Magikida for you also," Libby says as she hands me the softest feeling clothes I've ever felt. I see the hilt of her Magikida sticking out behind her back, over the top of her head.

"They're so soft," I say, running my hand over the shirt.

"It's made out of a very special material that helps deflect Talents that can cause harm, like fire or being zapped from electricity. It never weakens over time. They can't completely protect you but it keeps the most painful Talents bearable. It's why we learn hand to hand combat."

Not thinking about being shy, I strip out of my clothes and throw on my new to me battle gear. It literally fits like a glove. I test out the flexibility and find it moves with me like another layer of skin.

"Let's go," Libby says. "Shae should be waiting for us with Malory. I really don't like that she's going with us but maybe she'll prove she's really not as bad as she's been acting lately."

We Run back down to the Hospital Wing and find everyone waiting for us. Ty walks over and puts a pair of boots down in front of me. Instead of just standing up, he starts to untie my shoes for me and helps lace up my new battle boots. They feel sturdy and well-built but light, as if I'm not wearing anything more than my socks.

He hands me a mean looking sword and says, "I know you haven't been trained with one of these before but it's pretty self-explanatory and hopefully you won't have to us it. Use your Talents, use this as a last resort."

I nod and take it. It feels really light and it's warm in my hands, I was expecting it to be cold. It's vibrating also.

"You guys sure you're up for this?" Ty asks us.

"Yes," we all say.

"Alright, I left a message for Meredith, Bill, Doc, and our parents. Emma, what do we need to do for you to Jump us?" Ty asks.

"I just need everyone touching," I say. "Where should I Jump us to?"

'Maybe the Gym, it's not likely they'll be in there and we can sneak up on them if Vanessa and the Rifts are already there," Ty says.

"Okay," I say. "Everyone ready?"

I look around and see everyone nod. I make sure everyone is touching their neighbor. Ty grabs my hand, I close my eyes, and think about the dark room that used to be the Gym. I take a step forward and instantly smell dirt and underground stale water.

There are gasps and when I open my eyes, I find out

why. It's pitch black, which shouldn't really surprise us, there's no electricity down here anymore.

"Which way is the door?" Clay asks.

"I'm not sure," Ty says, sounding perplexed.

"Hang on," I say. On each hand, I rub my index fingers and thumbs together is small, fast circles. I can feel static starting to build up. I flick my index fingers out, like I'm flicking a bug and I see balls of electricity fly to the walls. The lights flash on, brighter than they've ever been, hurting our eyes.

"How did you---" Clay starts to say.

"Do that?" Max finishes his sentence.

"I don't know, it's all so new and spontaneous. I just know what to do when the time comes to do it," I say, looking around. I feel like I keep repeating myself, I wish I had a better answer for them.

"Shae, Malory, Libby, Emma, you guys stay behind Clay. Max, get my six, let's go," Ty says, walking towards the door which happened to be behind us.

We make our way down the tunnel that leads to the Great Room. We stop halfway up the tunnel just before we get to the entrance, the electricity was leading the way.

"Can you stop it from here on out? Just until we get inside?" Ty asks from the front.

I snap my fingers and the lights go out.

"So stinkin' cool," I hear Shae say behind me.

We ease our way towards the entrance and stop

and listen to see if we can hear voices. It's dead quiet.

"Slowly," Ty says.

I'm so nervous, I can feel zaps of electricity flying between my fingers. As we walk in, it's apparent right away that no one else is here. We all straighten up and spread out from our line.

"Lights?" Ty asks. I flick my fingers out again and the balls of electricity fly out and the lights blaze back on.

"Should we check all the rooms?" Clay asks.

"No need, no one is here," I state, leaning against the wall.

"How do you know?" he asks.

"I Scanned The Pit, we're the only ones down here," I answer him. The sound of my voice sounds defeated.

"Oh," is all Clay says.

"Now what?" Malory asks.

We all look at Shae. She sighs and leans back against the wall. She slides down and puts her head in her hands.

"Give me a second, I've never tried to Look," she says.

"Look?" I ask quietly to Libby.

"She's trying to Look into the future instead of letting the visions come to her," Libby says as she sits down on the ground.

Every 5 to 10 minutes, Shae would twitch, like she was sleeping restlessly but in a sitting position. While we wait, we contemplate what Vanessa could have done to them and where they could have gone. There wasn't any sign of a fight. So did they go willingly or did they realize they didn't have a chance if they fought them?

"I've got it!" Shae exclaims. We all jump up and run over to her. She stands up and says, "They've gone to the Elders. I don't know why but Vanessa, Chris, and the Rifts have taken Charlie and Alysa to the Elders."

"Aren't they in Greece?" I ask, remembering what I had read and heard about them.

"Yeah, they are," Libby says.

"Have any of you been there?" I ask.

They all shake their heads.

"I can't Jump us unless someone has been there," I say frantically.

"Jump us back to The Estate and then we can take a jet. It's not as fast as Jumping but it's fast enough. We can also check in and see if Bill and the others are back yet," Ty says.

I nod. Once everyone is touching, I step forward and Jump us back to the driveway, in front of the mansion.

"Max, go get the jet ready. Clay, go grab Ray and his group, we'll need some extra hands. Girls, if you're going, stay here. I'm going to Run in and see if Bill's back," Ty says before he disappears.

"Why would Vanessa be going to the Elders? What

can they do for them?" I ask no one in particular but Libby is the one who answers.

"Nothing really. They're just the oldest of our people. The ones the Leaders look for, for advice when they've hit a dead end or if something serious has happened. The Elders don't really get involved unless it's something serious. They have been trying to track down Vanessa and Chris and the Rifts, to find their main hideout but they haven't had any luck."

We sit in silence, thinking about what they could possibly want with the Elders. Ty is back in five minutes with Clay, who has brought nine other guys with him.

"They aren't back yet. I'm starting to get concerned. It shouldn't have taken that long to search the island. But, we don't have time to worry about that, I know they can take care of themselves. Our priority right now is getting to Charlie and Alysa," Ty states.

"Malory, are you sure you want to go?" Clay asks her as he puts his hands on her shoulders, staring into her eyes.

"Yes, I want to help Alysa," she answers. Clay nods and then kisses her forehead.

"Libby, Emma, Shae, are you guys sure?" Ty asks.

We nod. No way was I staying home while everyone, I had come to care for, leaves to go save Charlie and Alysa. After everything they had done to me, I don't wish them ill or hate them, I just want to understand why they act the way they do and they can't explain if Vanessa kills them.

"Let's go then," Ty says. He leads the way down the drive just a bit before he Runs off to the hanger, we follow.

Max has a fast jet pulled out and ready to go. We climb up the ladder and take our seats. I look around for Ty but see him sitting in the cockpit with Max.

"Ty can fly?" I ask Libby as she takes a seat next to me.

"Yeah. As his Unit's leader, he chose to learn how to fly so that if an emergency arose and he needed to fly, he could. Good thing because today is just what he was thinking when he decided to do it."

Shae takes the seat across from us and closes her eyes. She looks like she's trying to Look. I can't imagine how stressed she must be. I know she's got to be on her last nerve because I feel like I am and it's not even my sister or Anima Gemella we're going after to save.

Ty and Max glide us up the runway and ease us into the air. It was the smoothest take off I've ever experienced. I look out the window and see our little sanctuary disappear behind us. There is nothing but blue water below us and blue skies above.

"How long should it take us to get to Greece?" I ask.

"On a normal flight, 17 hours but on this jet and Ty flying, it will only take 12," Clay says from behind us. He's holding Malory in his arms, she's just staring out the window, lost in thought.

"A lot can happen in 12 hours," I say frantically.

"It's the best we can do. The fastest way we can get there," Libby says, patting my hand.

All of a sudden, I feel lightheaded and extremely dizzy. I close my eyes and I can feel my head rolling around on my shoulders.

"Emma, what's the matter?" Libby asks. I can feel her kneeling down in front of me.

"I don't know, maybe motion sickness. I feel really dizzy," I say, leaning my head back against my seat so it would stop rolling. "But I've never gotten motion sickness before, so I don't know if this is what it feels like or if it's something else."

"It could be, we did get in the air awfully quick," Libby says. "Ty, come back here, Emma isn't feeling well."

"No, it's okay, it'll pass," I say. I don't want to take Ty away from flying for something as silly as motion sickness.

"It's not silly," Libby says.

Hmmm, I hadn't realized I'd said that out loud.

"What's wrong, Emma?" Ty asks, I can feel him beside me before he touches my shoulder. How crazy that our bodies are so in tune, that I can feel his energy before we're even touching?

"Just really dizzy," I answer with my eyes still closed.

"Open your eyes," he says.

I do as he asks but instantly regret it. It looks as if the entire jet is spinning in circles.

"Ugh... not good," I groan. I squeeze my eyes shut as tight as I can, willing the nausea to go away.

"That bad?" Libby asks.

"Imagine us being on the spin cycle in a washing machine," I say, it's the only thing I can think of that might compare to how I feel.

"Oh yeah, that's pretty bad," she says.

I hear a ringing in my ears, so I stick a finger in my right one and try to rub it away but it gets louder. I cover my ears with my hands. I can barely hear what Ty and Libby are saying, one of them is shaking my shoulder and the other is squeezing my hands. The last thing I remember before complete blackness takes me is the ringing getting so loud, I scream out in pain.

Light starts to form around the edge of my vision but I'm aware that I'm not on the jet anymore before I can see clearly. I can smell wet earth and trees. I look around and see that I'm lying on the ground outside what looks like mansions built into the side of a mountain.

The ringing in my ears that I remember hearing on the jet quiets, I hadn't realized they were still making that sound. As soon as it stops, I can hear screaming coming from all around me. The screams are coming from inside the forest and inside the mountain mansions. It sounds like they're coming from every direction.

Jumping to my feet I turn in circles, trying to find my friends and Guardians that were on the jet with me. Ty and Libby are nowhere to be found. Shae, Malory, Max, and Clay are gone and so are the nine Guardians.

Where is everyone? What happened?

I see someone running from the entrance of one of the mansions, it's an adult and she looks like she's shimmering around the edges. A man runs from the entrance and throws a ball of blue fire at her. It catches her in the middle of the back and she falls to the ground screaming in pain. The man walks up to her and I watch, frozen in place, as he engulfs her with fire. Her cries get louder before they slowly, painfully slow, drift quietly to silence. I see something like a sliver of white light lift from the middle of her body and float into the air until it mixes with sunlight and vanishes.

I can feel my face hanging open in horror and then I feel my rage for what I have just witnessed gets me moving. I run at the man. I expect him to Throw blue fire at me so I have my hands up and ready to catch what he Throws and Throw it back at him. But he doesn't even act like I'm there, he slowly turns on the spot looking around him.

Before I can get to him, he says out loud, "Tell Vanessa I got Selina, I don't think she was able to get a warning sent out."

I skid to a stop just inches to him.

"Vanessa!" I scream but he doesn't acknowledge me.

He turns and walks right through me.

What is going on!?

"Who are you?" I ask.

Again, he doesn't respond. He walks around a little more before placing a hand on the ground.

"No, I don't feel anyone approaching," he says to no one. "Have Levi and Jaydin come out. They can keep watch."

A minute goes by when a man and woman come Running out of the same door this man had come out of from the biggest mansion.

"Chris, Steven said you wanted us?" the man asks. I'm guessing this is Levi.

"Yeah, take the first watch," Chris says. Levi and Jaydin nod and start walking a patrol.

Is this *the* Chris? I don't remember seeing a picture of him in all the stuff I was given to read and look through. It has to be him. My rage flares and I try to run at him, but I again run right through him. He just walks back towards the entrance of the mansion and starts to enter it.

Breathing heavily, I follow him. Once I get into the mansion, I see destruction everywhere. Dead bodies lie all over the floor. The majority are wearing the same black battle gear that my friends and I are wearing but then some are wearing the same flowy, soft looking, white pants and shirt as the Elder woman, Selina, who was killed outside.

Standing in the middle of the destruction is Vanessa. Kneeling in front of her is a man dressed in the white clothes and off to the right a little ways, Alysa and Charlie are kneeling too.

"Do you see what happens when I don't get what I want?" Vanessa says in a sickly, sweet voice.

"I'll never tell you what we know," the man says. "Go ahead and kill me too. You'll never know our secrets."

"As you wish. I don't need to know the Secrets of the Elders anyways. There's a new way of life coming, no reason for old ways to be kept around," Vanessa hisses and with a slash of her hand, the man slumps to the ground, instantly dead. The same sliver of white light leaves the middle of his body, just like it had with Elder Selina.

Chris is by her side and I can hear him whisper in her ear, 'My darling, do you think that was wise?"

The saying 'If looks could kill' has never been truer than in this instant with the look Vanessa shoots her husband.

He hastily bows his head and takes a step back, away from her.

"Now, you two. Tell me what you know about my dearest daughter Emma," Vanessa says, turning towards Alysa and Charlie.

"Go to hell! We aren't telling you anything," Charlie snarls at her.

"I'm not so sure about that," Vanessa says before she raises a finger and points it at Alysa. A solid flow of lightning shoots out of it and connects with Alysa, right above her heart. She starts screaming and convulsing on the ground beside Charlie.

"You bitch! Stop it! Torture me, not her! Stop it!" Charlie screams and strains against whatever is holding him in place.

"All you have to do is tell me what I want to know," Vanessa loudly whispers. She stops torturing Alysa after another minute of her screaming and Charlie shouting curse words at her.

"Keep talking that way to my wife and see what happens," Chris says, taking a step towards him.

"Screw you, you coward! Are you guys too afraid of us to fight us fairly?" Charlie growls out under his breath. He shoots Alysa a concerned look out of the corner of his eye before returning his glare at the other two.

"We know you're Talents, we don't need you Jumping from here back to your little hidey hole," Chris snaps back.

"Just tell me what I want to know and I'll let you

go. Or better yet, join me," Vanessa says, I can hear the irritation starting to creep into her voice. "Alysa, you remind me so much of myself."

"Don't... tell... the... bitch... anything... Let them... kill me," Alysa breathes out heavily. "I'm nothing like you."

"Alysa," Charlie whispers out in a harsh, startled way.

"I'm... serious... Charlie... It's the least... we can do... for her... We owe her that... and so much more," Alysa groans out. She closes her eyes and I see a tear run down her cheek.

Charlie shakes his head and slowly bows it before he says, "Vanessa, you'll have to kill us both because we aren't telling you anything about your *niece*." --- he hisses the last word.--- "You won't know anything about Emma unless *she* wants you to know."

"Such a waste," Vanessa says as she raises her hand as she did before she struck the elder man dead.

"NO!!!" I shout out in one long, loud scream.

I sit up quickly, dizzy from it, and confused for a fraction of a second. I'm back on the jet.

"Emma!? What happened?" Libby asks, staring down at me, she's kneeling beside me. They must have lowered me onto the floor of the jet.

"I don't know. The last thing I remember is the ringing in my ears and then blacking out. I woke up, where I assume the Elders live. Vanessa and Chris were there and they killed them all. All the Elders were dead. She killed the last one because he wouldn't tell her the Secrets of the Elder's. She started torturing Alysa and Charlie because they wouldn't tell her anything about me. She was getting ready to kill them like she did the last Elder, just now, when I woke up. It was just a nightmare, right?" I ask, shaking. Ty sits down beside me and wraps his arms around me. The electrical current between us eases my panic.

"I don't think so," Shae says. She's lost all color in her face, she's gone completely white. "When I was Looking, I saw that they were at the Elders, but they were still all fighting. I couldn't see past that. I think you had a Vision."

"We have to get there quick, now!" I shout. I notice that the jet isn't moving. "Where are we? We've landed already?"

"We had to make an emergency landing in the Philippines. You were vibrating so bad, we thought the jet was going to come apart," Max says from behind Libby.

"I can Jump us. I know where the Elder's live, I've seen it, I can get us there," I say, standing up quickly and pulling Ty up with me.

"I don't think that would be a good idea, you just went through something obviously strenuous," Libby says.

"I wish you all would stop wasting time when I suggest I do something by arguing with me about it. I know it's out of concern for me, but I can do this, I've proven I can do it. So, we aren't arguing about it, grab hands, we're going," I state slightly more angrily than I had intend too.

They look at each other for a fraction of a second before grabbing hands. I grab hold of Ty's hand, he squeezes slightly, encouragingly. I close my eyes and take a step forward. The same feeling and smells hit me from my Vision. Only this time, there's no screaming.

We're too late.

CHAPTER 28 - DESTROYED

Heart racing, I glance around and see that Elder Selina is lying on the ground. I look towards the doorway I had gone through, following Chris earlier, and see the back of his shirt disappear.

"We're too late for Elder Selina but we can still save the Elder man, Charlie, and Alysa!" I exclaim.

"Who are you? Where'd you come from?" a voice comes from behind us.

We spin around and see Levi and Jaydin standing there. Before any of us have a chance to answer, Ty and Max Run at them and have them bound and gagged.

"Clay, do your thing," Ty says.

Clay walks forward and places his hands on Jaydin's and Levi's forehead, they start to protest but soon their muffled pleas stop and their eyes glaze over. Clay nods, Ty and Max let go of them. They sit back on their heels and just stare forward.

"What did you do to them?" I ask as I walk forward.

"Just something Bill's been having me work on. It puts them in a trance so that they can't fight us, or alert anyone that we're here. Not really a Hold but the same idea. They can't do anything unless I tell them too or I release them from it. If I can get to someone before they start fighting, Bill wants me to do this so we can have people to interrogate later. We all know that if we come across anyone who is sitting like this, we aren't allowed to touch them," Clay answers.

"Where to now?" Shae asks, bouncing on her toes. I can tell she's anxious. She can sense her sister and Anima Gemella are close by.

"This way," I say, leading the way to the entrance of the biggest mansions built into the mountain. "They'll be right inside here, so prepare yourselves."

I feel a ripple go through everyone before we continue inside. We can hear Vanessa talking before we see her.

"Do you see what happens when I don't get what I want?" she says in the sickly, sweet voice, the same thing I heard in my vision right before she killed the Elder man.

Heart racing, I hear his response, "I'll never tell you what we know. Go ahead and kill me too. You'll never know our secrets."

I speed up and when I see her, she's raising her hand, saying, "As you wish, I don't need to know the Secrets of the Elders anyways. There's a new way of life coming, no reason for old ways to be kept around."

"NO!" I scream and throw my hands out, she's

knocked backward. Ty Runs forward and grabs the Elder man and Run's him outside. I see all this in the weird slow-motion vision I have.

"What the..." Chris says, kneeling down beside Vanessa. She's slowly sitting up.

I flick my hands out at Alysa and Charlie and see them sag to the floor. For a brief second, they look completely surprised to see us. Then the realization hits that they aren't being held in the invisible field anymore and they Run over to us.

"Emma, we are so sorry," Alysa says. Charlie looks down, ashamed.

"Not now," I say, Vanessa has gotten back to her feet.

I suddenly feel Ty standing behind me, he's back from taking the Elder outside. He places his hand on my lower back, steadying me.

"Emma, my sweet girl, I was hoping I'd see you," Vanessa says sweetly but I can hear the underlying anger.

"I am not your girl. You lied to me my whole life. You acted like you got murdered in front of me. You let me believe you were dead. YOU SAT BACK AND WATCHED THOSE MEN BEAT ME! YOU WOULD HAVE LET FRANK KILL ME!" I'm shouting so loud, I can feel veins popping out of my neck. I can also feel the mountain trembling. Ty softly squeezes my upper arm.

"Easy," he whispers for only me to hear. His touch and voice simmers my rage.

"I can explain all that," Vanessa says, pleading in her voice. Before I can tell her I don't want to hear anything she has to say, she starts talking again. "I didn't want to resort to what had to be done but you weren't showing any signs of having Talents. My brother was a brilliant Demi and his wife also but I started to think they had produced a Dudmon, which is a Demi without a Talent or without Talents. The only way to force out Talents is extreme trauma. I thought maybe seeing me murdered would have triggered something but it didn't. The beatings were to trigger the self-protection side and make your Talents show themselves but nothing was working. I was afraid you truly were a Dudmon and not who we were looking for after all. Frank had asked for you as payment for insider information he gave us. I didn't know what he meant when he asked for you was that he wanted to kill you. I reassigned him after a few days. We haven't seen him in a while, he gave us false information."

I had started to shake my head at the mention of her brother and his wife, my father and mother. By the time she's done talking, I'm shaking with rage.

"I don't want to hear what you think is a reason for what you did. You... DO... NOT... TREAT PEOPLE LIKE THAT!!" I scream.

Dirt from the ceiling falls down on us. Somewhere in the house we can hear crashing. The walls are trembling and the lights are flickering on and off.

"Easy, Emma," Libby says from the other side of me.

"Emma?... This is you?" Vanessa asks surprised. She waves her hand out around her.

"Yes, it's me. It was also me who pushed you away from that poor Elder man. It was also me who cloaked us, all 100 plus of us, in Invisibility the day you and your *sheep* came to The Pit. Frank didn't give you false information, we were there, you just couldn't see us," I spit out. I am so angry I could cry. I have to ask a question that I've been dying to find out since I found out Vanessa wasn't my mother. "Did you kill my parents?"

Vanessa takes a step towards Chris, I feel Ty tense beside me. I didn't see her do anything, but I felt a wave, or vibration, go through the air.

"No, not your parents..." she answers, hesitating for a moment but I can tell she is lying before she's done talking.

"You're a liar," I say through clenched teeth.

"I didn't kill my brother, but I did kill his wife. Chris took care of him so I wouldn't have to," she says, sounding like she truly is upset about it.

"Why?" I ask in a whisper. I'm afraid if I raise my voice, my rage will explode out, and bury us under the mountain as it's still shaking.

"They weren't going to give me what I wanted, so I got them out of the way," she says it so matter-of-factly, like how someone would say the sky is blue and the grass is green.

Before I can say anything, we are surrounded. At least 60 of her Rifts have appeared out of the shadows. In one movement, Magikida blades are being drawn all around us. We draw our own but Ty catches my hand and puts it back down to my side before I can get ahold of mine.

"Use your instincts, use your Talents," he whispers into my ear. Nodding, I put my hands out in front of me like I had when the shark attacked.

"We don't want to fight you. Join us and we can change the way the world sees us. They'll actually get to see us and have to thank us for the work we do," Vanessa says through tight lips.

"What work? Evil has taken over the world because the Demi-gods have had to go into hiding because you've been killing our people for your own greed. Demi-gods haven't been able to do their jobs for years but that ends now," I say.

Out of the side of my right eye I caught a movement, I look over just in time to see one of the Rifts Throw what looks like a shimmering net at us. I swipe my hand into the air, like you would to clear the cobwebs out of the way, and the shimmering net dissolves into thin air.

"Impressive," I hear Vanessa say. "Don't hurt Emma, bring her to me, do away with the rest of them."

I instantly go into defensive mode and start blocking every Talent I can that is Thrown at us. Six Rifts at once were Throwing fire, two are sending shards of ice, and a handful were rubbing their hands together to create electric balls.

"Don't try to fight them all at once, we can fight as well," Ty says. "Work on what's in front of you or what's an immediate threat to yourself. You'll wear yourself out trying to take them all out."

I turn my focus back on what is in front of me and I see Clay and Max battling Chris. Malory, Alysa, Shae, and Libby taking on Vanessa. The nine Guardians are fighting with their Magikidas and deflecting Talents being Thrown at them. They're, also, using their own Talents. Ty and Charlie are fighting six Rifts as once.

I start to make my way towards Vanessa but I'm all of a sudden surrounded by 20 or so Rifts. I run my hands up over my head and down around my body, it must look like I'm dancing. They can't see it but I can feel it. I put a protective barrier between me and them, I know none of their Talents can hurt me. I send out the same barrier to my friends who were closest to me, which happens to be Ty, Charlie, and five of the Guardians. They shiver a little as it hits them but they don't stop their fighting. They start knocking Rifts aside with ease. Ty looks at me and smiles.

"Thank you," he mouths, he knows what happened.

"Let's get her," one of the Rifts says that's standing

in front of me.

They all start to converge on me. I flick my fingers, one by one, knocking them back, sending some tumbling backwards. I send out invisible ropes to tie them up as fast as I can. I have about half down and tied. Out of the corner of my eye I see a flash of light and stick my hand out just in time to catch a ball of fire. I catch it, turn in a circle, and Throw it back to its owner. I hear a surprised yelp. The rest of the Rifts back off a little after that.

I slowly look around, they all look scared.

Good!

I look around to check on my friends. I can see Malory lying on the ground in the fetal position. Alysa is sending fireball after fireball at Vanessa but she is deflecting them with a swipe of her hand. Libby has changed into a wolf and is stalking Vanessa, lunging when she sees an opening. Vanessa has her Magikida out and she almost catches Libby in the shoulder with it on the last lunge. Shae is making a waterspout and she just about gets it on Vanessa but Vanessa sends one of Alysa's fireballs into it and its strength lessens.

I look back at my crowd of Rifts and see them inching closer to me. I put my hand over my head and act like I'm swinging a rope. Instantly a lasso appears above my head but it's made out of bright white electrical energy. My circle of Rifts back up quite a ways and they all look at each other.

With my right hand, I keep my lasso going in a big circle around me but with my left hand, I start flicking little balls of electricity out at the Rifts. One by one, they fall to the ground, and start seizing, like they've been hit by a stun gun.

I move myself closer to the girls. Malory and Alysa are closest, so I send out a Barrier to them. The rest of the Guardians are in reach now too, so I send it to them as well. I'm not quite close enough for Shae but I stretch myself mentally and send it to Libby. She changes into her human form and looks around, she can tell something's changed. Vanessa was doing something to her but now she's not.

I look back at Ty, Charlie, and the other guys and they're all still fighting. It seems as if more Rifts are coming out of the woodwork. When I look back at Vanessa, I see she's caught in Shae's waterspout. Shae is smiling gleefully and starts pulling it back towards her, tightening the funnel, hoping to suffocate her. Alysa wraps the waterspout with a fire funnel of her own. Libby has her Magikida raised.

There's a sudden sound like a dam breaking and water goes flying. Libby and Alysa are thrown backwards, and Vanessa is free from the waterspout. As if in slow motion, I see Vanessa turn towards Shae and cup her hands together like she's making a snowball. She then opens her hands out towards Shae and pushes whatever energy she made at her. Because of the slow-motion, I can see the ball of shimmering energy flying towards Shae. I know if it hits her, she'll die.

"Nooooo!!" I scream. I throw my hands up and out, knocking all the Rifts within 20 yards of me flying backwards. I accidently knocked some of the Guardians down as well. Chris, Clay, and Max go flying also. I send out a Cushioning Ward so they don't hit the walls or ground to hard.

As if I'm stuck in mud or time has slowed down so much, I can't Run fast enough. I see the ball of energy connect with Shae and she looks as if she's been punched in the stomach but then her arms fly out, like she's welcoming someone in for a hug. Her chest pushes out and she flies backwards and hits the ground.

My world breaks. As I'm Running to Shae, I throw my hands out to my sides in fists and open them fast, at the same time, bringing my hands together, clasping my fingers when my palms touch. And then, like I had with the shark, I throw my hands out but push all the energy around me out as I do it. It looks as if an invisible bomb goes off. Everyone that's standing, goes flying into the air. Part of my brain sends out the same Cushioning Ward as before, hopefully my friends aren't seriously injured from my... whatever it was.

I see Vanessa go flying into a wall across the room, away from Shae. I slide to my knees when I get to Shae. Her eyes are closed but she still has a look of surprise on her face somehow.

"Please, please, please," I plead as I check for a pulse with shaking hands.

Nothing.

"Oh my gods! NO!!!" I hear Alysa scream. She's beside me in a second. "Shae!? Malysa? Please, please! Open your eyes! Malysa!?"

"Shae?" I hear a cracked voice from somewhere behind us, Charlie. He's beside me in an instant too. "Oh gods, no! Shae please, please!" -He's pulling her head into his lap, bending down and kissing her lips.- "Please, Shae, please wake up!... Ty!... TY!... Libby, she needs Healed! Hurry. Please! Oh gods no!" tears are running down his face.

I look over and see Vanessa moving, Chris is crawling over to her. I stick my hand out and put an invisible weight on them, they can't move. As long as I hold it there, they can't move, they can't leave.

Ty and Libby are here with us now. They're checking Shae. Libby starts to cry.

"I can't... I can't find... no, no, no, no," she sounds on the verge of a panic attack. Max pulls her up and away, engulfing her with his big arms.

Malory pulls Alysa away and hugs her, Clay hugging them both. Charlie pulls Shae's limp body into his lap even more. He brushes her hair out of her face and kisses her checks, her eyes, anywhere he can reach while she's lying on his lap.

"She can't be gone, she can't! I love her!... Do you

hear me, Shae? I LOVE YOU!... I'm so, so, sorry! I've been so stupid. I want you, I've always just wanted you... I've been stupid and scared. Plllease come back to me, please!... You're my Anima Gemella... You are! You were right. You're always right! Please, please!" Charlie starts to sob.

I look back down at Shae in time to see the sliver of bright white light start to float out of the middle of her body.

"NO!" I scream. Making everyone jump around me.

I fan my fingers into the palm of my left hand and just as my pointer finger touches my palm, I turn it towards Shae. I can feel a zap when my hand connects with the sliver of light. I slowly push it back down but I can tell I need both my hands. "Someone get Vanessa, I need both hands."

"What? What do you mean?" Ty says. He sounds choked up too.

"I'm holding... Vanessa and Chris... down... but I need... my other hand... to save... Shae," I pant out. I'm using all my power to keep the sliver of light in Shae and Vanessa and Chris in one place.

"You can't, she's gone," Ty says, sniffling.

"Yesss, I can!" I grunt out. "Get... Vanessa."

Just as Ty stands up and walks toward Chris and Vanessa, I feel the little sliver of light that I know is Shae, start to push up on my hand. I release Chris and Vanessa and use my other hand, and all of my energy, to push it down. But I didn't see the Rift standing off to the side of Chris until it was too late. As soon as Chris sits up straight, the Rift grabs Vanessa and Chris and vanishes. They Jumped.

Damn it!

Refocusing my concentration on Shae, I tell myself to forget about Vanessa, we'll catch her later.

Keeping my left hand on the sliver of light, I put my right hand over her heart. Making a fist with that hand, I close my eyes and reach out with my mind, feeling all the energy around me. The energy from the mountain, from my friends, from everything. I send all the energy to my hand and when I open my eyes, I see a ball of energy so bright, it makes sunlight look dim. I open my hand and force it into Shae's heart at the same time that I push the sliver of light back into her body the rest of the way.

Shae's body arches off the ground but Charlie holds on to her with all his might. I pull in more energy from the mountain and send another ball into her heart. She arches again. One more time. Third times the charm, right? Pulling in energy from the trees outside, the water from the river nearby, and more from the mountain, I send the brightest of the balls of energy into Shae and she arches so bad I fear she might break her back.

When her body relaxes back down onto Charlie's lap, we see her take a breath in. Charlie quickly looks at me and then back at Shae.

"Shae? Can you hear me? Shae?" he pleads.

"Mmmm," she says sleepily.

"Oh my gods!" Alysa and Libby say together and they're back beside us.

"Shae? Can you hear us?" Libby asks. She reaches down and checks for a pulse. "Oh.. My... Gods! She's... she's got a pulse. She's back! She's alive!"

"Malysa?" Alysa asks, touching her sisters face.

"Don't call me that," Shae chokes out. Relieved laughter breaks out around us.

"Oh, Shae," Charlie says, kissing her deeply.

When he pulls back, Shae's eyes are open and she's looking at him in amazement.

"What happened?" she asks.

"Vanessa killed you," Alysa sniffs. "You... you... you were dead."

"But how am I back?" Shae asks, looking around until her eyes fall on me. "You. It was you, wasn't it?"

I just shrug.

"Hell yeah it was Emma! She did some kind of thing with the brightest light I've ever seen and shocked you. She had a hand here," Charlie pointed to the middle of her body. "And a hand over your heart. It was the most amazing thing I've ever seen."

"How long was I... dead?" Shae asks shakily.

"It felt like forever," Alysa says.

"Maybe three minutes," Ty says, wiping his face on his shirt. He's been crying, too.

Shae looks over at Libby and puts a handout.

"Hey," she says. "Libs?"

Libby throws herself on top of Shae's legs, hugging her. Bawling, she says, "Shae that was the worst thing I have ever, ever experienced in my entire life."

"I'm back now," she says, starting to cry herself.

I go to stand up but can't seem to feel my legs. I go to put my hands out but they feel numb, too. The world tilts suddenly and I'm lying on my side. I see Ty rush to me but once again, I can't hear anything. I look down and see a bright light around the middle of my body and then darkness takes me.

A special thank you to my Beta readers;
Nancy Laney, Stephanie Mays, Melissa Kendall, Kristy
Backlund, Jennifer McGuire, and Pam Maxwell.
Thank you for taking the time to read my book
and give me notes, I truly appreciate you all.

*To find out what happens next, stay tuned
for book 2 of the Emma Hart Series*

www.ingramcontent.com/pod-product-compliance
Lightning Source LLC
Chambersburg PA
CBHW020628020726
47494CB00001B/97